THE
SIGN
OF THE
DEVIL

Oscar de Muriel was born in Mexico City, where he began writing stories aged seven, and later came to the UK to complete a PhD in Chemistry. Whilst working as a translator and playing the violin, the idea for a spooky whodunnit series came to him and Nine-Nails McGray was born. Oscar has now written five Frey and McGray titles and splits his time between the North West of England and Mexico City. *The Sign of the Devil* is the seventh book in the Frey & McGray series.

THE SIGN OF THE DEVIL

OSCAR DE MURIEL

ORION

An Orion paperback

First published in Great Britain in 2022
by Orion Fiction,
This paperback edition published in 2023
by Orion Fiction,
an imprint of The Orion Publishing Group Ltd.,
Carmelite House, 50 Victoria Embankment
London EC4Y ODZ

An Hachette UK company

1 3 5 7 9 10 8 6 4 2

Copyright © Oscar de Muriel 2022

A CIP catalogue record for this book
is available from the British Library.

ISBN (Paperback) 978 1 4091 8771 4

Typeset at The Spartan Press Ltd,
Lymington, Hants

Printed and bound in Great Britain by Clays Ltd,
Elcograf S.p.A.

MIX
Paper from
responsible sources
FSC® C104740

www.orionbooks.co.uk

The seventh one's for all o' youse,
for putting up with mah clishmaclaiver till the very end.
I owe youse all a wee dram.

Let drunkards grim and wither'd hags,
with their foul mouths and wicked nags,
prattle about that nine-nail'd man.
A dreary story;
hear them talk and ye'll feel sorry
for the McGray clan.

Nae long ago they rose to fame,
alas! most wretched is their name;
husband and wife snuffed like a flame.
What a dreadful sight!
Hear all about the gore and shame
o' that tragic night.

Their wee young daughter went dead mad;
butchered and sliced her mum and dad
and ran off laughing with the blade.
She seemed unrattled,
and with bloody hands she cackled
at the mess she'd made.

Her brother fought her to nae gain:
she thrust the knife without restrain
and poor Adolphus howled in pain.
A horror he'd nae seen before –
his finger hanging by a vein,
his blood spilt all over the floor.

The stars shut down their dwindling light,
Adolphus passing from the fright.
And right before his world went black,
(though he'd never tell)
he saw the Devil rushing back
to his mirky Hell.

'Lament for the McGray clan'
Trad.

1883

The tune was quite vulgar, clearly born in the depths of a stinking tavern, but Lady Anne hummed it with pleasure. The roof of her narrow cabriolet carriage, the smallest she owned, was folded up, so no one would hear.

How fast the wit of the mob worked. Mr and Mrs McGray were not yet cold in their graves and already there were songs about them. Then again, their tale was juicy.

The carriage halted by the entrance to that drab inn, abandoned long ago by its morose tenant. Only one of the grimy windows glowed, golden amidst the cerulean shades of the midsummer night.

In the distance, the lights of Dundee shone in the same amber hue. Far closer than Lady Anne would have liked. She must not be seen in the vicinities of that common town. Not so soon.

The light, two-wheeled carriage bounced and shook as her manservant jumped off, his feet stomping heavily onto the ground. Jed, a six-foot-three, broad-shouldered man, stepped to the inn's door and knocked softly. There must have been some reply Lady Anne could not hear, for Jed turned the latch and pushed the door slightly open. He peered inside for a moment, and only then did he come back to open the coach for his mistress.

Lady Anne covered her aging hands in thick leather gloves and had the prudence to remove her conspicuous hairpiece, custom-made and decked with long pheasant feathers dyed in black. She was famous for her extravagant hairdos. People would recognise her silhouette even in the dark.

Jed handed her an ebony walking cane and Lady Anne Ardglass made her dignified way to the grimy, woodworm-infested door. Fortunately, she'd only have to venture a few steps into that pigpen.

Her contact, Procurator Fiscal Pratt, was already there, seated in the wide hall, which only a few months ago would have been packed with intoxicated tradesmen. Now there was only a tattered table, a few rickety chairs and a threadbare armchair by a dark fireplace.

Mr Pratt jumped to his feet as soon as he saw her come in. His head, completely bald, reflected almost to perfection the flame from the one lit sconce. That was how Lady Anne had first spotted him: a gleaming scalp in the dull courts. And then she'd heard his cunning tongue, and instantly she knew he'd be the right man to carry out her dirty work. She'd already defrayed a significant proportion of his son's education – more than enough to secure the man's loyalty for life.

'Lady Anne,' he said with a bow, 'have a seat, if you—'

But the woman was already installing herself in the armchair, after her servant had spread a blanket on it to protect his lady's fine dress.

'Jed,' she said, pointing at the empty hearth. The large man needed no further instruction and began building the fire.

Pratt wrung his hands as the infamous 'Lady Glass' produced a hunter's flask from her little purse. A most expensive silver piece, with leather lining and a detachable cup. Lady Anne poured herself a measure of aromatic cognac and had a very noisy slurp. Manners were for the common and the young.

'Is the chap here?' she asked.

'Yeh – yes, ma'am. But I asked him to wash before meeting you. He stank of—'

'Nonsense. Bring him in.'

Pratt rushed to a nearby door, just as the hearth burst with light and heat. Most efficient was Jed. And loyal. It was a pity he would die relatively soon.

The hall already felt warmer when Pratt returned, and behind him came a young fellow. He must have been be in his early twenties, short and scrawny, but his lean face and arms were already weathered by the elements. Pratt elbowed him when they approached Lady Anne, and the young man at once took off his soiled flat cap.

'So you are the McGrays' gardener?' the woman demanded.

'Aye, ma'am,' he replied, a little too sure of himself for her taste. 'Only part-time. They keep this other lad—'

'What's your name?'

'Billy, ma'am.'

Lady Anne took a sip, thinking that there was a cheeky spark to the man's eyes. He might be useful.

'Is it all they say at the inns?' she asked, and Billy whistled.

'Aye, ma'am. Worse even! I saw the lass myself and what she did to the young Master Adolphus. Well, that was before that lunatics' doctor—'

'What happened earlier?' she snapped. 'During the day. Before the girl shouted she'd been possessed by the Devil.'

'Well, I spent the best part o' the day working in the gardens. I finished by dinner time and went to the kitchens to get my meal. The family ate in the big hall. Before that I'd seen them get in 'n' out the house. Mrs McGray, rest in peace, had been arranging flowers. I plucked a few roses for her myself.'

'And her husband?'

'I didnae see much o' him at all, ma'am. Only two, three times that I walked past his library window. He was there since the early morning, bent on his papers.'

Lady Anne clasped the silver cup a little more tightly. 'Did you see anything else going on in that room?'

'Nae, ma'am, but I ken what ye mean. That's where the lass lost her mind.'

'But you saw her earlier in the day, did you not?' Lady Anne pressed. 'Did she look insane before?'

Billy shook his head. 'Nae, ma'am. I heard her laugh with her mum in the morning. And after dinner she went out riding with Master Adolphus, her brother. I was outside havin' a fag when they left, so I saw them go. They looked quite happy.'

'And then?' Lady Anne asked, leaning slightly forwards. Her hand, blotched and bony, clenched the armrest like a talon.

'Well... Mr McGray, rest in peace, asked auld George to tell us to go to the pub. He even gave us money for our drams.'

Lady Anne chuckled. 'Did he do that often?'

Billy twisted his mouth. 'Every now and then, when he wisnae cross. Usually 'round Christmas time and in summer. Thought it did us good, but between youse 'n' me, we were never too keen. The pub's a couple o' miles away; bonny walk, but a wee bit long. Especially when ye have to come back half blootered.'

'So that's where you all were,' Lady Anne said. 'You were at the pub while your master and mistress were being butchered by their own daughter.'

Billy bit his lip. 'Aye.'

'Was there anyone else in the house?'

'Only auld Betsy.'

Lady Anne blinked. 'And who's that?'

'Och, aye, ye don't ken her. The housekeeper. She's getting on in years, if ye take my mea—' Billy saw that Lady Anne's creases deepened at any mention of advanced age. 'She doesnae like long walks anymore, let's say.'

Lady Anne took a long drink. 'So all you know for certain is what that woman saw.'

'Aye.'

'Tell me,' Lady Anne asked, her pale eyes glimmering with eerie intensity, so much so that Billy took an involuntary step back.

'She – she said she stayed in the kitchens, having a wee nap. She has a nice rocking chair there. Said she thought she heard horses arrive; she thought it was Miss Amy and Master Adolphus coming back, but ... it couldnae have been them. Master Adolphus only came back after—'

'Don't jump ahead,' said Lady Anne. 'Tell me things in order. She heard horses, and then?'

'She didnae make too much of it and went on napping, and then ... well, then it all happened. She heard mighty screaming at the library. The lass Pansy – Miss McGray, I mean – seemed to have gone mad. She just burst into the kitchen, grabbed the biggest cleaver, the one Betsy uses to cut through bones, and ran back to the library. Poor auld Betsy said she almost died o' the fright.'

'Did she follow her?' Lady Anne asked.

'Aye, and she heard Mr and Mrs McGray screaming too; trying to control the lass, ye'd think.'

Lady Anne was on the edge of her seat, even ignoring the drink. 'Did she see anything? Did she go into the library?'

Billy shook his head. 'She said she only made it to the door. It was a wee bit open but the lass closed it when she saw Betsy getting close.'

Lady Anne arched an eyebrow. 'Did she lock the door?'

'Aye, ma'am. And then Betsy heard Master McGray telling her to go away. Cannae blame him. If a child o' yers went mad, ye wouldnae want the servants to see and go telling—'

'*Oh, go on!*' Lady Anne shrilled, her voice echoing across the

5

hall. All three men started, even the tall Jed. She noticed she'd just spilt half the drink on her skirt, and forced herself to take a deep breath.

Lady Anne knew *plenty* about mad offspring.

Jed – the only one who understood the reason for the outburst – refilled the cup for her.

She downed it in one gulp and cleared her throat. 'Go on.'

Billy drew in some air too. 'Betsy couldnae get into the library and she kent the rest of us were at the pub, miles away, so all she could think o' doing was to go out and look for Master Adolphus. She—'

Lady Anne raised a hand. 'Did she hear anything? Anything the McGrays were talking about? Anything that would explain why the girl had lost her wits?'

'If she did, she'll never tell. The McGrays are the apple o' her eye. Auld George's too.'

Lady Anne nodded at Mr Pratt. They might have to find that woman, but it must be a careful approach, if she was indeed so loyal to the family.

'Go on,' she said. By then there were beads of sweat on Billy's upper lip.

'Auld Betsy found Master Adolphus soon enough. He was just by the lake. She told him there was trouble and he rode like the wind back to the house. Betsy ran after him, and it was about that time that we came back. We found her running and weeping on the footpath. She told us what was happening; I remember her words very well. She said wee Pansy was screaming as if some devil had got inside her. I remember very well 'cause – as youse ken by now – she later—'

'Don't jump ahead,' Lady Anne said again. 'I presume you and the other servants also ran to the house?'

'Aye, o' course, ma'am. Auld George the butler; me; Conor, the

6

other gardener; and Mary, his wife, who also helps in the house. And we heard the shrieks well before we made it to the house.'

'Did you see the horses?' Lady Anne asked. Billy felt as if those veiny eyes could see right through him.

'Aye, ma'am. Master Adolphus's brown horse, and Miss Amy's wee foal.'

Lady Anne parted her lips, as if about to say something, but instead she looked sideways, staring into the crackling fire for a moment. She wanted to ask more about the horses, but realised it would be far too risky. In the end, she raised her silver cup, and Jed refilled it.

'Continue,' she said before taking another sip.

Billy had to use his flat cap to wipe the sweat from his face.

'We found the main door wide open, and I remember the door to the library was still flapping. We – we saw her then.'

The young man shuddered, a tendon popping on his neck.

'The poor lass was running about, shrieking 'n' swearing and – och, she *did* look like the Devil. Her dress was all stained with blood … she was all pale like the dead, and – och, ma'am, those eyes! I still see her when I close mine. And she still had that nasty cleaver in her hand. It was dripping blood everywhere!'

Lady Anne had listened without blinking or breathing.

'Did you go after her?'

Billy winced. 'N-nae, ma'am. I thought I was soiling myself! It was auld George and Conor who ran after her. Mary and me were too frightened …' He blushed intensely, and then lifted his chin. 'But it was good we stayed put! We heard Master Adolphus moaning in the library.' He shuddered again. 'Youse can imagine the mess. The poor lad was on the floor, all stunned – all … covered in blood too. And his mum and dad lay dead right behind him …'

There was a moment of sombre, almost respectful silence, as

if the McGrays' ghosts had descended to hear their own morbid story.

Billy cleared his throat.

'We managed to get Master Adolphus to the kitchen. Mary gave him some spirit, but –' his blush became a greenish hue – 'it was only then that we saw his hand, all butchered. Mary and me were too scared to do anything, and yet the poor master kept bleeding all over the floor!'

Lady Anne remembered the rhyme. This Billy must have been prattling to others.

He looked down. 'The poor master had to bandage himself with a kitchen rag. It was then that he told us what had happened. I'm nae sure he even realised he was sayin' it out loud. He said it had been his wee sister. That she had killed the masters and then chopped his finger when he tried to hold her still.

'We heard more screaming when he was talking. Then George came round and said the lass had gone to her room. Conor was holding the door in case she tried to go out again; she'd tried to stab them too. Betsy came by with the keys, but she nearly fainted. It was me who went upstairs and locked the door.'

Lady Anne lounged back, taking another deep breath as if she had just gone through the ordeal herself.

'Did the girl try anything after that?'

'Nae. She went deathly quiet, ma'am. We all did. No one spoke for the rest o' the day. Master Adolphus, blood and all, carried his parents to their bed. Betsy went to clean them and in the meantime Master Adolphus went to Dundee for the undertakers. George wrote to the lunatics' doctor in Edinburgh. I myself took the message to the telegrapher in Dundee.'

Lady Anne raised a suspicious eyebrow. 'And Dr Clouston arrived the following morning, did he not?'

'Aye. Before sunrise. He must've travelled through the night. We were all asleep then, worn out like auld boots. It was George and Betsy who received him. But—' the man smacked his lips loudly, his mouth dry. He eyed Lady Anne's little cup. 'Can I have a wee drink o' that?'

Rustic, common folk! Lady Anne thought. Then again, so had been the late James McGray and his slut of a wife. So was his vulgar son Adolphus. And Amy, the only one in that family who might have had a few redeeming qualities, was now lost forever.

While Lady Anne mused, Jed pulled out a flask from his own pocket and handed it to the trembling gardener. Billy had a couple of long swigs, wiped his mouth and shook his head as he felt the burn of the cheap whisky.

'We all woke up to the lass's scream,' he finally spluttered, his eyes fixed on the fire. 'It was demented, ma'am. It was – I've never heard anything like it. We heard her all the way to the servants' rooms. Like an eagle or a – banshee or something from hell.

'And she screamed the Devil's name. We all heard her. If we had any doubts the lass was mad, that sealed it.'

Billy had another drink before handing the flask back.

'It was then that the doctor took her away,' Mr Pratt added. 'Straight to the lunatic asylum. As we now know.'

'Aye, sir,' Billy said.

'The asylum…' Lady Anne mumbled to herself. She knew that no good could ever come from that arrangement, but there was nothing she could do about it. Not yet, at least. She had the last of the drink and looked back at Billy. 'And you will declare all this at the Sheriff's Court?'

'Aye, ma'am, every word under oath as I must. Unless – well, unless ye want me to add or take something, and…'

He slowly rubbed his thumb and first two fingers together.

Lady Anne sighed, all weariness. 'You can go for now. Mr Pratt was right; you stink like a mule.'

Billy bowed and walked away, to one of the inn's many empty rooms.

Lady Anne stared at the fire, holding the fragrant liquor under her nostrils.

'What happens now?' she whispered.

'They will try to class the girl as insane,' Mr Pratt said. 'Avoid a full trial.'

Lady Anne at once shook her head. 'From what I just heard, the girl *is* insane. And if Dr Clouston is involved, I'm sure he will follow all the legal procedures to certify it.'

And manage he would, she thought. Even if Scotland had one of the strictest lunacy acts in the civilised world.

Mr Pratt pulled over one of the rickety chairs and sat closer to the fire.

'Insane she may be, Lady Anne, but wouldn't it be most convenient for you – if she was *not*?'

The woman looked up, like a hound that has just caught a scent. 'Do you mean ... have her tried for murder?'

'Indeed. Show Clouston's incompetence. Or a conflict of interests. He is, after all, very close to the family.'

Lady Anne sighed. 'I cannot be involved in any scheme of the kind. Dr Clouston knows all about—' she said, mouthing the words 'my son', with a hand obscuring her lips, in case Billy were prying in the shadows.

Mr Pratt pulled his chair a little closer.

'No one needs to know of your involvement, ma'am. If you leave things to me—' He gulped. 'If I play our cards right, this could finally pay my debt to you. And you will finally have your revenge on the old McGray.'

Part One

Dear Friend, for Jesus' Sake, forbear
to dig the Dust enclosed here.
Blest be the Man that spares these Stones,
and curst be he that moves my Bones.

Ledger stone found at St James's cemetery,
London, dated 1802

1890

19 February

'Bonnie night to undig the dead!'

The coarse whisper sounded amidst the sheer, solid darkness, along with the frantic thuds of spades on dirt.

Eyes open or shut, it made no difference; the night was so black the two snatchers could not even see the borders of the grave. All they had for guidance were the ruffles of their clothes and their chattering teeth. And even if the skies opened – which was most unlikely – there'd be no moonshine to speak of.

'Reminds me o' the night we dug up poor Bessy MacBean. Nice lass. A milk lass. We did a wee bit o' hornpipe dancing, if ye take my meaning. Didnae know it was her grave till we opened the box. Imagine my yelp when I saw her face! Still plump 'n' pretty. A wee bit green, but nae wormy yet.'

His companion dug a little faster.

'I do feel bad about her, don't ye think me a beast. I knew she was for the dissection table, to be cut open 'n' her bits put in crocks, but the trade's the trade. Uhhh! Maybe ye've seen her eyes in the college! Floating in one o' yer jars? Green, they were, and she had this odd speck in—'

'Oh, do shut up!'

'Uhh! Gittin' scared, lad?'

A snort was the only reply.

'And I've nae even told ye 'bout the real scary nights! Like those times the witches got there first and helped themselves to fingers 'n' scalps 'n' livers—'

'*I said shut up!* Do you not—?'

There was a clank then. Metal on metal. One of the spades had just hit the hinges of the coffin.

'Shallow grave,' said the coarse snatcher after a satisfied whistle. 'Yer lucky. That auld sexton must've been desperate to go home before his arse got frozen.'

Blindly, they scraped the loose soil from the top of the coffin. They heard the spades scratch what must be wrought-iron ornaments.

'A dear box!' said the snatcher, producing a crowbar from his coat's inner pockets. He wasted no time and removed the lid with little noise and no ceremony.

The younger man in turn produced a handkerchief, but before he had a chance to take it to his nose—

'Not even a waft of stench yet,' he mumbled as they heard the coffin crack open. 'It must be the cold.'

'Told ye, lad. Bonnie night for our trade.'

The younger man struck a match, lighting the ditch with a glow that seemed blinding in the pitch-black night.

'*Och, put that out, for fuck's sake!*'

'It has to be the right corpse!' the young man retorted, bending over the dead body.

The first thing he saw was a pair of yellowy, bony hands, as dry and creased as an old parchment. The pale skin appeared to glow, resting on an old, black dress, and clutching sprigs of evergreens and a little prayer book.

The young snatcher moved the light towards the face, saw the glint of a thin gold necklace, and then looked up to—

'*God...*'

His gasp came from the bottom of his stomach, as a nasty tingle spread along his spine.

He could say no more, for the older man shushed him, pulled up the match and smothered it in his bare hand. The darkness encircled them again, and they listened out.

They waited for a few moments, perfectly still and breathing cautiously.

Silence.

'We better hurry, lad,' said the snatcher, already shifting the corpse.

'The face...' his companion whispered, not yet recovered from the fright. 'The face has this – this... never mind.'

The older man pocketed the fine leather prayer book and the necklace, and then they lifted the limp body. The thin, aged lady somehow felt too heavy. Their hands must be numb.

The pair scrambled out of the ditch and felt for the shroud they'd left already spread on the snow. They laid the body on it and wrapped it hastily. The glow from a very distant street light at least let them make out their own silhouettes.

The older man looked up, almost spraining his neck. His companion waited, holding his breath, and then he too heard the noise.

'We have to go now,' the old man urged.

'But the tools—'

'*Nae time!*'

They lifted the poorly wrapped body and ran across the graveyard, panting. They saw the wide Greyfriars church, a shade darker than the surrounding snow, and as they turned around its corner, the lights of the Grass Market tenements emerged in the distance.

They heard the noise again, this time louder, and ran faster, with the shroud slipping from their sweaty hands. The iron bars of the back gate appeared before them, the outline of their cart right behind it. The horse, already restless, stamped a hoof on the frozen slates.

The old snatcher pushed the gate, and with the creak of rusty hinges came a booming shout, cutting the air and bouncing all across the graveyard.

'*I see youse, wee bastards!*'

At once they recognised the roaring voice of Nine-Nails McGray.

There was a gunshot, and then the sounds of whistles and hooves trampling the snow. The peelers were coming on horseback from the front gate.

The snatchers tossed the corpse onto the cart without even looking. The young man leapt on, just as his companion took the driver's seat and whipped the horse. The cart darted ahead and the young man had to hold on to the boards with both hands, the corpse sliding back and nearly pushing him off the edge.

He had a quick glance over his shoulder, just in time to see another gunshot detonate in the dark.

'*Stop!*' Nine-Nails howled, his voice fading as the cart charged towards the gardens of George Heriot's Hospital. The building, a solid castle-like block, rose to the skies like a forbidding wall.

The cart entered the hospital's snowed lawns, wide and open, the perimeter illuminated by gaslights.

'*Are you mad?*' the young man screeched, hearing the whistles and the shouts of the peelers, but then the snatcher steered the horse to the right, to some blackened rose beds, and animal and cart trampled frantically on thorny bushes and specimen shrubs. The horse neighed and jolted, but the snatcher whipped it on, and just as they heard another gunshot behind their backs, they made it to a narrow side gate. The pathetic picket fence was no match for the frenzied horse, the old wood giving way as the cart passed through.

They entered a dark, narrow alley that stank of piss and stale beer, with only a faint, yellowish spot of light marking the other end, many yards ahead.

The snatcher whipped the horse again and the cart moved faster. Again the young man felt the corpse sliding backwards, pushing him to the edge of the cart. He growled, clenched the side boards with both hands and kicked the dead old woman towards the front. He propped himself more firmly, and only then did he notice that the peelers' voices could be heard no more.

He allowed himself a sigh of relief, and then the cart stormed into the long esplanade of Grass Market. The tall tenements he'd seen from the graveyard were now right before them; and beyond, as if floating in the sky, he saw the many specks of light coming from the narrow windows of Edinburgh Castle, blurry in the night mist.

The older snatcher steered the horse north, to the safety of the darker alleys, but then an explosion of voices, whistles and hooves came from his right.

The young man gasped at the sight of four horses charging in their direction, and the glow of lanterns and many simultaneous gunshots. He crouched down, as the snatcher turned west swiftly.

'*Where the hell did they come from?*' he shouted.

The horse's hooves skidded over the frozen cobbles, the wheels creaking as some of their tattered rods burst into splinters.

They rushed on, crossing the unpaved, muddy land that led to the wide road of Johnston Terrace. The young man could only see a solid patch of blackness in front of them – the steep cliffs of Castle Rock. And the peelers were right behind them. And the cart now creaked as if about to fall apart.

A gunshot came, followed by the pained scream of the snatcher.

The young man knew all was lost. The darkness was his best

chance. But he had to act now, before they made it to the lit road, even if that meant Nine-Nails's horse might crush him to death.

He took a deep breath, jumped off the cart and landed on cold slush, rolling uncontrollably on the ground as the sound of frantic galloping and men's yelps finally surrounded him.

Something hit him on the head – and he knew no more.

McGray heard the clash of wood against rock, then the neighing of the poor horse, and then hooves trampling manically.

He spurred his black horse Onyx and squinted as the officers shed their lights ahead.

The jagged slopes of Castle Rock were much closer than he expected, and amidst the shadows he distinguished the outline of the cart, now half sunken into a muddy ditch, a broken wheel still spinning in the air.

The horse was desperately trying to jump out, twisting its body but still strapped to the shafts.

McGray stopped his horse right by the cart, fanning his gun from left to right.

'Release that poor beast,' he told the officers as soon as he was sure there was no threat.

Young Constable McNair and another man jumped off their horses to do the work, while McGray stared at the blood-covered temple of the body snatcher.

'Damn!' he said as he dismounted. 'The poor sod's dead?'

Constable Millar came by with a lantern and touched the man's head. It turned limply to one side.

'Aye, sir, but nae from yer shot. Looks like the auld man banged his head against the rock.'

'How fucking inconsiderate!' McGray snorted. He'd been meaning to question the rascal. He looked around. 'Look for the other bastard. Cannae be far.'

Millar nodded and turned on his heels, the beam of his lantern shaking across the field.

McGray turned back to the horse, just as McNair cut the straps in one clean blow. At once the animal jumped onto the road, shaking its mane, and McGray rushed to seize it by the terrets. The horse shook and neighed, but McGray pulled it to him and sheathed his gun to pat it on the back. Its wide, glassy eyes were fearful, and McGray felt sorry for the poor creature.

'There, there, don't stomp on my feet! He's dead now!' He then shouted over his shoulder. 'McNair, check the cart.'

McNair did so, though not too enthused. Inspecting unburied bodies in the middle of the night was not something he particularly enjoyed.

'Old woman,' he said, shedding light on the corpse after lifting the shroud. 'Looks like – God, it's just what ye feared, sir; the widow from the asylum.'

'*Bastards!* Ye sure?'

'I ... I think so, sir.'

'I'll have a look in a moment,' McGray said, running a hand – his mutilated one – on the horse's mane. It was a surprisingly good horse; wide, muscly and well-fed. The chestnut coat reminded him of Rye, the last horse his late father had ever given him, and he felt a pang in the chest.

'They helped themselves to the jewellery, Inspector,' McNair added. 'And from those marks in the neck they must have ripped – *God!*'

The last word came out as a shrill.

'What?' McGray asked, giving the horse one last pat. He approached the cart and looked over the side board. McNair was panting.

'There,' he whispered, a trembling finger pointing at the woman's face.

McGray at once felt a chill on the back of his neck.

'*What the hell is that?*' McNair asked, even if the horrid mark on the dead skin demanded no explanation.

It was the Devil's work.

Caroline Ardglass felt a stab of fear.

The shout had come from far too close – no more than two rooms away. It had been a tearing, tortured wail, like that of a dying woman.

She looked up, still holding Miss McGray's hand in hers. There were footsteps and murmurs, the old asylum awakening.

And she was not supposed to be there.

Miss McGray stirred in the bed. She'd been about to fall asleep, her dark hair and long eyelashes standing out amidst the pristine white sheets. Her eyes, as brown as Caroline's, opened wide, and she looked from side to side in fright.

For an instant she did not seem to recognise her surroundings – the high ceilings or the curtains around her four-poster bed. And when she realised where she was, Edinburgh's Royal Asylum for the Insane, she whimpered. Caroline squeezed her hand a little tighter.

'It's all right,' she said. 'It's all right, Pansy.'

That was the girl's childhood nickname, given to her by her late mother, who told every acquaintance her daughter's eyelashes made her look like her favourite blooms.

Hearing it seemed to work. Pansy's pupils moved a little in Caroline's direction, not quite making eye contact, and she exhaled with some relief.

Caroline did too. Somehow, they could easily soothe each other without words.

But then there came another scream, and neither young woman could contain a gasp.

Caroline turned to the door, feeling Miss McGray's hand quiver.

'I'll be back,' she whispered, giving Pansy a quick kiss.

She rose, her heart racing, and reached for the doorknob. She could already hear the orderlies running up and down the corridors, so she only opened the door an inch before cautiously peering out.

The hall was still pitch-black, a cold draught caressing her face. Caroline took a deep breath and stepped out. She looked in both directions, the echoes of nurses and orderlies bouncing all around her. Though she could not make out what they said, the air was laden with an oppressive sense of doom.

She walked amidst the darkness, but she'd only taken a few steps when she clashed against an oak cabinet, its contents shaking in a loud rattle. She grunted in pain, and then an icy hand seized her by the arm.

She shivered from head to toe, turned on her heels, and just as she was about to let out a scream—

'You have to go, Miss Ardglass! Now!'

It was Cassandra Smith, the head nurse, her pale face lit by a shaky oil lamp, and Caroline allowed herself a sigh.

'What's happening?' she asked, but Miss Smith was already pushing her.

'*Now!* If Dr Harland sees you—'

Too late. They heard the doctor's unmistakable voice, shouting orders just around the corridor's corner.

Caroline froze, seeing the glow of the doctor's lamp grow brighter. She only moved when Miss Smith pushed her towards the cabinet – the very same one Caroline had just hit – in a desperate attempt to hide her from view.

The doctor appeared, and Miss Smith rushed to meet him.

'Dr Harland! Have you heard?'

'Of course I bloody heard! The damn lord provost must have heard!'

Caroline pressed her back against the cold wall, realising that the hem of her black dress was sticking out by the base of the cabinet. She did not dare move, staring at the long shadows of the doctor and the nurse, projected sharply on the floorboards.

'Who were you talking to?' the doctor demanded. 'Miss McGray?'

'A – aye, doctor.'

Dr Harland sighed impatiently. 'Another *fit*? Do I need to—?'

'Oh, no! She was just – upset by—'

'Well, then, come with me. This is ugly.'

Caroline could see the hesitation in Miss Smith's shifting shadow. 'Erm ... can I make sure Miss McGray—?'

'Sod Miss McGray! Someone's just been killed!'

Caroline had to cover her mouth, else she would have let out a cry. She saw the doctor's shadow move in her direction, and then past the cabinet, mere inches from her. She could even smell his cheap cologne. He halted for an instant, and Caroline's heart skipped a beat.

But then the tall doctor walked on to the next corner without looking back.

Miss Smith followed him, taking the light with her. She cast Caroline a brief glance.

'She'll – she'll have to fend for herself this time, I suppose!'

Caroline recognised the slightly raised tone: those words had been meant for *her*, and just as she realised it, the head nurse disappeared. The glow of her little lamp faded almost at once, and Caroline found herself in complete darkness.

Alone.

In the middle of that dreadful asylum where someone, apparently, had just been killed.

She'll have to fend for herself, she heard again in her head.

She forced in a deep breath and blinked hard, trying to make out what shapes she could in the dark. She would have to grope her way out. Thankfully, she'd walked along those corridors many times, even before she found out that her half-sister was an inmate there.

Caroline took a step to Pansy's door, thinking she'd take her cloak and say goodnight, but then she heard a cacophony of voices, so close she started.

'He's dead, I tell youse!' someone cried. '*Mighty stabs in his chest!*'

With no time to think, Caroline dashed along the corridor, feeling her way on the wood-panelled walls. She had to get out of there before the entire building became a pandemonium. If someone was indeed dead – stabbed! – they'd summon the constables, and among them would be—

She shook her head, scuttling across corridors and servants' stairs. She made it to the ground floor, to the airy hallway that overlooked the back gardens. The lawns were lit by one single gaslight, which shed a faint glow into the room through the wide windows.

Caroline could only just make out the outline of the long hall, and the door to the back storerooms that would finally lead her to the gardens. She rushed on, groping the wall, seeing more and more light filtering through the windows as she moved. The asylum's many rooms were coming to life one by one, their lights bouncing on the gardens and into the hall.

Then she felt a shiver and halted.

Her hand had rested on something warm, slimy and repulsive. Only then did she realise that she'd also left her gloves in Pansy's room.

Caroline drew in a breath and looked up. By then, the light filtering through the hall's windows was bright enough to let her see what she'd just touched.

This time she could not contain herself. She let out a piercing scream, stepping back and staring at the dark, red smear on her fingertips.

She looked at the wall again. Her jaw dropped and she nearly touched her face with her stained palm. Instead, she let out another scream and ran to the back door, with that ghastly mess imprinted in her mind.

On the wall's white plaster there were four stains painted in thick blood: a pair of menacing little eyes, like squinting slits, and they were crowned by long, wide horns.

I

My father's death was most unexpected.

Elgie, my youngest brother, had to wire me the news, for the February blizzards prevented all travel for the best part of a fortnight. The postman himself barely made it, and I received a wet, smudged piece of paper where the message could only just be read.

It had been a sudden seizure, apparently, which in itself was no surprise. The old Mr Frey had spent the past fifteen years indulging in brandy, claret, pastries and boeuf en croûte.

His death struck me far more than I would have expected, I must admit, and not only because of my rather shaken mood.

I'd been recuperating in my Gloucestershire home for the past five weeks – repose I truly needed, after the dreadful case that had nearly sent me to my death last December.

My broken wrist had now healed, but the bones still ached in the damp and cold, and I could not yet flex my right hand as before. I still had nightmares of guillotines falling to my neck, and green and blue torches coming after me in the dark – thankfully not every night anymore.

I took a train to London as soon as the weather allowed, wrapped in my thickest black coat and armed with an unusually large hip flask – my valet Layton seemed to judge my needs better than I did myself. He'd also packed my finery, for he knew I'd be facing the worst upper-class hyenas in all Christendom: the Frey family.

I'd not been back for the past fifteen months, so it shocked me that London looked so grim and blackened, the dome of St Paul's like the face of a chimney sweep.

Had the place always looked like that? Or had last year's soot been particularly unkind? Perhaps it was simply that the city became a little darker and gloomier year on year, noticeable only to those who, like me, spent a long time away.

Even the white-plastered façade of my childhood home in Hyde Park Gate looked dull – grey, almost, amidst the bare, blackened branches of the maples that adorned the street. The city itself seemed to have festooned herself for mourning.

Catherine, my stepmother, like any respectable lady of her class, was 'prostrated with grief' and unable to see me, for which I was only glad. I cannot emphasize enough just how much contempt I feel for that woman. My half-brother Oliver was also *unfit* to receive (as the butler put it), and Elgie, as I shall mention shortly, now had his own lodgings. I thus had a lonely supper and then spent the night in one of the guest rooms – the small one, which overlooks the backyard with the stable and the outhouse. Catherine knew very well how to tell people they are not welcome.

The following morning I rose early, donned my best black suit and my dear emerald signet ring. I had a cup of ghastly tea (whether Catherine has appalling taste, or she told the servants to get me the cheap stuff, I cannot tell) and, not waiting for the rest of the household, I asked a footman to call me a cab. In my haste I even forgot my gloves.

The air was cold and dry as I walked into Brompton Cemetery, the sun only just risen in the south-east.

I walked around the domed mortuary chapel, its elegant

26

sandstone walls bright even in the dim morning light. My father's coffin would be brought there for the service before the burial, but at the moment the gate was still locked, the cemetery quiet and desolate. The dull noises from the city could be heard in the background, though; one low, uniform, ever-present growl, that made me miss the utter peace of my Gloucestershire estate.

A couple of ravens cawed. I looked up with a twitch and saw them glide right above my head. They perched themselves on the twisted branches of a nearby ash. Their keen eyes instantly put me on edge.

'Ian!'

I shook at the sound of my own name, but recognised the voice within an instant. I turned and saw the slender figure of Elgie, also clad in black, coming hastily to join me. He looked paler than usual, with dark rings under his typically carefree eyes. On that bleak morning it was hard to believe he would only turn twenty the next summer.

'I went to Mother's house,' he said, breathless, as soon as he was within hearing distance. 'They told me you must be here already.'

I was going to rant about Catherine's cold reception, but decided not to. Elgie too had just lost his father.

After an affectionate pat on the back, I invited him to join me for a stroll around the snow-covered graveyard. 'How are you?' I asked him.

He sighed as we walked, and I saw, poorly concealed under his white scarf, the reddened mark of his violin's chin rest. He must have spent the best part of the night playing.

'I'm shaken,' he admitted. 'Nobody was expecting it. I was supposed to have supper with him that evening! I was going to invite him to the new place so he could—'

He choked and looked away. I wanted to ask how the old Mr Frey had reacted to him leaving the family home, but again I refrained. For almost ten years Father had moaned bitterly of my departure to join the CID. I had spent just over eight years in my rented lodgings near Scotland Yard, which he did not visit once, despite my recurrent invitations. Then, a little more than a year ago, I'd been forced to move to *Edin-bloody-burgh* (as the old man enjoyed calling it), and though Father *had* visited me there twice (for reasons that must be explained elsewhere) I cannot tell whether he'd ever truly approved of my choices.

Right then, on his burial day, I could not stomach hearing how he might have praised Elgie's apartments.

My young brother had recently rented quarters in some fashionable stretch of Pont Street, where most of the theatre luminaries lived and threw their post-premiere soirées. Elgie, now first violin at the Lyceum Theatre orchestra, would be constantly rubbing shoulders with the likes of Sir Arthur Sullivan, Oscar Wilde and Bram Stoker. That made me even happier that I'd managed to avoid Catherine, for she would have prattled on and on about the scintillating triumphs of her youngest child.

We paced on in uncomfortable silence, Elgie most likely guessing my thoughts.

'I last saw Father in Edinburgh,' I said at last. I heard the flapping of wings above our heads but did not look up, fearing the ravens might be following us.

'Oh yes,' Elgie answered. 'The gypsy's case.' He half smiled. 'I heard he spoke of nothing else at the club when he came back. And he also brought it up almost every dinner time, if only to upset Mother!'

We both laughed, and how refreshing it was, but it was unavoidably followed by a pang of sorrow. I had only begun to like the old man, with his acidic frankness, his razor-sharp tongue and his relaxed manners. He had also just begun to imply he 'tolerated' my career – now all but abandoned.

'Will you stay for long?' Elgie asked, but I only shrugged. 'You can always stay at my place, of course. I am hardly ever there these days! And you must come to the theatre one evening to see *The Dead Heart*.'

I wrinkled my nose. 'Henry Irving playing some fervent, fried-potato-munching Parisian *révolutionnaire*, and Miss Terry some weeping, generously-cleavaged French trollop?'

Elgie arched an eyebrow. 'Somewhat accurate. But with full orchestration and real fire on the stage.'

'Tempting, but I'd better not. Imagine the tantrum that Henry Irving would throw if he spotted me in the audience.'

'But Bram – Mr Stoker, I mean – he might be glad to see you.'

I chuckled. 'That will *not* be so. Remember that I once questioned him while he was stupefied with laudanum.'

'Oh, that's right.' Elgie nodded. 'Well, he tells me he still keeps in touch with Mr McGray. He is penning – don't tell anyone I said this – he is penning some gothic something or other.'

'And I am sure Nine-Nails will be a bottomless pit of information on the odd and ghostly!'

'Do not say it so disparagingly. You must know almost as much as he does by now.'

'Hardly,' I lied, the ingredients for a witch's bottle at once coming to mind.

Elgie looked away, towards the snow-capped tombstones. He let out a sigh.

'Are you really not going back?'

I nearly tripped when I heard that.

'What? To Scotland?'

'Yes.'

My laughter travelled along the path. 'Whatever for? I do not even have any possessions to salvage from up there.'

'Yes, but – you once told me you had a sort of *need* to prove your value. To do something useful for—'

I kicked the path's icy gravel. 'It is astonishing how a single year of trials and misery can diametrically change your views.'

We walked on in silence for a moment, towards the northern end of the cemetery, where the graves looked more crowded and the trees less manicured. Moss and brambles grew all around the headstones, most of them speckled with yellowish lichen. The trees too seemed a little wilder, their branches more twisted and their trunks more gnarled.

'So what will you do now?' Elgie asked me. The air must have been getting colder, for his breath began to condense as he spoke. 'Will you simply stay in Gloucestershire, cut off from the world, downing whiskies and brandies for the rest of your days, while someone else manages your estate?'

'Gosh, you make it sound even more tempting!'

Elgie shook his head. 'I'm sorry, that's not like you.'

I said nothing, all weariness. I only twisted my lips in derision.

'I know you,' he insisted. 'This has all happened before; after you came back from Cambridge all disillusioned by the law degrees. You could not stay idle at home for long. You're not an Oliver.'

I chuckled at this, picturing our plump-faced brother whiling away his days in the comfort of Catherine's parlours, ever nibbling on cheese and biscuits.

Elgie smiled. 'You'll be up to something in no time. I give you a fortnight.'

'Let's go back,' I said, partly to change the subject, but also because this end of the graveyard was becoming too grim for my liking.

We began to turn on our heels, but then something seemed to shift in the air. I cannot describe it. We both *felt* it and, a second later, we heard hundreds of wings flapping above our heads.

A flock of black birds rose from among the tombs and undergrowth, crossing the cemetery and fleeing southwards.

I turned my head and, perfectly outlined against the fresh snow, saw two figures clad in black, their faces obscured under hoods. One was tall and slender, the other short and broad.

My heart skipped a beat. My breath, like Elgie's, began condensing before my eyes, as if my very innards had also gone cold.

'Go away,' I told my brother.

'What?'

'*Now!*'

I had to push him hard, and then he saw the figures too. Memories of twisting shadows lurking in the dark, ready to get him, must have come to him, for he did not argue and hurried away.

My heart pounded, and instinctively I reached for my inner pockets, looking for a gun.

Of course I had none. I was no longer a CID inspector. I had not carried a weapon in weeks.

The figures approached with long, hurried strides, their cloaks waving in the wind as they passed the rows of neglected tombstones. They were the witches from my nightmares, but as real and tangible as I'd seen them not two months ago. I expected ravens to perch on their shoulders; to see them produce torches of green fire or vials full of horrendous acids to throw at my face.

Yet, somehow, I could not move.

I remained there, my feet firm on the ground, facing them without blinking. I only looked back once to make sure Elgie had gone. When I looked ahead again, the women were a mere ten yards from me, the shorter one already lifting a hand to remove her hood. And when I saw her face, I could not believe my eyes.

2

'Joan!' I cried.

Indeed, my former maid, as plump as ever, stared at me with affectionate, yet exhausted eyes.

'Master Frey!' she said with her thick Lancashire accent as she made a deep curtsey. Most unusual of her. I noted a hint of irritability in her voice, and when the taller figure pulled her hood back, I understood the reason.

Caroline Ardglass.

'*You!*' I cried again. 'Why is it always bloody you?'

'Mr Frey,' she said with a bow of the head. 'Always the gentleman.'

Her cheeks were a tad more sunken than they'd been in December, a slight furrow beginning to set between her brows. I realised how much she'd resemble her infamous grandmother when she grew old. Thankfully that would not happen for another few decades at least.

'What are you doing here?' I asked, too flummoxed to think of civilities.

Caroline looked sideways, regarding the graves with a grimace.

'I know this is the worst possible time,' she murmured. 'My – my condolences.'

Her voice quivered as she said it. She too had lost her

demented father one year ago. I'd been with them the moment the man died.

'Thank you,' I said. 'But... how did you know?'

'It's in all the papers, sir,' Joan intervened. 'I'm so sorry.' She then broke all protocols and reached for my hand, which she squeezed in an almost motherly fashion.

She probably was about to comment on how cold my fingers were, but then the wide emerald on my signet ring caught her eye.

'Handsome stone, sir! Was it your father's?'

I blushed at once, and in the cold morning I feared my cheeks might produce steam. Caroline's face was mighty red too, for she had given me that ring last December. It had belonged precisely to her late father. Without any surviving male relatives, she'd handed it to me.

Joan shook her head. 'Sorry, sir. You know what I'm like.'

I nearly said I would not have her any other way, but the encounter was already turning a little too sentimental.

'Not that it is not good to see you,' I said, 'but what brings you both here? You are a long way from Scotland.'

Their faces turned sombre.

'Oh Lord,' I moaned. 'Who is in mortal danger now? No, do not tell me. Miss McGray again?'

Caroline clutched her hood and wrapped it around her neck, as if struck by a sudden chill.

'Yes, she is,' she whispered. 'In terrible danger. And me too. And – Dr Clouston, if things get messy.'

I pinched my nose. 'Oh, pray stop! I know where this is going. Allow me to guess – some dreadful incident at the asylum?'

Their faces, grimmer if possible, were all the answer I needed. I shook my head and growled as I sat on a nearby tombstone.

'And I suppose you need me up there for some inescapable reason, do you not?' I added with my most grating cynicism.

Caroline took a step forwards. 'I beg you! I have never begged, but I am begging you now.'

Surprisingly, Joan placed a reassuring hand on Caroline's arm.

'We all beg you, sir. If you let the missus explain—'

'Why should I get involved?' I interrupted her. 'I do not work for Nine-Nails anymore. I do not even live in Scotland!'

'Are you not his friend?' Caroline said.

I laughed, and instead of answering I pointed at my deviated septum: McGray's masterstroke. If he'd been present, I am sure he would have remarked something in the lines of – *Och, ye still mad about that wee tap?*

'Master Adolphus would swing by in a jiffy if he knew you were in trouble,' Joan said.

I looked at them from the corner of my eye, unconvinced.

'If things are as dire as you claim, how come he did not come and ask himself? Why did he make you travel all the way to London rather than sending a wire?'

Caroline exhaled in frustration. Clearly she had expected the question.

'A wire you could ignore. Also, the situation is complicated. There are certain . . . *facts*, which Adolphus – Mr McGray simply *cannot* know. And without those pieces, his sister is all but doomed.'

My frown deepened. 'Which facts can you possibly know that Nine-Nails must not hear?'

Caroline wrung her hands, almost tearing her black leather gloves.

'It is a very delicate matter, Mr Frey,' she said as her cheeks blushed. 'I will only tell you if you agree to help us. On our way to Scotland. And I shall do so most reluctantly.'

I raised my chin, and though I was certainly intrigued, I spoke with caution. 'If – *if* I agree – when would we have to leave?'

'The Scotsman departs in two hours.'

34

I nearly fell backwards. 'What – *today*? Miss Ardglass, it is my father's burial!'

'I know, I know,' she said. 'It is a big ask, and truly unfair, but once you hear me you will understand.'

'Then speak quickly.'

Caroline looked around, her eyes flickering with anxiety. 'As I said, I shall tell you all on the way to Scotland.'

I let out a piercing '*HA!* You *must* be joking!' I turned my eyes to Joan. 'Do you know what this is all about?'

She opened her mouth, ready to prattle, but Caroline placed a hand on her shoulder and, for the first time in her communicative existence, Joan managed to bite her tongue in time.

Caroline's eyes seemed to go a shade darker. She stepped a little closer to me and whispered.

'I *beseech* you, Mr Frey. As soon as you hear me, you will agree all this secrecy is justified. I can assure you of that.'

Joan nodded vehemently, her lips tight, as if fearing that the moment she opened them everything would spurt out in a torrent.

I felt sorry for them, I truly did, but I needed to keep my stance. For the past year my compassion had dragged me to unimaginable lows, and I mean it quite literally – from ancient caves and stinking sewers to the most modern underground heater flues. The mere memory of the latter made me decide and, without speaking, I rose to my feet and headed back to the chapel.

'You cannot look forward to this service!' Caroline shouted behind me. 'Your eldest brother will surely show up.'

I halted at once, a sudden burst of anger in my chest.

'And his fiancée will not miss such an opportunity to show herself on his arm,' Caroline went on. 'Do you want to see your brother being comforted by the woman who left you at the altar?'

35

'*She never left me at the bloody*—!'

'*And,*' Caroline interjected, 'she will do so in front of all your late father's relatives and connections.'

Joan sneered. 'And I'm sure the smug floozy will flaunt her engagement ring as much as she can.'

I had a vivid picture of young Eugenia – the insufferable social climber who'd broken our engagement as soon as my luck turned sour – pressing a hankie to her bone-dry eyes, moving her hand to find the perfect angle for her offensively large diamond to catch the chapel's candlelight.

I growled, thinking of the scornful stares, the whispers, the triumphant sneers from my eldest brother – all that as background to my father's last rituals. I'd never say it out loud, but secretly I had looked for a genuine reason not to attend the funeral. And here it was, landing before me almost wrapped in ribbons.

I turned around very slowly, feigning struggle, for I did not want Caroline to think that my ulterior motive was simply to save my last dregs of dignity.

'Is this business – *truly* life or death?' I asked.

Caroline bit her lip. 'Well ... not yet. It may not come to that if you help us. But we must act quickly.'

The chapel's bell chimed, reminding me that my father's mourners would start flocking in very soon. I had but an instant to make up my mind.

In the end (and I hope the reader believes me), it was not the potential shame amidst my old London circles that made me decide. It was Caroline's gaze. She could not help eyeing her father's signet ring, perhaps an instant too long, before forcing herself to look sideways. I cannot quite describe the gesture. Despair, sorrow and even a hint of guilt all seemed to boil in her at the same time.

I let out a hissing breath, turning on my heels and pointing to the ground.

'Wait here,' I grunted. 'And if this turns out to be some trifle...!'

I did not finish the sentence, rushing back to the chapel. Elgie ran to me as soon as he saw me, his face almost as pale as the snow around him.

'Are you all right? Were those really witches?'

I smiled wryly. 'Some people might say so.'

'What did they—'

'Elgie... I have to go.'

My poor brother blinked a few times, struggling to take in my words.

'*What?* But Father's coffin is not even—'

I raised a hand. 'Yes, I know, but apparently there is some urgent matter to solve in Scotland; life or death, potentially.'

'But you don't work there anymore!'

'*I know! I just said so myself!*' I snapped, my voice travelling all across the cemetery. I took a deep breath and smoothed my coat. 'But it seems they really need me.'

We heard the distant sound of a whip, and then hooves. We turned our heads and saw a very familiar carriage parking some thirty yards away. Our eldest brother had arrived.

Elgie looked at me with a quizzical brow. 'Are you only agreeing to go because Eugenia and Laurence will—'

'*No*, I am bloody not! Make sure people know that!'

'How? What should I tell them? Mother will be the first one to suggest—'

'Just say it is CID matters. And –' I could not help myself – 'tell them you overheard that the Prime Minister himself needs me. *Again*. And – erm – that you heard something about Queen Victoria being involved too.'

I gave him a hasty one-arm hug, and when we stepped apart I saw him tensing his lips, trying not to laugh.

'What is so amusing?'

Elgie smiled. 'You've really beaten me this time. I gave you a fortnight, not fifteen minutes!'

I wanted to retort, but then we heard Eugenia cry something like, 'Oh, this odious slush!'

'Go,' Elgie said.

I nodded, adjusted my hat and strode towards the wilder end of the cemetery.

Just as I did so, the skies rumbled again in a long, dull thunder. A portentous omen, some would have said.

3

'Just look at them collars!' Joan cried when she pulled my shirts out of the trunk, so loudly even the train's steam whistle was no match. 'No starch in the middle, but the tips are so stiff you could stab a filthy cracksman with 'em.'

'You do not have to do that here,' I protested, massaging my temple.

I had paid extra to secure a first-class compartment, where I thought at least I could have some peace and quiet. I had not counted on Joan's old grudge against Layton, my 'stiff-lipped-fire-poker-of-a-valet', as she called him. She kept rummaging through my trunk; the only one I'd carried from Gloucestershire. I realised Layton had only packed my mourning clothes, so I'd be wearing nothing but dull black in the coming days. Then again, I *was* in mourning.

'Course I have to do this now!' Joan answered, brandishing one of my undergarments as if it were a flag. 'And look at these! Those filthy southrons don't know how to wash their—'

I had to jump on my feet and snatch the damn thing from her hands, for Caroline had just stepped into the compartment. I quickly plunged the unmentionable back into the trunk, but Caroline's slight blush told me she'd seen more than enough.

'Oh my!' she said rather theatrically, pointing at the shirts in

39

Joan's hands. 'You will have to redo those, Joan. Mr Frey cannot possibly show up in Edinburgh wearing *that*.'

Joan perked up proudly. 'Told ya, sir. Even the gal that hasn't rinsed a stocking in her life can tell!'

And she walked out with her chin high. I was going to ask her where she'd be taking my shirts. Did they even have pressing rooms on a train? (In all fairness, I did not even know where the washing rooms in my own home were.) Caroline stood in my way, mouthing 'Let her go', and closed the sliding door at once.

She sat in front of me and attended the tea service with exaggerated focus. I was about to ask why, but then I noticed that a generous fraction of my undergarments were still sticking out of the trunk. I closed it with a furious kick and pushed it under the seat.

'I had to send her away,' Caroline said at last, though looking a good deal tenser. 'The things I need to tell you .,.'

She sighed, and I saw a slight quiver as she poured a splash of milk into her cup. It struck me that she still had her gloves on.

'I thought Joan knew,' I said.

'Only the half of it,' Caroline answered, taking the cup to her lips.

'Would you prefer something for your nerves?' I offered, already reaching for my flask, but she raised a hand.

'No, no. I need a level head for this. Besides, it's not even noon.'

I was already pouring some for me into one of the teacups. 'My father just died and I am being dragged back to Scotland. Lulling the senses is a necessity.'

She took a quick sip of tea, her hands trembling even more. I could tell she was about to share some momentous information, and I felt a pang of sympathy. What could be worse than all the secrets I already knew about her and the ill-fated Ardglass family? Her insane father, secretly locked in Edinburgh's asylum;

the dubious businesses of her drunken grandmother; their dealings with the ruthless Lancashire witches...

I picked another cup, poured a small measure and casually placed it next to the scones.

'Just in case.'

Caroline looked at the golden drink for a moment, as if mesmerised by it. It was around then that the train rolled into a rainy patch, and streaks of water began to run down the windowpane. Their shadows were like freckles on Caroline's face.

'I'd better start from the beginning,' she said after a sigh. 'A month or so ago Adolphus – Mr McGray – was recruited by that new superintendent.'

'Trevelyan?' I asked. 'What for?'

'He wanted Mr McGray to keep an eye on Greyfriars Kirkyard.'

'The cemetery?' I asked with a frown.

'Indeed. Too many graves had been desecrated throughout the winter. Too many – *resurrections*.'

'And I assume McGray was all too happy to help.'

'Yes. Especially when he checked the dates. The diggings had coincided with the past three new moons. He thought it might be—'

'Witches looking for potion ingredients?' I said, seeing her hesitate. 'I know that some of their remedies call for things like livers and hands exhumed at specific lunar phases.'

I could see Elgie in my head, mocking my now extensive knowledge on the occult.

'Yes, Mr McGray said that very same thing. He began investigations right away. He already had a few contacts who knew about the resurrections market, so he made good progress. It all seemed almost routine, until...' She was about to pull off her glove, but seemed to think better of it, and reached for her tea instead. 'One of his contacts told him that on the next new moon the body snatchers would definitely be at work again.'

'The next new moon?' I asked. 'Do you mean – last night?'

'Yes.'

'How did you make it to London so quickly?'

'I took a steamer. Do you remember Captain Jones?'

'How could I forget him? Did he take you to London?'

'No, his ship wasn't ready. But a friend of his, a merchant, was about to sail off. Sadly they could not take us back. After London their route was—' She shook her head. 'It doesn't matter. What you must know now is that this digging and the new moon also coincided with the death of one of the inmates at the asylum.'

I leaned slightly forwards. 'Did it?'

'Yes. The deceased was an elderly lady whom Mr McGray knew very well. I understand she lost her wits years ago, out of sheer fright after she walked into ... an attic, I think.'

I raised my eyebrows. 'Why, I remember that case! Nine-Nails claimed the attic was haunted. That some evil spirit dwelled in there and frightened people to death. The woman's husband did die upon entering that room.'

Though I did not recall their names, I could never forget that the house in question was near the Botanical Gardens. McGray had forced me to inspect it once, at night, when the stars were in the right *alignment*. Ghastly experience it had been. I shall never speak of it again.

'Pray continue,' I said.

'The poor lady died,' Caroline went on. 'Natural causes, as far as we know. Dr Clouston, of course, informed Mr McGray at once, since he'd been so invested in the woman's case. That is how he heard that in life the lady had arranged to be buried in the Grayfriars' cemetery, next to her husband. Mr McGray feared that the snatchers might have their eyes set on her. He was right.'

'Of course,' I agreed. 'Did he catch the snatchers?'

'One of them. Well – the man got himself killed when he was trying to flee. His accomplice ran away.'

'And did McGray manage to recover the body?'

'Yes, and that is where things become complicated.' Her eyes flickered, as if trying to solve a mental puzzle, so I gave her time. 'The body – well, it was not what we might call *intact*.'

The way she said it made me feel a slight shiver.

'I do not like where this is going,' I muttered. 'Had some witches taken something?'

'No, no,' she said quickly, trembling at the very mention of the word. 'Rather . . . the woman's face had been marked.'

I frowned. '*Marked?* How?'

Caroline shook her head. 'Mr McGray doesn't know yet. I didn't see the poor woman, of course, but I understand it was not something done with knife or ink or fire. It was some sort of *stain*.'

'I do not follow.'

'Neither did I. That is all I heard: the lady was buried with an unblemished face, yet when she was disinterred, this mark was on her skin.'

'Intriguing indeed,' I muttered. 'Are you certain she was not—?'

'That's all I know. The last I heard was that the body had been taken to the morgue and that a Dr Reed was to look at it.'

'I see,' I said, lounging back and already thinking of the possibilities.

'I do know the mark's shape, however.'

Caroline spat that phrase, as if fearing she might not have the courage if she waited for too long.

'What was it?' I asked. 'I have paper. You can draw it if—'

'It was the Devil's face,' she spat again.

Either the rain became harder then, or it wasn't until that moment that I noted the insistent drumming on the glass.

'The Devil's face?' I repeated, already pulling my little notebook out of my breast pocket.

'Yes,' Caroline said as she put the teacup down and took the notebook. I also passed her a little pencil. 'Two long horns and two slits for eyes—'

She rubbed the pencil on the paper in an anxious manner, nearly knocking the teapot over, and then pushed the sketch back to me.

'This,' she said. 'It looked exactly this.'

I picked it up and looked at the drawing. She'd almost torn the page with her tracing. It truly looked like a squinting, horned demon, but also...

I tilted my head, realising something. 'This is very detailed,' I remarked, lifting the notebook and arching a brow. 'Yet you just told me that you never saw the dead woman yourself.'

Caroline could not blink for a moment, a gesture of utter guilt taking hold of her face.

I knew that expression. She'd told me far too many lies in the past, and this was the gesture she pulled whenever she knew herself cornered.

'The same symbol was found somewhere else that very night,' she said finally.

'I see. Where?'

'At Edinburgh's asylum. Right after an inmate was —' she gulped – 'murdered.'

'Murdered? How?'

'Stabbed, I heard.'

I lifted the sketch again. 'And this very same symbol appeared at the asylum?'

'Yes. Drawn in blood.'

'Oh, God!' I groaned. 'Typical!'

'And from Mr McGray's depictions of the old lady's mark,' Caroline went on, 'it was identical to what I just drew.'

'Did McGray also draw it for you?' I asked.

'No. He didn't want to discuss the murder in detail.'

I stared at her for a moment. 'So – how is it *you* know what it looked like?'

Caroline took a deep breath and looked out the window, at the grey, blurred landscape, unable to meet my eye.

'Because I was there when it was still on the wall.'

I nearly dropped my cup.

'*You were at the asylum?*' I cried. '*Again?* Whatever for? Your father died last year!' How could I ever forget that case? It had taken us all the way to the Lancashire wilderness and... and then something clicked in my mind and my jaw dropped.

'You used to visit him during new moons, did you not?'

Caroline looked at me with a mixture of fear and embarrassment. She had broken into the asylum for months, always on moonless nights and swathed in black cloaks, like the one she'd worn to the cemetery that very day. Despite her precautions, some of the inmates had managed to spot her from time to time, calling her *the new moon phantom.*

I stroked my chin, the implications of the case taking shape in my head. 'I see why you were so desperate to get my help. If it transpires that you were there that very night, and that you also visited the asylum before, in similar circumstances—'

Caroline looked through the window again. I realised she was pooling tears, and I felt terribly sorry for her.

I let out a long sigh, refilled my teacup (not with tea, of course) and lounged back. I wanted to give her some breathing space, but I could not. Joan could come back at any time.

'I must know,' I said softly, 'before you tell me anything else about this murder. What on earth were you doing there?'

Her lip trembled, as did the tears that had built up in her eyes, reluctant to run free.

'I erm—' She looked desperately for a handkerchief under her sleeve. 'I was visiting Miss McGray.'

She found no hanky, so I offered her mine. I almost wished I had not, for as soon as she touched it she finally broke down. Her face wrinkled in a miserable grimace and the tears came out like a burst dam.

Not once did she weep. She cried in silence instead, dabbing her eyes with shaking hands.

Foolishness. Recklessness. Those were the first words that came to mind; Caroline being thoughtless and embarking on some imprudent action for some silly reason. But . . .

'Why?' I asked. 'Why would you? Unfortunate as her situation might be, Miss McGray is nothing to you.'

The train entered a dense woodland, which darkened the compartment.

Caroline gulped, her face dappled with fleeting shadows, and answered with a broken voice.

'You're mistaken. Miss McGray is my sister.'

4

McGray's wide blue eye looked thrice its size behind the thick lens. To the opposite side, the view was far less pleasant – a ghastly, deep cut on human flesh, the blood now dry and blackened at the edges.

The clots framed a generous layer of yellowish fat, the splinters of a rib, shreds of sinew and the still shimmering edge of the man's right lung.

There had been many stabs to the chest. How many, McGray could not tell, for they'd all cut at the same spot with astounding precision, severing arteries and flesh and even denting bones. The blade, though clearly very sharp, must have been rather short too, judging from the marks on the lung.

McGray looked at the dead man's face again. He appeared to have been in his fifties, with sagging skin on his wide neck, a grey moustache and only a few strands of white hair on a blotched scalp. He might have been younger though; life at an asylum was not precisely an idyll.

As he thought so, McGray rose fully, feeling another shiver. Not because of the nude corpse that lay before him, but because of the draughty, unheated storeroom the asylum staff had used to keep the body in.

The sandstone walls were crammed with garden shears, spades

and pikes – ironic decor for a man who'd just been stabbed. McGray looked at them with squinting eyes, all the blades either covered with rust or dry soil. There was only one narrow window, the glass cracked and grimy, letting in very little light along with the icy wind.

The young nurse noticed McGray's squint and brought the oil lamp a little closer, to place it carefully on the corner of the wooden worktable.

McGray took a moment to inspect the three grim faces that stood by the corpse. To the left was the young nurse, so new at her post that McGray did not recall her pasty, freckled face. To the right was the creased, seasoned head nurse, Cassandra Smith. And in between them stood the tall, sour Dr Harland, who'd been on shift at the time of the murder. They all looked tense, though each in their own particular way. The only somewhat relaxed face was that of spindly Constable McNair, who stood stoically by McGray's side.

'Ye can cover him now,' McGray said.

Miss Smith nodded and the junior nurse rushed to extend the shroud. McNair helped her, seeing that she nearly retched at the sight of the wound. That poor lass would not last long in the asylum. Ironic that the staff came and went, and yet McGray's sister lingered. Just the thought of her made Nine-Nails shudder; this ordeal might prove disastrous for her. He shook his head and forced himself to focus on the more immediate facts.

'What was his name?' he asked, nodding at the body.

Dr Harland glanced at his pad. 'John MacDonnell,' he said, not bothering to conceal a slur of boredom.

'And the ailment?'

'Extreme delusions.'

The words hung in the air, the wind whistling outside as Dr Harland moistened his lips.

'*And?*' McGray pressed.

Harland let out an exasperated sigh, lifted the pad and began turning the pages most wearily.

'Och, am I bothering ye, ye daft sod?' McGray snapped. 'Anything more important in yer calendar?'

Dr Harland moved marginally faster.

'Extreme case of delusion,' he read when he found the appropriate page. 'He believes – well, *believed*, that there were foul vapours in the air, which, in his very words to Dr Clouston, "wasted his insides", whatever he meant by that.' Harland wrinkled his nose as he read on. 'In order to guard himself from those vapours he used to stuff nose, ears, mouth and – well, any bodily crevice, with paper and rags. Or anything at hand.'

McGray lifted the edge of the white sheet, picked up one of the man's icy hands and saw the chafed tips and nails. They must have looked red in life; now they were almost purple. McGray tucked it back in place.

'Did he ever get vicious?' he asked. 'Make any enemies with the other patients? With the staff?'

'I do not know,' Dr Harland said swiftly. 'He was not in my caseload.'

McGray snorted. 'Could ye be any more useless?'

'We have eight hundred and forty-six residing patients, inspector. I cannot possibly keep track of them all.'

'He was never vicious, inspector,' Miss Smith said, taking a step forward. 'MacDonnell, I mean. Kept himself to himself. He'd been doing quite well lately, to be frank. His last episode was in September.'

McGray arched an eyebrow. 'He one o' yer patients, Miss Smith?'

'No, but I do take a pride in my work.' She cast Harland an accusing stare when she said so. The doctor simply rolled his eyes.

'I guess it wasnae *ye* who brought him here,' McGray said,

looking at Harland, whose white coat and wavy blond hair looked pristine.

'I told two orderlies to do so,' he said, and McGray shook his head.

'Ye shouldnae have.'

'He was in the middle of the hall,' Harland protested. 'In the east wing, where our better-off inmates stay. Your own sister inclu—'

Miss Smith elbowed him discreetly, seeing that McGray was beginning to clench his fists.

'And youse also cleaned,' Nine-Nails grunted.

'We had inmates running to and fro,' Harland said. 'We could not let them wander into a butchered man and a pool of blood. Perhaps now Dr Clouston will listen to me and start locking the inmates in their rooms at night.'

McGray ground his teeth, his face slowly turning red. He had to take a deep breath not to beat the haughty doctor to a pulp there and then. He turned to the young nurse.

'It was ye who found him, right?'

The girl, who could not be much older than sixteen, nodded. Her two braids of bristly blond hair were dishevelled.

'What's yer name?'

'Evangeline, sir.'

'Inspector, not sir!' Harland corrected. 'And you have a surname.'

McGray raised a hand – the one with a missing finger, which the girl eyed nervously.

'What were ye doing in the corridor, Evangeline?'

The girl gulped. 'I was emptying some potties, sir – inspector.'

'That part o' yer job?'

The girl began stammering, and Miss Smith had to answer for her.

'Yes, inspector. She does her rounds twice every night.'

'There, there,' said McGray soothingly. 'I need ye to tell me what ye saw. We'll give ye a few drops o' brandy after this.'

Dr Harland let out an impatient scoff, and McGray did not punch him only because young Evangeline spoke just then.

'I only saw the dead man, inspector. I came 'round the corridor and found him there on the floor, just—' she seemed to run out of breath.

Miss Smith went to her and patted her on the back. 'Go on, darling.'

Evangeline gulped and took a few deep breaths.

'I – I only saw him for a wee moment, on the floor 'n' in a pool o' blood. I dropped the potty and I screamed. I also dropped my candle and I had to look for Miss Smith or Dr Harland in the dark. I thought I'd be next! I – I—'

'Calm down, calm down,' Miss Smith whispered, and then looked at McGray. 'She's telling you the truth. We found the potty and the light next to the man when we came by.'

'Did ye see anything or anyone?' McGray asked her.

Evangeline shook her head. 'No, but – it was dark. I dropped my candle, like I said, and it – it was dark.'

'Ye hear anything? Before or right after ye found him?'

The girl stared at the covered body, and then shook with a tremor.

'A gag, sir.'

'A gag?' McGray repeated.

'Aye, inspector. As if – as if the man were choking.'

McGray nodded. 'I see. Anything else? Did ye hear him fall? Any footsteps?'

The girl closed her eyes, doing her best to remember. 'No, inspector. Nothing at all. And I do have a good memory.'

'What about youse?' McGray asked Harland and Miss Smith. 'Where were youse when it happened?'

Dr Harland cleared his throat. 'I was in my study, as the girl can confirm. She found me there after she saw the dead man.'

McGray noted the slightly higher pitch of the doctor's voice.

'Did *ye* hear anything?'

'Nothing out of the ordinary. Orderlies coming and going, nurses gossiping and so on. The place had been rather quiet in the minutes preceding the – well, the minutes I presume must have preceded the murder.'

'And the lass came to ye and it was then that ye found the body?'

'Yes. I took my own lamp and followed the girl.' He sneered at her. 'As you can imagine, she was hysterical and made little sense. To be frank, I thought she had just found an inmate pulling some silly act. I only believed that the man was dead and soaked in blood when I saw him. Sadly, the child's screeches roused one of the inmates: Mrs Rochford, a very old, very wealthy patient. She peeked out, saw the dead man and howled like the maniac she is. Things spiralled after that; orderlies and nurses came by, more inmates got out of their rooms ... It was then that I went looking for Miss Smith, as things were getting out of hand.' He cast her a questioning look. 'I am surprised you did not come at once, with all that racket.'

'I was tending to Miss McGray,' she rushed to say. Nine-Nails felt a pang in the chest at the very mention of his sister.

'That late?' Harland probed.

'*Shut it!*' McGray hissed. 'I ask the questions here.' He looked at Miss Smith. 'It was nearly midnight, right? Did Pansy need ye that late?'

Miss Smith tensed her lips.

'I'm nae questioning ye, Miss Smith,' McGray said. Cassandra, who'd looked after his sister for so many years now, was beyond suspicion. 'Was Pansy all right?'

'Yes, yes, of course. I just heard her stir and went in to make sure she was fine.'

Harland's eyebrow arched further. 'Are you sure? When I found you I heard you talking to someone.'

Miss Smith glared at him. 'I told you then! I was talking to Miss McGray. I always do, even if she doesn't reply.'

Harland smirked. 'You'd do well to watch your tone with me – *Miss* Smith.'

Cassandra's face blushed with sheer anger; Evangeline's with embarrassment.

McGray could not repress himself any longer and threw the man a slap on the temple. Caught off guard, Harland crashed sideways against the wall, knocking secateurs and pots.

'*Ye* watch yer tone, ye silly turd! Talk to her like that one more time and I'll scour yer wee shrivelled baws with the rustiest rake I can find in here.' He waited for Harland to prop himself up again. 'Now tell me, where's the knife?'

Harland smoothed out his coat and his hair, all the while looking daggers at McGray.

'We didn't find one.'

'What?'

'That's true,' Miss Smith intervened. 'Either one of the inmates took it before we got there, or whoever did it took it away.'

'Oh damn!' McGray let out with a sigh. 'McNair, we'll have to do a proper search. Arrange it with the lads as soon as possible. If that damned knife's still in the asylum it might give us a track to follow.'

'We can help you,' Miss Smith offered. 'Your officers might alarm our patients.'

'Sorry, Miss Smith, but the lads will have to do it. Am sure ye understand. We don't want people at the Sheriff's Court claiming yer staff tampered with the evidence.'

She nodded, though reluctantly, and McGray saw how tense

she really was, the tendons on her neck flickering. Could she be hiding something? Protecting someone, perhaps?

McGray sighed. He might talk to her later. In private.

'Very well, I think I'm done here for the time being.' He looked at Harland. 'Make sure nobody touches the body until the constables arrive. *Nobody*. If I hear that even a sodding fly rested on the lad's belly I'll come to ye with that rusty rake. *Get it?*' He didn't wait for a reply. 'Now take me to that blood smear on the wall. I want to see it again.'

Silence.

McGray looked into everyone's eyes, but even Miss Smith could not meet his gaze.

'Och, what is it now?'

Miss Smith fidgeted with the folds of her skirt, quite at odds with her usual commanding manner.

'It will have been cleaned by now,' she spluttered.

McGray's jaw dropped. '*What?* Och, you have to be joking!'

The women looked down, Dr Harland sideways, and even Constable McNair held his breath.

McGray grunted and raised his hands, set as if ready to strangle someone. He would have punched the walls, but they were all crammed with dangerous blades.

'So youse moved the poor wretch,' he spat, 'cleaned his blood, cleaned the damned marks on the wall too, then ...' He rubbed his face in utter frustration. 'Did youse also give the gate keys to the inmates in case they wanted to go for a wee wander?'

Harland answered with a growl. 'We were following orders – inspector.'

'*Whose?* Who was the sodding idiot that—?'

'*That would be me.*'

An icy draught came in along with the voice. It was Dr Clouston, who'd just opened the door, his black overcoat contrasting sharply with the snow outside. He shut the creaking door hastily, his hands shaking from the cold. His cheekbones and shiny scalp were blushed, his bushy beard doing little to keep him warm.

McGray was taken aback not only by the sudden confession, but also because the asylum's superintendent looked terribly haggard, his eyes sunken as if he'd not slept in days.

'Why did ye do that?' McGray snapped soon enough. 'Ye of all people ken the sort o' work I'll have to do!'

Dr Clouston raised his chin.

'I'm sorry, Adolphus. I could not leave that ghastly mess down there to disturb my patients and staff.'

'Ye may have a bloody murderer at large in yer asylum! *That* will fuckin' disturb them!'

Clouston nodded, but instead of answering he looked at Dr Harland and Miss Smith.

'Leave us, please. We need as many hands in there as we can get. That is, if Inspector McGray is happy to let you go.'

McGray only waved a dismissive hand.

Young Evangeline was all too happy to go, as well as Dr Harland. Miss Smith hesitated, but Clouston nodded reassuringly at her, and the nurse blushed. Again, McGray felt the woman was acting oddly. She'd never been a shy violet.

'May I speak with Adolphus in private?' Clouston asked, looking politely at McNair. The constable in turn looked at McGray, who nodded in approval. 'Leave the light, please,' Clouston added, for McNair had already picked up the little oil lamp. He left it back on the worktable.

As soon as the constable shut the door, McGray burst out, 'Ye really should've left that untouched! This is serious!'

Clouston shivered in the cold. He had to hug himself and rub his arms.

'I thought Amy would be your main concern.'

There was a clear hint of a reproach there, and McGray had to bite his lip.

'*Of course* she is,' he said. 'The first thing I did was to ask about Pansy. Miss Smith told me she was fine.' Then, as if catching the chill from Clouston, he trembled too. '*Is* she?'

'Yes, yes,' Clouston said quickly. 'I checked on her as soon as the situation allowed me. She is perfectly fine. I didn't even need to sedate her.'

'Does she ken someone's been murdered near her rooms? Again?'

Clouston covered his brow. 'Don't remind me of that bloody Ardglass affair. Every day I regret my involvement.'

'Aye. Any involvement with an Ardglass can only end in a stushie,' McGray said with a roguish smile – the only one he'd pull that day.

'To answer your question,' Clouston said, 'she does seem to realise that something untoward is happening. This sort of agitation could not go unnoticed even by her. But she cannot know it was a murder. She'd be terribly anxious if she knew.'

'Is she awake, then? Can I see her?'

'She is awake all right, but I would not advise that you see her just now.'

'Why?'

'If she sees you, she'll know for sure that something very serious has happened. You have witnessed how your presence can distress her; kindly meant as it might be.'

Another reproach. McGray growled, knowing very well Clouston was right. He'd never forget the episode at the Orkneys clinic, where Pansy had been taken for a few months right after the 'Ardglass affair'. Clouston had decided to move her there precisely because McGray's constant calls seemed to upset the girl. Quite recklessly, McGray decided to visit her there, which, of course, had dreadful consequences. No one knew how, but the night after McGray's arrival, Pansy had managed to escape the nurses' watch, scuttle out of the clinic and end up on a nearby beach. They'd found her in the morning, staring at the sea, her bare feet plunged in the freezing waters.

McGray winced at the memory. The thought of his sister stepping into the endless waters never to be seen again...

'Besides,' Clouston added while McGray pondered, 'you won't need to see her or to inspect her room for your investigations. I can assure you – Pansy was most definitely *not* involved in this.'

McGray frowned, indignant.

'Of course she wasnae! The question never even crossed my mind! But *others*—'

McGray had to cover his brow, his worst fears finally coming to the fore, louder than any other thought.

His sister's madness was a thing of local lore – the lass who claimed she'd been possessed by Satan, right after going on a killing spree; the lass who'd never spoken again, forever locked in a mental institution.

And now there'd been another murder at her asylum. Devilish marks left behind. All mere steps from Pansy's room. All on the same night McGray had found the Devil's mark on an unburied body – the body of an inmate from the *same* asylum.

It would only be a matter of time before those facts reached the press. And as soon as it happened, people's imaginations would go wild.

'Ye ken what people will think,' McGray managed to say collectedly after a few deep breaths. 'Ye ken the sort o' gossip that'll follow a thing like this.'

'I do, Adolphus, I—'

'And ye ken I'll have to prove beyond doubt that she wasnae involved. *Beyond those court vultures' doubt!*'

Clouston pinched the bridge of his nose, a slight twitch in his shut eyes. McGray noticed that the man's crowfeet had deepened within a very short time, as if something were eating him inside.

'What might happen if I fail?' slipped off McGray's tongue; the question he'd promised himself he would not ask this early. But now that he'd said it, he could not stop. 'What might happen if she's accused of murder – *another* murder – and I cannae do anything to clear her name?'

Clouston's eyes opened wide. 'Adolphus, it is too soon to—'

'Tell me,' McGray insisted.

For a moment Clouston held his breath, and when finally he exhaled, it came out as a puff of vapour.

'She will not be jailed, for sure, but…' a deep sigh. 'But if the court determines she committed such an act under my supervision – other physicians might be summoned, which would be dreadful, since—'

Clouston gulped, and for a moment he seemed on the verge of tears.

'Since they'll most likely decide this institution is not fit to care for her. They'd take her away to another asylum, with *more secure* facilities… to be treated as a menace.'

McGray had somewhat guessed that would be the answer, but he still felt his face go cold and numb, as if life itself ebbed away.

He knew what those secure facilities looked like: tiny, grimy cells, with narrow barred windows, and as icy and damp as medieval dungeons. Inmates were not treated; they were taken there to die and be forgotten, visitors seldom allowed. McGray pictured Pansy crouching in such a place, cold and soiled, and a renewed wave of fear made him start.

'Don't torture yourself,' Clouston said. McGray saw him bite his lip, surely to stop himself saying 'just yet'.

For a moment McGray did not care how alarmed he looked. He rubbed his chest and allowed himself to breathe.

'Very well, doctor,' he said after clearing his throat. 'We'd better get in now, I can see yer arse is freezing. And I better get to work. I'll have to search the place and question all yer staff and yer more lucid inmates. It will take us the best part o' the day. And then I'll have to attend that other case at Greyfriars... Damn, I do hate my post sometimes!'

'We shall do all we can to assist you,' Clouston said, already rushing to the door. McGray was going to open it, but before doing so he nodded at the corpse.

'I told that sod, Harland, to keep the body well guarded until our lads can come and take it to the mortuary. Please make sure he does.'

'Oh! I... erm... I want to talk to you about that too.' Clouston placed a hand on the door, if only to pretend he could keep McGray from opening it.

'Do ye?'

Clouston looked almost meek – as unusual for him as it was for Miss Smith.

'Mac— MacDonnell's family wish to pay their respects,' he said, 'and I'd really like them to see him before he's been, well, *examined* and sewn back together. Could you please leave him here until tomorrow?'

McGray snorted. 'What? Did ye nae hear what I just said? This is a murder investigation! We have to do what we have to do!'

'Of course, of course. I am asking this as a personal favour. The man had two daughters and three very young grandchildren. The women have gone through unimaginable struggles to keep him here under proper care. I've condoned their debts whenever I could, and they've always had help from the asylum's charity fund, but I do need to keep this institution afloat.'

McGray sighed again, this time deeper and longer. 'Ye do get yerself in a lot o' trouble for yer patients, doc.' *Like he's done for*

Pansy, a little voice chided in his head, and he grunted. 'How long d'ye need?'

'I expect them to be here tomorrow.'

'*Tomorrow!*'

'Yes. I know it is too much to ask, but they live in the Highlands, where they all hail from. They are desperate. I had to pay for their train fares from my own pocket.' Nine-Nails was already shaking his head, so Clouston rushed to add: 'Show them some mercy, please. One day we might need someone to have mercy on your sister.'

McGray closed his eyes, those words stinging like needles. He went back to the body and lifted the shroud to have one last look at the man's face. Just as he did so, a particularly cold draught came in through the crack on the window.

'Well, he won't go maggoty in this weather; that much is sure.' He sighed. 'Very well, I'll pull a few strings. But the *minute* they—'

He noticed something then. Something he had missed before.

It was barely a shadow, perhaps highlighted by a small shift in the light. Perhaps McNair had left the lamp on a slightly different spot.

Whatever the reason, McGray saw a new shade now, outlining a small bulge on the man's cheek.

He brought his fingers to the cold, still sticky lips, and very gently pushed them open. They made a brief, repulsive sound.

'What the—'

'What is it?' Clouston asked, leaning over the corpse.

McGray saw a nauseating tinge of yellow, like bile, and then grey, like rotten meat, as he held the lips open. He winced and, with his other hand's index and thumb, pulled out a tip of that ghastly material.

'A rag,' he said.

Clouston assented. 'Johnnie … he used to stuff his mouth with—'

'Aye. Harland told me.'

McGray pulled and pulled. The nasty strip of damp cloth seemed to have no end. It looked like an old, frayed bandage. He'd pulled out a good eight inches of it when he found some resistance. Clouston had to help him, opening the man's mouth further.

A sickening waft came out, but Clouston barely reacted to it. He inserted his entire index and middle finger, worked out the bandage, and finally pulled out a slimy tangle.

'That lassie, Evangeline, said she heard a gag,' McGray said, seeing how Clouston spread the rag on the pristine sheet.

It was no bandage. It looked more like a piece of printed cloth; yellow stripes against a once-white background. It was now soaked in ghastly bile: MacDonnell must have vomited, the rag keeping it all in like a revolting cork.

'There is a stain here, Adolphus,' Clouston said.

'Of course there is! The poor sod must've—'

'No, no. There is *writing* here!'

'What?'

McGray grabbed the lamp and shed light on the rag.

Not that he needed it. He could see the letters clearly; the dark, bluish ink, seeping on the cloth like a fungus. And yet the words could not be clearer.

Why won't you die?

5

'Sis – sis – *sister!*' I squeaked.

'Half-sister, rather,' Caroline mumbled, still staring out the window, even if it offered nothing but a grey blur.

I cannot tell for how long I sat there, motionless, simply looking at her. It was my teacup, half full of whisky and slowly sliding through my fingers, which brought me back to the present.

'Half-sisters…' I repeated, all the cogs and bolts in my head reeling. As far as I knew, they could not possibly have had the same mother. In which case…

'Lord Joel?' I said, again in high-pitched tones. 'Lord Joel and the late Mrs—' my mouth opened in a perfect 'O'. *'Lord Joel and McGray's mother?'*

'I will not draw you a family tree,' Caroline snapped, pushing her teacup aside and grabbing the measure of whisky I'd poured for her. 'It was a very sad affair. My grandmother must have bribed every servant and their dog to keep it all quiet.'

I only half heard her. 'Miss McGray is about to turn twenty-two, is she not?' I counted in my head. 'Yes, she went into the asylum aged fifteen, which was six – six and a half years ago. That makes her ten years younger than Nine-Nails. The age difference always struck me, but never to consider—' I looked back at Caroline, a new question imposing itself above many others. 'How long have you known?'

Caroline had her first sip of Scotch, twisting her mouth at the taste.

'I only learned last December.'

I frowned. 'During our last skirmish with the witches?'

Caroline gave a quick nod.

'Your old nanny Bertha?' I guessed. 'Did she tell you?'

'Yes. Right before she died.'

'Of course,' I mumbled, allowing myself a long sip of liquor. 'She looked after you since you were a new-born. She would have been aware of any extramarital—'

'*Stop!*' Caroline hissed, putting the cup down with a clank. 'Remember it is my father you speak of.'

Your father the mad murderer, a voice whispered in my head. I'd always thought that insanity ran in the McGray family. Could it be that it in fact came from the Ardglass side?

'I am sorry, Miss Ardglass,' I said. 'I did not mean to treat your family affairs as mishaps out of a penny dreadful. But I do need to know—'

'You need to know no more,' she cut off. 'I was at the asylum when the murder took place, for the reason I have just explained. The head nurse can vouch for me, if you need it. She helped me get in and kept my presence secret. I know nothing else about that death, so you need to hear nothing else from me.'

I tilted my head. 'On the contrary. If I am to investigate this matter, I will very well have to—'

'I am telling you, you do not. And if you call yourself a gentleman, you will not demand any more details.'

'Miss Ardglass, all I—'

'All you must know is that Pansy had nothing to do with that death or that ghastly smear of blood on the walls. She cannot have. I was with her all the time.'

I arched a brow, the details of Pansy's madness coming to mind.

'The last thing she ever said was that the Devil had possessed her,' I said sombrely.

'Yes.'

Caroline said no more, that one syllable leaving everything implied.

Amy McGray, so close to not one but *two* deaths seemingly connected to the Devil. Not only would the press have a field day with the story, but the McGrays' enemies (and there were a couple I could think of) would make the most of it. Clouston too might be declared unfit for his post, allowing such things to happen under his watch. And Pansy… what might become of her, if the good doctor could not treat her any longer? Where would she end up, accused of two more deaths? Also – how devastated Nine-Nails would be! The things he'd be capable of doing, if it came to that!

The thought was so dreadful it took me a moment to focus again.

'So,' I said, 'it will be up to me to investigate the inmate's murder, in the light of Miss McGray having a solid alibi.'

'Precisely. Also, you cannot tell Mr McGray how it is you know. He would ask me questions and I could not—'

She bit her lip all of a sudden, her cheeks turning red, which I found rather strange. I would have understood the embarrassment from anyone else (discussing one's father's philandering can hardly be a pleasant endeavour), but the late Joel Ardglass had committed much worse felonies.

And there was something odd in Caroline's expression. I could tell that her tension stemmed from something else; something she would not share with me.

'Do you expect McGray never to find out about this connection?' I asked. 'Even if you do keep visiting his – *your* – half-sister? What will you do if someday he finds—'

'I shall cross that bridge when I come to it.'

She glanced at me for an instant and then looked at the tea service.

'It will have gone cold,' she said, and at once she stood up and left the compartment. In her haste she left the sliding door slightly open. I stood up and followed her, but then stopped under the threshold, seeing the manner in which she scurried away. Her head was bent down, the young woman possibly shedding more tears now that she thought I could not see her. I'd better give her some space.

I shut the door and went back to my seat, suspecting I would not hear from her for the rest of the journey. At least I could use the time to ponder.

I remembered looking into a comprehensive file on Joel Ardglass, which covered his insanity and his life before reclusion. I did not recall the finer details, though. Those records had been in my hands a little over a year ago, and I'd not precisely had a quiet time since.

That file might still be in McGray's—

I let out a growl, remembering that after our very last case, the Prime Minister – yes, the Prime Minister – had raided our office and seized most of its contents.

Nine-Nails, as far as I knew, had been able to salvage some of his most prized artefacts (witchcraft books, anomalous specimens, treatises on the occult and the like). I could only hope that he'd also had the sense to look after our most valuable records. In fact, I should look for those documents first thing.

I did not know what I expected to find there, but the story was intriguing indeed. The Ardglasses and the McGrays... ever sailing on a sea of murky dealings.

It piqued my curiosity as much as that devilish mark, seemingly pulled out of a grave.

6

The weather worsened as we moved north.

We travelled across Cambridgeshire under grey skies; by the time we passed Darlington there were thunderous clouds, and then a thick fog received us when we crossed the Scottish border. It went on and on as far as the eye could see, as if settling all over the country as the day came to an early close. When we approached Edinburgh's improvised Caledonian station, all that could be seen of the castle were the tips of its battlements and main tower, rising well above the mist like floating ghosts.

Joan came back then, with freshly pressed and starched shirts (I have no idea how she managed it) and she forced me to change into one of them. I cannot tell whether it was the scent or the texture, but as soon as I put it on, it took me back to the days she'd looked after me, back when I still lived in my rented chambers in London's Suffolk Street. Sadly, the immaculate shirts only highlighted my mourning clothes.

The moment I stepped off the train I was hit by an icy draught, which sent a stabbing pain to my right wrist. I could not hide a wince as I clenched it with my other hand. It was right then that Caroline reappeared, emerging from another compartment just in time to witness my discomfort. To my surprise, she did not mock me.

'Are you still able to shoot?' she asked, keeping an eye on the young chap who unloaded our luggage.

'I have not even tried since they took the splints off,' I said, and then arched a suspicious brow. 'Why? Do you think I will have to?'

She only shrugged.

Joan rushed to her and threw a heavy, black bearskin coat on her shoulders.

'There, Miss. Don't make me tell you again! Last thing you need is to catch consumption now.'

Caroline groaned. 'You do not just *catch* consump— *Oh, keep off, I can do it!*' And she pushed away Joan's hands as the stubborn woman attempted to button up the coat for her.

They began a rowdy quarrel, and only then did I have a head to ask:

'How did you come to be travelling together?'

Joan interlaced her hands, pushing out her lower lip. 'Master Adolphus didn't want the gal going up 'n' down the country by herself like a common—'

Thankfully, a steam whistle drowned the epithet.

'Nine-Nails concerned about virtue?' I mocked.

Joan opened her mouth wide, again ready to prattle, but Caroline interjected.

'Do you know where you'll be staying, Mr Frey?'

'I do, in fact. I will take lodgings at the Palace Hotel.'

'Oh, will you?' Joan moaned. 'I had already arranged to bake you them fruit scones you like so much!'

I cannot express just how tempting the offer was, but I had already concocted a plan. It would be far easier to gather my own evidence and compile my own notes if I could be based away from McGray's snooping eyes.

'I am so sorry, Joan. I do not want to be distracted until this matter is solved. In fact, I should leave presently; if there are no vacancies, at least I will have time to look elsewhere.' I turned to Caroline. 'Miss Ardglass, are you staying at your grandmother's house on Duke Street?'

'Gosh, no! I took—' She cast Joan a tired look. '*We* took an apartment on Charlotte Square. One of my grandmother's empty rentals.'

'Empty rentals?' I asked. 'The good Lady Anne holding on to idle assets?'

Caroline scoffed. 'These days she does nothing but moan about how difficult it is to get reliable tenants – people that don't burn her properties to cinders.'

'Oh, Lord! *You* of all people know that I had nothing to do with the fire that—'

'She is selling many properties as we speak,' Caroline interjected, 'and putting her money in the old quarries – so that *others* make the money for her. Here, Mr Frey.' She handed me a little card. 'This is my address in case you need me.'

I gave it a glance and put it in my pocket. 'Very well. I shall be in touch very soon.'

After a quick bow I threw a sixpence at a cab driver, who'd been standing nearby waiting for business, and we walked away. At once I could hear Caroline and Joan arguing again. I nearly said something along the line of needing them both alive, but preferred not to face their combined wrath.

I followed the driver to the road, full of go despite the inclement weather. He found his nondescript cab with outstanding speed, secured my luggage and opened the door for me.

'Did ye say the Palace Hotel, master?'

I looked back to make sure Caroline and Joan were not within hearing range.

'No. Take me to the City Chambers first.'

The man frowned. 'The police headquarters?'

'Indeed. I have work to do.'

The night had drawn in properly by the time the cab made it to the infamous Royal Mile. The fog, thick and unmovable, turned the street lights into milky, yellowy blurs that diffused into nothingness.

The road, as expected, was deserted; we only saw the occasional late worker rushing home, and a couple of intoxicated men swaying their way from the nearby pubs, like the Ensign Ewart, McGray's den of preference. I heard some drunken chants coming from within, right before the contents of a chamber pot splashed dangerously close to my window.

'The usual welcome,' I sighed.

Very soon I saw the façade of the City Chambers emerge on my left-hand side, right in front of the shadows of the ancient Mercat Cross. The sandstone arches were barely lit, only darkness behind them.

I opened my door and jumped out as soon as the driver halted.

'Wait here,' I told him. 'I shan't be long.'

I crossed the courtyard hastily, feeling the cold seeping despite my thick coat, and saw that a single constable guarded the main entrance. I did not recall his name, but his face was definitely familiar.

'Inspector Frey!' he said in a thick Scottish accent. 'Are ye back, sir?'

'Only briefly,' I said, and nodded at the door with authority. The chap opened it without question.

Unsurprisingly, the headquarters were almost as cold as outside, and just as dark, with only a few gaslights left burning. I had to go to the constables' cupboards and take a lantern. The room I was heading to would surely be pitch-black.

I descended some narrow, steep stairs, feeling the damp and the cold increase with each step. The door I found was ajar. I pushed it open and shed light into what had been, not that long ago, the *Commission for the Elucidation of Unsolved Cases Presumably Related to the Odd and Ghostly.*

The basement, however, was now desolate. My footsteps even echoed as I looked around. No furniture, no files, no books or spooky artefacts. The one article that remained was a very tall Peruvian totem, so ugly and voluminous I was not surprised Nine-Nails had left it behind.

I saw the barred windows, just below the ceiling line, that faced the courtyard, and I also recognised the section of wall I'd once thrashed in desperation. It had been coarsely boarded-up and an icy draught filtered through the slats, bringing in the saltpetre smells of the abandoned passages that ran underneath Mary King's Close. Nine-Nails believed that ghosts meandered through those alleys – tortured souls trapped underground centuries ago, forever wailing in disgrace. Pretty much like me, when I worked there.

I stepped closer to those boards, already thinking I'd have to look for the Ardglass files elsewhere, but also strangely fascinated by that cold current. I took off a glove, stretched my palm and ran my fingers along the damp boards.

For an instant I imagined a white, willowy shape, ebbing from between the cracks in the wood to come and whisper into my ears. And I felt a nasty shiver.

'Mr Frey!'

I gasped and turned on my heels, nearly dropping the lantern, and I saw a lanky shadow right in front of me. A pair of impassive auburn eyes glowed under the beam of light.

'Superintendent!' I cried, recognising the thin and ever-composed features of Robert Trevelyan, head of the Scottish police.

I was very close to bowing to him, but stopped myself just in time. He was no longer my superior, after all.

'Mr Frey,' he saluted, and it was odd not to hear him call

me by my former rank. 'I see Inspector McGray succeeded in recruiting you.'

'Oh, he did not *recruit* me,' I said at once. 'I am merely here to help out in—' I tilted my head. 'Are you – excuse me, are you working this late?'

He raised his chin a little. He too must find it odd that I should question him so freely.

'I was just leaving,' he explained, 'but McCloud told me he saw you come in.'

'McCloud!' I whispered. 'That's the name!'

'I did find it strange that you came here at this hour,' he said, and then nodded at the empty cellar with a side smile. 'Do you miss your old workplace?'

'*Oh, indeed!* The scant light, the damp and the dust.' I pointed at the corner where I used to sit. 'Particularly my dear old chair, but I see that it has been taken too.'

'I think we only saved a desk. The rest of the furniture was so decrepit it went for firewood.'

'Thank goodness that seat cannot hurt anyone anymore!' I saw that Trevelyan's gesture was still inquisitive. 'I came to see if any of our files had been rescued. I might need them for Nine-Na— for Inspector McGray's investigation. *Your* latest assignment to him, I understand.'

'Yes. Unfortunate case. Unfortunate that his sister is involved.' He was soon to correct himself. '*Presumably* – presumably involved.'

I raised my eyebrows. I had not expected people to be thinking of Miss McGray as a potential suspect already. That could not be good.

Trevelyan cleared his throat and hastily changed the subject. 'Which files do you need?'

I paused. I did not want to draw attention to the Ardglass family.

'Did you manage to save any at all?' I asked instead, and Trevelyan sighed.

'*We* did not. The Prime Minister's men came here in the middle of the night and took almost everything that was not nailed to the walls. Thankfully, Inspector McGray had foreseen it. He'd already taken away a good deal of documents and his – well, I don't know what to call them…'

'Collection of mermaid and goblin foetuses suspended in formaldehyde?'

'And the like, yes. He will be your best chance to find – whichever information it is you need.'

So he *had* noticed my evasive answer.

'I am glad you have been persuaded to help,' Trevelyan added. 'Inspector McGray will need all the assistance he can get, with the asylum story hitting the papers tomorrow and—'

'Tomorrow! Already?'

Trevelyan twisted his mouth.

'They held it back as a personal favour,' he said. 'Two days is a long time for them, as you surely know.'

'Indeed,' I said. 'I am sorry. You must have gone through a lot of trouble to arrange that.'

He simply tensed his lips, an unprecedented awkwardness rising between us.

'You must understand,' he said, his voice tense, 'that your not being an officer will present certain – limitations.'

I frowned. 'If I am to be of any help, I shall need access to the evidence, the morgue, the witnesses…'

'Indeed, and I shall grant it, merely as a favour to Inspector McGray, but we cannot expect that to last. In fact, all I can do is turn a blind eye to your presence. As soon as people start to question it…' He sighed. 'And Inspector McGray's involvement will also be put to question, I can see it already.'

'Of course,' I said. 'Investigating a crime that, in people's eyes, might involve his own sister...'

Trevelyan's brow flickered when I said *might*. Could he genuinely think that Pansy had been involved? I preferred not to ask.

'If – no, *when* the conflict is brought to my attention,' Trevelyan said, 'I will have no choice but to remove you both from the investigation at once.'

I took a deep breath. 'Of course. Does McGray know about this?'

'He does, Mr Frey. And you can imagine how he took it.'

I nodded, not needing more details. 'How long would you say we have?'

Trevelyan blew inside his cheeks. 'Impossible to tell for sure. Perhaps two, three days.'

'Two or three *days*? Are you *joking*?'

'I wish I were,' Trevelyan said while my voice still bounced between the walls, and I felt a nasty churn in my stomach. Things were far more desperate than I'd expected.

'In that case, I'd better leave now,' I said with a slight bow of the head. 'The earlier I start tomorrow, the better.'

Trevelyan nodded, and since he had no lantern himself, we had to walk upstairs together in a very tense silence. I put the light down at the first opportunity and left the building as quickly as I could. However, as I crossed the courtyard, I heard Trevelyan's voice behind my back.

'Be careful, Mr Frey,' he said, in a tone I could not ignore. I stopped and turned my head back.

'Careful?' I asked.

'Yes. You may find that the city has become somewhat – hostile.'

7

Nine-Nails let out a long, exhausted sigh as he dropped onto his library's tattered sofa.

What a long, dreadful day it had been. And he'd not even managed to go back to the morgue and look at poor Mrs Brewster's body again. At least he could trust Dr Reed. The young man would have a report ready in the morning.

Feeling his mood, Tucker, his faithful golden retriever, went to him and rested his muzzle on McGray's knee. The dog let out a little whimper, and McGray tousled its ear affectionately as he poured himself some whisky.

'This is loyalty, Mackenzie!' he grunted at his other dog, the huge black mastiff that lay, drooling and half asleep, by the wide fireplace.

McGray stretched his feet, had his first swig of liquor, and then, just as the streets went quiet and his mind began to drift, the dreadful memories came.

He did not even flinch. They always came at this hour, punctual though uninvited. And they were worse in the dark; that was why he seldom bothered going to his bedchambers. Most nights he simply sat here, whiling his nights away with a drink. Sometimes sleep came; sometimes not.

The memories, on the other hand, were ever present.

He always saw that glint first: a spark reflected on steel. The steel of a fire poker in his late father's library, in their country house just outside Dundee. The instrument that had killed his mother.

And then all the events came to him in quick succession, and he could do nothing to stop them. Once more he saw Pansy's frenzied eyes and the blood-stained cleaver in her hand. Once more he fought her. Once more he saw his severed finger; his phalanxes flailing about, hanging by a thin shred of torn skin, and the white bones surrounded by bleeding flesh. That image also came with the vivid memory of the searing pain.

He was used to it by now, after six and a half years reliving it night after night. He even stared mockingly at the stump of his missing finger, before bringing the tumbler to his lips.

The image that came next, on the other hand, never failed to give him a pang in the chest.

He had seen that – *thing*.

Right after gazing upon his bleeding hand, as he was about to pass out from the pain and the many shocks, he had looked up. And there it had been, making its way to the open window.

A deformed, twisted figure moving with the jolts of a bird of prey.

He had seen the horns too, large and twisted, and though the rest of his vision had been blurred, the horns could not have looked sharper, clearly delineated against the darkening sky.

Just like the old rhymes said.

And the more he tried to remember, the more he tried to focus on the image, the more confusing the memory became.

He'd seen that before hearing Pansy's last words to Dr Clouston; before knowing she'd said everything had been the Devil's work. How could it be? How could he deny the fact?

They had both seen it. Perhaps their mother and father had too, taking the secret to their graves.

McGray had felt that very same fright the night before, upon seeing that dreadful mark on the dead woman. The bloated horns, crowning two slits for eyes.

He felt a shudder, which he could only placate with a long swig of whisky.

He could hardly believe how different his life had been six years ago, just a few hours before those incidents. That very morning he'd woken up to a perfect summer day, riding his favourite horse, teasing his loving mother and sister, sharing drinks and stories with his irritable father... Had that world ever even existed?

McGray shrugged. If it had, it was as lost as his dead parents. Pansy was the last vestige of that life, though locked in an asylum, alone and forever silent, her fate sometimes seemed worse than a quick death. She had already lost what ought to have been the most cherished years of her early womanhood, and McGray could only stand by, watching her as the years slipped through his fingers. He thought he'd lost hope many times, and yet on each occasion something tantalising happened – a look, a faint reaction, her allegedly talking to another inmate, the promise of miraculous waters from some remote loch...

What a cruel thing hope could be; more like an illness, or like a scales in perfect balance, never deigning to tip one way or the other. More than a saviour, hope sometimes seemed like a sadistic executioner that rejoiced in delaying death.

McGray nearly dropped his tumbler as he entertained that thought. Tucker shook suddenly then, and turned his head to the library door, just a second before someone knocked.

McGray recognised the tired raps of auld George.

'Come in,' he said, and the door opened. 'Ye should be in bed, George,' McGray told him as the aging man approached. 'Who's going to cook my breakfast in the morning?'

It took some effort to say that without sarcasm. George did

his best, but his cooking was no match to Joan's. In fact, it was hardly edible, but McGray did not have the heart to tell him so.

George showed him a piece of neatly folded paper.

'A message, master.'

'A message?'

'Aye, sir. From the Ardglass lass.'

McGray instantly leaned forward.

'So soon? Didnae she leave last night?'

George shrugged. 'They're back. My Joan brought the note herself.'

McGray took the paper and unfolded it with impatience. He could only cackle at the opening line: *Mr Frey is here. Be kind to him.*

8

The sun had not yet risen, but a lonely figure already walked briskly along a silent Dublin Street, clad in a black overcoat, his face half concealed under a bowler hat.

The man stopped in front of Lady Anne's main residence; a large townhouse that took up almost half the street. He looked up at the wide, darkened windows, and saw that only one was lit from within. The old crone was already awake.

He climbed the granite steps that led to the gate and rang the bell.

The arrogant butler, as usual, took his time to attend the door. He opened only a narrow gap, just enough to show half his pasty face. Surrounded by darkness, he looked like a spectre.

'Mr Pratt?' he asked with a raised brow. 'I did not know the good lady had an appointment with you.'

'Her ladyship doesn't know I've—'

'She will *not* receive you if you don't have an appointment!'

The butler attempted to shut the door, but Mr Pratt pressed a hand against it. He was stronger than his creased face and his wide waist suggested.

'It is crucial she sees me.'

The butler chuckled.

'Crucial for *whom*?'

'*Open the damn door!* Your mistress will lash you to a mush if she finds out you sent me away!'

The butler looked Pratt up and down, as if gauging him, and after a derisive 'humpf', he finally let him in.

Then there was a pathetic race across the dim, high-ceilinged halls; both men trying to out-pace each other, yet neither daring to break into an undignified run. They reached a particularly darkened corridor on the first floor, as cold as the rest of the mansion.

'I will announce you first,' the butler whispered as he knocked gently at the door.

Pratt did not protest this time. Lady Glass did not react well to people breaking into her private study.

Her deep voice, bored yet commanding, responded from behind the door, and the servant stepped in. Pratt thought he'd use those moments to catch his breath, but there was no time; the butler emerged again almost instantly.

'My lady bids you—'

Pratt was already past the threshold, and he shut the door himself.

He took a deep breath as he saw the tall Lady Anne. She stood by the window with her back turned to him, her slender frame delineated by the glare from the street lamps. The woman was in her seventies, but her spine was still as straight as a mast, and her feathery hairpiece, spiky like a crown, made her look even taller.

She turned around slowly, her chin raised and her lips tense. The one lamp on the desk projected sharp shadows on her creased face, the skin stuck to her sharp cheekbones like one of those mummified corpses exhibited at Surgeons' Hall.

Pratt took off his hat at once, his perfectly bald scalp covered in perspiration, and made a bow.

'Lady Anne, you'll excuse the intrusion.'

The woman twisted her mouth. Instead of answering she went to the cut-glass decanter on her desk and poured herself a generous glass of ruby port. Pratt thought it looked like fresh blood. She savoured a couple of sips but said nothing, so Pratt moved closer to the desk.

'It's happening, ma'am,' he said, extending the newspaper on the desk. 'This is circulating on—'

Lady Anne raised a dismissive hand. 'I know. I've read it already.'

Pratt was open-mouthed. 'You alrea— excuse me? This is fresh from the—'

'I heard before it even went to the press.' And the woman rejoiced in Pratt's astounded face. 'You always assume we're all as inept as you.'

Those words were like fire in Pratt's gut. The man had lost more than one case against the McGrays, first in Dundee and then as a fiscal in Edinburgh, and they'd all been resounding humiliations. The court's young devils still laughed behind his back every time he entered the Advocates' Library, mocking his failure at the case against McGray's blasted gypsy friend. And much worse had been his failure at Dundee's Sheriff's Court, when he failed to have that little madwag Amy McGray tried for murder. He'd not even managed to have their country house searched.

Lady Anne cast an impatient glance at the newspaper.

'I rent lodgings to more than one of those famished pressmen,' she said. 'Printing words is a pauper's job. They're always in need of money and they know it pays well to keep me informed.'

Pratt gulped. 'Then you – you know the predicament!'

Lady Anne gave a crooked smile. 'Don't act so surprised, Mr Pratt. I told you this would happen one day.'

Pratt clenched his hat. 'Yes. Yes, you did. But—'

'Have a seat. Here, a drink too.' It must be expensive liquor, for she poured him a much smaller measure.

Pratt took the glass with a trembling hand and, even though he'd not even broken fast, downed it in one gulp.

'What can we do now? This was *not* supposed to happen. This – are you *laughing*?'

It was in fact just a side smirk, Lady Anne's teeth (enviable for someone her age) catching the light from her little lamp. An open cackle could not have been that eerie.

'You should be happy, Mr Pratt. This is a most fortunate turn of events.'

'*Fortunate?*' Pratt echoed, and again Lady Anne took delight in his incomprehension.

'Only if, for once, you do things right. And you must do *exactly* as I tell you.'

Pratt lowered his gaze and stared at his small glass.

He was in that blasted woman's hands again. And how he hated being at someone else's mercy...

Lady Anne leaned over her desk and pulled the newspaper to read the headline, even though she knew it by heart.

'"The Devil's Sign",' she read aloud. She poured herself a little more to drink, raised the glass and held it to her lips. 'Yes, this is good. Trust me. The Devil has always been kind to my kin.'

9

The bedroom curtains opened with a mighty racket, and before my eyes grew accustomed to the light, someone pulled my covers away.

'*What the hell!*' I roared.

'It's almost nine o' the sodding clock!' the rough, annoyingly familiar voice of Nine-Nails McGray snapped. 'And yer still in yer bloody nighties!'

After I rubbed my eyes I had a blurry vision of the man himself, his tall frame and his broad shoulders as unmistakable as his gaudy tartan clothes. He was pacing from one side of the room to the other, a newspaper crumpled in his four-fingered hand.

A slender porter rushed in then, his usually pale cheeks now red like ripe cherries.

'*Sorry, sir!*' he pleaded. 'We couldnae—'

'I know, I know,' I said, clumsily clambering out of bed. 'You may leave; I can deal with –' I eyed McGray – 'that.'

The young man did so. I put on a dressing gown and looked out of the window as I tied the cord. My bedroom had a lovely view of Castle Rock and Princes Street Gardens. Or there it must be – behind all the damned fog.

'How did you find me?' I asked, bleary eyed.

'Caroline told me ye were here,' McGray said swiftly, still pacing. 'So ye'll have heard the pit o' shite I'm in!'

I turned to him and took a moment to study his face. To my astonishment, his very square jaw was cleanly shaven, and his dark hair, peppered with premature strands of grey, looked practically decent. His blue eyes, though as fiery as ever, were also framed by rings as dark as bruises. He must be desperately worried about his sister.

'Very well,' I sighed, once more feeling sorry for him. 'Give me a few minutes to get dressed. You can wait in my breakfast parlour, just through that door—'

'*Breakfast!*' he squealed. 'They're selling this shite all over the city as we speak!'

And he jerked the sorry newspaper for me to see. I raised a hand, not even attempting to read the enormous headline.

'I know. We can discuss it all—'

'Over tea and jammed pikelets? Are ye mad? If I don't see yer lanky English arse in—'

'*Bloody hell, you are not in command!*' I roared from the bottom of my stomach, my voice bouncing across the room.

McGray made a fist, crushing his copy of *The Scotsman* and ready to punch me, but I stood my ground.

'I am here to help you, *not* to follow your orders. If that displeases you, I can have my things packed up again and—'

'Och, piss off!' he snapped, turning his back to me and leaving the room with long strides. 'See ye in yer sodding lassies' *parlour.*'

He really must be desperate, I told myself, to give in quite so soon instead of dragging me to the police headquarters in my nightclothes.

Still, I made haste, well aware that every minute was precious.

*

It must have taken me less than fifteen minutes to get ready, but by the time I stepped into the suite's parlour, Nine-Nails was already strangling the haughty waiter. Half my breakfast was spilt on the carpet and a bunch of files were spread on the expensive damask sofa.

I let out a weary breath. 'Nine-Nails, put that man down, if you please?'

The poor waiter gagged desperately, his spindly legs five inches from the floor.

'He's been a wee twat!' McGray retorted, squeezing the man's neck harder and lifting him a little higher.

'I am sure he has,' I said as I sat by the table, 'but do humour me. We have plenty to discuss.'

Again, he surprised me by consenting rather quickly. He dropped the waiter, who bent down and coughed loudly, both hands on his neck.

'Och, don't be such a lily-livered baby!' McGray grunted, giving him a kick at the rump. 'Am sure yer mama squeezed ye harder last week, trying to wean ye!'

The young man indeed could not have been that injured, for he straightened up and held his chin very high.

'*Outrageous!* I shall call the police and—!'

'Och, sod off! I *am* the fuckin' police!'

McGray picked up a cup and made to throw it at the waiter's face. Thankfully the young man had the good sense to dash away and slam the door shut behind him.

'Do you see what you have done here?' I moaned, laying a napkin on my lap. 'Now I will have to serve my own breakfast! What is left of it, that is.'

McGray sat down too, the chair's legs creaking under his weight. While I poured my coffee and buttered my toast, Nine-Nails chewed on his lips as if trying to make them bleed. It was not anxiety, but some sort of – embarrassment.

'What is it?' I asked and he sighed noisily.

'I'll put this out o' the way,' he said, and then gathered air as if about to confess to the most disgracing secret. The first word came out rather constricted. '*Thanks* for coming. We – *I* really need the extra hands.'

I only wish he'd said so at a more adequate time to gloat. I've seldom made firewood out of a fallen tree.

'I will not say it is a *pleasure*,' I said.

'If ye did, I'd ken ye'd be lying.'

'But I will do my best to help you and your sister. I pledge to it. And I shall act as fast as humanly possible. We may not always see eye to eye, and your methods and manners—' McGray had already put his muddy boots on the table and was helping himself to the crispy bacon with nothing but his hands, 'your methods and *lack* of manners do drive me insane. On the other hand, I cannot ignore the bonds of loyalty that we have—'

'Och, still wearing bloody jewellery!' he mocked, his mouth full, when he saw my emerald signet ring. 'And what the hell are those glossy lapels for? Who snuffed it?'

'My father.'

McGray gave a slight jolt, as if suddenly hit by one of those new-fangled electric devices. He put his feet off the table and, for the first time since I have known him, seemed abashed.

'Whah – really?'

I simply nodded and had a sip of coffee.

'Och, I'm sorry,' Nine-Nails said earnestly. 'I liked the auld sod. One o' the very few bastards who've ever told me to shut it and walked away without a limp!'

'Like I did just a moment ago?' I said, if only to ease the unexpected tension. Nine-Nails let out a cackle, and that terminated any soppy speeches.

'Tell me about the case,' I said. 'I know we may have very limited time. What do the papers say?'

McGray reached for his copy of *The Scotsman*. He must have been twisting it with clammy hands for a while, for it now looked like a soggy piece of rope. I struggled to extend it on the table.

'See? If you had not strangled the waiter I could have asked him to fetch me a freshly pressed copy.'

Thankfully it could still be read, especially the headline, which stretched from end to end of the sheet, with letters broader than my thumbs:

THE DEVIL'S SIGN APPEARS!!!!

'Oh, how imaginative!' I grumbled, and then skimmed through what little text they'd managed to fit on the rest of the front page.

'Is this accurate?' I asked.

'Some of it,' McGray said. 'Fat sod killed at the asylum; mark on the wall painted with blood; nae clear suspect; nae weapon or trail to follow.'

'No weapon?' I repeated, and McGray went on to tell me all he'd found out already: the missing knife, the young nurse who'd thought she'd heard a gag, the ghastly piece of cloth he'd found in the man's mouth, and how the staff had cleaned the crime scene and the smear on the wall – following Clouston's orders.

I let out a long sigh but made no remark, at least for the time being. Nine-Nails knew very well I had never fully trusted 'good' Dr Clouston. I focussed on the case, asking questions as I took copious notes.

'Do you suppose they gagged the man and then stabbed him?'

'Aye. Either that or they just let him stuff his mouth himself; he was known for doing that when he had his fits. Whichever the case, looks like they left him to bleed to death on the floor. Nae idea for how long.'

'What a horrid way to die ... And did you manage to question all the orderlies and the staff?'

'Aye. Everyone. They all claimed innocence and gave alibis, but many o' those are impossible to verify, especially as we don't ken for certain how long that poor MacDonnell lay there in agony.'

'And the asylum is a very large place,' I said, 'full of corridors and nooks and crannies ... It would be very easy to hide or simply scuttle away in the dark.' As I spoke, I pictured Caroline doing precisely that. 'And you say the inmates' rooms are not locked?'

'Only a few dangerous cases have to be, but aye, most of the rooms on the east wing are nae locked. Clouston fears that'll be used against him.'

I looked up. 'The east wing is for the more affluent patients, right?'

'Aye. The patients there each have their own chambers. On the west wing most of the inmates share common dormitories, but there are orderlies guarding them at all times. O' course there are some exceptions. MacDonnell was one o' them. He used to sleep in a separate room because o' his condition.'

'I see. Did they keep him locked in?'

McGray sat back, rumbling. 'They used to. Nae since January.'

'Oh?'

'Cassandra Smith, the head nurse, says he had nae fits since last September. He'd been improving quite a bit, so they decided he could be trusted.'

'Who decided that?'

McGray made a grimace. 'Clouston.'

There was a recalcitrant silence. I could not afford politeness any longer.

'The same Clouston who had the crime scene mopped up?'

'Aye. Make of it whatever ye want.'

I underlined the name. 'I certainly will,' and I looked back at my previous notes. I'd filled quite a few pages already. 'Going back to the weapon, I assume you made a systematic search?'

'Aye. It took us nearly all day yesterday. We found nothing, neither at the inmates' chambers nor at the staff's common areas. We also searched the laundry and the kitchens and even the bloody privies.' He retched at that.

'And you found nothing?'

'Quite a few kitchen knives and garden tools and medical instruments that would match the type o' stabs. None was covered in blood. But as I said—'

'The murderer would have had plenty of time to clean the blade,' I said. 'Or chuck it away or ... Oh God, this is complicated—' I let out a sigh. 'What else did you find inspecting the body?'

'Reed hasnae done the post-mortem yet.'

I nearly spat out my coffee at that. '*What?* Why?'

'The family want to pay their respects. I told Clouston we could wait.'

'McGray, for goodness' sake! This is already a needle in a bloody haystack!'

'Aye, I ken, but the corpse is in the gardener's storeroom, very well guarded. Trust me, it won't decompose. That room's colder than yer stepmother's bosoms.'

'When will the good doctor deign to release it for examination?'

'Today, nae matter what. I made that clear.'

'Very well,' I said, and again looked over my notes. 'We need to trace the man's steps. Look for any quarrels, enemies ... orderlies he might have crossed. Anything that will take suspicions away from Pansy. Did you search his chambers, his belongings?'

'Aye. All looked quite ordinary, but we can look again. I told them to keep that room locked.'

'Good. I'd also like to have a good look throughout the asylum. Just for good measure.'

McGray chuckled. 'I might have to get one of our lads to guard ye. The inmates have gone all—'

He went quiet. I knew the sort of word he'd been about to utter, and it was only consideration to his sister that restrained him.

'Restless?' I ventured.

'Aye,' he said in a low voice, and his face turned sombre.

'And how is your sister?' I asked, rather hesitantly.

He sighed. 'All I heard is she's fine.'

'Heard? Have you not seen her?'

'Nae. Clouston didnae let me get even close to her room. Said my presence might *distress* her.'

At least in that I agreed with the man. I knew Miss McGray's medical history better than I would have ever wished to.

'Well, I am glad she is fine,' I said, and then found the perfect chance to fish for details that might, at some point, incriminate Caroline. 'I assume someone checked on her after the mayhem?'

'Aye. Miss Smith told me she was with her when Harland raised the alarm.'

'Good,' I said, looking down in case my eyes betrayed me.

So, Miss Smith had lied to him. I'd have to question her very soon; ask her what she'd truly been up to. And Clouston too, for he must be aware of Caroline's visits and her connection to Miss McGray. And I did not like his behaviour at all, taking advantage of McGray's loyalty to get his way.

I looked for a blank page to take note of that, and in doing so my little notebook opened naturally on Caroline's sketch. That made me notice ...

'They do not mention the snatchers or the marked woman,' I said, pointing at the newspaper. I turned the crumpled page, but the rest of the article was just another sensationalist overview of the McGrays' tragedy. I'd read the story so many times I could tell they'd copied it verbatim from a previous issue.

'Aye,' McGray said. 'We've managed to keep *that* quiet so far. They're already slandering Pansy far too much. If they also hear about that poor auld – wait – ye drew that?'

I realised only too late that he was staring at the sketch, and he snatched it before I could pull it away. I bit my lip, remembering how Caroline had pleaded for my silence.

'Yes,' I lied. 'Yes... I drew it. This is what Miss Ardglass said you saw.'

The moment Nine-Nails spent staring at the page felt like an eternity.

'It's uncanny,' he said, finally handing it back. 'Ye sure ye don't have the inner eye?'

'I am no gypsy,' I remarked, and then feigned ignorance. 'Are you certain this was the mark?'

'Aye. I only saw it briefly before they mopped it up, but – it's like ye were there! The exact same shape, both at the asylum and on the auld woman's face. And now on yer sketches. It's like it's appearing everywhere!'

Thank goodness for his superstition, I thought, tapping the sketch with my pencil.

'Do you also recognise what I see here?' I asked. 'Though it looks like such, I do not think this is a devil's face at all.'

'Aye, yer right. It's a cloven hoof. The Devil's footprint.'

10

After a hearty breakfast we took a cab and headed off to the morgue.

McGray wanted to walk, but I'd have none of it – the weather was as foul as the night before, the sky only a little less dark. I could tell we'd have rain or sleet very soon.

We travelled in silence for a while, but then, as we ascended the steep road that led to the Royal Mile, McGray cleared his throat.

'Which files were ye looking for yesterday?'

I nearly gasped. 'E – excuse me?'

'Ye deaf? I said, which files were—'

'I heard you, but how do you know I was there?'

'McCloud told me. And that Trevelyan told him that ye were looking for files. What were ye after?'

I pretended to be scribbling a note, just to evade his eyes while I concocted a quick lie. 'Oh – yes. I wanted to look at my old notebooks. I may still have transcripts from our last case at the asylum. They might give me some perspective.'

Nine-Nails raised a brow, and for a moment I held my breath.

'If ye say so,' he said at last. 'Aye, I might still have them. I took most o' the files home. Ye can check them any time. They won't be in order, mind.'

'I should be able to find my way,' I said, and then let out a discreet sigh of relief.

We entered the busy Royal Mile, the poor horse's hooves skidding on frozen cobbles. And then, just like the night before, the contents of a chamber pot were thrown from the tall tenement buildings.

'And you wanted to walk!' I mocked.

To my surprise, the carriage did not turn into the high street, but instead went on south, towards the wide George IV Bridge.

'Are we not going to the morgue?' I asked, impatient to see the so-called Devil's footprint with my own eyes. Especially after Caroline had said it was no cut or ink or burn.

'Nae. We're going to Greyfriars Kirkyard first. I want ye to see the tracks we found on the snow.'

'Tracks on the snow?' I asked. 'Will they still be there?'

'Aye. I had the place locked up. There's a guard there. And I told the kirk's minister to keep everyone off the graveyard.'

'I was more concerned about the weather erasing them.'

'It's nae rained or snowed since. The traces should still be visible.' He pointed at the swirling clouds. 'Nae for long, though.'

'No cloven hooves, I hope!'

'Ye never ken. I didnae see them that night. That's why it's better to inspect the place now. It'll get dark early and—'

'The will-o'-the-wisps will come out and drag us by the feet to the underworld?'

McGray poked my sternum quite harshly. 'Don't milk it, Percy. I ken yer balls've finally dropped, but patience is nae my strongest suit.'

'Very well, very well,' I said, and as soon as he looked away I rubbed my chest, already picturing the future bruise. I was about to remind him how much I abhorred it when he called me by my middle name, but there were more important matters at hand.

'Miss Ardglass told me that Trevelyan originally asked you to investigate resurrections at that graveyard.'

'Aye. Three bodies have been stolen from there since last November. Mrs Brewster would have been the fourth.'

'And I understand they were all taken on new moon nights.'

'Aye. Too much of a coincidence. Even *ye* must admit that.'

'Indeed. I was thinking of—' I had to clear my throat to be able to say it, 'witches looking for potion ingredients.'

McGray looked wistfully at the grey streets. 'Liver o' blaspheming Jew... Gall o' goat, and slips o' yew... Sliver'd in the moon's eclipse, Nose o' Turk, and Tartar's lips...' he shook his head just as I was about to ask him to stop butchering Shakespeare. 'I also looked into the more mundane possibilities...'

I raised my eyebrows. '*Gosh!* Do you mean dull, earthly body snatchers?'

'Aye. That was the first possibility I looked into.'

For the first time I felt hopeful. 'You do have contacts in those – I shall call them *circles*.'

I winced at the memory of that ghastly night, in November 1888, when we had ventured into Calton Hill's cemetery, guided by one of McGray's *lads*.

'I did manage to get a wee bit of information out o' them, but they've tipped each other and now they all ken I'm after the sod that's been pillaging Greyfriars Kirkyard.'

'And I suppose they'll cover their own tracks.'

'Indeedy. They're like a guild. Their bloody clients too.'

'By clients, do you mean the college? Have you also investigated there?'

'Aye. I sent one o' the lads to Surgeon's Hall to make inquiries, but it was as pointless as asking *ye* to nail a horseshoe. It's an open secret that the professors still resort to snatchers, but nobody will ever talk. It'd be bad business for the colleges, and the students are either scared o' their professors or so keen to learn, they're happy to keep quiet. We've been trying to find a snitch, but ye can imagine we have to do so very discreetly.'

'Of course,' I said. 'Back in Oxford the police never became involved. Then again, the bodies hardly ever came from the local cemeteries.'

'Only high and mighty twats interred there?'

'That was one of the reasons, yes. I can tell you from my own experience – the bodies were never terribly fresh.' I shuddered at the disgustingly vivid memory of the smells. 'It will do no harm if I go to that Surgeons' Hall myself at some point.'

'Aye. The place is full o' patronising, arrogant sods. Ye'll be in yer element.' I was about to protest, but – 'Right now we should focus on the graveyard. Am fearing someone at Greyfriars itself might be colluding with the snatchers.'

'Are you?'

'Aye. These past months the graves have been getting shallower and shallower.'

That side of the city, I must admit, looked almost respectable, with its elegant Georgian sandstone façades, sadly begrimed with decades of soot. We turned right far sooner than I expected and rode past a fountain topped with the bronze statue of a rather ugly, straggly dog.

'That's Greyfriars Bobby,' McGray said. 'Some ten or fifteen years ago the wee doggie—'

'Oh, save it. My stepmother wept for days after she read the damn story in *The British Lady's Magazine*. What was so special about it? It was a silly bloody dog! Most likely lingering around for scraps and bones.'

McGray clicked his tongue. 'Yer dead inside.'

The cab halted by a short, narrow alley, and we stepped out swiftly. McGray told the driver to wait for us, and on we went.

Squeezed in between the sorry establishment of a picture

restorer and a row of unusually well-kept little houses, the pebbled lane led to the cemetery's wrought-iron gates. They were locked with a thick chain and padlock, and behind them was the stark gable of Greyfriars Kirk, with its plain walls and unadorned Gothic windows.

A very plump constable stood by the gate, guarding it with enviable stoicism.

'All quiet, Willy?' McGray asked him, and the man, his face clearly numb, answered with an unintelligible mutter which must have been an affirmative. McGray rang a little brass bell and we waited.

'We caught the snatchers in the middle o' the night,' he said, 'so all we could do then was have a quick look to make sure none o' the bastards had decided to hide in between the tombs. I wanted to come back the morning after to inspect, but, like I told ye, they called me from the asylum. I had to attend the murder case first.'

I only nodded, more concerned by the foul smell of the alley. That narrow passage was surely a popular pissing stop for the city's drunkards.

Fortunately, we did not have to wait for long. A plump man, clad in a thick black suit, emerged from the church. His footprints were the only ones on the otherwise pristine snow.

'Inspector!' he said when he reached the gate. 'Thank goodness you came. I was expecting you earlier. I had to give my service at the public house!'

As he opened the gate I studied his perfectly round face. His nose was broad and red, his hair a neat crown of white locks surrounding a pale scalp. The man gave off a strong scent of bay rum, perhaps to guard himself from the odours of the surrounding alleys, and his pale blue eyes had an undeniable twinkle – one which the ladies of his flock most likely did not appreciate.

'Sorry, rev'rend,' said McGray, stepping in. 'Yesterday was murder.'

'Reverend Andrew Hunter, at your service,' the man said, offering me a hand to shake, which I found most forward. 'Minister of this humble temple and Professor of Divinity at Edinburgh University. And you are Inspector...?'

'Ian Frey,' I answered promptly, happy to let him believe I still acted as a police inspector. However, I soon regretted volunteering my name.

'*The* Mr Frey?' Reverend Hunter repeated, and he pulled his hand away swiftly.

'He's nae Devil worshiper,' McGray rushed to say, 'if that's what yer thinking.'

'*Devil worshiper?*' I cried. 'Are people still saying that?'

McGray whistled. 'Ye've nae idea. Tell ye later.' And he passed inside in the most nonchalant manner.

'What do you mean by that?' I asked, but both he and the minister had moved on. I looked at Willy. 'What did he mean by—? Oh, forget it.'

'Ye kept the place untouched?' McGray was asking when I caught up with them.

'Yes, inspector. And the coffin is locked in the sacristy, like you instructed.'

He led us along a broad gravel path covered in rock salt. The snow to both sides, mostly untrodden, seemed to glow under the grey sky.

There were evergreen yews dotted all across the cemetery, their canopies black under the gloomy winter light, like protecting arms hovering over the haphazard rows of tombstones. Beyond were the more elaborate family crypts, like the one in which my own father would have been laid to rest the day before. I felt a twinge of guilt over having not been there.

'Have you lost someone recently?' the minister asked, eyeing my mourning clothes.

'Yes,' I said sharply, making it clear I'd not welcome any further questions, and just then we turned around the kirk's western corner.

The grave we looked for, some ten yards ahead, could not have been more conspicuous: a dark, square hollow, the snow around it trampled and speckled with dirt. I even saw the two spades and the pickaxe the snatchers had left behind.

McGray halted, raising a hand in front of the minister.

'Can ye wait inside, rev'rend? We'd rather do this on our own.'

The man tensed his jaw a little. 'Of – of course, inspectors.'

'But stay within the grounds,' I told him. 'We need to ask you a few questions.'

He simply nodded and rushed back to the church. McGray waited until he saw the man disappear through one of the church's doors.

'A graveyard's the last place ye'd like to be inspecting right now, I guess,' he said as we approached the open pit.

'I can visit my father any time,' I said, trying to convince myself more than him. 'I am of more use here, helping the living.' I tried to ignore the fact that I was looking into a desecrated tomb.

I bent down to inspect the clumps of disturbed snow. The weather had smoothed the edges, but the main trails were still discernible.

'Those are mine and the lads',' McGray said, pointing at a set of footprints that went to and from the gravel path in an almost straight line, 'from when we carried the coffin back to the kirk. And those are obviously our horses' hooves. The rest o' the footprints are the snatchers'.'

As he said so he took a few measured steps, trying not to

deface the other trails, and then compared those prints to his own.

'Ye can tell the heavier ones,' he said, pointing at the deepest, most chaotic trail. 'They were fleeing with the corpse there. But these over here must be from before.'

'Indeed,' I said, and then saw an even shallower trail. 'They were much lighter than you. Particularly that one over there.'

'That must be the poor sod that got himself killed that night. Really skinny fella and as rough as an auld leather boot.'

'Identified?'

'The lads are on it.'

'So it is this trail we should watch,' I said, looking at the other set of prints, slightly deeper, and I pictured the movements in my head. 'They first came this way.'

'Shame the wind's blurred them,' McGray mumbled as we examined them. 'More than I'd expected.'

We went through the deeper prints one by one, looking for the best preserved one.

'They were clearly walking blindly,' I said. 'Meandering left to right. It makes sense, on a new moon night...'

We saw then that the track ran underneath one of the gnarled yews. The thick canopy had sheltered that spot from the elements, the prints still distinct in the half-frozen mud.

'Good!' McGray let out, hunkering down.

Though of similar sizes, the two sets of prints could not have looked more different. One was flat and neat, the other – the lighter one – was that of a very worn-out sole, with a very deep crack on the heel, visible in almost all the prints of the man's right foot.

'That's definitely the dead sod's,' McGray said. 'His boots were a sorry mess.'

I focussed on the other track.

'Look at the edge of the heel here,' I said. 'It is a straight line where it goes deeper than the rest of the foot.'

'Aye, very sharp. Those were brand-new boots.'

'Precisely. Who wears his new boots to a midnight jaunt in the snow and mud?'

'Some rich, vain sod like ye.'

'Exac— What?'

'So, an upper-class bastard working side by side with a seasoned snatcher,' McGray mumbled, stroking his cleanly shaven jaw.

'A university student, perhaps?'

'Aye. Professors won't bother coming here; nae if they can send a minion to do their dirty work.' He arched a brow. 'This might make things a wee bit easier... a snatcher and a prim 'n' pretty accomplice will be more memorable. I'll tell my contacts that's what they need to look for.'

'Good,' I said. 'Seems that for once we are making some progress.'

'Och, why did ye have to say that? Now ye've jinxed it all.'

I would not admit it, but I feared he might be right. I saw him pace around, stooping and examining every little blemish on the snow.

'What are you looking for?'

'Cloven hoof prints.'

'Oh, for goodness' sake! Because you think the Devil decided to stroll by and trample on that poor woman's grave?'

McGray went on searching, undeterred.

'I ken the lady's face wasnae marked before she went into the ground. And it makes nae sense for the snatchers to brandish their goods. It's best for them if the corpses are nondescript. Also, have ye heard of the Devil's footprints of Devon?'

'I can proudly say no.'

'It happened thirty or so years ago, in February too, after a terrible blizzard. People all over Devon found these really odd tracks o' footprints.'

'Uhh, the Devil's!'

'Och, listen, for fuck's sake! They were cloven hooves, and they cut so deep into the snow they almost cleared it to the ground.'

'The Devil's blazing feet melting the ice?'

'Aye, and I wish ye could hear yerself when ye pretend to mock these things. Yer voice makes me think of a throttled fart that's trying to sound *inquisitive*. Now, before ye say those tracks were left by some bored twat with stilts—'

'Or a goat?'

'Whatever did it was two-legged. And the tracks appeared at several places; they covered almost a hundred miles. Nobody could've walked that distance in one night.'

'Perhaps a team of bored—?'

'*And* the tracks went on through walls and appeared on roofs too. Sometimes they stopped in front of a wall only to continue right on the opposite side, nae marks o' climbing or them walking around the obstacles. How can ye explain that?'

'I cannot. I did not see those prints myself. And also, I do not care.'

I left him to inspect the snow and went back to the open grave. The soil was flat at the bottom, compressed by the coffin. The only marks I recognised were those left by the constables, where they had secured the straps to lift the box out.

The daylight was quite dim, so I could not see the finer detail. I looked for a suitable spot, a side of the pit with many rocks and protrusions, and very carefully clambered down into the grave. My gloves became soiled at once, nonetheless. I took the right one off and inspected the walls, feeling them with my bare fingertips. The soil was compacted and frozen, so I could still see the dents made by the shovels and pikes, but not much more. The pit was utterly empty; no items of clues left behind.

'Nice view?' McGray asked me, looking down from the edge of the hollow. He was holding the snatchers' shovel.

'There is one way in and one way out of here,' I said as I turned in circles. 'Are you certain the body was not marked during the service or the burial?'

'That's what they told me. The mark must have appeared while the auld lady was under the ground.'

'Not that I distrust you, but I shall ask the minister directly,' I said, and I looked for supporting points on the wall. My feet slipped on the frosty stones, and so did my hands when I tried to pull myself upwards – far easier to get in than out.

'McGray, give me a hand, will you?'

Nine-Nails gave me a roguish grin, resting his weight on the shovel as if it were a cane. 'Have I told ye about these Devil's footprints in Devon?

'McGray ...'

'*Feel like mocking them now?* See, that's the throttled fart sound I was talking a—'

'McGray!' I grunted, my hand stretched upwards.

He raised the shovel again, bringing it closer to his eyes and inspecting it inch by inch.

'Auld tool,' he mumbled. 'Nae marks or names or anything to trace it ... Shame.'

'Were you expecting them to be engraved with the snatchers' name and address?'

McGray tossed the shovel aside.

'Still mocking me? Even from doun there?'

I jerked my hand. 'Do not be a child, Nine-Nails! Will you help me now?'

He chuckled for a few seconds, savouring the moment. In the end he did lower a hand and pulled me up as if I were made of hay.

'Thanks,' I said, shaking the mud off my gloves. 'No need to dwell in the realm of the dead. I'll spend plenty of time there one day.' I headed to the church. 'Now let's talk to that minister and whoever dug that pit.'

'Aye,' McGray said, eyeing it with concern. 'It really was quite shallow for a Christian grave.'

II

To my surprise, the interior of the nave was bright and airy, with large stained-glass windows shedding light from all four cardinal points. The air was misty with incense, so the dim daylight filtered in through the broad Gothic arches in milky streams. And the place was mighty cold, our breath condensing before our faces as much as it did outside.

We found Reverend Hunter by the wooden pulpit, his back turned to us. He was talking heatedly to a tall man with a long, white beard, so wiry and bushy it seemed solid. His skin, I noticed even from afar, was as gnarled as the bark of the graveyard's yews. It was that second man who first saw us. He nodded in our direction, and as we approached I noticed the old black hat he held by his chest, wringing it with nervous hands.

The minister turned to us.

'Inspectors!' he said with exaggerated enthusiasm. 'Are you done outside? Would you like to talk to me now?'

Whatever they'd been discussing, he seemed very happy at the interruption.

McGray did not answer, his eyes on the other man. 'Ye the sexton?'

'Aye, sirs. Jimmy Stevens,' he answered with a polite bow, though he could not quite mask a slight tremor in his voice.

McGray nodded, looking at Jimmy's baggy trousers. The material was scuffed and faded at the hems and knees. He clearly spent a lot of his time kneeling on mud.

'Can we talk to yer man first?' McGray asked the minister, though his tone implied he was not requesting permission.

'Oh? Well ... yes, of course,' the minister said, somewhat offended. He only moved when McGray cleared his throat so noisily I thought he might expectorate onto the slabbed floors.

He waited until the man disappeared, and then spoke to the old sexton.

'Take a pew?'

The man bowed again and went to the nearest bench. I noticed a slight limp, and when he sat his joints made all sorts of noises.

'How come I'd nae seen ye around before?' McGray asked him as he sat near him. I remained on my feet, pacing to keep myself warm.

'A good sexton is never noticed,' the chap said with a hint of pride, 'or that any part o' the kirk needs his attention.'

'What d'ye do here?' McGray asked. 'Normal sexton duties? Cleaning the nave, ringing the bell?'

'Aye.'

McGray squinted a little. 'Digging the graves?'

Jimmy made a sour smile.

'Aye, sir. Only to find that some damned bastards have been undoing my work lately.' He looked at the altar and made another quick bow, as if asking forgiveness for his profanity. 'They dig so quick they'd put me out o' business if they wanted!'

'That new grave,' McGray said. 'A tad too shallow, don't ye think?'

The sour smile widened. 'The ground's frozen, sir, as you must have seen,' and he looked at my soiled gloves. 'I do what I can, but—' he opened and closed a fist, and we saw his knotted knuckles and joints. 'Each time it gets a wee bit harder.'

'Do you mean to say – that you dig all those graves without help?' I asked him.

'Budget doesnae allow for help, I keep hearing.' He raised his voice a little, clearly hoping that the echoes carried his words to the minister's ears. 'That's what we were talking about just now.'

'Ye sure that's the only reason?' McGray probed. 'We'd hate to find ye've been getting a few bob under the table to make the job easier for the resurrectionists.'

'Och, I'd never!' he cried. 'I've worked here since before either o' youse was born. I've dug more graves than I can remember!'

'All right, all right,' McGray said, lifting both palms. 'We did have to ask. Now tell us...' He stroked his jaw, perhaps missing his stubble. I knew he did not want to mention the *Devil's mark* to anyone who did not strictly need to know. 'Did ye notice anything odd in the auld lady? Before she was buried, I mean.'

The man frowned. 'Odd, sir?'

'Did ye see her during the service?' and McGray pointed at the altar, where the coffin would have been then.

'Aye. Nae that I pry into people's coffins, sirs.'

'Course nae. What d'ye remember about her? Anything that caught yer eye?'

The sexton fidgeted with his hat. 'Erm... All I can think of is that very pretty pendant 'round her neck. Nae that I took it!'

'I ken,' McGray said. 'We found it still on her. Well – let's just say we found it. Anything else?'

'Nae sir. Auld lady, very wee, very skinny. Ordinary black dress. Nae relatives. That's all I can think of.'

McGray shifted uncomfortably on the pew. 'It's nae the sermons that keep me out o' the kirk; it's the bloody seats! Now, Jimmy, from what ye've told me, ye sound like an honest lad...'

'Course, sirs!'

McGray looked around, making sure we were still alone, and then leaned closer to the sexton. 'Tell me... Did ye see anyone getting close to Mrs Brewster? Doing anything...' he went on in a whisper, 'strange?'

The sexton did not blink for a moment, both unsettled and confused. I could not even guess what he might have been thinking.

'Nae, sir. Who could've? The service was very sad; only the rev'rend, me ... and that nurse woman.'

I looked up at once. 'A nurse?'

Jimmy nodded. 'Aye. Said she'd looked after the auld lady; that she felt sorry she had no mourners.' He frowned more deeply as the scene appeared to come back to memory. 'She *did* get close to the coffin before we nailed it. To pay her last respects, it seemed. I saw her squeeze the lady's hand.'

I felt a twinge of excitement. 'Really? Did you get to hear her name?'

'Och, nae.'

'What was she like?' I asked.

'Nae young or bonny, for sure; around forty, I'd say; with brown hair. Also ... Grumpy. Bossy. Like she was in command.'

That could only be Miss Smith, I thought. I discreetly produced my notebook and jotted the fact down. McGray noticed it but made no comment.

'What about the minister?' he asked, still in low voices. 'Did he get close to the missus? Closer than he needed, I mean.'

'I don't think so, sirs. I mean, he did have to bless and anoint her, but that's done for all the dead.'

I also took note of that and underlined it.

'I think that is all we need for the time being,' I said. 'Unless my colleague says otherwise?'

'Nae. I've heard enough.'

'Shall I guide youse to the sacristy?' the sexton offered.

'Nah, we'll manage, Jimmy,' McGray said.

The sexton then excused himself and left the nave, and

McGray and I headed in the direction we'd seen the minister go, albeit slowly.

'McGray,' I whispered, 'from what you asked that man – you *do* admit someone must have tampered with the body before it went into the ground.'

'It could be, I grant ye that. But—'

'It *must* be. And I do not like the fact that Miss Smith was present, or that she even touched the—'

'Inspectors?'

The minister's voice startled me. The man had approached us as stealthily as a fox. We'd not even heard him open the thick oaken door to the sacristy.

'Oh, do excuse me,' he said. 'I've been told I have a very light tread.'

'Indeedy,' McGray replied. 'Can we talk to ye now?'

Hunter showed us the way to the airy sacristy, where he kept a neat office. The whitewashed walls contrasted nicely with the dark varnish of the ornate furnishings: a solid desk, a chest with a thick iron lock and a table with a cut-glass decanter prominently displayed.

'May I offer you a drink?' he said, pointing at it. 'Or tea, perhaps?'

'No, thank you,' I replied, and we all sat down around the minister's desk. I saw that a copy of the day's *Scotsman* lay among his other paperwork, but I did not want to be the one to draw attention to it.

'Are you finished now inspecting the graveyard?' the man asked, staring at the trail our dirty boots were leaving on his expensive rug.

'Aye,' McGray said. 'Ye can have yer flock back now.'

'How delightful. I am sure they will be happy to come back here for the evening service. Although … they might be a little frightened.'

'Frightened?' both McGray and I said in unison.

'Yes,' Hunter said, and then reached for the newspaper. 'Excuse me, but I have to ask you – Does this have anything to do with that ghastly death at the asylum?'

Reverend Hunter was looking at the stump on McGray's hand. Like everyone in Edinburgh, he knew Nine-Nails's story and the fact that his sister was an inmate at the asylum in Morningside. Now he must be jumping to his own conclusions, just like many others in the city.

McGray stirred, interlaced his hands and lounged back. His eyes were burning with indignation.

'I'd rather ye didnae ask those sorts o' questions.'

'Oh, I'm sorry!' Hunter said. 'I didn't mean to be nosy, but one does wonder! This poor woman's grave desecrated... then this death – murder, it was! Both were inmates at the same institution. And then this horrendous business of that devilish...'

'Did ye touch Mrs Brewster's body before she was buried?' McGray jumped in, purposely truculent.

'I – I beg your pardon?'

'Which word o' that did ye nae get?'

'I – well...'

'We understand you had to anoint her,' I intervened before McGray turned the desk over.

Reverend Hunter gulped, both hands pressed on the edge of his desk.

'I... I do. I mean, I did! That is part of the funeral rituals.'

'May I see the oil you used?' I asked.

Hunter ruffled like a cornered cat, his crown of white hair standing on end. He was about to protest, but McGray again cleared his throat very loudly.

After a moment's hesitation, the minister stood up and went to the ornate chest. He pulled a chain he wore around his neck and produced the key. After he unlocked the chest he only lifted the lid a smidgen; just enough to seize a small silver-plated box, which he placed ceremoniously on the desk. He opened it and, nestled in purple satin lining, I saw a small bottle with a glass stopper. Reverend Hunter took it out with both hands, as if it were the most delicate child, and showed it to us. It must have contained less than an ounce of pale golden oil.

I stretched a hand to take it, but the man recoiled.

'Oh, inspector, I cannot. This is the most sacred—'

'Give him the damned thing!' McGray snapped, but Hunter still wavered.

'I will be very careful,' I said.

After a resigned sigh, the minister finally handed me the bottle.

I held it with respect, once more thinking that my own father would have been anointed in his coffin the day before. I opened the bottle, at which the minister flinched, and I took a cautious sniff.

'This is olive oil, am I correct?'

'Indeed, inspector. Sanctified and perfumed with frankincense and myrrh.'

I was going to dip a finger in it, but thought better of it and put the stopper back on.

'May we take this, reverend?'

'Oh, absolutely not, inspector. That is consecrated oil!'

McGray rose from his seat, ready to *persuade* the man, but I lifted a hand.

'Perhaps just a few drops?' I said.

'Impossible,' Hunter said again.

McGray snorted. 'Och, yer too soft, Percy!'

He yanked the bottle from my hands and shoved it most casually into his breast pocket. 'We're taking it. Like it or lump it.'

Hunter jumped up and banged his fists on the desk.

'This is an *outrage!*'

'Don't scratch yer desk,' McGray said.

'You *will* hand that back and—'

McGray stood up, rising to his full height. 'And *what?*'

Hunter raised a finger, with much more bravery than good sense. He was so incensed he could not bring himself to speak.

'You will have it back, reverend,' I had to intervene. 'And I will make sure it is treated with respect.'

The man was shaking from sheer anger, but eventually he lowered his hand.

'We need to see the coffin now,' McGray said, still hostile.

The minister exhaled in grumbling snorts, opened one of his drawers and produced a set of larger keys. Without words he stepped out of the office and led us to a nearby door. It led to a darkened storeroom, crammed with broomsticks, buckets, broken pews and other bric-a-brac.

'We need light,' McGray commanded, and the minister, still fuming, went off to get it.

'Why do you always have to do things like this?' I hissed while he was away.

'He's a gossip-mongering twat!' McGray snapped.

'I know. He is a minister, after all. But still—!'

Reverend Hunter returned then, bringing a small oil lamp. He pushed it into my hands and immediately turned on his heels, mumbling something that sounded like 'If you need me ...'

'Better that way,' McGray said, already stepping into the storeroom.

I shed light on the narrow coffin, which rested on two very old benches nobody had ever bothered to repair.

'An expensive item,' I said, looking at the thick hinges and the polished wood.

'The Brewsters arranged their funerals years ago,' McGray said. 'Or so I was told. Clouston might have chipped in too.'

He pulled up the lid and we saw some of the thick nails still sticking out. McGray touched the sharp tips.

'That Jimmy may have dug a shitty shallow grave, but he made sure the snatchers had it hard trying to open this.'

He propped the lid against the wall and I lowered the light, bringing it closer to the white lining. It was corrugated satin, like the one that had protected the sacred oil. Though of a lower quality, it was still a very decent niche, compared to what I had expected. It even had a little pillow trimmed with white lace, now stained with dirt and smudges.

'They were wearing gloves,' McGray said, delicately touching one of the stains near the pillow. Indeed, the parallel marks were too thick for bare fingers, and there were more marks where the woman's calves would have rested. I felt a shiver as I pictured the two men lifting her limp body in the dark.

I reached for the pillow, but somehow I could not bring myself to touch it. I spotted a few strands of white hair still resting on it, and my discomfort increased.

'D'ye feel it too?' McGray asked.

'Feel what?' I said, feigning contempt.

McGray whispered with something akin to reverence. 'It's like she's still here...'

I'd been stirred by something, indeed, but rather than it being a tormented spirit trapped within the coffin, I felt as though we were prying into a lady's bedchamber; invading her privacy. After all, what place can be more intimate, more sacred, than one's last resting place? That space was meant to stay sealed forever.

I let out a sigh, opened and closed my hand, and mustered the courage to pick up the pillow – that sensitivity was what made me quit my medical degree in Oxford.

At first I thought the material was wet, and nearly gasped. Then I realised it was just terribly cold. I looked at the fabric and the lace; no stains or marks of any kind. At least not that I could see under that light.

Much to my discomfort, I had to bring the pillow to my nose, careful not to touch the strands of hair. Even McGray wrinkled his nose.

'Damp and incense,' I murmured. 'Not even a trace of the odours of decay.' I arched an eyebrow. 'No sulphurs from Hell either, I am afraid.'

We looked at the rest of the lining, McGray running cautious fingers on every corner and fold. Other than the muddy stains, the most suspicious thing we found was a small twig of yew caught in the seams.

McGray picked it up carefully and brought it closer to the light. It was just over an inch long.

'It still looks fresh,' I said.

'Aye. Yew sprigs can last for days and days. One o' the reasons it symbolises eternal life. That's why they always plant them in graveyards.'

'Do you think it was left there by a mourner?' I asked. 'Or that it just fell in there after the snatchers opened the coffin?'

'There was only one mourner,' McGray said. 'It won't be hard to find out. Still, we should take it. D'ye have one o' yer hankies with ladies' Belgian lace?'

'I will disappoint you on the lace,' I said, producing my plain handkerchief and carefully wrapping the twig (I did do my best to conceal my initials, embroidered in purple and green).

'Anything else ye'd like to see?' McGray asked, but I shook my head.

'I am not sure. I definitely need to look at that mark on the body, otherwise I have no idea what to look for here.'

'Aye, we should head to the morgue now. But trust me – the mark will only puzzle ye even more.'

He was correct.

12

After gathering the evidence – the sacred oil and the yew sprig – and telling Reverend Hunter nobody should touch the coffin until we said so, we finally set off to the City Chambers.

I was glad we had looked at the tracks in the snow first, for the skies were now shedding a persistent sleet all over the city. It only worsened as we approached the Royal Mile, and by the time we reached the police headquarters, Edinburgh was a grey blur of mud and slush. When I jumped off the cab I had to hold my bowler hat firmly, lest it flew away in the wind.

A beggar boy and girl, both drenched and covered in dirt, approached me with their palms extended, wheedling for alms. I pulled a few coppers out of my pocket, but when I looked up, someone in the distance shouted something I could not quite make out. As soon as they heard it, the children screamed and ran away in panic.

I saw several fishwives and pedlars along the road, all looking at me with various degrees of hostility. A man in particular, just hopping onto a cart full of coal, cast me an eerie glare.

'Come on,' McGray told me, giving me a pat on the back that felt more like a commanding push, and we stepped into the muddy courtyard.

'What was that?' I asked. 'Why was everyone staring at me?'

Nine-Nails, with the bag of evidence under his arm, simply shrugged.

'They think yer... Satan or something.'

'*What?*'

'Can ye blame them? That witchcraft ye performed at Calton Hill Jail, with a crowd behind ye—'

'*Witchcraft!* The entire point of that display was precisely to refute—'

'Och, stop screeching! *I* ken, but d'ye think they care? If an ignorant wretch likes a story, he doesnae give a damn about wee details like *logic.*'

That was as infuriating as it was true. I only answered with a snort, and McGray looked at me with a slight frown as we stepped into the building.

'And... well, there's that other matter.'

'What other matter?'

'Remember the house ye burnt down?'

'*The house I*—' All the officers and clerks in the main hall turned their heads to me, so I had to lower my voice. 'You know I had nothing to do with that! In fact, I lost some of my best merino wool suits and some very valuable cufflinks!'

'Course I ken! I was around when it all happened. But someone spread the rumour that it was ye 'n' yer devil-worshipping friends that set it on fire. No wonder those poor little brats ran away from ye. They must expect their flesh will rot off if ye touch them.'

I let out a weary sigh. 'Was that rumour circulated, by any chance...?'

'Aye, that auld bitch Lady Glass. She spread all sorts o' slander after ye burned her house and never paid her a penny.'

I let out an exasperated growl. 'Why was I supposed to pay her? Did *I* start the bloody fire or—?'

'Told ye,' Nine-Nails said as we walked down the stairs. 'Ye should never've gone into business with that auld coo! She's the Devil incarnate. Tried to swindle me and my auld dad too.'

'What was I supposed to do? She happened to own the only respectable properties in – oh, never mind.'

We reached the morgue, and I shivered as soon as we stepped into the small reception room. The place was mighty damp too, its tiled walls jaded and cracked after years of constant cleaning.

The very young Dr Reed was already there, jotting notes on a pad, his white coat ever stained in red at the stomach and the cuffs.

'Inspector Frey!' he said as soon as he saw me. When I'd first met him, fourteen months earlier, I'd thought that he looked like a fidgety cocker spaniel, with his plump cheeks and his wide, watery eyes. Now he looked at least a decade older. 'I thought you had quit!'

'I am back just for this one case,' I told him, purposely holding back the details.

'So he says,' McGray mocked, and I'd rather not dwell on that.

'Inspector McGray tells me you have already looked at this corpse,' I said. 'Mrs ...'

'Brewster,' said Reed, showing me the pad. 'Yes, I was just tidying up the report.'

'May we see her?' I asked.

'Of course, inspector, follow me. You *are* still an inspector, are you not, sir? Or what should I call you?'

McGray opened his mouth, a roguish twinkle in his eye, and I snapped. 'Say nothing! Mr Frey will do. Shall we?'

Reed led us to the small dissection room, which as usual smelled of a mixture of laudanum, formaldehyde and a hint uncomfortably similar to that of a butcher's shop. There were a few bodies on the tables, all covered in white shrouds.

'Has Clouston sent the inmate's body?'

'Not yet, sir,' Reed answered. 'But I hear Constable McNair

and others are already on their way to retrieve it. Thankfully it's winter.'

'Indeed,' I said, remembering that ghastly murder case last summer, when the body began to decompose in the balmy weather.

Reed went to the nearest table and drew the cloth with a solemn, respectful look. I'd grown to like him; despite the pressures, the young man had not yet become cynical about his job.

Reed uncovered just the face of an old, now yellowish-looking woman. My heart skipped a beat, for I recognised her face at once. I had seen her at the lunatic asylum, prostrated in bed and stunned with laudanum. Although she now seemed relaxed, as in a pleasant sleep, the wrinkles that cut deeply through her face spoke of her many months of insanity.

'Where is the mark?' I asked, and Reed turned the head with a gentle touch. I reached for one of the nearby lamps, leaned closer, and held my breath.

There it was: the exact shape Caroline had sketched in my notebook, and yet so sharp and clear, as if traced with a scalpel, that it sent a stabbing prickle up the back of my neck.

'The cloven hoof,' I muttered.

'Indeedy,' said McGray. 'Touch it.'

I looked up, frowning at the odd request, but I obliged in the end, placing a hesitant finger on the woman's skin.

'Excuse me, madam,' I whispered, again feeling like an invader.

I then understood the reason for the request. The mark did not feel swollen or indented. Like Caroline had mentioned, it was clearly not a cut or a burn.

'Did you try to wash it off?' I asked, staring at the greyish colour.

'I did, sir,' said Reed. 'Soap first, then oil and then white spirit. Nothing worked.'

I stretched the creased skin a little, and the mark stretched with it. It was as if...

'It seems to be part of the skin itself,' I said. 'Almost...'

'As if coming from within,' Reed completed for me.

I looked on for a moment, my eyes mere inches from the woman's skin. I rose only when the damp air made my wrist ache again.

'Very odd,' I mumbled, rubbing the tips of my fingers, which tingled as if I'd just touched something infected. 'Very odd indeed.'

'What d'ye think?' McGray asked, but I would not answer immediately.

I stared at my fingers, rubbing them a little harder.

'Do you have an ewer and basin?' I asked Reed. I knew it was all in my head, but still I felt as if the tingle increased.

'Of course, sir,' he said, and led me to it.

I lathered rather anxiously, rinsed my hands and accepted the towel Reed offered me, all the while pondering.

'That greyish colour...' I began. I did not want to say it out loud, but I could not avoid it. 'It looks as if—' I sighed. 'As if the flesh is rotting a little faster, but only at that point – only to shape that mark.'

McGray raised his chin. 'The Devil's mar—'

'Pray, do *not* say again that the Devil marked her while she was underground!'

'I was going to say,' McGray grunted, 'that the Devil's mark must have appeared on the asylum walls at about the same time we were chasing the snatchers.'

'At least *that* mark did not come from the netherworld,' I said, my mind swirling in the sea of possibilities. 'It is still disturbing that the same shape should appear in two places at once.' I shook my head. 'We must indeed keep this quiet,' I added, looking directly at the young Reed.

'I made an oath, sir,' he replied, his chest swollen with pride.

'Of course,' I said, and then looked back at the woman's corpse. 'There are two things I want you to do.'

'Yes?'

'Do you have a microscope?'

He bit his lip. 'There is an old one in the store, sir, but I'm not sure in what state it might be. Hasn't been used in months.'

'The last time I saw ye use it,' McGray said, 'was back when that sod Bram Stoker was here.'

Reed nodded. 'Oh, yes! Those blood samples he was so keen to—'

'Yes, yes,' I interrupted. 'If the microscope works, I want you to take a sample from this woman's skin. Inspect both the mark and some of the unblemished skin too, for comparison.'

'What are ye expecting to find?' McGray asked.

'For once, I have no idea,' I admitted. 'First of all, I want to see how deep that mark goes. It could still be some sort of indelible ink, in which case the colouration should be superficial.'

I gently covered the woman's face with the cloth, as if embarrassed by what I was about to suggest.

'How certain are you that Mrs Brewster died of natural causes?'

Reed's lips parted a little. 'Well, I … I hadn't even questioned the fact,' he stammered after a moment. 'There are no obvious marks of violence; no wounds or bruises.'

McGray was frowning. 'Are ye suggesting she could've been murdered?'

'All these happenings, the marks … the snatchers … they do cast some doubt. Sadly, she would not be the first person to die very conveniently when a corpse is needed at the medical schools. It would not be a mad idea to carry out a full post-mortem.'

'I can definitely do that, sir,' Reed said, but at once turned to McGray. 'I mean, if you agree, inspector.'

McGray stroked his chin, visibly worried. If Mrs Brewster's case also turned out to be a murder, it would require a full investigation, and that would be far more difficult to keep quiet.

And with MacDonnell's murder at the asylum already in the papers – again I shuddered at what people might conclude: not one but *two* killings, both under the same roof where McGray's sister dwelled, the same mark appearing twice on the same night. Even the nosy Reverend Hunter was already piecing things together, and he only knew a fraction of the facts. I could already imagine a crude engraving on a newspaper's front page: Pansy with a dagger in her hand, lurking in the middle of a darkened corridor, defacing corpses and smearing the walls with satanic symbols.

A shadow grew on McGray's face. He must be entertaining very similar thoughts. 'Do what Percy says,' he told Reed. 'We need to find the truth.' And he bit his lip, as if to contain a gloomy, 'whatever that truth turns out to be'. He then produced the little bottle from his breast pocket. 'Oh, and have a look at this too.'

'What is it?' Reed asked as he received it.

'Anointing oil,' I said. 'Tell us if it could have been used to mark Mrs Brewster. You might want to try it on a skin sample. But keep in mind we need to return it.'

'And don' touch it,' McGray warned. 'It might nae be as hallowed as we think.'

13

I held up the twig, the better to catch light from the oil lamp, but even through the magnifying glass I could see nothing of consequence.

'It has a little talon,' I mumbled. 'It was definitely torn from the tree; not cut – so we still cannot be sure whether it went into the coffin by accident or by design.'

McGray only answered with a growl, as he rummaged through his piles of books and assorted rubbish. We were now in his library, which had once been the ballroom of his grand house at Moray Place. The space, ever crammed with McGray's most precious books on the occult, looked much worse now, further packed with all the files, artefacts, ghastly specimens and formaldehyde jars he had managed to save. The only surface free of books, papers or haunted trinkets were the rugs by the wide fireplace, where McGray's two dogs now lay, sleeping in enviable bliss. Even McGray's armchair was full of loose sheets and half-read books (sitting on top of them did not seem to bother him at all). The low coffee table was even more cluttered, with a bottle of whisky proudly topping a precarious tower of leather-bound books.

This was the one room Joan was not allowed to clean. One notorious exception had been the time McGray dropped a one-gallon demijohn containing the preserved foetus of a donkey with a deformed skull (which he claimed to be a baby unicorn).

'Put the twig here,' McGray said, passing me a little vial. 'In case we want to look at it again.'

'Most likely to be useless,' I said, but I obliged nonetheless. I put the little vial on the crammed mantelpiece. When I turned, McGray was already penning hasty notes. 'Are you writing to your contacts in the resurrection business?'

'Aye. Telling them we're potentially looking for an upper-class sod who's been working with a really skinny sack o' bones. Am sure no one will talk to me now, but it's worth a try. By the way, the files from our auld cases are over there, if ye want to have a look.'

He pointed at a pile of old crates, all packed with creased folders. I had almost forgotten I'd asked him if I could see them; the records on Lord Joel, which might shed more light on Pansy's true parentage and the old, perhaps turbulent connections between the Ardglasses and the McGrays. I felt a twinge of genuine excitement as I faced the boxes.

'What did you do to these?' I asked, pulling out one of the files. The covers were caked with dry dirt. 'Did you wade through a cesspool with them?'

'It was raining bloody cats and dogs when I took them out! Three in the fuckin' morning; right before Lord Cecil's bastards arrived.'

The files, as I'd been warned, were not sorted at all. I could picture McGray pulling them out of my carefully indexed drawers and hurling them blindly into these very crates. Thus I was pleasantly surprised to find Mrs Brewster's file right away, sitting close to the top. Nine-Nails must have consulted it recently. I put it aside and discreetly looked at McGray, still engrossed in his messages. I dived back into the crates, for I'd never have a better chance to retrieve Joel Ardglass's records.

I found a hefty file on Bram Stoker, an even thicker one on Madame Katerina, a treaty on the miraculous waters of Loch Maree, and a catalogue of all the known cursed violins of the seventeenth century.

At last, between Queen Victoria's astral chart and a log on seasonal observations of will-o'-the-wisps, I found a folder with the asylum's stamp. I recognised it immediately as the one I'd held in my hands just over a year ago. That file detailed the life and tribulations of Pansy's real father.

I held my breath as I opened it. More than half the sheets were dedicated to notes on witchcraft. I put them aside and took out just the ones that looked like medical records. After one last peek over my shoulder – McGray was now addressing the envelopes – I shoved those pages into Mrs Brewster's file.

'I will first reacquaint myself with the case of the Brewsters' haunted home,' I announced. I was going to give further explanation, but McGray had already nodded distractedly, so I thought I'd not stir things further.

A moment later he whistled stridently and George, his aging butler (and Joan's – I shudder as I pen this – *lover*) came in.

'Mr Frey,' he cried in the thickest of Scottish accents. 'Yer back!'

I shook my head. 'I would not say *back*, George.'

'If we didnae have to keep it quiet, I'd get tar and paint that phrase on yer forehead,' McGray said before turning to George. 'Can ye take these messages to the Ensign? Tell Mary to pass 'em on as usual.'

George hesitated. 'Och, master, can I wait till the sleet stops?'

The man turned his head to the window, the storm drumming on the glass, and McGray twisted his mouth. He knew we had very little time to act, and yet poor George was not getting any younger.

'Send Larry, then. And tell him this is very important.'

George bowed and took the messages, and McGray saw him walk away with understandable affection. That man had been at his side through thick and thin; he'd even been around the night Pansy had gone insane, and then stayed on with Nine-Nails when everyone else in Edinburgh turned his back on him.

'How long do you think it will take them to bring the second body to the morgue?' I said after a brief sigh. We'd asked the constables to send us a note as soon as the corpse arrived from the asylum, and I wanted to inspect it before Reed carried out the post-mortem.

'Clouston assured me the relatives would be there today. They might have dispatched poor MacDonnell already.'

I saw the little box of stationery where he kept his ink and paper. There was also a bobbin of twine. I took it as casually as I could and used it to tie the folder – both to make sure I lost nothing, and so that McGray did not get to see what I was taking.

'It might be a good idea to question them too,' McGray said.

'Erm – who, sorry?'

'MacDonnell's daughters! Are ye daydreaming?'

'No,' I said promptly, and then rushed to tie the string. 'I was just – running through all the pieces in my head. This case is so convoluted.'

McGray chuckled. 'Indeedy, and all those morning brandies must be taking their toll on yer brains.'

I did not even register his words. I sat back, a little more relaxed now that the file was tied up. I pressed my fingertips together and began to reflect.

'For instance,' I said, 'I agree with you: I doubt very much that the snatchers had anything to do with that mark. In fact, the unearthing of Mrs Brewster seems to have been a happy accident.'

'I thought that too. Without the snatchers, that Devil's mark would've stayed underground.'

'Remind me of the name of those very famous Edinburgh resurrectionists from a century ago? The ones who murdered haphazardly.'

'Burke and Hare? That wasnae a century ago! Just about fifty years. But aye, I also thought o' them when Trevelyan assigned me the case. Those two rascals killed for over a year; pedlars and prostitutes and street children. Even their wives were in the game. Disgusting.'

'So,' I said, 'it would not be impossible that someone at the asylum – some orderly or nurse or ... doctor—'

'Let's just say *someone* at the asylum,' McGray interjected.

'Someone,' I conceded, 'was in league with the body snatchers and procured them bodies that nobody would miss.'

'I thought o' that too,' McGray said. 'Harland or one o' the orderlies. But—' He shook his head. 'It's those damned marks again. It's almost as if ...'

'As if somebody were trying to draw attention to those deaths?' I completed.

'Aye. That's exactly what it looks like.'

I arched an eyebrow, slowly leaning forwards. 'What if someone else at the asylum found out what was going on? And they decided to expose the deaths? Marking the victims and the scenes of the crimes so they could all be linked in our investigation?'

McGray bit the inside of his cheek, barely nodding.

'Yer sort o' making sense, Frey. I'm glad Caroline thought o' calling ye.'

So it had been *her* idea to summon me, not McGray's. The thought made me feel unexpected butterflies.

'But if yer right,' McGray spoke on, 'why don't they simply come to us and *tell* us there's a murdering bastard afoot?'

'Fear of retaliation, perhaps?'

McGray pondered for a moment before shaking his head again. 'Aye, but there's also MacDonnell's family. He's nae the typical resurrectionist target. He *would* have been missed. And Clouston also followed his case closely, especially as his illness was such a strange—'

He went silent. A moment later he snapped his fingers and jumped on his feet.

'What is it now?' I asked, seeing him rummage through a small chest of drawers.

He came back with a bundle of yellowish cloth, only a little bigger than his fist, and lay it on the mess of books at the coffee table.

'I should've shown ye this from the very start,' he said as he opened the bundle.

'What is it?'

'The rag we found inside MacDonnell's mouth.'

'*Oh, for God's sake!*' I cried with a retch. 'McGray, did you keep that in your home, right where you—?'

It was pointless to end the sentence, for McGray was already unrolling the nauseating rag on the table. The wintry weather had kept it damp.

'That was inside a dead man's throat!' I protested, covering my mouth and mentally vowing never again to touch the books underneath the cloth.

'What d'ye make o' this?' McGray asked, and he pointed at the eerie writing.

I looked as closely as my nostrils allowed. There was a bilious whiff to it. I still managed to see the pattern of the cloth – yellow stripes against a once-white background. Like most bandages for the poorer patients, the piece had been torn from some used garment.

'Is this why you said the murderer might simply have let MacDonnell gag himself?'

'Aye. MacDonnell feared the air poisoned his insides.'

'Yes, I remember. I also remember he vomited all over me on the very first occasion I visited the asylum.'

'Ha! So ye *do* remember that!'

'How could I forget? That was a very expensive suit! I threw it away the morning after. But again, I digress. Do you think the man was *taunted*?'

'Aye. It's very odd that he happened to have a fit like this after five or six months of good behaviour.'

'Indeed,' I said. 'And he also left his dormitory and wandered all the way to the asylum's more affluent wing. There must be a story behind that.'

Again, I thought of Clouston, my suspicions growing. He knew the man's medical history very well, *and* he had manipulated McGray to let him keep hold of the corpse for much longer than he ought to have done.

I only sighed, opting to keep those musings to myself for the time being.

I looked at the rag and the crude writing. *WHY WON'T YOU DIE?* It was as though someone were shouting the words at my face.

'This is clearly disguised,' I said. All the letters were capitals and traced with straight lines, so they almost looked like ancient runes. 'And look at the seeped ink. This must have gone into MacDonnell's throat when the writing was still fresh.'

I was about to lift one of the corners, but then pulled my hand back with a spasm.

'Och, no wonder they kicked ye out of Oxford!'

'They did not kick me out; I quit!'

'Is that any better?'

I sighed, begging the heavens for patience. 'I hesitated to touch it because I fear this might be poisoned.'

'Poisoned? But I—'

'Poisoned or daubed in something that either lulled MacDonnell or sent him into a frenzy. Whatever the case, I would advise you to stop touching the damned thing with your bare hands.'

For the first time in history, McGray followed my advice without objection. He reached for a pile of dirty dishes (peppered with the leftovers from last week's dinners), picked a fork and used it to roll up the rag again.

'Any way to find out what sort o' shite might be in here?'

'It will depend on the substance.'

'Useless to sniff it,' McGray said. 'It only stinks o' bile and boke.'

I nearly gagged at the thought. 'It will be easier to spot in the post-mortem, especially if it is opiates they—'

Someone banged at the main door then, the rapping startling us both. Even the dogs raised their heads. McGray sprinted to the window and drew the curtain, the sleet still falling heavily behind the glass.

'What is it?' I asked.

'One o' the lads. Cannae see his face.'

I heard George's quick steps along the entrance hall. McGray did not even get time to follow him: just as he opened the library door, a young constable rushed in. The man was drenched to the marrow and he stammered unintelligibly, unable to catch his breath.

McGray went to him and seized him by the shoulder. 'What is it, laddie? Breathe.'

The young man did so a couple of times as he wiped his forehead.

'The – the body at the asylum, sirs.' He gulped. '*It's gone!*'

14

The rain and sleet pelted over our heads as Nine-Nails led a dozen police officers into the asylum's grounds. I crouched and held my borrowed umbrella at an angle, barely protecting my face from the elements, as I marched behind the constables.

Indeed, it felt like a march, our feet splashing on the muddy gardens in almost military synchrony, Nine-Nails at the front. He was shouting orders at the constables, sending half to search the gardens and surrounding grounds, the rest to guard the asylum's corridors.

Clouston came out of the main gate, his face terribly pale as he saw the men storm into his building.

'What is this?' he cried, right before one of the beefier officers pushed him aside.

I was expecting McGray to be as sympathetic with him as ever. Instead—

'*I trusted ye!*' he barked, raising a hand as if about to smack the doctor across the face. 'I kent I should've taken the body yesterday, and now ye've—!'

He clenched a fist, as if about to throw a punch, but then lowered his hand and forced himself to take a deep breath.

'Shall we step inside?' I said, holding the door before the wind closed it behind the last constable.

'Of course,' Clouston said, sleet-soaked after even those moments by the gate. He walked in briskly and we followed him, only to find that the corridors were already a mayhem of confused nurses, patients and busy officers.

'Tell us what happened,' I asked as I closed my umbrella. McGray was so incensed he could not speak for a moment.

'We kept the body in the garden storeroom,' Clouston replied. 'It was well locked. And Tom, one of my orderlies, kept an eye on it every now and then.'

'Fucking good job he did!' McGray snapped.

I lifted a palm, begging him to have patience.

'What happened then?' I asked Clouston.

'We don't know!' he said. 'I sent Tom to bring MacDonnell back in, so that we could have him ready for his daughters. I didn't want them to see their dead father on a potting table. Miss Smith even got hold of a tweed jacket, so they wouldn't find him in —'

'Pray, move on,' I said, fearing McGray might slap the man.

Clouston produced a handkerchief and mopped his temple. 'It was at that time I sent a message to your headquarters, for someone to take the body to the morgue. I calculated they'd arrive just after these women had made their peace with their father. Only...'

'Only what?' McGray pressed, and Clouston nearly tripped.

'The corpse wasn't there. It had just vanished!'

I chuckled. 'Dead bodies do not vanish, doctor. You should have allowed the investigation to proceed.'

'I was only thinking of these poor people! My intention was never to hinder—'

I raised my palm again, for Clouston's explanations were only pushing McGray to the edge.

We walked to his office in tense silence. The door was open, and there we found Miss Smith, her hair dishevelled and her face pale. She was pouring tea for a couple of rustic women seated by the window. They were both in their mid-twenties, though their skin was weathered by the harsh Highland winters. Their dark coats, though frayed, were meticulously patched-up in places, so they must be their Sunday best. One of the women had a very young baby in her arms.

Standing in a corner, his face half cloaked in shadows, was a tall, brawny man. I did recognise his face.

'You are Tom, are you not?' I said. 'And these ladies are Mr MacDonnell's daughters?'

They all nodded nervously, their eyes on the irate McGray.

'What did ye do with the body?' he snapped at the orderly.

The younger woman, wearing an old hat with tattered feathers, brought a hand to her mouth, muffling a sob.

'Tom is beyond suspicion,' Clouston said. 'He is one of my most trusted men. And if you please, these ladies have just lost their father!'

'*Ye*'ve lost their father,' McGray snapped back.

The younger lady finally burst into tears, and her sister – the one with the baby – had to put an arm around her.

'Take them to the little parlour, please,' Clouston told Miss Smith. The head nurse bowed and gently led the MacDonnells into the corridor.

'I *need* to talk to you at your earliest convenience,' I whispered to her as she passed close to me. She understood everything I'd wanted to convey with my tone, and her eyes flickered.

'Ah – aye, sir,' she whispered back, only to quicken her pace and shut the door behind her. I had never seen her so anxious.

'So ye were guarding the storeroom,' McGray said to Tom.

The young man, despite being as tall and broad-shouldered as Nine-Nails, fixed his eyes on the floor.

'Aye, sir. But ...'

'But what?'

'Well, I didn't guard it all the time. I just checked on it every now and then during the night. One last time at five in the morning or so. MacDonnell was still there.'

McGray snorted.

'And the shed was still locked,' Clouston intervened. 'The latch and the door are intact. There was no way—'

'Can we see the room?' McGray cut in.

Clouston nodded, but he too looked down. For an instant I felt sorry for him. It was not only the tension; the man, for some reason, also seemed dejected.

'Follow me,' he said, patting his pocket. 'I have the key. And—'

Whatever Clouston was about to say, he thought again when he looked into McGray's eyes. He simply reached for the door and led the way in utter silence.

For once, McGray did nothing to ease the doctor's tension. It was sad to behold – the chasm between him and Clouston growing wider at every turn of events.

'It is true,' I said, my eyes but an inch from the lock, the rain drumming loudly on the roof. 'This looks intact.' I rose, wincing from the aching bones in my wrist. I looked around, while McGray inspected every nook and cranny of the cluttered storeroom.

'Who else had keys to this door?' I asked.

'Nobody,' Dr Harland replied. He had joined us on the way there, and now stood, sullen, by the empty table where the body had lain. He looked as if he had not slept at all that night. 'There is only one copy. The gardener usually keeps it, but as you can see, this is not the season to be mowing the lawns.'

'He hands the key to me in winter,' Clouston explained further. 'I had it with me the entire time. I only handed it to Tom when I asked him to retrieve the body.'

I glanced at the tall orderly, who again had picked a shady corner to stand in. At once he turned red.

'I did nothing, sir, I swear!' he cried, and then pleaded with Clouston. 'Doctor, you must tell them!'

Clouston looked for McGray's gaze, but he'd turned away, still inspecting the place. The doctor had to appeal to me.

'As I said, Tom is beyond suspicion. I have trusted him with –' he gulped – 'well, some of the most delicate matters of my career.'

I knew precisely which cases he meant. Tom had been aware of Lord Joel's madness and the shady deals Lady Anne had resorted to in order to keep her son's insanity a secret. Those deals still loomed over Clouston; a threat to his professional reputation if Lady Anne were ever to reveal them.

Tom shifted his weight from one foot to the other, his jaw clenched. I wondered how far his loyalty might take him.

My doubtful gesture did not go unnoticed by Dr Harland. He opened his mouth to say something, but right then McGray let out a victorious '*Aha!*'

'What is it?' I asked. I saw he was leaning over the mucky glass of the room's only window.

'Look, Percy,' he said, pointing at a thin crack across the pane. 'I remember I felt a draught when I came to see the body. It came from here. Look at this dent.'

I approached, feeling the cold waft on my face. The otherwise straight crack had a chip close to the window frame, where the gap was slightly wider, and some of the grime on the glass had been smeared. That smear went up, all the way to – the window's latch.

'Looks like they used something,' McGray said, 'a piece o' bent wire or something. They inserted it here and then pushed the latch up.'

He pointed at the sill. The sides – the sides only – were caked with cobwebs and dust and old mud. The middle, on the other hand, was rubbed almost clean.

'So... they pushed the latch up from the outside,' I said, looking at the piece of rusty steel. I tried it: it needed but a soft poke to come loose. 'And then they dragged MacDonnell out through here.'

'And they surely used the same wire through the crack to lock the window again,' McGray added.

He opened the window and we both looked out, the rain lashing the backs of our heads. There was a pile of mud on the other side, the heavy drops splashing all over. All tracks had been erased long ago.

'Blast!' I cried, pulling my head back in before I became drenched. I looked at Clouston and his men. 'Did none of you know there was a cracked window?'

Clouston and Tom looked embarrassed, but Harland gave me a mocking smile.

'There is also a crack on those boards over there, inspector. And the nails on that corner of the roof have been loose for months.'

McGray ground his teeth. 'D'ye have a point, or yer just being an arse?'

'Did you want us to keep MacDonnell in a sealed vault?' Harland retorted. 'How could we have expected someone would break in to steal the decaying body of a murdered nobody? Who would have wanted to do that?'

I could not repress a sardonic laugh. 'Oh! Perhaps – the *murderer*? Attempting to conceal evidence? Or maybe—'

'A body snatcher,' McGray jumped in. He looked sideways, his eyes half shut, and his voice became a mumble. 'Especially if they lost their last bounty the night before.'

Indeed, I thought. If Mrs Brewster had been destined for a good client, then the resurrectionist would have required a quick replacement.

The faces of the three men distracted me then. They'd all opened their eyes wide and I studied them one by one: the superintendent who'd been in charge of the victim's treatment, who had been in possession of the key to the storeroom through the night, and who had begged McGray not to take the body until the day after; the young doctor who'd been on shift the night of the murder, with full access to all the rooms and corridors; and the orderly who'd been in charge of looking after the corpse throughout the night, with ample opportunity to break in. How fortuitous that they all happened to be here at once, crammed into the frosty storeroom from where the body had disappeared.

Nine-Nails too looked at them with suspicion. 'Get out now,' he told them. 'And tell one o' my lads to come here.' Clouston was the first one to nod, more than happy to go. Harland and Tom, for some reason, hesitated. '*Now!*'

They started at the shout and hurried away.

'I should nae have said that out loud,' McGray mumbled once we were alone, pinching the bridge of his nose. 'Now they can go and warn their buyer.'

'Do you suspect them all?' I asked. 'Even Clouston?'

McGray did not reply. He only shook his head, unable to admit it out loud.

I looked up, feeling as if a cog in my brain had just turned. 'This may not be the worst thing to have happened ...' I said with a sudden twinge of excitement.

'What?'

'We must check at the college. *Right away!* If the body is to appear somewhere, it is bound to be there. And MacDonnell's corpse is not that fresh anymore; if the snatchers want to get paid, they will act quickly.'

'True! Frey, yer almost worth yer pay.'

'I am being paid nothing for—'

But McGray had already opened the door and was running across the lawns. I ran behind him, not even being able to reopen my umbrella. We crossed the asylum and found Dr Clouston by the main entrance.

'Is there anything I can do?' he asked.

'Just let the lads do their job,' McGray said curtly, pointing at the men who were searching the lawns inch by inch, and rushed to the carriage before Clouston could answer. I lagged behind for a moment, taking a discreet step towards the doctor.

'I know about Miss Ardglass and her visits,' I whispered swiftly into his ear, and the poor man jolted.

'I … I have no idea what you're—'

'Oh, don't play the fool! She told me herself.'

Clouston opened and closed his mouth, but no sound came out. I had no time for further explanations; as far as I knew, MacDonnell's body could be being sliced into an unrecognisable pulp as we spoke.

'Here,' I said, giving him a card. 'Come and see me at the Palace Hotel at your earliest convenience. We must speak. And bring Miss Smith. If you don't, I will come to you.'

Clouston simply stared at the card – and gulped. I could tell he would ignore my request, but I had no time to press him, for McGray was already calling me in florid language. I ran to the carriage and, just before I hopped in, I looked up.

One of the front windows, on the second floor, was Pansy's, and I caught a glimpse of her dark hair and pale forehead. From that angle I could not see her eyes, but I pictured them in my mind, so similar in colour to those of Caroline Ardglass.

As ever, Pansy did not move, surely staring absently at the gardens like she'd done for the past six and a half years.

So quiet, so oblivious … and yet at the core of all things.

15

'Is it already dark?' I cried, looking out of the carriage window. The lamplighters were already lighting the posts along the wide avenue of Bruntsfield Place.

McGray kept tapping his boot on the carriage floor, as regular and insistent as a ticking clock. I wanted to tell him he'd make a hole, but I knew better these days. The day's drawing to a close did not escape him, nor the fact that things were far more tangled and desperate than at the start of our investigations, that very morning. We were not even sure how much time we had before Trevelyan had to pull us away from the case.

'I hate the college,' McGray finally grumbled, as if to distract himself. 'It's full o' those upper-class bastards that belittled my family when we moved to Edinburgh. Ye ken the type – inbred auld clan chieftains that now boast they hosted lardy Queen Vicky and taught her how to dance *Strip the Willow*. They all chant how Edinburgh's at the top o' modern medicine, but still most o' them feck off to London as soon as they graduate. And, down there, their *science* only serves them to stuff smelling salts into debutantes' nostrils whenever the stuck-up bitches feign to swoon. Do they treat our poor locals? Fuck nae! They only ever come back for parties to boast "*uhh – I treat Lady Della-Twat-Della-Pom-Frit!*" Pricks.'

I arched an eyebrow. 'Are you quite done?'

He returned the look. 'Ye'd fit in there perfectly. Think about it. It's never too late to quit a third degree.'

I simply tapped the coach's front window, so that the driver sped up. Not that he had to; we were already riding frantically along the muddy South College Street. The grand buildings reminded me of the Oxford colleges, only these were much newer – and yet already covered in the city's thick soot. Two constables followed us on horseback, and I could hear the hooves galloping right behind our backs.

As we turned right, into Nicolson Street, we caught the first glimpse of Surgeons' Hall, with its extravagant Roman façade, colonnaded and topped with an elaborate gable, the carvings in fact highlighted by the grime encrusted in every cleft.

The carriage skidded on the street puddles as we halted. I jumped out hastily, just as the two officers reined back and dismounted next to us. I looked up at the building, and it was as if its stones put up a defiant face to scare us away: a grand, wealthy institution that had stood there since the dawn of civilisation.

The illusion, however, shattered as soon as we passed through one of the twin granite archways. The walls behind the façade were coarse brick, as were the tenement buildings that looked over the little courtyard, with naked pipework and crumbling mortar. Someone in those tenements must be boiling a ghastly meat broth, which made me nauseous at once.

We strode briskly across the muddy yard. A lanky student, with pasty skin and the thickest spectacles in the world, had the misfortune to cross our path as he ran for shelter. McGray grabbed him by the back of his collar.

'Where's the theatre, lad?'

The poor young man looked up, trembling at the sight of Nine-Nails. 'The-the—?'

McGray snorted. 'Och, is yer mum also yer sister? *The theatre!* Corpses. Lectures. Snip-snip. *Where?*'

The student shook like a leaf, barely managing to point at the wide gate.

'First – first floor—'

McGray let him go and we rushed into the building.

'At the end of the hall!' the young man, still trembling, cried behind our backs.

An old porter was about to stop us, but he stepped aside as soon as he saw the uniformed peelers (and McGray's fist).

We entered a long, airy hall, loaded with the smell of books and wood polish. The central corridor was flanked by glazed cabinets, displaying all manner of gore preserved in formaldehyde, as well as skeletons hanging by hooks. A couple of them were so deformed I shivered.

A deep hush fell throughout the hall, and people went so perfectly still I even caught the gentle sway of a brain suspended in a jar. I saw many female students and academics too. Some of them covered their mouths; others frowned at the intrusion.

McGray never stopped, his strides the only sound amidst the silence, and then there came a sudden rattle. I turned to my left and saw a young professor making a blatant run to the stairs, trying to overtake us.

'*Stay there, laddie!*' McGray roared at him, his voice causing gasps and yelps among the crowd.

The man froze on the spot, gulping as we rushed upstairs. My heartbeat quickened a little when I saw McGray draw a hand to his breast pocket, as if readying himself to pull out a gun.

We stepped into a long, darkened hall that led to a heavy double gate. McGray pushed it with both hands, the oak cracking as it slammed open. Behind it, a cacophony of voices gasped in shock.

We stormed into a wide chamber, its ceiling dotted with

windows that must provide good light in summer. Right then, though, they only clattered with the sound of heavy rain. The room was instead lit by many gaslights, reflected on the pale faces of at least fifty students, most of them clad in black. They were all crammed in three tiers of seating stands; horseshoe-shaped benches that encircled not one, but two dissecting tables already drenched in crimson.

All the students stared at us, as did the two young assistants who'd been rushing around the tables with buckets to collect the oozing fluids (one was already half full of blood; the other contained some greyish, milky substance which immediately upset my stomach).

The one person who did not stare at us was the lecturer, who stood at the heart of it all, his back turned to us: a medium-height man, strongly built, with his light brown hair tied in a tight pigtail.

'*Nobody leaves this fuckin' room!*' McGray cried, if possible accentuating even more his Dundee inflections. '*My lads don't care which sodding Duke shagged yer great-grandmamas; they'll still beat ye to a pulp if ye give us trouble!*'

There were pants and gasps, but no one protested. Their faces, rather than alarmed, were contemptuous.

The lecturer took his time to reach for a rag and wipe his blood-stained hands. He then tossed it furiously at one of his assistants and gathered breath as he turned to face us.

'*Get out of my theatre! You blasted—!*'

He stopped when he saw the uniformed officers. His apron, almost black with dry blood, nearly made me retch, and I saw that his tight pigtail was not doing his receding hairline any favours.

He bared his enviably white teeth at us, half indignant, half confused.

'What is this? *A raid?*'

McGray approached him. 'What's yer name?'

'Professor Carl Grimshaw.'

'Grim and grimy indeed,' McGray replied, and then pointed a finger at the man's face. 'Stay where ye are.'

The professor did not reply, but shamelessly eyed the empty space where McGray's missing finger would have been.

Nine-Nails, far too used to this, simply turned to the two corpses on the dissecting tables. Only then did I see that both were already beyond recognition, their ribcages cut open with saws, and I shall not describe what was left of their faces.

McGray walked around the nearest body, the students watching his every move. The scene looked like an eerie convention of carrion birds, all craning their necks over their next meal.

After a few vexed snorts, McGray moved on to the second, rather bulkier corpse. He lifted the man's hand – we could still tell for certain that the corpse was male – and gave it but a brief look.

'It's him,' he said, and there was a general gasp.

'Are you sure?' I asked, stepping closer.

He showed me the hand, still not dissected, and pointed at the bruised fingertips.

'I saw these,' he whispered. 'They're unmistakable.'

'Chapped by his constant...?'

'Stuffing,' Nine-Nails completed for me, and I raised a brow.

'Did they not say that it had been months since his last fit?'

McGray gave the briefest of nods. The professor cleared his throat loudly and we remembered where we were.

'Someone put back in whatever Professor Grimy took out,' McGray told the assistants. 'And make sure youse don't mix the stuff. I'll come back and twat youse if the mortician tells me he found more than two bollocks.'

He turned to the students and I saw several of them lower

their faces and cover their brows, like older men caught by their wives in the cheapest brothel.

'The lads here will take yer names and addresses,' McGray barked. 'And if youse lie to them, I'll make youse envy these poor carcasses here.' He snatched a notepad from one of the front students and gave it to the officers, before telling them in whispers, 'As soon as yer done with that, take the body to Dr Reed. Make sure nobody else tampers with it.'

'If that makes any difference now,' I said, seeing how the assistants unceremoniously crammed entrails and viscera back into the man's torso. It reminded me how, at the end of a long trip, one's suitcases always seem to have shrunk.

'*I don't know where the bloody bodies come from!* How many times do I have to tell you?'

Professor Grimshaw was scrubbing his hands so furiously I feared he'd scour them to the bone.

We were in a little tiled room, adjacent to the main theatre. The one window looked over the sad courtyard, and from there I saw how the constables took the body away in an open cart, poorly covered with a blood-stained shroud. Students, professors and gossip-mongers lined all around it. So much for a discreet intervention.

'Does it not bother you at all that the man you were dissecting was murdered?' I asked. 'Did you not notice the stabs on his chest?'

Grimshaw let out a hissing, grating sigh.

'I've seen all sorts of corpses, inspector. You have no idea. I couldn't do my job if I dwelled on womanly sentimentalities all the time.'

'*Sentimen*—! You encourage a barbaric trade!'

Grimshaw tossed his towel on the aquamanile and growled. 'We *save* lives here! Models and diagrams are no use to a surgeon's training. How can a man operate if he's never *felt* the insides of the human body? How else would you expect the students to learn what's soft and what's firm? What's spongy and what will squirt fluid if you mess with it? Criticise me as much as you wish, but you're nae better than me!' He had to bite his lip when his Scottish accent slipped to the fore. 'The day you need to get your gout drained, you'll thank me for my *barbaric* teachings.'

I was going to protest again, but McGray raised a hand, for once the peacemaker.

'So how does it work?' he asked. 'People just bring in corpses? Or do youse go out in search of them?'

Grimshaw bit a lip. He seemed more intimidated by quiet questioning than by direct recriminations. 'We receive – we call them donations.'

'Donations?' McGray repeated, not even pretending to believe the man.

'Yes, and most of the donated cadavers come from the police itself, as you ought to know. Your officers bring us unidentified beggars from the streets, or convicts either executed or dead in their cells, or people without relatives or friends to pay for their burial. That sort of situation. And we are banned by law to offer payments or any kind of rewards – *precisely* to avoid the sort of wrongdoings your colleague is implying.'

McGray nodded. 'And *ye* are the head anatomist?'

Again, Grimshaw hesitated, as if fearing he might be stepping into a trap. 'Y-yes.'

'So yer the one in charge of those *donations*, right?'

'I am to be notified, yes. Whether to accept or reject them.'

'Reject them?' I asked.

'Indeed. People like to believe we are always short of speci-mens, but that's rarely the case. Sometimes we do have to send them away. Those corpses then go to the communal graves.' He raised his voice slightly. 'In fact, wintertime is when we have the highest surplus of bodies, with all the sickness around and the homeless freezing to death in the closes.'

I chuckled. 'And yet, our murdered man was here. And you have just admitted that you are in charge of—'

McGray raised his hand again.

'If I wanted to donate a *specimen*,' he said, to my surprise, rather calmly, 'where would I bring it, initially?'

Professor Grimshaw opened and closed his mouth, for a moment unable to talk.

'It'll be easy to find out,' McGray added, 'even if ye don't tell us.'

Grimshaw answered only after a reluctant rumble. 'We have an antechamber at the back of the building.'

'Antechamber!' Nine-Nails mocked. 'How grand-sounding. Can we see it?'

The professor let out another beleaguered sigh. Without speaking, he raised a hand, inviting us to the corridor, and led us back to the ground floor.

After a labyrinth of narrow rooms and passages, very much like servants' quarters, we made it to a long chamber. Its dimensions and the worm-eaten gate that led to the streets made me think of a small stable. The floors were dark terracotta tiles, surely to mask bloodstains, and all the windows had shutters, left open to keep the room as cool as possible. The windows also let in that nauseating broth smell from the streets. I was about to mention it, but the view distracted me.

Before us there were a dozen high-wheeled tables neatly lined up; however, only two of them were occupied by bodies, both covered with off-white sheets. That did not look like the overabundance Professor Grimshaw had just referred to.

'So, people bring the bodies here,' Nine-Nails said before I could make any remark. He went to the gate and weighed the thick padlock. 'Who brought the ones ye were dissecting just now?'

Grimshaw snorted. 'I could not possibly tell.'

'Don't play games with me, lad!'

'I said I am informed when the bodies arrive. Not that I am present and take note of every bloody detail.'

'So ye cannae tell who brought which corpse and when?'

'I'm glad you have been paying atten—'

McGray banged a fist on one of the empty tables. 'I need ye to say *yes* or *no*.'

The professor started, his face sterner. 'No. I cannot.'

'How fucking convenient,' McGray snapped. He leaned closer to one of the corpses. 'D'ye ever look into their faces?'

'I try not to. It makes my job easier.'

McGray lifted one of the sheets with unexpected delicacy and looked at the person's face; a middle-aged, scrawny man. His skin was leathery and greyish, his cheeks hollow, and he only had a few strands of hair left, still speckled with small clumps of snow. His eyelids were not fully shut, a yellowish sliver of his eyeballs visible. The cold seeped to my bones.

'Do you keep records?' I asked.

'Records?'

I sighed. 'In want of a more respectful word – an inventory?'

Grimshaw let out a condescending laugh.

'No, inspector, we do not. We count the bodies and we remember. It is usually a one-figure number. Your butler surely does the same with your flour stocks.'

My valet Layton in fact kept a comprehensive ledger for our pantries, but I saw no need to mention this. 'Can you tell at least *when* the body in question arrived?'

'No, I could not. I know they arrive but not who is who. As I told you, I try not to look at their faces until I dissect them. Quite frankly, after a while they all start to look the same.'

McGray covered the dead man's face.

'Yer treading on very thin ice, professor,' he said. 'I hope ye ken that. And all ye've said so far sounds like porkies to me.'

'I have an entire institution to back me,' Grimshaw said, raising his chin. 'If you believe I went out and murdered a man, when we can simply stroll into the street and find a dead beggar—'

McGray took a step closer to him, his boots stomping loudly on the tiles. He breathed in and out like a hissing engine, and this time even the arrogant professor gulped.

'Very thin ice indeed,' Nine-Nails said again, and then poked Grimshaw at the sternum. 'I wouldn't want to be in yer shoes when we find out the truth.'

We remained in a tense silence for a while. It could have gone on for much longer, but then a foul waft came in through the open shutters; a meaty, revolting stench that stabbed at the nose and the mouth. This time even Nine-Nails grimaced at it.

'Och, what the fuck is that?'

Professor Grimshaw pulled a mocking smile as he went to the nearest window and opened it wide. It looked out over the college's backyard, where I saw half a dozen students gathered around a fire. One of them was stirring – I blinked twice before I believed it – what looked like a large witches' cauldron. Something yellowish popped up amidst the nasty froth, and I felt a prickle all across my spine when I saw it was a human skull. That was no paupers' pottage. They were boiling a human skeleton.

'A new specimen for the main hall's display,' Grimshaw explained. 'The chaps have to use strong lime to get rid of every last shred of tissue.'

As he said this, one of the students used a pair of long iron tongs to pull out a clean, almost glimmering femur.

It also brought out a cloud of billowing vapours, and the sight and stench of that ghastly brown soup was more than I could bear. I retched noisily and darted to the nearest door, a hand pressed on my mouth.

McGray followed me, shouting at the professor something about *nae leaving town*.

'Cannae blame ye, Percy. That was truly vile!'

I finished gargling and spat the whisky out of the carriage window. More than embarrassed, I was furious at my sorry display. A lady lecturer had had to offer me a draught of quinine after I emptied my insides into a basin, and I pray I never have to face again the youngsters that celebrated the event with whistles and cheers.

Another professor led us to a small study, so I could recover in private, and in the meantime McGray summoned Grimshaw's assistants – the ones who handled and prepared the bodies.

The young men, all from Scotland's upper and middle classes, told us the exact same story:

There were four corpses in the antechamber that morning. They cleaned and prepared one. They *had* noticed the chest wounds, but assumed that the legalities had been taken care of (and, like Grimshaw, they all proudly professed to have seen much worse).

That was all. They'd not been around when the bodies had been delivered and, allegedly, never had anything to do with the procurement of cadavers.

'It could be any o' them, Frey,' McGray groaned as the carriage took us back to the City Chambers. '*Any* of them. All young and wearing shiny new boots even on the nights they go out to desecrate graves.'

'Indeed,' I said. 'And regardless what he claims, Grimshaw *must* pass money and favours in exchange for those corpses. If

Edinburgh's College works anything like Oxford, he must be the one coordinating the entire procedure.'

'And he'll never confess.'

'No. He will lie for his students and his students will lie for him. And even if we managed to trace the rascal who did it, I doubt we could gather enough evidence to convict.' I looked wistfully at the tall tenements as we entered the Royal Mile. 'The answer will not be there, McGray. It will be either in the asylum – or in the corpses themselves.'

16

We had a quick meal – how I managed to eat after seeing that foul mush of boiling bones, I do not know – and then we went back to the morgue.

We found Dr Reed bent over a small brass microscope. The room was as dark as a cave, the young doctor lit by only one tall oil lamp. MacDonnell's bulky body was already behind him, now covered with clean sheets. Next to it, dwarfed in comparison, was the body of Mrs Brewster.

I hate it when corpses pile up on us.

Reed perked up, the rim of the microscope stamped around his right eye. 'Inspectors! I've found the most interesting evidence!'

'Och, finally!' McGray cried, rubbing his hands in anticipation.

'Is that Mrs Brewster's skin you are looking at?' I asked him.

'Yes, inspec— Mr Frey. I took samples, as you requested. Luckily the microscope just needed a few tweaks to work. But before this, I did a thorough post-mortem on the lady.'

'And?' McGray urged.

Reed looked broodingly at the woman's covered body. 'I found no injuries or bruises or upset organs… except for the lungs. She had fibrotic lesions.'

'Pneumonia?' I asked.

'Indeed, sir. That is the most likely cause of death.'

McGray let out a weary sigh. 'So she could've died naturally, or some devilish bastard left her windows open to give her a wee push.'

'Which would be impossible to demonstrate beyond doubt,' I said. I was going to look at her again, but preferred not to. Instead, I nodded at the microscope. 'Can you show us the samples now?'

'Of course.'

Reed again looked into the eyepiece, repositioned the oil lamp ever so slightly, and adjusted the little disc mirror that redirected light onto the glass slide.

'I cut out a sample as thin as I could,' he said, pointing at a little pewter dish, covered with a cloth. 'Here, have a look.'

I rushed forwards, itching with curiosity.

The first thing I saw was a bright pinkish smear. I adjusted the lens and, very slowly, the finer features began to emerge.

'Good cross-section of the skin,' I said, recognising the porous, flaky sheets of the epidermis. As expected, the sample was rather pale on the outermost layer, then progressively pinker and darker, the undulating rows of cells stacked together with mathematical grace. It still amazes me how our flesh is so similar in colour to raw pork. 'This is the healthy section, is it not?'

'Yes, sir. I took the samples from the edge of the – ahem – Devil's mark, as you told me. Move it to the right and you shall see—'

I gasped. 'Here it is ...'

The familiar pinks and whites turned into a slightly darker hue, so gradually that it was hard to tell where the change began. Then there was a thin, whitish layer, after which the tissue turned the sickly grey we'd seen on Mrs Brewster's face. I moved the glass slide around, looking into the deeper layers of the skin, but the grey spread on and on, all the way to the fatty tissue. I pushed the slide further down, to the very edge of the sample. The stain would have continued beyond.

'How deep was this sample?' I asked.

'I'd say an eighth of an inch,' Reed said. 'All the way to the muscle – which also seemed slightly stained.'

I looked back at the midsections of the sample. The grey varied in hue, following the natural undulations of the cells.

'It looks like something that grew slowly,' I mumbled. 'Almost... biological.'

'Let me see,' McGray said, bending down over the microscope. I was surprised by the delicacy with which he moved the slide and adjusted the fine focus peg.

I pulled out my little notebook. 'So the mark went all the way down to the fat and muscle,' I mumbled as I scribbled. 'We can discard inks, then.'

'And burns too,' Reed said. 'The epidermis is not scorched at all.'

'It gets more disgusting the further down ye go,' McGray remarked after a loud whistle. 'As if it sprouted from within!'

'Not necessarily, sir,' Reed said. 'The inner tissue is more delicate. The outer layers of our skin are dead cells, designed to withstand the elements.'

I wrote that comment down and then pressed the back of the notebook against my chin. 'Did you find anything untoward under the skin? Perhaps something on the inside of the cheek, like the mark of an injection?'

'Oh, I did check, sir!' Reed said proudly (it is rather endearing how he still tries to impress us sometimes). 'I found nothing. The muscle was intact, and so was the inside of the mouth.'

I shook my head with frustration. 'I have never seen a stain like this.'

'Neither have I,' Reed agreed. 'I can only tell that it was clearly done after death. Otherwise we'd see scarring and inflamed blood vessels.'

I took note of that too, far more confused than ever before.

Reed cleared his throat. 'There is – there is something else, sirs.'

'Something else?' McGray echoed. Reed nodded and went to the corpse. Very delicately, he pulled one of Mrs Brewster's hands from under the sheet. He was kind enough not to uncover the rest of the body, now stitched back together after the post-mortem.

McGray and I approached, as Reed folded the arm and placed the hand on the lady's stomach, over the shroud. He extended her fingers, and I felt both sad and revolted at the now greyer tones of the flesh.

'I must have thought it was a blotch on the skin on the first inspection,' Reed said. Indeed, the woman's hands were peppered with blemishes, natural at her age, but then Reed separated the index from the middle finger, and right at the joint—

'Another stain!' McGray cried, instantly bending closer.

Indeed. There it was, the same odd grey as the mark on the lady's face. I had to blink to believe it. I also saw a long cut, the joint carefully stitched back.

'I cut out a sample and looked at it under the microscope too,' Reed said. 'It is of the same nature, no doubt.'

I took the dead hand with utmost care and split the fingers slightly further apart, squinting. McGray looked closer too.

'It looks familiar,' he said.

'I thought so too,' I mumbled. 'It reminds me…' it took me a moment to complete the phrase, desperately searching for the memory in my head. 'It reminds me of an ink stain. Like when one is writing and spills ink on one's fingers…'

I looked up at once.

'The holy oil?'

Reed shook his head. 'I checked it, sir. It is just oil. I even daubed some samples of skin from another corpse. Nothing happened.'

I rose and took a deep breath. How could all this evidence become more and more puzzling each time we looked?

And Reed was not done yet. 'MacDonnell's corpse was also quite interesting,' he said, turning to the man, 'even if there was very little I could do with him. Besides the obvious dissecting, he's been washed and scrubbed all over. They even infused him with camphor and eucalyptus.'

McGray snorted. 'I bet the poor lad never smelled that good when he was alive.'

We all bent around MacDonnell's face as Reed lifted the shroud, and I could not repress a flinch.

Reed had done his best to reassemble the body, but even his fine stitching could not disguise all the cuts. One ran right down the middle of the forehead, all the way down to the tip of the nose. It joined horizontal cuts on the forehead and cheeks, so that the face's skin could be opened like the pages of a book. There were also cuts around the eyelids and on either side of the mouth to examine the jaw and the teeth. Now stitched back, it looked as if MacDonnell gave us a gruesome, eerie smile.

'I cannae let his daughters see him like this,' McGray whispered. He pointed at a section on the left cheek, where Reed had had to stretch and pucker a fold of skin that somehow had not fit back into place. 'He looks like a darned sock! Nae offence, laddie.'

'None taken,' Reed said. 'It's precisely that spot that caught my eye. A section of the skin from his cheek was missing.'

'What!' McGray and I cried in unison.

'It was quite noticeable,' Reed said, running a finger over the stitches. 'All the other cuts were straight and precise, evidently by a very seasoned hand: the skin could be put back together like sewing patterns. Except for that spot there.' He reached for his writing pad and showed us a careful sketch. 'This is the shape and size missing; a rough oval, some two and a half inches wide.'

'Shite!' McGray snapped.

'To state the obvious,' Reed said, 'it looks like they found the same stain and cut it off. It was even on the same spot as Mrs Brewster's mark.'

McGray growled, massaging his temples.

'Perhaps they removed it not to scare the students?' I ventured.

'Or 'cause they recognised it,' McGray said. He shook his head. 'He had nae mark when I saw him at the asylum, Frey. I'm sure. It's impossible to miss something like that!'

'I know,' I said, and then raised an eyebrow. 'So it would have appeared overnight. While he was still at the asylum...' Clouston, Harland, Tom the orderly, Miss Smith... their names flashed in my head. 'Someone must have applied it then.'

'It would have been ideal to have that sample,' Reed said. 'To compare them.'

'Sadly, whoever cut it off will have had hours to dispose of it,' I mumbled.

'*Damn*, it's right there!' McGray blurted out, making us jump. 'It's right under our fucking noses and yet we've nae idea who did it all!'

I pondered for a moment, while McGray sulked, all the pieces at play dancing in my head.

'You studied at Surgeons' College, did you not?' I asked Reed. 'Do you still have contacts there?'

McGray shook his head. 'Forget it, Frey. Reed was the first one I came to see when Trevelyan gave me the case.'

'A few professors and assistants will still remember me,' Reed said, 'but they won't talk to me about these matters. They know that I work for you.'

'True,' I whispered. 'But still...' I tilted my head. 'Did you ever meet one Professor Grimshaw? Haughty? Pigtail, yet going bald?'

Reed nodded. 'The head anatomist. Of course.'

'What can you tell us about him?'

Reed looked sideways, suddenly tense. 'Well... he *loves* teaching.'

'Do you mean, he loves feeling arrogant and superior?' I asked.

'Look who's talking,' McGray added after a chuckle.

'He is quite arrogant, yes,' Reed continued. 'He was very pedantic too. If you made a mistake, no matter how trivial, he'd remind you of it until your graduation day.'

'Good memory, then?' McGray asked.

'Oh, yes! Like an elephant's. I bet he still recalls how many arteries I mistakenly tore in my last dissection.'

'It ought to have been none,' I said, and both Reed and Nine-Nails cast me infuriated looks.

'So he's lying through his teeth when he says he cannae remember the faces of the corpses he dissects?'

Reed sighed. 'I would not be so sure. He isn't likely to look at them with too much attention. He must see them like a farmer does his cattle.'

'That's what the sod said,' McGray muttered. He then looked at Reed with a twinkle in his eye. 'So – when *ye* were a body snatcher—'

Reed started, took an involuntary step back and bumped into the table on which MacDonnell lay.

'I told you! I only did it two or three times! And I'm certainly not proud of that. I was struggling to keep up my college fees, so I had to. I didn't even get money; just a prorogue of my payments.'

McGray raised a conciliatory hand. 'Aye, I ken, laddie. And I won't blame ye. If anything, yer wanderings have helped us in the past.'

'Who did you deal with?' I asked at once. I would have done so much earlier, if I'd known Reed had studied there. 'Was it Grimshaw? Another professor?'

Reed sighed. 'No, no. One of the senior students was always in charge. He approached us – well, he approached the less well-off pupils, or the ones who needed favours.' He slowly clenched his hands in tight fists. 'It won't surprise you that those senior students were the ones who got the best posts after graduation; the ones who were introduced into the right circles.'

His silence was recalcitrant. It left so much implied.

'You refused to play the game?' I asked softly. 'They did not get to owe you favours?'

Reed only sighed again, which was confirmation enough. McGray gave him a gentle pat on the shoulder.

'Did ye take the bodies to the ante-chamber?'

'Oh, you know about it already? Yes. They'd give us the keys and tell us where to meet the *professional* resurrectionists. We helped them dig up the bodies and delivered them in the early hours, before anybody arrived, so the professors could always deny any involvement. If they offered you money, you were paid by the senior students. And we were told never to bring up the matter in front of the lecturers, else we could be expelled or even handed to the police. The same went for all the other students if they blabbed.'

'Very tight, very neat system,' McGray said. 'Unfair to everyone but the damn college.'

'Even unfair to *them*,' I whispered, looking at the abused bodies on the dissecting tables. 'Disrespected even after death ...'

Again I pictured my late father, now alone in his grave, and the thought nearly made me gasp.

'Let's go,' I whispered. 'Our minds will be fresher in the morning.'

*

'That cab will charge us a bloody fortune,' McGray grumbled as we walked through the darkened courtyard.

'Indeed,' I said, looking at the patient driver. The rain had turned into a mere drizzle, but the poor chap was still soaked to the bone. 'You should tip him well. He has been servicing us all day.'

'*I should!* Ye cheap bastard.'

'Cheap? Excuse me, each night I spend at the Palace Hotel costs more than your bloody Scotch distillery!'

We were crossing the arches, just a few steps from the cab, when a man planted himself before us. A broad-shouldered figure, wrapped in a black overcoat.

I'd not seen him in months, but still I recognised him at once. It was impossible to forget the name George Pratt, or his scalp, as smooth and shiny as polished wood, or the way my father had humiliated him at Edinburgh's High Court. Impossible also to forget his old grudge against the McGrays.

'*What the fuck?*' Nine-Nails snarled the moment he saw him. 'Go away! I'm having a rotten day. The last thing I need right now is dealing with fat-twat Pratt!'

The man never failed to wince a little whenever Nine-Nails called him by his surname.

'Believe me,' he replied with his rich, petulant voice, 'it is no pleasure having to deal with the likes of you.' McGray made to walk round him, but Pratt raised his voice. 'In fact, I was shocked to hear this investigation was assigned to you two – the brother of a potential suspect and his recently sacked minion.' I nearly tripped when I heard that. This was exactly what Trevelyan had predicted. 'And the cracks in your approach are already beginning to show: I hear you briefly lost a corpse, didn't you?'

McGray looked livid. 'How did you hear about—?' I began, but McGray interjected.

'We just found it, *Pratt*.'

A vein popped on the man's temple. 'I need to know the details as to—'

'Piss off.'

McGray walked on, more decidedly this time, but Pratt raised his voice further.

'You also failed to inspect your own sister's chambers, Inspector McGray. Or so I heard. Biased and unprofessional, would you not say?'

The street was still busy, many eyes turning to us as soon as they heard the name McGray.

He went back to Pratt, seized him by the collar and hissed, inches from his face. 'What the fuck are ye playing at? Trying to accuse my sister of murder again?'

Pratt made a side smile and whispered, 'It would be best for her that you let go of me.'

I nodded at Nine-Nails. People along the street were staring at us, and we had enough trouble as it was. After a muffled growl, McGray obliged.

'You and your officers inspected every room in that madhouse,' Pratt said. 'Every room except Miss McGray's. Why was that?'

McGray raised a fist and I had to seize him by the shoulder.

'There was no need,' I intervened. 'Miss McGray was not involved in the matter. I know!'

Pratt arched his eyebrows. '*Oh, you do!* How?'

I bit my lip, cursing my rashness. 'That is not something I can divulge while our investigation is on-going,' I said as casually as I could.

'Mr Frey, I am a procurator fiscal. I have the right to know—'

'Ye have the right to *fuck* yerself!' McGray growled, pushing the man and making his way to the cab.

'I must concur with that,' I said. 'You have no right to demand any information from us. Not yet. This is not an inquiry.'

'Oh, but an inquiry *will* follow. Very soon. And I'll be sure to mention that you failed to inspect the chambers of a potential suspect. And I will also remark how irregular it is that the investigations are being handled by you, an Englishman who's just been sacked from the Scottish police.'

I nearly shouted that I had resigned, but there were far too many people around, and it would do no good to admit that I had no official authority to investigate.

'I suggest that you do,' I retorted instead. 'As it is, we do not even know if the inquiry will be assigned to you. Good evening.'

I also rushed to the cab, but Pratt followed me and spoke right before I hopped in. His voice dropped an octave.

'You two should be careful. I hear the Devil has made his mark.'

I turned to Pratt so fast I pulled a tendon on my neck, and McGray, already on his seat, leapt back to the cab's door, ready to jump out. Thankfully, he managed to contain himself, and neither of us said a word. We simply stared at the bald man, dumbfounded. People had also stopped around us, casting inquisitive stares at us.

Pratt savoured the moment. He gave us the most sardonic, most infuriating smile, and then donned his bowler hat.

'You are not the only ones investigating this case, gentlemen. And it would seem my sources are just as informed as yours.'

And with a tip of his hat, he turned on his heels and walked away.

17

I shall not transcribe the avalanche of foul language that McGray spurted out on our way home.

'There are a dozen ways he could have found out,' I reminded him as soon as he paused for breath. 'People may have seen MacDonnell's body while it was taken to Surgeons' College. Students must have seen the mark, perhaps other lecturers too.'

McGray only snorted and went back to his most inventive swearing.

Neither of us dared pronounce our main fear – that Pratt already knew the culprit. And if he did, he would have time to twist evidence and coerce statements to incriminate Pansy. That might be the only reason he'd not requested the case was taken from us – our activities would be one more irregularity he could milk at the Sheriff's Court when he tried to incriminate Pansy.

I shook my head at the thought. It would not do to fill my mind with all the terrible possibilities we might have ahead.

A few minutes later the cab halted by the Palace Hotel. A porter ran to open the cab door for me, bringing an open umbrella.

'How very civilised this is,' I said as I alighted, doing my best to lighten the mood. 'Long gone are my days sleeping in the Lancashire wilderness.'

'Yer forgetting something,' Nine-Nails said behind me.

I looked back and saw him handing me the tied folder with Mrs Brewster's records – and the files of Joel Ardglass.

I had completely forgotten about them! I'd taken them into the cab back when we first set off to the asylum, right after hearing about the missing body. That had happened earlier that same day, but I felt as though it had been weeks ago.

'Why, thanks!' I cried, and I snatched the papers, as if fearing that McGray could read through the folder.

'Try to rest,' I said, even if I knew McGray would most likely spend a sleepless night.

He mumbled a barely discernible 'good night', and I saw with some melancholy how the cab rode on into New Town.

I clenched the files as the porter led me in, thinking those pages were very likely to contain crucial clues as to the origins of Pansy and Caroline, and they might also tell me so much about the McGray and Ardglass families.

It was as if they burned my fingertips.

My neck was sore after that encounter with Pratt, so I ordered a bath and some brandy as soon as I made it to my room. I was amazed by how quickly the two footmen installed a copper tub and filled it with hot water. They also set a little foldable table next to it, where they left a decanter, a tumbler and some very appetising butter biscuits.

Once on my own, I basked in the perfumed oils, letting the heat seep into my sore tendons. After a few blissful minutes I was a new man, ready to take my mind back to the case.

I opened the Ardglass file while still in the water. I looked at my signet ring, formerly Joel's, and began reading.

The files were mostly typed, but with side notes in Clouston's characteristic hand. I remembered that the good doctor used to type his reports in triplicate with carbon paper. In fact, he used to hand McGray copies of Pansy's records, and he continued to do so for years, without a hint of a change in her condition. Nine-Nails himself, perhaps too weary after reading the same sad diagnoses time after time, decided to put an end to it.

I sighed and focussed on the first page. The records began with a brief account of Lord Joel's early years. Only child of Anne Ardglass, herself a descendant of ancient Lancashire aristocracy, who'd married a Scottish baron so that her family title would not become extinct.

Apparently, Lord Joel had been a quiet boy, who preferred his own company and had a natural predisposition to sadness. He'd also been remarkably intelligent and resourceful – which, towards the end of his life, only turned him into a terrifying menace.

The next few paragraphs I remembered at once, especially the passages I'd underlined myself a year ago, when Lord Joel had murdered a nurse and fled from the asylum.

Joel's life had changed dramatically at twenty-three, when he'd attempted to kill himself by drinking rat poison. The date of the incident was 18 August 1858.

McGray had been born but a fortnight before.

'Of course!' I mumbled.

It was clear now. McGray and Pansy's mother – *must* have been Joel's great love.

Learning that she had given birth to someone else's son must have been the cause of his suicidal thoughts.

I turned the page swiftly and read the long list of medications prescribed and shipped to France, Bavaria and Italy. The long trips were only logical – the man would have tried to escape the memories of his lost sweetheart.

I found one of my own notes between two consecutive entries dated 1862 and 1868; a six-year gap in the medical records, without prescribed medications or suicide attempts. My scribble read:

Caroline Ardglass born early 1863. Brief period of family bliss? Joel would have married Lady Beatrice around 1862.

Lady Beatrice had, of course, been Caroline's mother.

There was another annotation, this one in red ink, made by McGray next to the lady's name. It read: *Died 1868*.

That date coincided with the next suicide attempt by Lord Joel. And also...

I lifted my chin and ran through the McGrays' ages in my head.

Pansy was ten years younger than Nine-Nails. She would have been born in 1868, in May, if my memory did not fail. She would have been conceived in 1867. Mere months before the death of Joel's wife.

So there *had* been a rekindling of the affair between Lord Joel and McGray's mother – while they were both married to others!

Lord Joel had had a pretty eventful time. Love affair, dead spouse, attempted suicide, birth of a love child – all within a few months.

I felt a renewed chill when I reread '*Died 1868*'. Could it be possible that Joel had murdered his own wife? That he'd murdered Caroline's mother? Could Caroline herself have her suspicions? After all, Lord Joel *had* murdered a nurse a year ago, right before fleeing the asylum.

As I thought so, my eyes went to the signet ring. I remembered vividly the day Caroline had presented it to me. I also remembered that it had an inscription inside the rim, so I put the files on the little table, pulled the jewel off – with some resistance, for I'd indulged a little too much over the Christmas period – and brought it closer to the light.

I'd always known it was a well-worn piece: all the edges were eroded, and there was a nice patina on the gold and the exquisite flat emerald. Joel must have sported it at all times before being locked in the asylum.

I squinted, trying to make out the two tiny engraved letters. The first one was clearly an *A*, which I had assumed to stand for Ardglass. The second, more worn out, I was only able to decipher right then. It was a faded *D*.

Despite the hot bath, I shivered. All this time I'd been wearing a ring Lord Joel had received as a present from – McGray's mother!

The woman's maiden name had been Amina Duncan. I knew it. I had seen it in the records of the inquiry that followed her death and her husband's.

An inquiry led by George Pratt, a little voice said in my head, and I nearly dropped the ring into the water.

Could he also be linked to all this mess? It seemed too much of a coincidence that he'd come to us with threats just now. But – *how?*

Could he perhaps know more about the enmity between the Ardglass and the McGray families?

I rubbed my eyes, too strained from reading in the dim light, and ran through the story in my head one more time.

Lord Joel had married a woman he did not love; that much was certain. The McGrays had been new money in town, snubbed by the aristocracy. The late Amina Duncan must have been of a similar background. If so, it made sense that Lady Anne would have been opposed to her marrying her son; maybe the old woman had even instigated his union to that mysterious Lady Beatrice. Then again, how come Joel had given in? A man capable of murder would not have surrendered to his mother's whims so easily.

And then there was his madness – a madness triggered by so-called witches, whom Lady Anne had angered by seizing her family's ancient manor in Lancashire, which the witches had occupied unlawfully for decades...

My mind swirled. I knew I was about to open yet another can

of worms, just while the case at hand was becoming more and more convoluted: MacDonnell's murder, his corpse being taken, the marks on his body and Mrs Brewster's face, the myriad of potential suspects at the asylum and the college ...

I growled, resting my head on the edge of the tub and closing my eyes.

As I let my body sway gently in the water, I felt as if I were drifting in a sea of confusion. All alone.

I could not talk to McGray and discuss my musings, which – it pains me to admit – always helped me think. I could not speculate with Caroline either, her father's insanity and infidelity at the core of the matter. I had occasionally confided in Dr Clouston, but now that was out of the question too.

My dear Uncle Maurice, to whom I always turned when in doubt, was now gone, the very thought of his passing still a raw wound. And now I had also lost my father, whose sour character had always been on a par with his sharp wit and—

I opened my eyes.

Elgie.

Of course. I could always confide in my youngest brother.

I nearly pushed myself out of the bath, but there was no need to rush: any telegram I penned would not be dispatched until the morning.

I savoured the last of the brandy as I came up with the message in my head. I also thought that the trip might do Elgie some good; take his mind off our father's death.

The mere prospect of seeing a familiar face, someone I could trust amidst this jumble of intrigues, was enough to reanimate me.

After I penned the note, my eyes itching with tiredness, I also made a plan for the morning.

I must rise very early and carry out my own investigations. And I would do so away from McGray's eyes for as long as I could. There was far too much I had to keep from his ears, and I'd never get anywhere if I was not free to ask the most pressing questions.

I'd first visit Miss Ardglass's apartment and extract as much information from her as her temper allowed. She was my only reliable witness, and might have seen or heard crucial details during her visits to the asylum. Every trace of information would be precious.

If I had time before Nine-Nails found me, I'd also confront Miss Smith. I had not yet asked her why she had been at Mrs Brewster's funeral or why she looked so uneasy these days. And I would also try to question Dr Clouston, even if I had to chase him to his family home and pull him out of bed.

I donned my nightclothes and, out of habit, reached for the signet ring. Only this time I hesitated. I stared at it, thinking of all the stories behind it; all the despair, all the misery it embodied. I was tempted to chuck it out the window.

Then again, McGray had seen me wear it and had made a joke of it. Its absence would only invite questions. From Caroline too, who'd seemed so pleased to see it on my hand – she could not have known its provenance.

I sighed. I would have to keep on wearing it for the time being – but thankfully not right then.

I tossed it onto the bedside table, thinking I would never wear it at night again.

18

I rose as early as I had planned, made a brief stop to ensure that the concierge dispatched my telegram to Elgie, and left the hotel just as the sun shed its first rays of pathetic Scottish light.

I did not even wait for the newspapers to be delivered to my room – something I'd come to regret.

Charlotte Square, where Caroline and Joan lodged, was only a couple of streets away, so I did not bother calling a cab.

I took the broad George Street, fringed by imposing sandstone houses and already bustling with horses and carriages. I felt a twinge of nostalgia for my former lodgings in New Town, I must admit, but at least the brisk walk and the crisp air awakened me.

Caroline's apartments were on the north-west corner of the sumptuous square, in a particularly large townhouse Lady Anne had partitioned into three independent dwellings to stretch the profits. Thankfully, very few landlords descend into such abominable practices.

The porter led me to the apartments on the first floor; the ones with the largest windows and the best views of the square's gardens. Even as we went upstairs, I caught the sweet sound of a violin. The notes were slow, long and melancholic; one of Mozart's adagios, from memory.

I only realised the music came from Caroline's chambers

when the porter knocked on her door, and I nearly gasped. I had completely forgotten that she played the violin, which, in itself, was a small act of defiance. Until rather recently, violins were not considered suitable instruments for women; respectable ladies were expected to play the pianoforte, the harp or the flute, which did not demand the brash, tomboyish movements of a bow.

To my surprise, it was not Joan who opened the door, but a young scullery maid. A very inexperienced servant too, for she let me in and led me to the parlour without asking my name or announcing me first.

Caroline was playing by the window, in front of a music stand, but in the overcast morning she still had to light the scores with an oil lamp. I also recognised the violin she was playing: a very expensive Guadagnini. It was an inheritance with a very dark past – like most things in her life.

She turned slightly in my direction and started as soon as she saw me, nearly dropping the precious violin to the floor.

'*Mr Frey!* What are you doing here? I mean – so early?'

She cast the young maid a murderous look and then began fidgeting with the instrument, as if, suddenly, she did not know what to do with her hands. In the end she hid the violin behind her back.

'Do excuse me, Miss Ardglass. I must expedite my investigations.'

I eyed the maid, conveying we needed privacy.

'Tilly, bring us some tea,' Caroline told her, and the girl left at once. 'Do be seated, Mr Frey.'

I sat on one of the very elegant velvet sofas while Caroline put the violin away. She joined me, though sitting at a distance. She seemed on edge, clenching her right hand around her left. Her jaw and lips were tense too.

'What a diligent musician you are,' I said, in an effort to ease the mood. 'Even my youngest brother does not play before nine o'clock!'

'If I don't rise early and get myself busy –' she sighed – 'my head fills with demons.'

She went silent then, and for a moment I could not speak either. The more I looked into her face, the more I saw the resemblance to Pansy; the same soft jaw – nothing like McGray's – the same long neck, the fine lips and the dark irises. How had I not seen it before? They were also the exact same height and build: Caroline had even borrowed some of Pansy's clothes at one point!

Never had I scrutinised her features so carefully. Suddenly, I was fully aware of her harmonious lines, of the smoothness of her skin. I could also see, clearer than ever before, that firm poise and elegance with which she carried herself: her back straight and her chin up, despite all the heartbreaks life had thrown at her. It was just her eyes that gave a hint of her inner struggles, and that only on close examination. Poor Caroline was disillusioned, tired and a little broken.

Just like me.

Perhaps, once all this mayhem was behind us, and if the situation was right, I might even—

I realised I was blushing at my own thoughts. I shook my head and cleared my throat.

'You were right to ask what brought me here so early,' I said. 'I need to ask you a few more questions. Quite urgently. During our trip here, you did not—'

'I told you all you need to know,' she snapped. 'If you are here to pester me with personal questions, you are wasting your time.'

I closed my eyes, for a second struggling to contain my frustration. How quickly she was able to shift my mood!

'My questions will have nothing to do with your – family. But

168

I need to ask them now. Especially as I might be banned from the investigations very soon.'

She tensed her lips further, looked out the window and took a deep breath, but said nothing.

'Everyone at the asylum is either a potential suspect or a biased witness,' I said as I produced my notebook. 'You are the only one I can trust.' I threw in a risky joke. 'Assuming, of course, that you are not a resurrectionist yourself!' Luckily, Caroline showed a faint smile, even if just to mock my clumsy humour. 'I need you to tell me exactly what you saw and heard that night. Everything. No matter how trivial.'

Caroline sighed. 'I'm not sure how much help that might be. I saw very little.'

'First of all, how did you get there? I presume you did not walk from here to Morningside on your own, especially so late at night.'

'No. I always hire a driver. The same man every time. I pay him handsomely to take me there and back.'

I took note of that. 'Is this also the driver who used to take you there when you visited your late father?'

'Yes. One of my grandmother's former coachmen.'

'Trustworthy?'

'Absolutely. He was very discreet then and I am sure he is now.' She sneered. 'Well, he knows his silence pays better than any indiscretion.'

'I see. How did you keep your arrivals in secret? Besides travelling on moonless nights, that is.'

'The driver would take me to the edge of the north gardens. The asylum abuts a large estate – Myreside, I believe it's called. It is desolate, so I could always make my way in without being seen. I would cross the gardens using the same wooded path the inmates use for their daily walks.'

'Were those gardens...?'

'As quiet and dark as ever? Yes, and of that I am sure. I always stay alert when I cross them, in case I need to flee. If anyone was going in or out of the asylum, it was not on that side.'

I took note of this.

'Did someone let you in?'

'Yes. I could have continued going there in hiding, as I did when I visited my father, but I preferred to look for help. After my father's –' she gulped – 'after he escaped and all that nasty affair happened, Mr McGray had to tell Dr Clouston the outcome of the case. That included telling him about my secret visits.'

'So you asked for his aid.'

'Indeed, and it made it all so much easier and safer. In fact, I was surprised by how quickly he agreed to help me and how easy it was to arrange the visits. He could not help me himself, though; people would have been suspicious if they saw the superintendent wandering the halls on his own so late, so he asked Miss Smith to let me in. He trusts her unconditionally. She would wait for me at one of the back doors; one that leads to the long gallery that oversees the lawns.'

'I see. On the night in question, did everything go as – let us say *normal*?'

'I was not seen and I do not recall hearing anything, if that's what you mean. Miss Smith received me and took me to Pansy's room.'

Somehow I could not picture the dependable Miss Smith, so committed to her job, suddenly allowing clandestine visitors into the asylum.

And she'd been at Mrs Brewster's funeral, holding the old lady's hand. The same hand Reed had just found to be suspiciously stained.

'How was Miss Smith that night?' I asked. 'Was she nervous? Did she say or do anything unusual?'

'No. She was quiet, but she always is when I'm near. She only mentioned her daughter had a cold.' Caroline looked up quickly, slightly flushed. 'You do know Miss Smith has a young girl, don't you?'

'Yes, she told me herself. I also know she is not married and supports the child on her own. And she also maintains her elderly father.'

Caroline nodded. 'I knew that as well. I feel for her. I tried to give her money the first time she helped me, but she turned it down. She could not have looked more insulted.'

The maid came back then with the tea service. Such expediency could only mean she was hunting for gossip.

'Thanks, Tilly,' Caroline said as soon as the girl placed the tray on the low table. 'You may go now. Wait for Joan in the kitchen.'

The girl curtsied and left, always followed by Caroline's keen eyes.

I thought she would serve the tea, but she did not. She simply kept her hands clenched in her lap.

'So you made it to Miss McGray's room without incident?' I asked, not bothering to pour myself a cup.

'Indeed. I brought her whisky fudge. I hear it's her favourite, even if I've never seen her eat it. We ...' Caroline cleared her throat. 'I assume you don't need the details of my visit.'

'We can move on to the main matter, if you prefer.'

Caroline took a deep breath, as if gathering strength.

'I heard a cry. A woman's voice. Then murmurs and footsteps. The noises stirred Pansy – she'd been about to fall asleep. After a moment we heard a second scream. This one came from much closer. A different person. It was then that the racket came from all directions. You can imagine how scared I was, so I went to the corridor –' She shut her eyes, trying to picture the details. 'I remember I stumbled on some cabinet just before Miss Smith found me. She told me to leave at once, only –' she grimaced – 'this doctor also came by.'

'Which one? Do you know the name?'

'That junior doctor, arrogant and very unpleasant... Harland?'

'Yes, I know he was on duty. Did he see you?'

'No. I hid next to the cabinet I just mentioned.'

I raised a quizzical brow. '*Next* to the cabinet, you say? How close did he get to you?'

'Oh gosh... at some point it must have been inches!'

'And he did not see you?'

'No. It was dark and – well—' She grumbled. 'Back then, I was sure he hadn't seen me. Now...' She went silent.

'Did he say anything?' I asked.

Caroline tilted her head, again closing her eyes. 'He acted – well, he questioned Miss Smith. He'd heard her talking to me and he asked about it, but she lied. She said she had been talking to my sister.' She opened her eyes wide and let out a little gasp. 'He – he may have seen my hem. I remember now; the cabinet wasn't deep enough to conceal my skirts.'

I frowned. 'And yet Harland said nothing?'

Caroline shook her head. 'Nothing to suggest he'd seen me, no. He said that someone had just been killed and then asked Miss Smith to follow him. If he saw me –' Caroline shuddered – 'he kept it to himself.'

I lounged back, mystified. 'Why conceal it?' I said out loud, but all I could do was take note of the fact. I would have to question Harland very carefully not to give away Caroline's secret, in case he had truly failed to see her.

'What happened next?' I asked her.

'I made my way out. I heard all sorts of voices. The entire place was in chaos.'

'Did you see anyone else trying to escape?'

'Thankfully not. Miss Smith had always taken me through

the least-transited halls and passages. She couldn't guide me that night, of course, but by then I knew the way by heart.'

'And it was then that you saw the mark.' I consciously avoided mentioning the Devil, in case the girl Tilly was eavesdropping.

'Yes. As I told you on the train.'

'And you saw no one in the gardens? On the streets?'

'No. The place was deserted. And again I looked in all directions as I ran away. I was terrified someone would see me. The streets were desolate too; not a carriage or a horse in hearing range.'

'It was very late, was it not?'

'Yes.'

'The streets would have been quiet indeed,' I said, and then looked through my notes. 'You left through the back of the estate. Now ... if someone had been trying to escape at the same time, they would have used a similar route; not the main gates. So, if you saw nobody, whoever did this –' I breathed in – 'is very likely to have remained at the asylum. At least during the immediate aftermath.'

'Seems logical.'

I sighed with some frustration. Her statement narrowed my search, but only a little.

'Is there anything else you might remember? Again, it does not matter how inconsequential it might sound.'

Caroline frowned. She took her time, looking upwards, then closing her eyes.

'I'm not sure this will be relevant ... I had to leave in a terrible rush. I did not have time to go back for my cloak and gloves.'

'You left them in Miss McGray's room, I suppose?'

'Yes. Has nobody mentioned that?'

'No. But neither McGray nor the officers have set foot there. I assume Miss Smith would have had the sense to take them away discreetly. I will ask her, for your peace of mind.'

'Thank you, Mr Frey. It was a black cloak, rather thick, and black leather gloves, if it helps to know. Sadly, I cannot think of any other—'

The door slammed open then. We both started and saw Joan storm in. She looked furibund.

'*The flagging I'll give that Tilly!*' she cried. 'Letting you receive men without a chaperone!'

Caroline rolled her eyes. 'Oh, yes! Mr Frey was making violent love to me!'

Joan turned all the shades of red. 'Don't even joke about that, miss! *You're engaged now!*'

It was one of those cries that change the world forever.

Caroline gasped.

I felt my jaw drop, and with it all the warmth in my chest slipped away. I felt as if my entire body scattered apart, like a bag of sand suddenly slashed at the base.

Only then did Caroline relax her hands, and I understood the reason for her nervousness.

She'd been clenching her left hand to conceal a diamond ring.

My first thought was that it was a vulgar, obnoxiously large stone, and of a rather shoddy cut. No wonder she'd kept her gloves on, even in the train's compartment.

A deep hush followed. It took Joan a moment to realise the extent of her indiscretion, and only because of the rage burning in Caroline's eyes.

'He didn't know?' Joan squealed, shamelessly pointing at me.

'Does that flabbergasted face of his suggest he did?' Caroline snapped.

Joan twirled a foot as if trying to dig a hole in the carpet. 'I – I thought by now—'

'En-en – engaged?' I jumped in, too conscious of my stammering. 'To whom?'

Caroline blushed, but raised her chin nonetheless.

'Mr McGray.'

I thank God I was sitting. And that I'd only had a light breakfast.

My jaw dropped further, my mouth opening so wide I could have swallowed my fist.

'*What!*'

I caught my reflection on a nearby mirror and forced myself to shut my mouth. I tried to speak but only managed to spurt out unintelligible babble.

'I shall pour you some tea, sir,' Joan said, rushing to the pot.

'Sod the tea!' I growled, finally able to articulate – sort of. '*Why* – why – why didn't you tell me before? Whe— when? *How?* Is this the reason the blasted Nine-Nails has started shaving and washing all of a sudden?' I noticed my voice was reaching notes even the Guadagnini would envy. 'Wait!' I said, now in a suitably grave tone. 'Are you and he not brother and sis—?'

They are not, a voice said in my head. Pansy shared one parent with each of them – McGray's mother, Caroline's father – but McGray and Caroline themselves had no lineage in common.

I realised I'd raised a finger and was drawing the family tree in the air; I nearly stomped my foot on the carpet like a stroppy child.

Caroline's cheeks were now as red as ripe cherries. 'Mr Frey, if you will allow me to explain—'

'There – there is no need.' I cleared my throat and jumped to my feet, now prattling at full speed. 'I did not come here to discuss personal matters, as I very well said. I – I must... congratulate you, I suppose. And wish you a life of happiness and – erm – so on and so forth. Now, if you'll excuse me, I must go. I have lunatics galore to interrogate.'

I dashed to the door, but just as I reached it, I heard Caroline rise.

'Mr Frey, please! May I ask you a favour?'

I am far too English to have ignored her. I turned back, but only managed a brief nod.

'Could you keep this to yourself?' she pleaded. 'Just until it is properly announced? I beg you.'

Again I cleared my throat. 'I ... of – of course. *Of course!* You and McGray – I understand. It does take courage to admit to a thing like that.'

'*Mr Frey, I—*'

'Good day, Miss Ardglass. Joan.'

And I stepped out as quickly as I could.

Thankfully, I tripped only after the door had shut.

19

'Of course!' I grumbled loudly as I walked in the middle of the road. 'Of course they're bloody engaged!'

I was getting odd looks, so I rushed to Princes Street and jumped into a cab. I barked at the driver to take me to the lunatic asylum in Morningside (to which he nodded with far more understanding than I liked), and then I was finally able to sulk in private.

It was all so clear now. How could I not have seen it? Even the timings of the current case spelled it out.

Caroline had been at the asylum just before midnight, yet she'd met me in London the morning after to advocate for the sodding McGrays. For her to have time to get to the harbours, contact Captain Jones, secure transportation and be in London by morning – she and McGray would have been in touch right after the events. They would have met at midnight!

Which perhaps implied—

'Everything all right, master?' the driver asked me. I realised I had just let out a deafening growl.

'Yes, yes. Just drive on.'

As to why Caroline had concealed the engagement – that was easy to guess. She must have realised, even before I did so myself, that—

I growled again. Was I so transparent? I probably was.

And Caroline knew that telling me the truth would only put me on edge. She probably thought I'd even refuse to look into the case at all.

I had been shamelessly manipulated into helping them.

I felt an uncontainable fire in my stomach, and despite my best self-control, I could not help picturing the blossoming of the affair.

Last December, after the ghastly case that nearly cost us our lives and took us to some of the furthest reaches of the British Isles, McGray and Caroline had returned to Scotland together.

They would have been as drained and exhausted as I'd been. More, even, their sad pasts considered.

Caroline had lost her dear maid Bertha, and her one surviving relative was – Lady Glass. And Nine-Nails had been shunned by all of Edinburgh after his sister went insane. How similar their situations seemed now. And living in that hostile town, without any relatives or friends, they naturally would have turned to each other.

I pictured the occasional visit. The unavoidable 'ooh, poor you, Mr McGray!' The unescapable 'och, it must've been a terrible time for ye, lass'. Then the accidental – or not so much – touch of the hands when reaching for the teapot... McGray winking an eye.

Caroline had nearly called him *Adolphus* more than once on the train.

I rumbled again, feeling like an utter fool. Here I was, on my way to an asylum, hundreds of miles from my home, to help them clear the name of *their* disgraced half-sister.

I was tempted to tap the roof and tell the driver to take me back to the Palace Hotel, pack my trunks and return to Gloucestershire, no explanations. I even raised my hand, but then thought better of it.

That was a coward's choice; a wet, undignified way out. It was beneath me.

Besides, Miss McGray did not deserve such behaviour.

I felt, if possible, sorrier for her than I usually did. On top of her madness, her confinement and her lost parents, she might also, one day, come to look a lot like the sour Lady Glass.

I'd conclude the investigations, see the case to an end, and then return to my not-so-humble estate, never to set foot in Edin-bloody-burgh ever again. The challenge now would be not to get too distracted by my bitterness.

Rather foolishly, I wished I'd encounter some major emergency at the asylum, if only to distract me from the matter.

Those wishes would be quite quick to come true.

The façade was smeared with all manner of filth. The lawns had been trampled. The wrought-iron gate was bent in places. It was as if a battle had just taken place within the grounds of the asylum.

When we made it to the iron gates a police officer planted himself in front of the cab, his hands raised. As we halted I recognised the bright ginger hair of Constable McNair.

'What happened here?' I asked him, leaning half my torso out of the window.

'Oh, inspector!' he said, straightening his stance. 'Angry mob, sir. They came at break o' dawn, right after the papers began circulating.'

'The papers? What did the papers say?'

McNair sighed. 'The superintendent will explain better than me.'

He stepped aside and the cab took me to the main entrance, where I recognised a group of familiar faces.

Miss Smith, a mop in her hands, was shouting orders at the junior nurses, who diligently brushed the walls. There were smears of – I want to believe it was mud – and also stains of rotting vegetables thrown at the door and windows. A couple of panes were shattered. Two brawny orderlies helped them, scrubbing the filth at the highest points.

Dr Harland and the orderly, Tom, stood on either side of the main entrance, the latter holding a rifle, the former a revolver. They both stared at the grounds with the weapons at the ready, as if expecting the mob to return at any time. I could not tell whose eyes were the more enraged. There were another two constables nearby, their gestures a tad more relaxed.

'The bastards won't come back, inspector,' one of them told me as soon as I alighted. 'Nae with us here, and—'

'They were bloody cowards!' Tom shouted from the entrance. 'Threw the stones and ran. I wish I could've taken a few down!'

His gesture was chilling, as was the way he gripped the rifle, his finger hooked on the trigger. I preferred not to reply.

'Good job,' I told the constables instead. I paid the driver and walked on to the entrance steps.

There I found poor Dr Clouston, staring at the mess with the most dejected grimace. His spectacles were askew, his beard dishevelled. I can only compare his gesture to that of a father who finds his new-born dead.

'Were you here when it happened?' I asked him. 'What did you see?'

Never taking his eyes from the façade, he handed me a crumpled newspaper, half torn and trampled. The mob must have thrown it at the gates.

It was not *The Scotsman*, but one of the more sensationalist publications that abound in our times. Most of the cover was taken up with a crude, amateurish illustration of an old woman's face. It could have been anyone, only she was branded with the Devil's mark.

'*How could they know that?*' I screeched, and at once my mind flooded with possibilities: Pratt, the snatchers, Reverend Hunter, his sexton, or even ... people here at the asylum.

I scanned the article quickly – the sections not covered in mud, that is. It told, in the most bastardised language, that the same mark found at the asylum had also appeared on Mrs Brewster's face. It told how the police – we – had concealed the fact, how the inspector in charge was none other than Nine-Nails and how he might be concealing his own sister's involvement. Despite the appalling quality of the newspaper, they had all the facts right, down to the victims' names.

It took me a moment to take in the words. Things were taking a very dark, very dangerous turn. Even sooner than my worst predictions.

'Is Nine-Nails aware of this?' I asked.

It took Clouston a moment to answer, his voice distant. 'We sent for him. He should be here soon.'

I became aware of how tightly I was clenching the newspaper, and forced a deep breath. 'Was anyone injured?'

Clouston shook his head slowly. 'No ... No. Only the broken glass.' He brought a hand to his brow. 'The things they shouted at us—'

I studied him for a moment. The poor man was not even blinking. He seemed rather – *too* affected.

I could partly understand it. He had led the institution for the past seventeen years; he'd devoted his life to those patients and their ailments; he saw his staff as family. But still, Clouston had faced much worse than a few broken windows and some debased slurs.

'Doctor,' I said gingerly, 'I know you are quite upset right now, but – I need to ask you a few delicate questions.'

Clouston glared at me. '*Oh, not now, Mr Frey!*' His voice travelled across the lawns and all eyes turned to him.

He covered his mouth, instantly regretting the outburst. Then he raised his other hand, as if about to explain something, but could not bring himself to speak. He rushed into the building with long strides. Miss Smith took a step in his direction, her face full of concern, but did not follow him in.

Dr Harland came over to me, never lowering his gun.

'It's in all the papers,' he said, casting a derisive look at the front-page picture. 'Most without that Michelangelo, of course.'

'Why is Dr Clouston so altered?' I asked.

Harland shrugged. 'He kept mumbling something about bringing doom to this place himself. This being his fault and so on.'

His tone was clearly accusing, and I noticed his eyes were reddened, as if he had not slept at all the previous night.

Tom heard everything Harland said and took an involuntary step forwards, the rifle quivering in his hands, his teeth clenched.

'You may lower those now,' I said, and thankfully neither man argued.

As soon as the weapons were down, I looked back at Harland. 'I must talk to Dr Clouston, but perhaps I should give him some time. Meanwhile, can I ask *you* a few questions?'

Harland cast me a challenging look. 'About what?'

I chuckled. 'I will paraphrase, doctor. I *have* some questions, which you *must* answer. It is best for you that we do it now, rather than wait for the public inquiry.'

Harland snorted, but again, he obliged without further quarrel.

I caught a glimpse of Miss Smith and Tom as I walked in. They both looked at me from the corners of their eyes. Only then did I notice that Tom had a bandaged hand, and he was quick to look away when our eyes met.

Harland led me to his office; a small, nondescript room on the first floor, the sky grey behind the frosted glass windows. We were not too far from Pansy's room, I noticed.

We sat by his narrow desk, every square inch of it covered by neat stacks of documents and patients' records. I dropped the newspaper on top of them and took a quick look at the office.

What a depressing sight it was: poorly lit, claustrophobic and crammed with files. It seemed to go well with the man himself. I studied him carefully for the first time, and noticed his elegant, though faded, clothes, as well as his scuffed shoes.

Even his desk spoke of decline: an ancient piece of walnut in the Queen Anne style, now scratched and ridden with wood worm. All the legs, which would have been carved as gracious paws or padded feet, had been replaced by crude blocks of unvarnished pinewood.

'This ought to be restored,' I said. 'It must be a hundred years old at least. Is it yours?'

Harland simply tensed his lips, and I left the niceties aside. I asked him to go through the events on the night of MacDonnell's death, which he did almost lethargically, glossing over the facts as if it were all a bland speech he'd been forced to memorise. I listened carefully to his every word, trying to catch anything he said that might involve Caroline, but he gave me no clues. He mentioned Miss Smith just tangentially; Miss McGray not at all.

I lounged back when he was done, considering my next words very carefully. 'You have a very soft accent, doctor,' I said after a while. 'Very soft Lothian.'

He sneered. 'Is that intended as a compliment?'

'Somewhat. I am sure it will have gone well with your lecturers.'

I waited for a comment but he made none. His lips, in fact, tightened a little more.

'You studied at Surgeons' College, here in Edinburgh, is that correct?'

For a moment he did not move a muscle. I could not believe a face could stand so still. I was about to remark how easy it would be for me to check this fact, but he must have thought the same.

'I did.'

He barely moved his mouth to say it. I had expected it to be so, but the confirmation still pleased me.

'A most prestigious institution. Do you still keep in touch with your professors? With your erstwhile colleagues?'

Again he took his time, and again he only just parted his lips.

'With a few of them, yes.'

I narrowed my eyes, lowering my voice a little. 'Did you enjoy your anatomy lectures?'

He scoffed. 'How is this relevant?'

'It must be difficult – seeing your former classmates set up their own practises, moving off to London, completing more advanced degrees ...'

'While I remain here, looking after lunatics and wiping their shit and vomit off my clothes?'

'If you want to put it like that. I mean no disrespect but – yours is probably not the best paid of jobs,' I softly kicked one of the desk's improvised legs as I said so. 'Clouston's post may be, but you are still years away from such a promotion, *if* the opportunity ever materialises. Clouston will only leave upon retirement; I give him another ten, fifteen years.'

Harland did not reply, but the resentment on his face was clear. He took a distracted hand to one of his cufflinks. They were cheap brass.

'Frozen, infirm cadavers abound, especially in this season,' I went on. 'On the other hand, it must pay handsomely to deliver a healthy body to the—'

Harland let out a hiss. 'Inspector, if there is something you wish to say—'

'I believe I am saying it. No one had freer access to all the corners of this building that night. Or to the patients' medical histories.' I nodded at the stacks of files. 'You had ample time and opportunities to spare.'

'Yes, I could have had many chances and routes and methods. More than you could come up with. And yes, I did have an expensive education that has given me next to nothing in return. But you have no way to prove I had anything to do with MacDonnell's murder. You have no evidence against me – or anyone else for that matter! You are just stabbing in the dark. You know nothing.'

I allowed myself a little smirk. 'Oh, but I do,' I said, knowing I was about to tread on thin ice. I leaned forwards, and delivered my best bluff. 'I know that something else happened that night. And I know you are concealing it.'

His eyes glowed with understanding, but to my shock he did not seem nervous. Instead, his lips parted in a macabre smile. He leaned forwards too, interlacing his hands on the desk.

'I *am* concealing something. Yes. And you will wish you never pressed me into saying it.'

I pulled back a little, as if someone had just waved a hot poker too close to my face.

Harland enjoyed the moment. He stared directly into my eyes, and when he spoke he savoured every word.

'I saw her.'

'Her?' I let out, my mind suddenly numb.

'Yes. *Her*. Guided by Miss Smith.' Harland smiled, making a pause for dramatic effect. His teeth seemed to be glinting. 'Miss McGray.'

'*Miss McGray?*' I echoed, almost in a trance, and Harland lounged back.

'I didn't believe my eyes, but it wasn't entirely a surprise. Since the beginning of the year, a few inmates had been telling me they'd seen Miss McGray wandering the corridors, always at night. At first I thought they were talking nonsense, like they usually do. That is – until the night MacDonnell was murdered. 'Miss McGray was outside her room. I saw her.'

'*You saw her?*' I cried as a torrent of thoughts flashed through my head – the gloomy corridor, Caroline being the same height and build as Pansy, their similar hair and faces. No wonder Harland, in the dark, had mistaken one for the other. Even McGray had mistaken them once!

'Yes, inspector,' he replied. 'I saw her like I see you now. The stupid girl tried to hide behind a rather slim cabinet.'

Oh no, a little voice said in my head as I lowered my eyes.

'Why are you so surprised, inspector?' Harland mocked. 'You just said that you *knew*. Were you just trying to trick me?'

I knew I could not look more stunned. The shock made me feel queasy. I would have to lie and feign ignorance.

'I do not know what you talk about. Miss McGray out and about on the night of the murder? I find that hard to—'

'I saw her! And I am prepared to state that under oath!'

I snorted, feeling the blood throbbing in my head. 'And what did you do? Did you take Miss –' I nearly said 'Miss Ardglass' – 'Miss McGray back to her room?'

'No.'

'Did you ask Miss Smith – or one of the other nurses to take her to her room?'

'No.'

'Why? Why did you not confront them?'

'For two reasons. First, I had a corpse and a troupe of other inmates to deal with.' He went silent for an exasperatingly long time.

'*And?*' I pressed.

'Inspector,' he said after a sigh, 'someone had been stabbed to death and I'd just confirmed that those two women were up to something. I did not want to be their next victim.'

'Oh, you cannot seriously believe Miss McGray did it!'

Harland sneered. 'Why not? All those journalists are speculating about her,' he nodded at the creased newspaper on the desk, 'and they don't even know what I saw!'

I shook my head. 'Dr Harland, this is – this is illogical. Why did you not say anything before?'

I regretted asking the question. The last thing we needed was him telling the world he thought he'd seen McGray's sister so close to the crime scene.

Harland let out a bitter laugh. 'I was tempted to, after the initial shock that night, but I've changed my mind. I know how life works. If I speak, that damned Nine-Nails will tamper with the evidence, or threaten me. Or he might even try to incriminate me, just to save his sister's neck.'

He turned to stare wistfully at the window. I wondered why, as it was frosted glass.

'I *do* feel curious, if I'm honest,' he mused. 'I would perfectly understand Miss McGray murdering someone. She has done it before – her bloody parents too! – and she is insane, so she needs no reasons. Miss Smith, on the other hand –' he shook his head – 'there is a lot you don't know about the good *Miss* Smith.' He looked back at me. 'Still, I don't want to know. It is up to *you* to find out. Just don't come to me asking more incriminatory questions. If I speak, things would get pretty grim for the McGrays.'

I felt a burning in the pit of my stomach.

'Are you blackmailing me?'

Harland grinned.

'Oh, do not call it that, inspector. I *will* keep quiet. For as long as the situation allows. But if I see fingers pointing at me, accusing me of what that crazy little bitch might have done in my corridors, I will have no choice but to defend myself.'

I could only snort, conscious of how heatedly I was breathing. I would not win this round.

Harland rose to his feet then, his voice unduly jovial.

'Now, do excuse me, inspector. I must do my morning round. The patients will be agitated. But feel free to stay here; you really do need to compose yourself.'

I pushed a stack of files aside and put an elbow on the desk, covering my brow.

'Oh, just don't touch those files, inspector. I spent all night sorting them.'

20

'Oh God, oh God...' I kept mumbling. The more I dwelled on the situation, the more tangled it seemed in my head.

I could not tell McGray any of this. If I did, I'd also have to tell him that Caroline had been at the asylum; he would ask why; I'd end up telling him that his late mother had been an unfaithful trollop. He'd punch me in the face...

Also, this did not change my suspicions. Harland might still have been involved. He had the motives, the connections and plenty of opportunity. Mistaking Caroline for Pansy would simply have given him better leverage than he could ever have hoped for. We could not accuse him of anything unless we had solid, unquestionable evidence against him. And even then, the populace might still want Pansy's blood.

Nine-Nails, I realised, must know the truth. There was no way around it. Not only would it help the investigation, but it would also keep him from asking Harland impertinent questions.

Caroline has to tell him, I thought. For once, it was not up to me. This was now, entirely, a family matter.

'A nice first hurdle in their married life,' I mumbled bitterly.

'Inspector Frey?' a ghostly voice said behind my back, and I nearly fell off the chair.

It was Cassandra Smith, looking at me with concern.

'Excuse me, sir. Were you talking to yourself?'

I blushed. 'Erm... *yes*, but do not lock me up here just yet.'

She met my joke with a wooden face (and people still wonder why I am always stiff-lipped).

'You said you wanted to talk to me,' she said, raising her chin a little. 'Yesterday, when you were here.'

'Oh, yes. Thank you for coming forward. Have a seat, please.'

'But Dr Harland—'

'He shan't be back for a while, I am sure.'

She cast the office a suspicious look, then stepped in and took Harland's chair behind the desk. I wondered if she did so to seem a tad more authoritative – not that she needed to. She was steeled, ready for the questions she knew I would ask her.

I produced my notebook. 'If you could please give me a moment before we start—'

'Of course, inspector.'

I only pretended to search through my notes, while I decided the best course of action. Harland had said he did not want Miss Smith to know he'd seen Miss McGray. And though I was not in the slightest inclined to take orders from him, I feared what he might do if he noticed a sudden change in Miss Smith's demeanour, especially right after our conversation.

I closed the notebook. I'd wait. And if I had to tell her anything, it would be away from the asylum, so she might have a chance to process the news.

'How are your father and your little girl?' I asked.

'Fine,' she said, expressionless.

'I hope your father keeps well, despite the season.'

'Thank you. He manages.'

'You live near The Meadows park, if I remember correctly?' I asked.

'Yes, in a small tenement on the south side.'

'That is quite far from here, is it not?'

She cleared her throat. 'Excuse me, sir, I don't mean to be blunt but – you don't have to ease things for me. Ask what you need to ask and I shall answer.'

'Oh, I did need to ask you those questions. Especially since I hear you were at Greyfriars Church. For Mrs Brewster's funeral.'

For the briefest of instants, even the composed head nurse seemed taken by surprise.

'Yes,' she said, but it sounded closer to a question. The fine creases around her eyes deepened a little.

'May I ask the reason?'

'The reason?' she repeated.

'Yes. I admire your fortitude, Miss Smith. I do not believe I could manage a life as busy as yours – a child, an elderly parent to look after, all the pressures of your post here, travelling all the way to Morningside, except, I suppose, when your duties force you to spend the night here.' I saw her tense her lips, perhaps thinking of the nights she'd helped Caroline sneak in. 'And yet you find time and energy to attend a patient's funeral. You do not do the same for all the inmates that sadly pass away under your watch, do you?'

'Of course not. I went there out of compassion. The poor lady had no relatives; no next of kin. Even her son died before her. Other than the minister and the sexton, I was the one attendant. To think that we can spend so many years in this world, and still end our days so alone… It made me terribly sad.'

'Terribly sad indeed,' I said, unexpectedly realising that I myself might very well end up like the poor Mrs Brewster, my connections leaving me one by one, like my late mother, uncle and father. I cleared my throat and pulled my attention back to the case. 'The sexton told me that you got very close to the coffin.'

'Yes, to pay my respects.' Miss Smith looked down, as affected as if standing before the open coffin again.

I felt so sorry I had to ask her the following, even more since I had to do it in an impassive tone. 'Did you tamper with the lady's body?'

Miss Smith looked up at once. 'Of course I didn't!'

'Did you *touch* her during the funeral?'

She let out a little gasp. 'I – I did. Yes. I touched her hand.'

'Her hand?' I repeated, thinking of the little stain also found there. 'Nothing more?'

Miss Smith tightened her lips and only nodded. I leaned back on the chair and studied her for a moment. She was staring at some point on the wall, avoiding my gaze.

I pointed at the newspaper, still on the desk. 'Did Mrs Brewster bear that mark when you last saw her?'

'No, not at all,' she rushed to say.

'Are you sure?'

'Absolutely. I wouldn't have missed that.'

'Indeed. Who prepared the body?'

Miss Smith nearly choked. 'I – I did. Mrs Brewster left no money for a mortician or proper embalming.'

'Can you give me the details?'

'Well, it was all very mundane. I washed her, dressed her, did her hair in a very simple plait, put on her favourite locket and brought her psalms book. That was all. Oh, and Dr Clouston came by then; we said a little prayer and he put a wee sprig of laurel and yew in the lady's hand.'

'Did he?' I asked, at once recalling the sprig we'd found in the coffin. 'Tradition?'

'Yes. He would have put flowers too, but it being winter...'

'I see. Laurel *and* yew, you said? Two sprigs.'

'Yes. They symbolise eternal life.'

I remembered McGray saying the same when we found the yew in the coffin. I scribbled *Missing laurel*. 'What happened next?'

'That was all. We left her to rest until the coffin arrived. I went back to make sure that the orderlies handled her carefully.'

'Which orderlies were those?'

'This young lad, Stephen –' she paused – 'and Tom.'

I arched an eyebrow and took note of that. The name Tom kept appearing here and there. Being Clouston's most trusted orderly was not paying off.

'Was she taken straight away?' I asked.

'Yes. Directly to the kirk. I went on the driver's seat. Mighty cold it was!'

'And nobody touched the coffin on the way?'

'No. Again, I would have noticed.'

I mused over my notes. 'I presume you found nothing different when you saw her again at the church.'

'She looked exactly as she did before we closed the coffin here. The sprigs may have shifted a little on the journey, but that was all. No marks.'

'And you are entirely sure you only touched her hand?'

Miss Smith let out an exasperated breath. 'Yes! Are you accusing me?'

'From what you tell me, you were the last person to touch Mrs Brewster before she was buried; the last person to see her without the mark. You surely understand why I must ask.'

'Why would I mark that poor woman's body?' she replied. 'You've known me for a while now, inspector. I'm offended that you'd even consider I'm capable of something like that.'

I smiled wearily. 'I do not seem to know anyone anymore.' I shifted in my seat. 'Miss Smith, you and Dr Clouston inspire the same conflict in me. You two seem so professional, so poised, so trustworthy…'

Her face turned stern. 'And yet?'

'And yet there is something else about you. Something I cannot quite fathom. Something – lurking underneath.'

Miss Smith said nothing. She avoided my gaze, which only seemed to confirm my point.

'For instance,' I said, 'you have lied to Inspector McGray.'

She shut her eyes. 'I guess you're talking about Miss Ardglass.'

'Indeed.'

'How do you know that? Did she tell you?'

'Yes.'

Miss Smith snorted. 'The times she made us swear we'd say nothing! And in the end it was *she* who—'

'She had to tell me. That is the only reason I came back to help. But I digress. As I said, you lied to McGray about—'

'We *had* to,' she snapped. 'For the same reasons that *you* lie to him now!'

I sighed. 'Yes, but it is a very risky lie. And those night visits—' I was tempted to tell her about Harland, but forced myself not to. 'I am surprised that you agreed to oversee them. You will have had to stay overnight on all those occasions; away from your daughter and your ailing father. All for the sake of protecting the family secrets of an upper-class young woman entirely unconnected to you.'

For a moment, Miss Smith's eyes were vacant, her mind miles away.

'I did it for Dr Clouston,' she said in a sigh. 'He begged me to. But, mostly, I did it for Amy. Over the years I've come to care a great deal about her. All the poor girl lost in a single blow... her family, her freedom... her—' Miss Smith sighed. 'Her sanity. God, she was a child when she came here. Her life was just about to begin, and yet now she is a woman. And she's still here. She deserves better than this place.' She glared at the narrow office, as if all of a sudden the walls repelled her. 'And Miss Ardglass was always very kind,' she added. 'Very well mannered and very grateful. Inspector McGray will be very happy.'

I felt my cheeks heating up. Even *she* knew!

'Speaking of Miss Ardglass,' I rushed to say, 'on the night of the murder she left her cloak and gloves in Miss McGray's room. Have you retrieved them?'

Miss Smith frowned. 'Did she? No. Where exactly did she leave them?'

'She did not say.'

'I haven't seen them, inspector.'

'But you *have* been to her room?'

'Of course. Quite a few times since then. Perhaps Miss Ardglass left them in the wardrobe – or one of my girls saw them and put them away, thinking they were Miss McGray's.'

Or someone else took them, I thought, and barely managed to repress a shudder.

'May we check?' I asked, already on my feet. 'Right away?'

'Yes. Do you think there might be trouble?'

'Perhaps.'

At once we left the office and rushed to Pansy's bedroom.

I could not conceal my anxiety. My encounters with Miss McGray had never ended well.

21

'I thought you didn't like to keep her locked in,' I said when I saw Miss Smith turn the key.

'I don't, but with all that's happened...' She was about to open the door but then hesitated. 'Do you mind if I step in first? Just to make sure—'

'I am sorry, Miss Smith. I must see that room as it is. You understand why, surely.'

'She might be distressed to see you.'

'Then we will have to deal with it,' I snapped. I hated myself for it, but this was not the time to be the exemplary gentleman.

She let out a long sigh and brought her face closer to the door.

'Pansy?' she said softly. 'It's me. I'm – I'm coming in. With a visitor.'

She listened out for a moment, an ear pressed to the door. There was no sound that I could hear. Miss Smith finally opened the door and stepped in.

I took a deep breath, and then followed her.

My heartbeat quickened at once. The air inside was decidedly colder, and I thought I heard a slight, dull murmur. It reminded me of the sound one hears in a conch; like a long sigh that lingered on an on, its echo never quite vanishing.

I'd heard it before, also near Pansy.

'Is there a current?' I asked.

As Miss Smith went to the window to check, my eyes were drawn to the back of a wide armchair. It faced the window, a little table next to it, on which I saw a small box of whisky fudge and a vase with a little white rose – an expensive present at this time of year.

From where I stood I could not see the chair's occupant; only the side of a small, pale hand on the armrest.

The fine fingers twitched with anxiety.

Miss Smith ran a hand along the windowsill, all the while showing a warm smile to Miss McGray. The nurse then looked at me, her face hardening in a blink.

'I can't feel any draughts here,' she said. 'But I'll bring the excluder just in case.'

She went to the wardrobe and opened its two doors as I stepped closer. I felt embarrassed to be inspecting Pansy's clothes, but I had no choice.

The girl owned a wondrous variety of fine dresses, bonnets and ribbons. Presents from her brother, surely; all in soft, pale colours.

I saw no black cloak, though. And such a garment would have stood out among those whites and pastels.

Miss Smith opened the wardrobe's bottom drawers. I nearly yelped at the sight of Pansy's underclothes, and I had to swallow all my decorum while Miss Smith rummaged through them.

She found nothing there either.

'Where did those lasses put that excluder?' Miss Smith said, her mouth turned in Pansy's direction, in an almost apologetic manner. I wondered why.

Could Miss McGray become upset it she knew we were searching her possessions?

I'd rather not find out. I had witnessed a couple of her worst fits. The last one, which had involved scissors, still made me shiver.

Miss Smith went on to search in a chest of drawers, even if the compartments would not have been large enough to contain a cloak. I could see her grow more and more agitated as she opened and closed them. I too was beginning to feel a slight prickle of fear.

'They might have put it under the bed,' Miss Smith said. She made to bend down and check, but I rushed towards the four-poster bed.

'Do allow me.'

I went on my knees and lifted the bed skirt. I saw a small hat box, which I pulled discreetly and, feeling terribly guilty by invading the young woman's privacy, opened it. It only contained a very fine white bonnet with pink ribbons. It pained me to think that Pansy would only get to wear it for her summer walks around the asylum's lawns.

I pushed the box back. There was nothing else there, other than the astonishingly clean floorboards. I even pressed them, lest one might be loose, but that was not the case.

'Nothing there?' Miss Smith asked.

I rose and shook my head. For a moment all we could do was exchange puzzled looks.

Why would anyone take those garments? They'd only be useful to someone – I trembled – interested in accusing Caroline. And only a handful of people knew of her visits to the asylum.

Miss Smith sighed, perhaps thinking that she too would be in trouble if it transpired that she'd been letting Caroline in. After a moment's silence she snapped her fingers.

'Oh, silly me, there it is!'

I felt a brief excitement, but then realised she'd meant the draught excluder, which she retrieved from the top of the wardrobe. She'd clearly known all along where it was, and had only pretended the contrary so that Pansy did not know what we were up to. Could Miss Smith really fear the girl might become violent if she thought we were prying?

Miss Smith placed the soft excluder on the windowsill, though it would not make the room any warmer. She smiled at Pansy, and suddenly the seasoned head nurse seemed awkward, as if not knowing what to do next.

I went closer to the armchair, my heart quickening with each movement. I had always felt this ... odd presence around Pansy. It was as if she charged the very air that surrounded her with some eerie energy.

I took a deep breath and walked around the chair, recalling the first time I'd met her, some fifteen months earlier. It felt like a lifetime ago but also, quite strangely, as if it had been only yesterday: the same seat, the same mahogany table, the same window and the same grey landscape Pansy had stared at for the past six years. She might even have been wearing the same white muslin dress that day, with delicate lace trimmings.

And yet, when finally I saw her face, it was clear how much things had changed.

One year ago her stare had been completely vacant, her dark irises – Caroline's – looking into nothing; seeing but not seeing. Now her pupils flickered erratically, in the way that the eyelids of someone having bad dreams do. Only her eyes were wide open, as if the poor girl were staring directly into her nightmares.

Her hands, once demurely folded on her lap, now quivered on the armrests, clenching the leather as if clinging to the edge of a cliff. Even her dark, wavy locks, usually decked with flowers, now looked dishevelled and brittle.

Never had she looked so much like a ticking bomb just about to explode.

Her condition had declined steadily since Lord Joel's escape, which made me wonder – could he have told her the truth? Could he have told her that she was his daughter? And if he had, how much could she have understood? Would she be aware that her father had become a murderer and that his escape had unleashed unspeakable horrors? Would she know that she was now, in many people's opinion, the lead suspect of another gruesome death?

It was all plausible.

I felt a pang of sorrow, and then realised I could not simply stand there, staring at the poor young woman, so I cleared my throat.

'Good – good day, Miss McGray.'

Her eyes flickered my way for a second, then back to the window.

'I came to make sure you are doing all right,' I said softly. 'I – I *hope* you are doing all right.'

I waited for a little while, even if I was not expecting her to reply or move. I half raised a hand to bid farewell, and then she reacted.

Her gaze shifted a little, just enough to spot the signet ring on my finger, and at once her entire body jolted.

My hand froze, understanding at once. Lord Joel must have worn this very ring in front of her. And now she recognised it.

I nearly hid it behind my back, but then, for some reason, did the exact opposite.

I turned my hand, the better to show the emerald, until it caught a glimmer of the dull daylight, for an instant showing its rich, dark green.

'Do you like it?' I mumbled. 'It is—' I hesitated, as if about to jump into the same abyss as her. 'It is a family heirloom.'

Her first gesture was of utter confusion. For a while she did not blink or twitch or make a sound.

And then something built up in her eyes, which shifted into an unsettling glare. She gathered air, tensed her jaw, as if about to let out a desperate scream, and then—

22

'*What the fuck are ye doing here?*'

I jumped and Miss Smith gasped, our necks nearly spraining as we turned to the wide-open door. There stood Nine-Nails, struggling to catch his breath, his eyes bloodshot, and he came to me with long, thumping strides.

'I came to make sure Miss McGray is well,' I spluttered. 'I imagine you will have heard what happened—'

'Get away,' he snarled, pushing me aside with just one hand, yet nearly knocking me over.

He knelt next to Pansy, almost toppling the table, but then his entire attitude switched within a blink: he took one of her small hands with utmost care, looking at his sister with heart-breaking devotion.

'Look at ye,' he whispered. 'Yer so cold—'

'There was a draught,' Miss Smith said. 'I'll get her a hot brew now.'

And she signalled me to follow her out.

McGray hardly noticed us leaving. I caught one last glimpse of him holding Amy's hand, then raising himself up a little to whisper soothingly into her ear. And then Miss Smith shut the door.

'How very strange,' she whispered. I was about to mention

the ring, but she'd not meant that. 'Why would anyone take that cloak away?'

I pinched the bridge of my nose, forcing myself to gather my thoughts. 'It is troubling, yes.' I remembered how clean everything in that room looked, down to the floorboards under the bed. 'Could someone have taken it for washing?'

Miss Smith nodded. 'Oh, yes! Miss Ard – *she* had to cross the gardens. The cloak would have been muddy. I'll ask my girls.'

'Thank you. Could you do it subtly? Do not mention the specifics to them.'

'Of course not. I'll do it now, inspector.'

I saw her walk away, a little voice in my head still telling me I could not trust her fully.

I did not have much time to muse, though, for McGray came out of the room a few minutes later.

To my complete shock, his eyes shone with repressed tears. And he looked deathly pale, much more noticeable without his usual stubble. I immediately remembered the reason behind his grooming, and any sympathy I might have felt was overtaken by fire in my guts.

His next words did not help.

'Why did ye get in there, Percy? To try on one o' her shimmies?'

It was like a tiny spark thrown onto a mound of dynamite. His engagement, my foolishness, the death of my father – everything spun in my insides and I howled from the bottom of my stomach.

'*Oh, you can go rot in hell!*'

I nearly expectorated when rolling the R, then turned on my heels and made to storm away.

'Wait! *Wait!*' McGray said at once. He covered his brow and mumbled a word I never thought I'd hear from his lips.

'Sorry. Sorry, Frey.'

We both took deep breaths, struggling to tame our tempers. I was only glad he'd mocked me first; now he would not suspect my glaring at him with all my loathing.

'This is all turning really ugly,' he said in an exhalation, his stare fixed on the floor. 'These fuckin' headlines – the things they're saying about Pansy – it's finally getting to me. And she *must* feel something bad is going on . . .'

He rarely spoke so candidly about his fears. I could have said 'I understand', or 'Do not worry', but I did not. I simply stood there in silence.

It took McGray a minute to recollect himself, without any help as he'd always done.

'I take it ye were one o' the first ones to read the papers,' he said at last. 'Gettin' them delivered to yer princely suite.'

'Y – yes,' I lied. 'That is – the reason I came here.'

'We have to go to the newspapers, Frey. See who told them about the auld lady's mark. The only ones who could've seen it are ye, Reed, me and—'

'And the snatchers!'

'Indeedy. Whoever's feeding them the stories will lead us to them. We'll go to *The Scotsman* with a few peelers and beat the truth out o' them.'

'*The Scotsman*? Even after what happened the last time we questioned one of their reporters?'

'Precisely because o' that! They'll sing faster if they learned their lesson.'

I was going to say something, but then I heard Dr Harland, his unique voice coming from around a corner.

'Follow me,' I told McGray, 'quickly.'

'What?'

'*Now!*'

And I rushed to the nearest stairs, fearing that Harland might repeat all he knew – all he *thought* he knew about Pansy.

'What's got into ye?' McGray asked, forcing me to stop at the first landing.

I looked up and down the stairs, pretending to make sure we were alone. In reality, I was working out which pieces of Harland's testimony I could tell him without betraying Caroline's secret. In the end, I only told him about Harland's bitterness regarding his profession, the fact that he had studied at Surgeons' College, and that he might still have shady connections there.

'I cannot be sure yet,' I whispered, 'but I think he is our man. He has the links, the contacts and the motive.'

McGray chuckled, grinding a fist against his open palm.

'I can *clarify* things for ye in a second.'

He climbed the steps and I panicked, for there was nothing I could do to stop him. He stomped along the corridor, looking from left to right; we passed Pansy's room and went on to Harland's office.

I saw the door ajar, McGray stormed in and I felt a pang in my chest. I nearly tripped when I rushed behind him.

'*No, wait!*' I squealed, my voice travelling up and down the hall.

McGray's back obscured most of my view. I had to walk around him to see that Harland was not there.

'Where's that wee turd?' he shouted, just as he kicked one of the desk's makeshift legs. The crude chunk of wood tore off and the furniture fell askew.

'McGray, we should go!' I urged, keeping a nervous eye on the door. '*Now!*'

'Och, what the hell's wrong with ye?' McGray asked, and I felt a trickle of sweat roll down my back.

'I – I do not think we should confront him openly just yet.'

'Why the fuck nae? Ye afraid he won't bring the lavender oil next time he joins ye for a bath?'

I gathered air. Thankfully, my answer was no lie. 'He seems

crafty. He knows we have nothing solid against him; nothing other than circumstantial evidence. I very much doubt he'll submit to intimidation.'

McGray still looked unconvinced. And keen to punch a face, irrespective of whose.

'If he thinks we are on his track,' I added, 'he might flee, or destroy evidence, or alert his accomplices – and accomplices he must have.'

Nine-Nails pressed a fist against his palm, grinding his teeth as he let out a hissing breath.

I felt a trickle of sweat run down my spine, fearing Harland might appear at any time.

After a seemingly endless time, McGray nodded.

'I'll trust yer judgement this once,' he said, and then pushed me out of the office. 'But only 'cause I think—' He fell silent and waited until we'd made it to the stairs. 'I think I already have a trail that might prove the link between Harland and Surgeons' College.'

'Do you? What?'

'Nae here. I'll tell ye on the way to *The Scotsman*'s offices. We'll go there first to catch them off-guard. Then we can go to the college.'

'Wait, I also wanted to question Clouston. He was downright horrified after the attack on the asylum.'

'Don't bother,' McGray said. 'The lads told me they saw him leave just before I arrived.'

I nearly tripped when I heard that. 'Wha— *He left?* He knew I wanted to talk to him!'

'He probably was in nae mood for yer wit and charm.'

I did not have a head to reply. Clouston was clearly avoiding me, but why?

There was no time to ponder. Right then we stepped into

the corridor that led to the front gate, and we stumbled across Miss Smith.

She was carrying a basket of laundry, in which I recognised some lilac ribbons and white silks that undoubtedly belonged to Miss McGray.

'Keep an eye on Pansy,' Nine-Nails asked her, placing a gentle hand on her shoulder. Miss Smith nodded, but she did not reply. I noticed that her lips were quite dry.

She looked at me, then at the clean clothes – and then shook her head.

23

So someone had definitely taken Caroline's gloves away. And the cloak.

I thought of Harland, and at once all the clues fitted together. If he'd seen the garments, he would have thought they were Pansy's. Of course! Fine clothes, same size... and evidently worn outside on that same night. Could he have taken them to muddle the case? As further evidence to frame her? If he had, there would be no way to clear her name.

The thought made me shiver.

I must tell Caroline about this. She must confess everything to McGray. For an instant I thought of doing so myself but – was it my place to reveal such a delicate family matter against Caroline's wishes? I thought no, but then again, was that the real reason of my hesitation? Or was I secretly hoping that the revelation might cause an irreparable rift between her and McGray?

The situation made me dizzy. All I knew was that the investigation could not continue in this secretive and disjointed manner. Pansy would not stand a chance if—

'Och, are ye listening?'

McGray's protest came with a jolt of the cab, just as we crossed the long Meadows park.

'Sorry,' I mumbled, my mind blank. 'I was... thinking of...'

'Whatever,' Nine-Nails luckily interrupted. He rummaged in his breast pocket and pulled out a piece of crumpled paper.

'What is that?' I asked.

'The list o' snobby sods at Professor Grimshaw's lecture. Our officers gave it to me yesterday, while ye were puking yer spleen out. I only had time to give it a proper look last night.' He handed it to me. 'Notice anything odd?'

I began scanning the names, but Nine-Nails had no patience.

'That name,' he said, pointing alternately at two lines. 'It appears twice.'

Indeed, two entries read: *E. Murray*. One was halfway through the list; the other almost at the very end.

'Different handwriting,' I mumbled. 'So one of the students—'

'Didnae want us to ken his name. Must've jotted down the very first one that crossed his mind.'

'And your men did not notice this?'

'Nae. I *will* give them a good bollocking.'

I nodded. 'The college should have a register of students. Professor Grimshaw himself might—'

'Aye, aye, but ye just made me think – we don't want to scare the game. I think we should look for the real Murray first. Tell him this is evidence against him; scare him sick so he tells us everything he might ken.'

'McGray, this is no evidence against—'

'Och, I ken so! But if he's yer typical upper-class mummy's boy, never out o' daddy's hunting grounds, he'll believe any auld shite we tell him.'

A few embarrassing memories, from my first days at Oxford, flashed through my head. 'Fair point.'

The cab rode past Greyfriars Kirk. I caught a glimpse of Reverend Hunter, distributing charities among a crowd of homeless children. The sight reminded me of Miss Smith's statement, particularly the missing branch of laurel.

'I would like to inspect Mrs Brewster's coffin one more time,' I mumbled. 'I think we might have missed something.'

I told him all I could from Miss Smith's statement, mentioning the sprig of yew and laurel, and the fact that she'd been the one who'd prepared Mrs Brewster's body for the funeral.

'She left her unattended for a wee while, ye said?'

I had to check my notes. 'Yes, before the coffin arrived.'

McGray arched an eyebrow.

'Quite a few people saw her after that,' I said. 'Mrs Brewster still had no mark.'

'True,' he said in a sigh. 'All right, add that coffin to the list o' chores.'

A list which only seemed to grow, the more we investigated.

The cab crossed the wide George IV Bridge, entered the busy Royal Mile, and then continued down the meandering Cockburn Street, the road twisting both horizontally and vertically.

We alighted in front of *The Scotsman*. Their gilded sign, glossy only last summer, was in dire need of repainting. The day was still overcast, a dim light coming through the dark clouds, and I felt as if the entire city were coming down with decay.

The smells of ink and glue hit us as soon as we walked into the busy reception room, where reporters and tradesmen ran in every direction. However, that was not the usual bustle of a newspaper: every face I saw appeared to be on edge.

A clerk came to us. His irritated look suggested he intended to send us away; however, the young man instantly recognised Nine-Nails.

'Oh, inspector! We weren't expecting you to arrive so soon!'

McGray wrinkled his nose. 'Expecting? *What?*'

'Follow me, if you please.'

McGray and I exchanged puzzled looks, but obliged without comment.

The clerk led us to the first floor, one storey below the cramped little cubicles where the correspondents and copywriters worked day and night. Here the corridors were wide and airy, the smells of ink mixed with fine tobacco and brandy.

We walked into a large office with crimson carpets and dark wood panelling. The two tall windows, facing north, let in only the most pathetic light, and the gas lamps ensconced on the walls cast sharp shadows on the two men present.

One, behind a bulky mahogany desk, was a thickset, short man in his fifties, with just a few strands of wiry hair left on his scalp.

The other, standing in front of him, was Superintendent Trevelyan. His auburn hair seemed almost on fire under the orange glow of the lamps.

He turned to us and let out a sigh of relief. 'Good, they found you!'

'Not exactly,' I said. 'We were heading here by coincidence.'

'A lucky one, then.' Trevelyan nodded and then took a step closer to us, lowering his voice. 'Things are already getting out of hand. It won't surprise me if it's less than a day before I have to assign the investigation to someone else.'

McGray took in a hissing breath, but held it in, and the way he ground his teeth made me think of a dam just about to crack.

'Shut the door when you leave,' the thickset man told the young clerk, who obeyed at once. As soon as he closed the door, the air appeared to turn denser, loaded with smoke from the cigar the stocky chap clenched between his teeth.

'I'm glad your men are here,' he told Trevelyan. His voice was a hoarse baritone, roughened by drinking and smoking, and, to my surprise, he was English. He pointed at the two cushioned chairs disposed around the desk. 'Have a seat, please.'

Trevelyan and I sat down, but McGray preferred to remain standing.

'This is Mr Cooper,' Trevelyan said, 'chief editor here. Mr Cooper, this is Mr Frey and – well, I believe Inspector McGray needs no introduction.'

'Indeed,' said Mr Cooper. 'I appreciate that you all agreed to come here to—'

'Save the niceties for yer deaf granny,' Nine-Nails grumbled. 'What the hell's going on? And make it quick; we also have quite a few questions to ask ye.'

Mr Cooper was not taken aback. He was probably used to pugnacious meetings. The man simply cleared his throat and eyed one of the drawers on his side of the desk.

'We received a rather alarming parcel during the night.'

'Alarming?' Trevelyan asked.

Mr Cooper winced, puffed at his cigar for courage, and then produced a little box from the drawer. He placed it on the centre of the desk, and we all stared at the object for a moment.

It was about the size of a fist, the brown packaging paper carelessly rewrapped and tied loosely with twine.

'What's that?' McGray asked, and Mr Cooper scowled.

'I'd rather not touch it again.'

McGray standing behind me and Trevelyan being the senior party, it was down to me to pick up the little parcel and remove the wrapping. It was a cheap, inconsequential tea caddy, neither new nor too old, but when I opened it I could not repress a retch.

'*Oh God!*'

I stretched my arm, so that Nine-Nails and Trevelyan could see the ghastly contents.

Nestled in woodchips, as if it were a precious piece of china, lay a piece of human skin.

Of course branded with the Devil's mark.

24

'How the hell did ye get this?' McGray cried, snatching the caddy from my hand.

Mr Cooper pushed his chair back and turned his head to one side, as if we'd just opened a vial of the bubonic plague. 'As I said, we received it during the night.'

'Who brought it?' McGray asked.

'We don't know. Someone left it in the reception hall when no one was looking.' The man cleared his throat. 'It was addressed to me.'

I still had the wrapping paper. I turned it over and saw the name *Cooper* scribbled in smudged black ink. The straight lines and the childish, yet eerie shape of the letters very much reminded me of the rag we'd found inside MacDonnell's mouth.

I passed it to McGray. He gave it a quick scan and then cast me a meaningful look. He'd noticed the similarity too.

'Is this the same mark you found on that woman?' Trevelyan asked us.

McGray brought it closer to me. 'I'd say so. Frey?'

The first shock gone, I took some time to examine the piece of skin. It had the same greyish hue, the same dryness and the same whitish outline we'd seen in Mrs Brewster's sample. Perhaps the only difference was that this mark was a little more noticeable.

'Yes. No doubt.'

McGray pinched the piece of flesh with his bare fingers and flipped it over. Cooper, Trevelyan and I winced in unison. I saw that the skin was now dry, a wafer-thin layer of fat still attached to it.

'The cuts are very straight,' McGray said. 'Done with a very sharp blade and by someone quite dexterous.'

'Indeed,' I added, and then glanced at the editor. 'But we should discuss this away from snooping eyes and ears.'

'True,' Nine-Nails said. 'These gossip-mongering bastards will go tattling like turdy, twittering twats.'

Mr Copper banged a fist on the desk. '*Excuse me!* I will not allow you to—!'

McGray took a few stomping strides around the desk and planted himself, towering, right in front of the editor. 'Ye won't allow me to *what?*'

Mr Cooper gulped, but then held his stance with reckless courage. 'I am only trying to help you! That is the reason I sent for the police. I could have kept this quiet until we published a roaring—'

'Ye only sent for us 'cause things are getting a wee bit too gruesome and now ye want our protection!' McGray pulled the piece of skin out of the box and dangled it inches from the editor's nose. 'I can tell yer balls have been rattling like two half-farthings in a purse since ye saw this. Cannae blame ye, though. Nobody wants something like this showing up on their desks.'

Mr Cooper's face turned an unsavoury colour, and yet he could not take his eyes from the dead flesh, as if hypnotised by it. Nine-Nails promptly put it back in the caddy, but only because the man seemed to be about to become sick.

'We'll have to take it with us,' McGray said as he handed me the box.

'Please do,' Cooper grumbled, puffing at his cigar as if trying to cleanse a nasty aftertaste.

'And like we told ye before,' McGray said, coming back to our side of the desk, 'we kent nothing about this when we headed here. We came to interrogate ye.'

'Interrogate—?'

'Seems only fitting,' Trevelyan intervened. His tone could not have been firmer.

'And you have just declared how keen you are to help us,' I added.

Mr Cooper swallowed smoke and let it out through his nostrils and mouth, as if his insides were suddenly on fire.

'Very well,' he mumbled, and McGray got right to the point.

'Who's been informing youse about this case? Especially the Devil's mark.'

Mr Cooper looked at the parcel I'd just rewrapped. 'Same as for that thing. We received a note in a sealed envelope. Anonymous.'

'Of course anonymous!' McGray chuckled bitterly.

'Do you simply publish every single ghost tale that reaches your offices?' I asked.

'Of course not, inspectors! We did check the veracity of the basic facts.'

'And what are the basic fuckin' facts for youse?' McGray said. 'That there's an asylum in the city and that the superintendent is a lad called Clouston?'

Mr Cooper grunted. Nine-Nails had not been too far off.

'The asylum was attacked just a couple of hours ago,' I said. 'By people incensed by the stories you and your trade published today. There were smeared walls, broken windows, threatening slurs...'

Mr Cooper chuckled. 'You cannot blame me for the stones thrown by some ignorant thugs, can you?'

'It was irresponsible of you to publish that,' I insisted. 'It was ill-timed, exaggerated and terribly biased. Did you not stop to consider what that story might cause?'

'As I said, it is not my responsibility what others—'

'Och, save it!' McGray snapped. 'I really want to punch ye in the throat right now!'

Mr Cooper snorted. 'The note we received said all newspapers had been notified. Even if I decided not to publish, people would have read it elsewhere.'

'And ye would have lost some precious sales,' Nine-Nails said, all bitterness. 'I ken yer type. Dirty weasels that would pawn their mothers just to get some juicy scandal. And what for? By tomorrow yer stories will be good for nothing but catching bird shite!'

Mr Cooper jumped to his feet, his face livid, but Trevelyan intervened before the man roared.

'*Mr Cooper, sit down!*' He turned to Nine-Nails. 'And McGray, I understand your anger, but we will not debate the ethics of journalism here and now. Understood?'

McGray hissed and clenched his fists, but miraculously managed to compose himself. Mr Cooper smoothed his jacket and sat again.

I gave them a moment to breathe, and then spoke.

'On the other hand, Mr Cooper, you will surely understand it is in your best interest not to publish a word about this parcel.'

'What?' he snapped, and I allowed myself a smile on the side.

'Think about it. This is no different from the ghastly packages that flooded *The Times* in London just eighteen months ago, at the height of the Whitechapel murders. I am sure you will remember. You must have covered that story in detail.'

Mr Cooper made an almost imperceptible nod, and I knew I had him where I needed him.

I pointed at the caddy. 'Fuel people's anxiety and you might start receiving similar correspondence on a daily basis. And we'd hardly be able to trace them or do anything about it.'

Mr Cooper twisted his mouth, biting into his cigar so furiously he nearly split it in two.

'Very well,' he grumbled. 'We can suspend these stories for the time being. But I cannot answer for other newspapers!'

'Fair enough,' McGray said. 'One more thing. Yer informants' notes – d'ye still have those?'

'Yes.'

'Today's shite on Mrs Brewster and the asylum's news too?'

'Yes. We file all our source material.'

'Very well. We're going to need them.'

Mr Cooper chuckled. 'Oh, I'm afraid that won't be possible. We might need them for future reference. Unless you bring an official order, we—'

McGray was going to stomp around the desk again, but Trevelyan raised a hand.

'Mr Cooper, I am the head of police. *I* am the one who would sign such an order. I'd suggest you ask your clerk to fetch them now. Like Mr Frey just said, it is in your best interest.'

The editor crushed his cigar in the ashtray until it was but a clump of smoking flakes.

'I miss your predecessor,' he grumbled. 'Superintendent Campbell would have done things in the proper—'

'*My predecessor*,' Trevelyan snapped, his voice momentarily booming, 'gave you far too much leeway. I cannot believe all the humbug you published last summer about prophesies and banshees at large!'

Even Nine-Nails knew this was not the time to defend the existence of banshees.

'It was precisely that case that cost Campbell his post,' Trevelyan went on, 'and I shall not follow his steps. You *will* surrender those documents. Now. That is the end of it.'

Mr Cooper ground his teeth, but in the end had to oblige. He gave the order to his assistant and, a few minutes later, the man brought us a thin file. McGray snatched it from his hand and I could only smile. I had nearly forgotten what it was like to have a competent superior.

'Anything else?' Mr Cooper said through his teeth.

McGray looked at Trevelyan. 'Can we post one o' the lads here? To look out for rascals trying to deliver unsigned notes or bits o' chopped flesh.'

'I was hoping you'd suggest so,' Mr Cooper admitted, and Trevelyan nodded.

'I shall give the order myself.'

'See?' Nine-Nails mocked. 'It does pay to help us.'

'And I might also send officers to guard other publications,' Trevelyan added. He rose then, and barely nodded to the editor. 'Good day, Mr Cooper.'

'We'll be watching ye,' McGray warned, pointing at him with the file, and we followed the superintendent.

Even as we walked downstairs, McGray peered into the folder.

'It's typed!' he said with a laugh. 'Stupid twats. Typewriters are so damned expensive! There must only be about three in the entire bloody town. It will be even easier to track these!'

It took an instant for the words to settle in, but once they did, my mind whirled and I lost control of my limbs.

Only the night before I'd been reading through typed documents!

The files typed by Clouston.

I tripped and nearly rolled down the stairs. McGray caught me just in time and propped me back on my feet.

'Och, what is it, Frey?'

I was disturbingly close to spitting out everything.

He did not know I'd taken those files. He'd wonder why I needed to pry into Lord Joel's life. He'd ask—

'I – I just lost my footing,' I stuttered. 'I did not sleep well last night.'

McGray gave me a suspicious look, so I speedily shifted the attention off me. 'Can I see those?' I asked, reaching for the messages as we walked on.

I saw the nondescript paper and the slightly smudged characters, and from the few lines I scanned, it was clear that the newspaper had simply reproduced those messages word for word.

'Typewriters are very expensive indeed. I remember reading about that Yankee Mark Twain boasting about his Remington machine. You need to be very wealthy and well-learned to own one.'

'I heard we only ever had one in the City Chambers,' Trevelyan said. 'And that it caused more trouble than good.'

I was about to say that I had been the last person to use it before it broke down for good. I'd found it gathering dust in our basement office. But then McGray asked:

'What sort o' trouble?'

'Typing is a very female trade,' Trevelyan said, and I had to swallow my comment. 'Ladies seem to have far more patience and delicacy to fiddle with those tiny keys. Their wee fingers are better for that too. You can imagine what happened when they brought a female typist into a building bustling with boisterous officers.'

I would have blushed, but then, just as we stepped out of the building and into a soft drizzle, my mind went to Miss Smith. Could she be a trained typist? Could she be the one transcribing Clouston's notes? Had she in fact seen Mrs Brewster's mark at the funeral, and was now alerting the papers? And why? Could she . . . ?

'Wait,' McGray said, halting in the middle of the street, arching a brow. 'They have a typewriter at the asylum! Clouston used to send me typed reports on Pansy's—'

'*There goes Nine-Nails!*' someone shouted from afar, and a few giggles ensued.

McGray was so used to the epithet he did not even bother look for the culprit amidst the crowded road. He simply walked a tad more quickly to the cab that still waited for us.

'These notes must have come from the asylum!' he went on, pulling them from my hand. 'It's so clear! What are the chances that someone owns a sodding typewriter *and* kens all the details of the—'

Another shout came then, closer to us and far more guttural.

'*Burn the mad witch!*'

There were cackles and cheers, but to me the world seemed to go as silent as a grave. I watched how McGray's face changed colour and his hair seemed to stand on end, his eyes burning with a rage that chilled my blood. The dam, I knew, would burst right now.

He bared his teeth, dropped the files to reach for his breast pocket, and in a swift movement pulled out his gun.

'*Who the fuck said that?*' he howled, moving in circles and pointing to the crowd.

There was a panicked outcry. Some people ran and others froze. Some carriages halted and some riders galloped away.

No one laughed anymore. For a moment the only noise was the drizzle on the street's flagstones.

'*Face me!*' McGray roared as he spun on his heels. '*Face me, ye fucking coward!*'

I crouched, irrationally, fearing he might shoot me first.

Trevelyan did the same, raising both palms. I was going to approach McGray, but Trevelyan beckoned me to stay back.

He waited until Nine-Nails partially faced him – close enough to see the superintendent from the corner of his eye, but still pointing the gun in another direction. Trevelyan then took a ginger step towards him.

'It was just some pedlar,' he said softly, for a moment reminding me of Dr Clouston's better days. 'Hardly worth your time.'

McGray went perfectly still, but for a moment did not lower the gun. He breathed like a maddened bull ready to charge into the crowd, and his blue irises looked almost white amidst his bloodshot eyes. The stub of his missing finger quivered right under the trigger.

For a moment I stared at him without blinking. If anyone spoke or shouted, my mind registered nothing. The thought of McGray finally exploding and emptying his gun at random was all I could entertain.

Very slowly, my own panting breath crept into my ears. It grounded me, and I could finally take in the details.

'The – the files!' I stammered without thinking. McGray's eyes moved ever-so-slightly in my direction. 'You – you dropped the files.'

He looked down, at the open folder that lay on the wet flagstones, the pages flapping in the icy breeze.

Trevelyan seized the moment. He reached for McGray's wrist and pulled it down. He whispered something into his ear and gently pushed him into the cab.

I became conscious of people's whispers and noticed a young child staring at the file on the ground, so I rushed to pick it up. I gathered the sheets and ran to the cab, very nearly dropping the poorly wrapped tea caddy containing the piece of flesh.

'Get away,' Trevelyan whispered to me. 'Quickly.'

Even as we hopped on, people were already shouting at us.

'He's as mad as her!'

'Fuckin' peelers!'

The driver did not need instruction, and before I was even settled in my seat, we were already riding down the hilly street.

The cab's side and roof shook with the thuds of the pebbles and rubbish people were throwing at us.

As we rode away, I felt like a hunted heretic in the sixteenth century.

25

McGray bent down and buried his face in his hands, his breath hissing in and out, his entire frame still shaking with rage.

I knew my life depended on giving him space, so I kept silent as the mob's cries were replaced by the usual sounds of the streets. The lawns of East Princes Gardens appeared before us, the green grass incongruously bright below the stormy sky. That drizzle was just the overture to something much worse. I tapped the roof and the driver parked right in front of the fortress-like walls of the Bank of Scotland.

For a long while I simply sat there, perfectly still, my eyes fixed on the window. I did not even dare look at McGray, for his breathing still resounded like bellows.

When I gathered the courage to face him, I found him rubbing his eyelids, perhaps to dab tears of rage before I could see them. It scared me to think that the strain might be turning him mad too. If he reacted like this to the slurs from some cowardly thug, I could only imagine what his reaction might be when Caroline told him about Pansy's true parentage.

The drizzle became heavier as I waited, and I could almost feel the air around me turn colder.

McGray at last straightened his spine, and cleared his throat. 'That cannae happen again, can it?' he said.

I gulped. 'I – I would not advise it.'

He punched the side of the cab, nearly smashing the panel.

'Am leaving this soddin' town, Frey! I swear. As soon as I—'
He bit his lip, perhaps about to say *as soon as I marry*. 'As soon
as this fuckin' case is over. I can take Pansy to Aberdeen or back
to the Orkneys or—' He sighed and covered his brow.

Despite all my bitterness and admitted jealousy – and I
cannot believe I envied the man with the chopped finger, the
mad sister and the tartan trousers – I found it impossible not
to try to console him.

'I think we are tantalisingly close to the truth,' I said in all
honesty. 'These pieces; the slice of skin, these anonymous messages, the missing name in the students' list... I feel they are all
about to fit together. We might be but one witness away.'

McGray stared silently at the evidence scattered across the
cab's seat. He gave a barely perceptible nod, still somewhat
shaken, and I saw the perfect chance to – I'd hate to say *manip-
ulate* him.

'I can continue the investigations on my own if you need
some time,' I said, trying not to sound overly keen. Without
him around I could visit Caroline, tell her about the missing
cloak and gloves; urge her to come clean. I could also confront
Clouston about the typed documents. 'It might do you good to
take the afternoon—'

'Forget it,' he snapped. 'Ye heard what Trevelyan said: Pansy
might nae have an afternoon to spare.' He looked at the evidence
again. 'Where should we start?'

I was asking myself the same question. I wanted to run to the
asylum and demand to see their typewriter. I was also intrigued
by that piece of skin. And there was that list with, potentially,
one missing name. Then again, there were also the practicalities
of—

'We should go to Surgeons' College,' McGray said. 'Before

those inbred imbeciles can claim they don't remember who was there yesterday.'

He banged the roof, shouted the address to the driver, and the cab began to move sluggishly.

'*Quick, for fuck's sake!*' he roared, and it was as if he'd spanked the horse. The driver made a sharp turn and the caddy with the piece of MacDonnell's skin fell off the seat.

'We should take this to the morgue first,' I said as I picked it up. Thankfully, the lid was firmly in place. 'We cannot go about Edinburgh carrying a piece of human flesh.'

'I wouldnae say we *cannae*...'

'McGray! We are just a few streets from the headquar—'

'Och! All right. But we better nae show our faces. Nae after what just happened.'

'I will not argue that,' I said. 'We are fast becoming the most infamous characters in this dreary town.'

In the end we told the driver to park a few streets away from the City Chambers and asked him to fetch Dr Reed. The young man came out to meet us – quite agitated, for people at the headquarters already spoke of nothing but McGray's nearly murderous outburst.

We gave him both the piece of skin and the typed notes for safekeeping, and then rode on.

The drizzle turned into a frank storm, and by the time we made it to the college, the streets were a mess of mud and puddles.

We stepped into the courtyard, our feet squelching on the slabs. Despite the inclement weather, the place was rather crowded, everyone instantly staring at us. Many would remember our loud visit the previous day, others would have read the scandalous news, and the rest simply reacted to McGray's sophisticated fact-finding.

He pulled random students by the collar, barking at them, asking them whether they knew one 'E. Murray'.

'Could you be a tad more discreet?' I grumbled, even if I knew it was too late. One of the students had just called McGray an 'unmitigated brute', with consequences I do not care to describe.

We turned out to be quite lucky. The sixth or seventh young man Nine-Nails assaulted gave us some answers.

'*E.* Murray?' he echoed, nearly messing himself as McGray gripped his lapel. 'Eu – Eustace?'

'I suppose,' McGray snarled.

'He-he – I think I just saw him in the reading room.'

'And where exactly is that?'

I could not quite understand what the young man babbled, but McGray must have, for he pushed the student away and rushed to the main building.

We entered the main hall, leaving a muddy trail behind. Instead of taking the stairs like we'd done the day before, McGray walked on into a long corridor. It led straight to an airy gallery, the walls entirely covered with rosewood panelling and matching bookshelves. There were several rows of lecterns, less than half taken by male and female readers. Only a couple of heads turned in our direction; that is, before Nine-Nails planted himself under the threshold and howled.

'*Eustace?*'

His voice bounced off the walls, and at once half a dozen hands pointed at a lonely chap seated in the furthest corner. Away from the few windows, and clad in a black jacket, the young man looked almost like a crouching raven.

He saw us approach with befuddled eyes, his dipping pen hovering over a stack of paper. He had the tightest ginger curls I have ever seen on a grown man, and more freckles than our cab's mudguard.

'Ye Eustace Murray?' McGray asked, his frame towering right in front the seated student.

'Y-y-yes?' he stammered, momentarily paralysed, and then he jolted and hastened to cover the sheets on the desk. Not before we could steal a glance, though. Young Eustace had not been studying, but had been sketching unicorns, griffins and a very strange creature, half-bird, half-whale.

Nine-Nails shook his head, casting him an ever-so-slightly amused look.

'Makes sense. They picked the idiot of the class.'

'Ehhh? Excuse ... sorry?'

McGray lifted him cleanly by the back of the collar, as if carrying a cocker spaniel.

'Save the eloquence. Percy, bring his shite.'

I quickly gathered Eustace's effects and then followed McGray as he dragged the whimpering young man out of the room. I tried not to look at the many eyes that stared at us while the rest of the students whispered to each other.

People also stared at us in the main hall as McGray took the staircase and climbed briskly to the first floor, poor Eustace stumbling on the steps.

I thought Nine-Nails was heading to the main dissection theatre, but he turned at the last minute and we entered the small tiled room where Professor Grimshaw had washed his hands the day before.

McGray pushed Eustace into the window recess, and the young man crouched against the glass like a cornered cat. Behind him, the rain battered the pane.

Without tables or desks around, I had to put Eustace's belongings in the porcelain basin, now dry. He looked at his books and papers with utmost worry.

'We'll give ye yer hobgoblin shite back,' Nine-Nails said.

'Half your own possessions fall under that category, McGray,' I muttered, leafing through the collection of bizarre art.

'We just want ye to tell us the truth,' Nine-Nails said, ignoring my comment, and then he pulled the crumpled list out of his pocket. He unfolded it and waved it in front of Eustace's face. 'Ye were at yesterday's lecture, when we came to seize that corpse. Ye wrote yer name here, right?'

'I – I did,' Eustace mumbled, and then raised his voice to be heard amidst the drumming of the rain. 'But I had nothing to do with those bodies!'

McGray grinned. 'Ahh, so ye ken there's something wrong with them!'

'Of course! We all do, but we're told not to ask questions. We show up, look at the professors' methods, do our own dissections later on … the specimens are already here. As long as we pay our bench fees we don't—'

'Och, shut it now,' McGray cut in and held up the list. 'Look at the bloody list. Yer name appears twice.' Eustace tried to take the sheet, but McGray pulled it away. '*Look*, I said.'

Eustace leaned closer to the sheet, squinting.

'There and there,' McGray told him, pointing at the names. 'How did that happen, laddie?'

Eustace was open-mouthed. He went pale, which only made his freckles all the more noticeable.

'I – I don't know!' he muttered. 'This *is* my hand. Here, the first entry. But not that one. You – you can compare them to my notes!' And he pointed at his stack of belongings.

I pulled out a sheet with a cringe-worthy poem woven around the drawing of a sinuous kelpie, and McGray held the two sheets together. The shaky, spidery hand was unmistakable, but Nine-Nails still pretended to be unconvinced for a moment.

'I didn't write the second one, I swear!' Eustace cried, as if pleading to an angry mother. I realised he must be but a couple of years younger than our Dr Reed.

'Then who did?' McGray snapped, handing me back the sketch.

'I – I – How am I supposed to know?'

McGray chuckled. 'Yer clever, are nae ye?

'Ehh?'

'Well, maybe nae *too* clever, but clever enough to study in this stuck-up college.'

'Erm...'

'Read the list again. One o' yer sodding classmates will be missing from there. Ye must remember who was present; it was only yesterday.'

'Or you might recognise the handwriting,' I added. 'From your sketches, you seem to have a good eye. You'd be a fair anatomical illustrator.'

Eustace looked at me in awe, as if nobody had ever paid him a single compliment. McGray had to shake the list closer to the young man's face to bring him back into focus.

He scanned the names quickly and then raised his scanty ginger brows, his irises suddenly still.

Again, McGray smiled. 'Ye found the needle?'

Eustace opened his mouth, then closed it. Opened it again – and then a constricted sound came from the bottom of his throat.

'*Tell me!*' McGray growled.

Eustace crouched further, his back pressing against the windowpane. I took a few steps closer and held him by the shoulder, fearing he might break the glass and fall to his death.

'What is the matter?' I asked, even if I already knew the answer.

'They'll know it was I who told you!' Eustace whimpered. 'They'll make my life miserable—'

'Even more?' McGray said.

'*Yes!*' Eustace cried. 'They already pick on me and call me names. Now they'll ruin my future too!'

McGray gave me a push and seized him by the lapel. 'I'll ruin yer fucking *face* if ye don't talk!'

Eustace, on the verge of tears, let out high-pitched whimpers.

'McGray, let him go for a moment,' I said.

McGray snorted impatiently, but in the end obliged.

I leaned closer to the young man, my hands on my knees. I must have been around his age when I first left home – though I was sure I had *never* looked that helpless.

'I know how things work at a surgeons' college,' I said softly. 'Believe me. I went to Oxford and—'

'How can ye manage to work that into every sodding conversation?' McGray said.

I took a deep breath. 'As you well said, everyone saw us seize you. They will harass you with questions anyway.'

Eustace gulped, clearly not having thought of that.

'But if you talk, we can protect you,' I said.

'How?'

'The sooner we track these resurrectionists, the sooner we will be able to arrest them. This case in particular is not only about desecration of graves, but also murder. Whoever is behind this, no matter how high up, will not be able to get back to torment you or to ruin your prospects.'

Eustace looked sideways, his lower lip still quivering.

'We can even take you somewhere safe,' I added.

'*Can we?*' McGray cried, and I gave him a loud shush.

'Yes, we can,' I told Eustace, and saw how his eyes glowed with a rage accumulated through months – *years* – of bullying. Again he moved his lips, as if yearning to speak.

'It is your turn to give them what they deserve,' I whispered.

For the first time, Eustace looked straight into my eyes. And he mumbled.

'Mar – Martin.'

I nearly gasped with excitement. I sensed McGray getting closer, craning his neck over my shoulder.

'Martin who?' I pressed.

For a moment the only sound we heard was the pounding of the rain on the window as Eustace ground his teeth and gathered breath.

We did not expect the name he finally gave us.

'Martin Pratt.'

26

'*What!*' McGray shouted, a combination of anger, astonishment and elation on his face.

My mind, too, was reeling. I pulled back for a moment, while Eustace's stare went nervously from McGray to me.

'Pratt, you said?' I asked, and Eustace nodded. 'Do you know if that could be a son – or a relation of – George Pratt? The procurator?'

Eustace frowned. 'I – I think so. He does like to boast that his father works at the courts.'

'Makes perfect sense!' McGray cried. He was about to punch the wall, but the hard tiles made him think twice. 'That's why he came to threaten us! He must ken it wouldnae take us long to track his brat!'

'Indeed,' I said, and then turned to Eustace. 'Is Martin Pratt one of the students in charge of receiving specimens?'

He shook his head. 'I don't know if he receives them. But I do know he is in charge of cleaning them sometimes. And he is a favourite of Professor Grimshaw.'

I let out a sigh, not of triumph, but of relief. 'Good. We are getting there. Eustace, would you be prepared to state this in court?'

The young man would not have a chance to answer, for just then a booming voice shouted behind our backs.

'Get *out!*'

It was Professor Grimshaw, as if summoned by the mere mention of his name. He was panting with anger, his face red and his pigtail tied as tightly as the strings of a fiddle. A couple of tall, brawny students stood behind him.

'*Are ye stupid?*' McGray yelled back. 'We're the fucking police!'

They argued on, and as they shouted, I traced a line in my head: Grimshaw ordering the bodies, Martin Pratt and his late accomplice sourcing them wherever they could; one of his contacts being Dr Harland at the asylum... How convenient it would be, for all of them, if the blame were to fall on McGray's sister.

'I must protect my students,' Grimshaw snarled. 'Even the sad dimwits like Murray here.'

Eustace looked at his professor with sheer panic. I gathered his books and handed them to him.

'There's a cab waiting for us by the main gate. Tell the driver Nine-Nails McGray asked you to wait for us there.'

Eustace attempted to put on a brave face, which only made me feel sorrier for him. Grimshaw cast him a sneering look, and the two students shoved him and hissed slurs into his ears as he passed between them.

Once he was gone, Grimshaw put his fists on his hips, his chest swollen with authority.

'You need to ask questions, you come to me. Do you under—?'

'*Piss off!*' McGray barked. 'Who the blazing hell d'ye think yer talking to?'

Professor Grimshaw smiled insolently. 'To the mad inspector who randomly points his gun at women and children.'

McGray and I opened our mouths in almost perfect synchrony.

That had happened less than an hour ago! How fast gossip can spread. More effectively than an infection.

I'd not finished the thought when McGray moved like the wind and threw Grimshaw a mighty punch, all his frustration and rage condensed into that one blow. I could swear I heard the crack of bones, and the professor fell backwards, clashed against the nearby wall and dropped to the floor like a rag doll.

His brawny students stepped forwards, but McGray had already unsheathed his gun.

'*That mad enough for ye?*' he shouted, aiming alternatively at the three men.

Grimshaw sat up clumsily and glared at Nine-Nails, wiping blood from the corner of his mouth.

'*This is an outrage!*' he growled, his eyes bloodshot.

'What ye talking about?' McGray said. 'Ye just tripped. I have a witness.' He nodded at me. 'Now – where's that sod Pratt?'

The two students looked nervously at each other, and then at professor Grimshaw. He simply shook his head, kneading his swelling jaw.

'We'll find him,' McGray said, 'even if youse—'

We heard screams coming from the courtyard. I looked out the window and saw a thin man, clad in a heavy overcoat and a wide hat, elbowing people as he ran to the main gate.

'Someone is fleeing!' I cried, and McGray sprinted to the door. The taller, more brutish student blocked our way.

'Och, ye twat,' McGray grunted. '*Move!*' And he pointed his gun at the man's brow.

The chap only grinned, as defiant and arrogant as professor Grimshaw. 'Do you want to pass?' he mocked. 'Then *shoot* me!'

McGray laughed in earnest, his shoulders shaking, and then lowered the gun and did precisely that.

The shot boomed in the tiny room, overheard throughout the college, and there was a general cry from the gardens. The bullet hit the young man in the foot and he fell to his knees, squealing like a piglet. McGray pushed him sideways to make his way to the door. I went after him and we ran towards the stairs.

'*You shot a college student!*' I screeched.

'Nah. He assaulted me first. Ye were a witness!'

We rushed down the stairs, nearly skidding on our own muddy tracks as we crossed the main hall. People shouted and moved aside as they saw us come, and we stormed into the courtyard, to be instantly lashed by the thick rain.

We ran through the arch that led to the streets, to find our driver trying to keep his restless horse under control.

Eustace was looking out of the cab's window, his ginger locks now drenched.

'Where did he go?' McGray cried, and Eustace, open-mouthed, pointed south.

'There. Turned into Hill Pla—'

McGray was already running there. He turned left at the first corner and I ran after him.

We entered a narrow street that led to a small square, a neat lawn at its centre, surrounded by elegant townhouses and a little church.

Instantly my eyes fell on a dark, lonely figure on the opposite side of the square: the cloaked man, desperately trying to unlock the low wrought-iron fence that led to one of the house's basements.

'*Freeze!*' McGray shouted.

The man looked in our direction, dropped his keys and then ran towards the church. The wind blew his hat away and I saw a perfectly bald scalp, except for a flare of blond hair on his forehead.

As McGray ran after him I went to pick up the keys. When I looked up the man had disappeared, and McGray was just entering the small temple.

I ran there, already drenched and panting, and through the small Gothic gate.

I had to halt, the place so dim it took me a moment to get accustomed to the low light.

After a few blinks in the utter silence I made out the lines of pews, the ornate pulpit and the raised altar. The air was laden with the scents of incense and myrrh, and the hall was lit by countless candles.

I took a step forwards but McGray's shout made me jump. 'Stay at the gate!'

Only then did I see Nine-Nails, striding briskly towards a cluster of candles. He seized one and began inspecting the benches, row by row.

'*Ye better come out now!*' he roared, his voice bouncing time and again under the high ceilings.

I tensed my legs, planting myself as firmly as I could by the narrow gate, and scanned the grim nave from left to right.

I felt my heart thumping, the rain splashing on the back of my legs, and saw my breath steaming into the dark nave. I twitched with each jolt of McGray's body, ready to see a black shape emerge from the shadows and pounce at me.

Only it came from behind.

A mighty blow to my kidneys made me howl in pain and I dropped to my knees. My palms hit the cold marble floor and the set of keys slid away. I thought someone else shouted, but it was the echo of my own voice.

I looked back, my eyes tearing from the lingering pain, and saw the misty silhouette of a tall man darting away across the square's lawn. Grimshaw's other brawny student!

I heard stomping steps and McGray pulled me by the arm. 'Ye all right?'

I grunted and winced from the pain, but before I could answer I saw something behind Nine-Nails. A moving shadow.

'McGray!' I cried, pointing at the altar.

He looked over his shoulder, and we both saw the glint of shiny boots jumping over the altar's rail.

McGray sprinted there at once, shouting profanities and pointing his gun.

I scrambled to my feet, saw the keys and seized them before darting forwards, each stride sending stabs of pain up my torso.

Amid the candles I saw the same cloaked man, his glimmering skull disappearing through an ornate door.

McGray also jumped over the rail, the carved wood cracking under his weight, and I lost sight of him too.

I made it to the altar just as two shots resounded throughout the nave. The echoes bounced in my ears as I crossed the rail and rushed to the darkened door.

Only once I'd crossed the threshold did I realise my recklessness, storming in there unarmed.

It was a small, dim sacristy, very similar in size to Reverend Hunter's, only with a line of mullioned Gothic windows that looked onto the street.

There was nobody there. The door in front of me was wide open, flapping in the wind and letting in the lashing rain.

I ran outside, back into the storm. I looked left and right, and there I saw McGray, running like the wind after a black cab. He shot at it just as the horse turned around the corner. The bullet hit the wheels and there was a burst of splinters, but the cab still rode on, back to the small square.

Nine-Nails roared madly and chased them. I followed him as fast as I could, but still lost him momentarily around the corner. By the time I turned right, McGray was already on the other side of the square, the cab nowhere to be seen.

I saw him stop at the corner, where Hill Street joined the main road in front of the college. We'd run a full circle. McGray stomped and growled, passers-by quickly moving away from him.

When I caught up with him, completely out of breath, I understood his frustration.

At least a dozen black carriages and cabs rode along that muddy street.

'*Fuck!*' he shouted, jerking the gun in plain sight of the passers-by. Some people yelped and ran away. '*Always the fucking same!*'

I took a few troubled breaths, pressing my pained torso while the rain soaked us to the marrow.

'Not – quite – the same,' I panted, and raised the set of little bronze keys, a smile growing on my face. 'Now we have access to his lair.'

27

We did not take risks this time. McGray guarded the entrance to the townhouse's basement while I called for two constables. Eustace was still waiting for us, so I told the driver to take him to the City Chambers with a message for Trevelyan: the young man was likely to be a crucial witness, so we could not risk leaving him to the mercy of his professor and angry colleagues.

I returned to Hill Square followed by two peelers armed with truncheons, and as soon as he saw us approach, McGray unlocked the fence and rushed down the steps. The rain had continued, so by this point we were as soaked as if plunged into the sea, our boots begrimed with mud.

McGray unlocked the door with the other key, pushed the door open and burst into the dwelling, his gun at the ready.

The room was dark and damp, the smell of saltpetre mixed with stagnated sweat and stale liquor.

'Blatantly a student's flat,' I mumbled after a quick sniff. McGray was already rummaging in the semi-darkness.

One of the constables struck a match and the faint glow was just enough to show us a nearby writing table, crammed with all manner of books, papers, quills, pieces of days-old bread and a collection of grimy glasses, all with dry crusts of red wine. I noticed a sooty oil lamp and passed it to the officer to light it up. We then had an uncompromised view of one of the most disgusting bachelor's pigsties I have ever had the chance to see.

It was a single room dwelling, every square inch as crammed and disarrayed as the writing table. The bed was a stinking jumble, guarded by a human skeleton hanging from a hook. It had an expensive white scarf around the scapula, and a rather fashionable bowler hat perched on the skull. It very much reminded me of the chambers of the well-to-do Oxford students – especially the heap of crumpled clothes accumulated next to a stack of neatly folded shirts, fresh from the launderer.

'Here,' McGray said, standing by the opposite wall. 'Bring the lamp.'

The officer did so, shedding light on a collection of unpaid bills pinned to the wall and used as targets for dart playing. McGray ripped one off.

'They're all from liquor merchants and launderers and cleaners,' Nine-Nails said, and when he looked at me he was smiling from ear to ear. 'All addressed to Martin Pratt.'

I sighed. 'I hate to disappoint you, but that proves nothing, other than the fact that he resides here. Playing at being *independent*.'

'Don't forget the list,' McGray insisted. 'And the wee Pratt penning a false name and then running away from us.'

'He can always claim he was afraid that you'd single him out, given the rivalry between his father and you. And the fact that you've just shot someone...'

'There!' McGray interjected, pointing at a corner. 'New, muddy boots! Like the prints we found at the—'

'And nobody else in Edinburgh has muddy boots.'

'Och, for God's sake, Frey, d'ye want me to put a hole in yer trotters too?'

'I am simply telling you the arguments they will surely use

at court. We need to find something totally and unquestionably damning. Nothing less will do.'

McGray shook his head and we began the search. Though it was not a vast residence, we still found all manner of condemnatory items – lewd magazines, female undergarments, absinthe and even a few jars of laudanum, but nothing that spelled out resurrectionist.

'Nae even a soddin' spade,' McGray grunted while still stooped over the writing table and rummaging through the mess of books.

'He left his tools at the graveyard,' I said. 'Otherwise he might have brought them here.'

McGray straightened his back and let out a tired sigh. A moment later he raised an eyebrow, and I could tell he was concocting something. He turned to the officers.

'Can youse go to the wee church and see if there's anything odd there? We'll join youse in a moment.'

Clearly he wanted them away. The constables left the lamp on the table, and as soon as they shut the door, McGray came closer.

'I have an idea,' he whispered. 'Yer right, there's nothing here. I say we secure this place, claim we found "evidence", and then summon Martin for questioning.'

I frowned. 'Even if we have nothing against him?'

'Aye. He's clearly nae the sharpest knife in the drawer. He tried to "escape" and led us straight to his sodding home! And look at his shite!' He lifted a copy of the college's gazette. Martin had embellished the engraving of the professor on the front page with a drawn moustache, girlish curls and specs for the blind. 'I say we summon him, tell him we have conclusive proof against him and make him shit himself with fright until he sings the truth. I can break him. Ye ken I can.'

I pondered for a moment.

'It is not your brutality that I question. You do realise it is a dangerous tactic.'

'It is a dangerous time.'

I raised my chin, thinking. 'At least that would force Martin to come back. We have no way of knowing where he has gone, but if we issue a formal summons, he will *have* to come to us. Pratt senior knows how the courts work; he will know that refusing to attend will speak volumes against his son, regardless of the kind of evidence we have.'

McGray smiled again. 'That sounds promising!'

I stroked my chin, unable to share his optimism.

Pratt would also know all the legal tricks in the book. He'd be able to delay things and to prepare his silly brat. I wished my father were still around. He would have been able to outsmart Pratt's every move.

'We better get Trevelyan to sign that summons as soon as possible,' McGray said. He made his way to the door but then stopped. 'Go fetch the lads. One o' them will have to stay here until we can secure the place properly. I'll guard the door in the meantime.'

He raised his gun as he spoke, and I pitied any poor wretch that might want to break in.

We failed to find Trevelyan at the City Chambers (ours was by no means the only case on his desk), so all we could do was leave him an urgent message and beg him to meet us first thing in the morning.

McGray invited me to dine on 'neeps 'n' tatties' at the Ensign Ewart. I declined, not only because of the dire prospect of eating grease-dripping spuds among Scotland's most vulgar drunkards, but also because I still had much to ponder.

I went to the morgue to talk to Dr Reed, but he had already gone home. At least he'd had the foresight to leave the caddy with MacDonnell's skin in a bucket with ice. I took the brown paper in which it had been wrapped, and one of the typed sheets, and made my way back to the Palace Hotel.

After a much-needed bath – I'd been sodden since our little chase – I gathered the new pieces of evidence and went through them while indulging in claret and roast chicken (an expensive treat).

I arranged the typed sheet next to the brown paper, and tore a few pages from my notebook where I scribbled the other pieces of the puzzle: the rag in MacDonnell's mouth, his piece of missing skin, the mark of the Devil on both corpses, the statements of Miss Smith, the threats from Dr Harland...

I needed a sip of claret just to gather my thoughts.

I first looked at the piece of skin and the typed document, delivered to the same place but also utterly contradicting.

Why type a letter and then address the parcel by hand? It seemed illogical even for someone as thoughtless as Pratt Junior – who, I was almost certain, had been the one who'd sent the skin. He must have cut it out while he was preparing the corpses. From what young Eustace had said, Martin Pratt would have been the last man to handle the body before it was sent to the crowded lecture room.

Perhaps Harland had sent the typed notes and Martin had sent the skin? As a joint effort to incriminate Pansy?

'It makes sense,' I whispered. By sending the skin to the press, with handwriting that matched something we'd found at the asylum, they'd be throwing the scent away from themselves.

And if my musings were correct and they had indeed reproduced the writing on the rag used to suffocate MacDonnell...

I gasped.

They had done it! They had seen the rag before it went into poor MacDonnell's mouth.

I felt a sudden wave of excitement, but it faded as soon as it came.

How to prove it?

I had a long sip of claret and picked up the page. The characters were smudged and the corners were blackened too. That was a carbon copy, like the ones Clouston used to send to McGray. He – or Miss Smith, or whoever typed them – would simply stack alternative sheets of white and carbon paper as they typed, instantly producing reports in triplicate.

Again, that made perfect sense. The story had reached all the papers on the same day. Whoever informed them would have produced all the copies in one go. Those were lengthy accounts, impossible to copy so many times within such a short period of time.

They spoke of a methodical, very organised mind. The entire operation would have been planned very carefully.

I sighed in frustration.

All these pieces lay in front of me, all those clear clues and connections, and yet we did not have any physical evidence to accuse anybody.

They, on the other hand, might do already.

The thought of Caroline's gloves and cloak came to mind, and I could not repress a loud growl.

Nine-Nails might have seemed quite optimistic, but he did not know as much as I did.

Neither did Caroline.

I realised I'd not yet told her that Harland had seen her and thought she was Pansy. After all, I'd only spoken to the blasted young doctor that very day. It was as if time kept stretching, simply to take delight in torturing me.

Caroline must hear the facts, and soon. Once she knew, she would not delay telling McGray the entire truth, and then we could finally tackle the case together.

It was too late to visit her, so I called a footman and paid him handsomely to deliver her a sealed note at once.

I shall call on you tomorrow morning, first thing.
Be available. Situation truly dire.

I also ordered more coal for my fireplaces, for the room appeared to be getting colder and colder. Initially, I thought it was my nerves, but when I looked out the window, glass of claret in hand, I saw that the windowpanes were encrusted with ice, the entire city swathed in thick fog. And the clouds above, lit by the city's many lights, swirled like the contents of an inverted cauldron.

More than one storm would break the next day. And our lives would change forever.

Part Two

Some books are lies frae end to end,
And some great lies were never penn'd...

Robert Burns,
Death and Doctor Hornbook

28

The explosion resounded thunderously all across the chasm, a billowing ball of fire and smoke ascending elegantly into the dawning sky, filling the air with the sulphurous stench of dynamite.

Lady Anne could momentarily feel the blast; a gentle wave pushing the air and bringing an almost pleasant warmth to the gloomy February morning. The snowflakes were momentarily disturbed, before they went on fluttering calmly around her.

The septuagenarian stared at the spectacle from the other side of Craigleith Quarry. She stood at the very edge of the cliff, her silver and ebony cane planted proudly on the rock.

She saw how a mammoth boulder, the size of a tenement building, split off the quarry's wall. Sluggishly at first but soon gathering momentum, it plummeted into the darkened depths of the abyss. The noise that came then was surprisingly similar to the thunders that kept grumbling in the sky.

Lady Anne looked at the ever-growing crater and the flimsy-looking scaffolding precariously attached to the rock. Against the ancient sediments, layer upon layer deposited over millennia, those scaffolds looked like brittle twigs, and the steam-powered pulleys, though state-of-the-art, looked like tiny bobbins puffing cigarette smoke. For a moment she pitied the many unfortunate men, all covered in soot and dirt, who worked down there from dawn to dusk, even on those icy winter days. The quarry's previous owner had warned her there would be at least a couple of deaths every season, no matter what.

She uncorked her silver flask – difficult with her black chamois gloves on – and had a sip of brandy. As she savoured the burn of the spirit, she wondered which one of those wretched workers would be the unlucky first.

She heard horses hooves and carriage wheels behind her. When she turned she saw the now-familiar carriage, its roof still dusted with fresh snow accumulated during the night – nothing compared to what the skies still had in store.

The driver halted and the door opened with a kick. George Pratt alighted, stumbling on the slushy ground, and walked hesitantly towards Lady Anne. He did not get too close, though, staring fearfully at the deep void.

'Don't be ridiculous,' Lady Anne said, reading his fear.

Pratt held his bowler hat in place and took only the strictly necessary steps.

'Has it been done?' Lady Anne demanded.

'Yes, ma'am. All is in place, but—' He stopped, unable to take his eyes from the quarry. Even in the inclement weather, a bead of sweat rolled down the man's temple.

Lady Anne sighed impatiently and walked away from the cliff, the spiky feathers of her elaborate headdress flapping in the wind.

'But what?' she asked as they headed to their carriages.

'They're getting so close,' Pratt whispered.

'But of course they are! You're all a pathetic pack of fools.'

Pratt took off his hat, his smooth scalp shining with perspiration.

'Oh, pull yourself together!' Lady Anne snapped. 'Things

should unfold by themselves at this point. *If*, of course, you have done everything as I told you.'

Pratt drew out a handkerchief and mopped his sweat.

'I have, ma'am.'

Lady Anne sneered. 'I hope so. You are the one who has the most to lose.' That was not necessarily true, but she'd rather have him believe so. Fear was the best motivation. 'What is it?' she asked, seeing the man biting his lips. How could he keep his composure at the courts? His entire career must be one pathetic act.

'Speak!' she cried, and Pratt jolted.

'They've been to my son's chambers,' he spluttered.

Lady Glass stood motionless for a moment, her lips, moistened with liquor, slightly parted.

'What do they have?'

'I – I don't know.'

'What *could* they have?'

Pratt's lips again trembled. 'My son – he's not quite sure.'

'Why, you blasted *idiots*!'

Her last shout was like a whip, the echoes travelling across the quarry. She raised her cane, wishing she could lash the man to a pulp. '*How could you botch things up like this?*'

She rushed to her carriage, sticking the cane on the ground as if it were Pratt's tender parts, and nodded to her footman. The man at once opened the door and helped her in.

'Hop in,' she told Pratt as she got settled in the seat. 'It is time for more drastic measures.'

She covered her knees with a woollen blanket, and as she had another sip of brandy for warmth, the very earth shook gently. Another explosion. Again Lady Anne felt the warp in the air an instant before she heard the blast and, a moment later, the wind also brought the desperate wails of a wounded man.

Lady Anne sighed.

So there was the first…

29

As instructed, the porter woke me long before sunrise, so I'd have time to dress. I was just adjusting my Ascot tie when he rushed in again.

'You have a visitor, sir,' he said, panting.

'A visitor?'

'Yes. A young lady. She is waiting for you downstairs. Said it was an urgent matter.'

'Indeed,' I answered. I donned my black jacket and dashed out.

Once in the main breakfast parlour I was met by an arrogant maître d', who led me past the marble tables with the stiffest upper lip.

'Ellen Terry stayed here last summer, sir,' he said in the most condescending manner. 'Did you know that?'

'I may have heard,' I said curtly as I spotted Caroline at one of the furthest tables. Only a few other guests were already there, their keen eyes following me while they pretended to butter their toast.

'Miss Ardglass!' I said with a bow. 'I see you got my message.'

'I did,' she said as I sat down. 'You sounded so serious I could not wait for you to visit, so here I am.' She had a steaming cup of tea in front of her, but she had not touched it, and from the dark rings around her eyes, I could tell she had hardly slept. 'Coffee for Mr Frey,' she told the maître d'. '*Now*, if you please.'

The man bowed and walked away, not even attempting to hide a sly smirk.

Caroline lowered her voice, glaring at him. 'You should have seen the faces he pulled when I told him I was here to see you.'

'I can imagine,' I said. A young lady calling on a man at his hotel would be seen as most scandalous. 'Did you come here on your own?'

'Why, of course not. They made Joan wait in the servants' rooms.'

'Indeed.' I said, suddenly growing anxious. 'I must admit – I wish we could have had this conversation at your apartments.'

'I shan't make a scene,' she assured me, but her stare went blank when I told her Dr Harland had seen her. I could almost see the desolation spread on her skin, her cheeks losing all colour as the news sank in.

The moments that followed felt like an eternity. I held my breath, wishing I could do something – anything – to ease the blow. At a public place, however, I could not even reach for her hand.

'Of course,' she mumbled at last. 'Of course he saw me! How stupid, *how stupid* I was to think he had not!'

Her shrill voice caught the attention of the other guests. I saw the maître d' approach, bringing the coffee himself.

'Get away!' I barked at him. When I looked back at Caroline, she had buried her face in her hands. I could only see her quivering lower lip, her chest swelling like bellows.

I did not want to add to her grief, but I had no choice.

'There is also –' I gulped – 'the issue of your cloak and gloves.'

Caroline looked up at once. 'What? Please don't tell me...'

'We could not find them,' I said before I lost my resolve.

'Oh God, it cannot be!'

'Miss Smith searched the room in my presence. I looked under the bed myself. She also checked the laundry. Nothing.'

Her head swayed, as if stricken by sudden vertigo, and for a moment I thought she would drop to the floor. She pressed both hands on the edge of the table, the tension on her knuckles visible through her black mittens.

'I'll be the very reason of her downfall,' she mumbled, and then her tone became darker. 'The Ardglass curse; the family curse. Of course it has touched her too.'

'Miss Ardglass, you know there is no such thing as—'

'Can you doubt it now?' she blurted out, and all the heads in the parlour turned to her. Caroline snorted, her shock becoming anger.

'We have no idea who could have taken them,' I said, lowering my voice. 'For all we know, one of the other inmates might have sneaked in that night, during the racket. Or—'

Caroline shut her eyes. 'Don't try to play things down for me. I understand very well what might happen now.'

She stared at the tea service, hatred brewing in her expression, as if the very existence of such trivial things as tea strainers and painted china were an insult to her misfortunes.

I had to take a deep breath to deliver the last part of my message.

'Miss Ardglass ... you must tell McGray.'

I said it slowly and almost in a whisper, fearing this might finally break her apart. Instead, Caroline bared her teeth, once more looking a good deal like her grandmother.

'Are you insane?'

'I fear McGray might confront Dr Harland. He nearly did so yesterday. And the man will, in turn, tell everyone all he – all he *thinks* he knows. He has only remained quiet to protect his own skin. This entire situation is like a house of cards.'

'Can you not persuade Adolphus to keep away from that man Harland? Come up with some reason to—?'

I shook my head, still wincing a little every time I heard her say *Adolphus*. 'By now you must know him better than I do. He can be a train wreck. Also, investigating has been cumbersome to say the least, having to conceal crucial facts and not being able to discuss things with Nine-Nails. We simply cannot protect –' I only mouthed '*your sister*' – 'without sharing all the facts.'

Caroline sat back and let out the most tired of sighs. 'I had intended to tell him,' she mumbled after a while. 'Someday – well in the future.' A smile flashed across her face, gone before I'd been fully conscious of it. 'I imagined I'd have to draw him a family tree to show him we're not related!'

'He is not so terribly dim-witted, is he?'

We must have laughed together for a mere couple of seconds, but even that seemed to lift some of the weary load off my shoulders.

'Leave it with me,' she said, already standing up and readying herself to leave.

'It cannot be delayed,' I insisted.

'I know, I know. I will find the moment. I—' She briefly looked at the emerald ring I still forced myself to wear. She still did not know it had been a present from Pansy and McGray's mother. 'Thank you for everything.'

She blushed slightly, an undeniable look of guilt on her face, and turned on her heels to dash away. The maître d' gave her a sardonic bow, and she finally exploded.

'Are you insolent *and* inept? Go and fetch Mr Frey's coffee! *Now!*'

I laughed unabashedly, and a few minutes later, as I sipped my well-earned coffee, I pictured how apocalyptic the domestics between Caroline and Nine-Nails would inevitably be.

I might turn out to be the luckiest one of the three.

30

Reed intercepted me as soon as I set foot in the City Chambers.

'Mr Frey! So good that I've found you. I need you to approve something.'

'Me? Has Inspector McGray not arrived yet?'

'Oh yes, but the superintendent called him and they've not returned. May I show you?'

'Yes,' I said, and followed him down to the ice-cold morgue. The moment he opened the door I perceived the sweetish pong of decay.

'Those corpses need to be buried, sir,' he said, pointing at the tables where the covered bodies of MacDonnell and Mrs Brewster lay. 'They are becoming a risk to myself and others.'

'Despite these cold days?' I asked as I covered my nose with my hankie.

'Indeed, sir. I can show you how they've—'

'Hardly necessary,' I said just when he was about to lift Mrs Brewster's shroud. 'Release them, only—' I snorted, remembering I had not yet inspected the lady's coffin. And with McGray surely sorting out the summons at present, I might not have time to do so until the following day. 'Tell that man, Reverend Hunter, that if I do not meet him today, he can proceed with

256

the burial, but he must keep the old coffin for us to inspect. I shall reimburse him if he needs to get a new one.'

'And the man? I understand his family...'

'Send him to Reverend Hunter too and ask him to take care of the man's burials. Just make sure you send word to the asylum, so his daughters know where he has been taken. I do not want any of the suspects laying hands on him again.'

'Yes, sir.'

'Is that all?' I asked, seeing that Reed had the microscope all set on a nearby table. Next to it was the small bucket of ice with the ominous tea caddy, and also a porcelain dish covered with a white cloth.

'I just looked at this new sample,' Reed said. He lifted the cloth and I saw the ghastly piece of MacDonnell's skin, now stretched and with a neat cut running through one of the mark's edges. 'I compared this skin with the corpse's. It definitely belongs to him. And I also compared it with the mark on the lady. Would you like to see?'

'Oh, indeed,' I said. I rushed to the microscope and took a long look.

It was clearly the thicker skin of a younger person, but that was the only difference. There were the grey hues and the deep stain, spread all across the dermis and reaching the layers of white fat.

'Very similar, are they not?' Reed said while I moved the slide under the lens.

'Indeed. Do you still have Mrs Brewster's samples?'

'Yes. I'll fetch them.'

A moment later he was back with the set of prepared slides, neatly arranged in a box full of ice.

'Thankfully, it is still winter,' he said. 'Ice is really expensive in the summer months.'

'And the hotels hoard it to cool oysters and champagne,' I added.

We compared the samples, both of us looking alternatively at them. After a few rounds I reached for a nearby stool and sat to ponder, while Reed sketched the new findings.

'In both cases it seems that the stained areas have corrupted a little more quickly,' I mused. '*Almost as if coming from within*, you said the last time.'

'Yes,' Reed answered. 'But there were no marks to suggest anything had been administered through a cut, or even injected.'

Another voice came to mind; McGray telling me the city's children feared their flesh would 'rot off' if I touched them.

I foolishly pictured the Devil's hooves doing precisely that – spreading corruption everywhere they trod.

'It does seem to sprout from inside,' I mumbled, 'and yet it is so well defined... like a true *print*.'

Reed was running his pencil on the sketch, attempting to reproduce the fading hues of grey.

'Are you sure the lady's mark only appeared while she was buried?' he asked me, and I could only sigh.

'Three different people have vouched for that. I may not trust them individually, but put together... I cannot see how they'd all tell me the same lie.'

I leaned closer to MacDonnell's sample and ran my fingertips just over the Devil's mark, following its contours but not daring to touch it.

'Clearly applied after death,' I said, 'hence no swelling or reddening. And if these sections of the skin were rotting more quickly... it is almost as if it was –' I felt a prickle on the back of my neck – 'partially digested.'

'Like the acids in the stomach do?' Reed asked.

'Yes, but – again, an acid burn would appear instantly, not the morning after. It is almost as if this has done the exact opposite of what we would expect it to.'

My hand went still. I held my breath and looked up at once. Reed did too.

'The opposite—' he muttered.

We both jolted at the same time, as if the obviousness of the matter had hit us in the head like a mallet.

'Of course!' I mumbled. '*Of course!* This must have been done with—'

'Inspector Frey!' someone cried at the door, and Reed and I shouted in unison, '*Not now!*'

'*Dammit!*' Reed added, and poor Constable McNair had to take a step back.

'Sorry, sir,' he panted, 'but you must come at once. The super—'

We heard shouting coming from the staircase, McGray's inimitable voice uttering a torrent of vulgarities that made us all blush. Even McNair.

'All right,' I grunted as I pulled out my small notebook and began scribbling. 'I suppose you can conduct a test to show at court. Do you have other corpses you might take skin samples from? These will not do anymore.'

'I – I think so.'

'If not, get some pork from any butcher. It is standard—'

'Standard for tests. I know, sir.'

I passed him the notebook. 'Do these iterations. When do you think you can have them ready?'

Reed nodded. 'Well . . . tomorrow, if I start straight away. That would give us a representative—'

The shouting became louder.

'Good job,' I told him. I had to leave the notebook in his hands, no time even to tear the page out. I then followed McNair upstairs, to the dim ground-floor corridor that led to Trevelyan's office.

There we found the superintendent himself, his arm lifted firmly in front of McGray's chest. Nine-Nails was livid, his fists clenched, and snorting and shaking like a boiling kettle. A group of officers and clerks had gathered around them, their hands ready to contain Nine-Nails if needed.

I was rather shocked when I saw they faced a single man; middle-aged, short and broad, with a very pale face (albeit a red nose) and wiry beard and mutton chops. In sharp contrast with McGray's temper, the man seemed rather bored.

'Frey, good you came,' Trevelyan said, clearly to take the edge off McGray's temper. 'This is Sheriff Principal Blyth. You might remember him from the trial against Miss Katerina Dragnea.'

As soon as he said it, I remembered the man – he'd looked just as bored at his court – and I could not repress a snort. I could already tell what was brewing: our chances had just come to an end.

'What brings you here, sir?' I asked nonetheless, and the man sighed.

'Oh, do I need to explain the entire matter again?'

'*Ye can go fuck yerself!*' McGray barked as he charged against the sheriff. Two officers had to seize him by each arm.

'Do tell us again, for Mr Frey's benefit,' Trevelyan said, while Nine-Nails grunted. He only seemed to be doing so to give time for McGray to calm down.

Sheriff Blyth spoke with a deep, throaty voice, as if addressing the courts with a memorised speech.

'It has been brought to my attention that Inspector McGray, here, might not be the best choice to conduct these investigations.'

'Brought to your attention by whom?' I asked.

'It hardly matters,' Blyth replied, brandishing yesterday's newspaper – the evening edition, which detailed McGray's outburst. 'This case is anything but inconspicuous. Also, I hear Inspector McGray shot a young man yesterday.'

'Minor details!' McGray barked.

Sheriff Blyth lowered the paper and folded his hands almost demurely.

'The young man is nephew to the city's Lord Provost.'

'Oh, God!' I cried.

'They will press charges,' the sheriff said. 'Though that is not the only issue that brings me here.'

'What else, then?' I asked.

'The asylum. I hear you have not inspected the place as thoroughly as the investigation demands. That you searched every room in there, except for the chambers occupied by Inspector McGray's sister.'

McGray stirred again, so I had to raise my voice.

'Who told you that?'

'Is that report incorrect?' Blyth said instead.

'Absolutely,' I answered at once, my heartbeats quickening. 'I inspected that room myself only yesterday and found nothing of consequence.'

Blyth furrowed his brow. '*You?* I understand you are no longer an active detective inspector. Is that correct?'

For a moment I was lost for words, so Trevelyan had to speak for me. He too sounded as if he'd prepared the argument well in advance.

'Mr Frey is helping with the investigations, given his experience with similar cases.'

'In what capacity?' Blyth asked. '*Consulting detective?*' He chuckled, and then looked directly into my eyes. 'See, Mr Frey, it bothers me that you, someone so close to the McGrays, have been allowed, unchecked, into all these sensitive places. Our very own morgue! How can I guarantee a jury that you have not been tampering with evidence in your friends' favour?'

'To what purpose?' I asked. 'Are you suggesting that Miss McGray is part of the resurrectionist trade?'

Blyth gave me a disdainful look. 'It's not the body snatching that concerns me. It is the murder.'

The word lingered in the air. With one final pull, McGray managed to set himself free and strode irately towards Blyth.

We all gasped, thinking he'd beat the man to a mush. I had to pull the sheriff away, and the officers sprinted from both sides to seize McGray. Trevelyan planted himself between them, his arms outstretched.

'I am not *yet* accusing the young lady,' Blyth said, on his toes to see McGray over my shoulder. 'But as it stands, the integrity of the investigation will be put to question at court.'

'What is it you want?' I asked. Though I already knew the answer, I needed to hear it from the man's own lips.

'That you two stand aside and let the rest of the case be followed by an unclouded party.'

McGray let out a deafening cackle.

'Ye cannae force us!'

'I cannot,' Blyth said, 'you are absolutely right. But your opposition will only compromise your sister's case in the courts. Ideally, neither of you should meddle with the evidence any further as of this moment.'

'I must ask again,' I said. 'Who told you all of this? Was it Fiscal George Pratt? Because his son happens to have suspicious links to—'

'Och, of course it was him!' McGray snapped. 'The senior Pratt went running to the sheriff like a whining bitch as soon as he saw we were gettin' close to his slobbering child.'

'I am aware of Martin Pratt being a future surgeon,' Blyth said, 'and all which that implies. And when this inquiry comes to my court, I shall evaluate whatever evidence against him that is presented to me. And if I may suggest, the new inspectors should commence their investigations with a thorough inspection of Miss McGray's chambers.'

I brought a hand to my brow, my worst fears materialising before my eyes; worse even than being pulled out of the investigation. There was one reason they'd insist so much in inspecting Pansy's lodgings. I pictured Caroline's cloak and gloves. This would be the perfect chance to bring them to light.

McGray did not need to know what I knew to become wary. 'We'll have to be present,' he prompted. 'To ensure yer inspection is truly *unclouded*.'

'That seems more than reasonable,' Trevelyan said.

'And nobody from the courts,' McGray added. 'Nae *Pratts*.'

He purposely spat with the last consonants, and Blyth twitched at the impact.

'Expediency is crucial,' he said as he produced a hanky to wipe himself, for the spit had landed dangerously close to the corner of his mouth. He turned to Trevelyan. 'If you can arrange for inspectors from Leith or another neighbouring borough—'

Right then we heard a high-pitched screech. It came along with an icy draught, straight from the City Chambers' main gate.

We saw a young girl rush in, her head wrapped in a shawl peppered with melting snowflakes. She stumbled from side to side, a constable having to hold her by the arm lest she drop to her knees.

'What is it?' Trevelyan asked when they approached. The girl's shawl fell back, revealing a dishevelled blond braid and a pallid, freckled face.

McGray recognised her at once. 'Evangeline?' he cried, pushing Sheriff Blyth aside. 'She's one o' the asylum's new nurses.' He went to her and lay a hand on her trembling shoulder. 'What is it, lass?'

The girl panted, both hands on her chest. '*Miss – Miss McGray, sir!*'

Nine-Nails lost all colour. 'Pansy? What happened to her?'

I could see the tendons on his neck, the veins bulging on his temple.

The girl forced a gulp, and then spoke.

'She's gone!'

31

'*What!*' McGray howled, grabbing the girl by the arms. 'What d'ye mean? *What's happened to her?*'

Poor Evangeline burst into tears and could say no more. The constable next to her, who had clearly escorted her from Morningside, was the one to answer.

'Miss McGray attacked a doctor – or so this lass told me on the way here. The place was in uproar.'

'Gosh!' I cried.

McGray was so shocked he even swayed. 'We need to go there,' he spluttered at once, already sprinting to the exit. Without even asking for Trevelyan's permission, he called several constables by name and they followed him. Sheriff Blyth mumbled something about joining them, he too trotting behind, and Trevelyan began barking orders I did not hear.

For a moment I simply stood in the middle of the hall, truly paralysed by indecision.

I knew what we'd find there, and that it was too late for explanations. I would have no time to warn McGray about his fiancée's gloves, Harland's misunderstanding and his sister's true parentage. Even if I did, and he managed to listen to me right now, how would he react to the story? How would he react to news like his own mother's infidelity, while his sister had just gone missing?

After an instant of pulling at my own hair, all I could do was run after the troupe of constables.

'Brace yourself for a tempest,' I mumbled.

And as if the sky had heard me, the snow turned into a violent blizzard as soon as I set foot onto the street.

I jumped on a cart along with four officers, McGray and the driver squeezed together on the front seat.

A second cart with more officers followed us, and behind it, a cab carried Superintendent Trevelyan and Sheriff Blyth. I could hardly see them, though. The snow fell mercilessly in almost horizontal blows, turning everything around us into diffuse, milky shadows, and it lashed our faces as the roofless cart bounced madly downhill. I could not even cover myself, my hands gripping the slippery wooden boards.

We darted along the pebbled esplanade of Grass Market, nearly clashed against a wagon loaded with beer barrels, and after nearly tipping to one side, we went on southwards. The horses must have galloped almost blindly, and with each bump I thought we'd hit a wall or a carriage or a confused pedestrian.

I could not help but feel I'd been here before, one year ago, rushing to the asylum after a nurse had been attacked, and another inmate – Pansy's father no less – had fled.

After what seemed like an agonisingly long journey, we made it to the broad roads of Morningside, and the silhouette of the asylum finally emerged in the distance.

The two carts and the cab halted right by the building's main gate, the lawns already covered in a thick blanket of snow. McGray was the first one to jump to the ground, and before I could even alight, he was already leaping up the entrance steps.

The officers and I ran after him. I had a quick look around, but I could not even see the end of the lawns; the entire world had become a pallid blur.

'Someone stay by the garden gates!' Nine-Nails shouted, and the officers from the second cart did so.

We stormed in and all the inmates and nurses looked at us with fear. This was the second time in less than three days, that a group of constables marched in.

An orderly I did not know ran to receive us.

'This way, sirs,' he said.

'Where's Dr Clouston?' McGray asked him as we rushed upstairs.

'I don't know, sir, but I'm sure he'll join youse soon.'

The racket increased as we approached the next floor. The corridor leading to Pansy's room was a mess, with nurses running to and fro. Another two orderlies wrestled with a choleric male inmate, and they almost crushed me as I passed by.

'There's the bastard,' I heard McGray cry just as we reached Pansy's door. There we found Dr Harland, being tended by a nurse. Someone had fetched him a chair, and the man was pressing a blood-soaked rag against his left cheekbone.

McGray pulled him cleanly off the seat.

'What did ye do to her?' he snarled, but Harland answered back with just as much rage.

'What did *I* do? *She attacked me!*'

'Bollocks!' McGray spat.

'*It's the truth!*' Harland roared, his eyes bloodshot. 'I thought I heard noises coming from her room. I went in and the moment she saw me she pounced at me! See what she did!'

He briefly uncovered his face and we all gasped at a deep gash that ran all the way from his nose to his ear.

'How could she do that?' I asked.

'She had a scalpel,' Harland grunted. McGray grabbed him by the lapels and shook him.

'*Ye fucking liar!*'

'Why don't you look at the room?' the incongruously calm Sheriff Blyth suggested from behind us.

McGray turned to him with a glare that chilled my blood, and for a moment there was nothing but deathly silence. McGray let go of Harland, pushed the door and went into the room. I stepped in right behind him, Blyth and Trevelyan after me.

I saw that the bedding was a mess, the little table by the window had been knocked over, one of the windowpanes was cracked and the wardrobe was wide open, some clothes spilling out.

My eyes, like everyone else's, were soon drawn to the rug by the bed. There lay the scalpel, Harland's blood smeared on the blade and spilled on the fabric. And something else. A clump of black material, caked with dry mud.

And a pair of black leather gloves.

'God,' I mumbled as I covered my brow. A prickle of fear expanded across my chest as McGray and Trevelyan knelt by the dark clothes. They lifted the valance and I saw the disturbed floorboards. A piece of torn dress lay on the edge of the hollow – white with pale yellow stripes.

'What is that?' Blyth asked, looking precisely at the bright material, but he would not get an answer.

'The gal was retrieving those when I walked in,' Harland interrupted, pointing to the cloak. 'She took the scalpel from under those boards. She must have had it there since God knows when.'

'*That is a lie!*' I shrieked. 'I looked under that bed yesterday!' for an instant I doubted myself. It felt as though it had been weeks ago. 'Those floorboards were undisturbed, I am sure! I even tried to pull them!'

Harland snorted. 'Good job you did!'

McGray's pupils flickered madly from one piece of evidence to the next.

He stretched a hand towards the scalpel, but—

'Don't touch that!' Blyth snapped. McGray nearly charged against him, but Trevelyan blocked his way.

'Do as he says. You don't want them to claim you tampered with it.'

Nine-Nails grunted, but had to step back.

We all stooped around the scalpel to inspect it. Under the room's dull light I could hardly see the detail. Then Blyth leapt right behind me.

'There's dry blood,' he said, pointing insistently at the blade. 'There's dry blood there, under this doctor's blood!'

'We never found the blade they used to kill MacDonnell,' Harland said with acrimony.

'There must be at least a hundred scalpels in this building,' I told him.

'Indeed. Hundreds of chances for the girl to get hold of one.'

'Ye did this!' McGray cried. '*Ye planted all this shite here!*'

Harland started to pull a mocking smile. I barely saw it, for McGray punched him right on the open wound. Even I winced at the man's tormented screech. Harland curled in on himself, his knees bent as he wailed like a wounded child.

McGray seized him by the collar and lifted a fist, ready to strike again. Trevelyan and I had to join forces and pull his arm back.

'*Where did she go?*' McGray howled. Harland shook his head, a trickle of blood running down his cheek.

'I don't know! She ran out screaming like the mad crow she is.'

McGray slammed him against the wall. 'And ye didnae follow her?'

'My face had just been sliced open! She wasn't my first priority.'

McGray looked at the door. Nurses and orderlies had clustered behind the constables, craning their necks to see what happened.

'And none o' youse has even tried to find her?' McGray roared.

Sheriff Blyth rolled his eyes. 'It seems nobody is in charge here.'

Nine-Nails walked ominously towards the staff, clenching his fists so tightly they quivered. His paroxysm in Cockburn Street flashed in my head and I instantly went to him.

'McGray, listen to me! *Listen!*'

I had to slap him at the last word, and he stared at me with befuddlement rather than pain.

'Did ye – *did ye just smack—*?'

'Pansy might still be near,' I rushed to say. 'Either in the gardens or the neighbouring streets. With this weather she cannot have ventured far.'

'What d'ye mean?'

'You are not thinking straight, McGray. You know it. But you can still help. Go and look for her.'

McGray frowned, suddenly staring at the scalpel, torn with indecision.

'I will witness the questioning here,' I said. 'You can trust me. You know you can.'

McGray looked down, his breath more and more agitated. I could read his expression like a book – he knew I was right, and hated himself for it.

'The sooner you go,' I whispered, 'the more chances of finding her.'

He sprinted forwards then, elbowing people aside and telling constables to follow him. As we heard their steps fade away, we all sighed with relief.

'Go get some stitches,' I told Harland, and then turned to the nearest officer. 'Close this room, and make sure nobody gets in to disturb the evidence.'

'Including *you*,' Sheriff Blyth said between his teeth as he followed me out.

'And where is Dr Clouston?' I asked loudly.

'I saw him in his office,' a young nurse said. 'I can show you.'

'I know the way, I—' I saw the handful of staff staring at us, motionless. *'What the devil are you all waiting for?'* I yelled, for they continued to stare at us. *'Look for Miss McGray!'*

They all sprang into motion and I walked briskly down the corridor. Trevelyan and Blyth followed me closely.

'You will not be able to preside over this inquiry,' Trevelyan told the sheriff as we descended the stairs. 'You have become a witness now.'

'Indeed,' Blyth answered, 'but don't think that improves the girl's chances.'

The asylum looked like a disturbed anthill, everyone running and shouting, no one there to tell them what to do. I shivered – how easily a place can plunge into utter chaos.

The door to Clouston's office was ajar. I pushed it open and found the man behind his desk, his face bent over the polished wood, both hands on his temples.

Miss Smith was by his side, squeezing his shoulder with one hand, and with the other offering him a small glass of spirit. She jumped when she heard us burst in, and we looked at each other for an instant. I saw her lips tremble, her features distorted with undeniable guilt.

'They need you out there,' I told Clouston. 'Your staff are out of control.'

Clouston raised a trembling hand, though he kept his face bent.

'I need – I need a minute.'

'We don't have a minute!' I shouted. 'Miss McGray might still be around!'

As I said so I noticed a speck of fresh blood on Clouston's otherwise snow-white cuff, and I felt a most unpleasant chill.

I took a small step sideways, hoping to block that speck from Blyth's view.

'Can you give me a moment with him?' I asked Blyth and Trevelyan.

'Absolutely not!' Blyth cried. 'This is—'

'*Get out!*' I howled, pushing the man away. Thankfully, he was not too strong for me.

Trevelyan gave me a nod, his eyes somehow telling me he trusted my judgement – but only just. He shut the door himself.

At once I went to Clouston and grabbed him by the wrist. Miss Smith pulled my hand, perhaps thinking I was about to beat the man.

'How did you get this?' I said, pointing at the speck of blood. It still glimmered under the light of the desk lamp. 'Is it Harland's? Have you seen Miss McGray after she attacked him?'

Only then did he look up, and my heart skipped a beat. He also had blood smeared on his collar.

'*Dear God!*' I whispered. 'What have you done?'

Clouston's entire face became distorted with grief. He pulled his hand away and again pressed his temples as if he wanted to crush his own skull.

He himself appeared to have gone mad.

Miss Smith stared at him, and she had to cover her mouth to muffle a sob.

'What have you done?' I asked once more.

Clouston stammered for a moment, and when he managed to speak his voice came out as a moan.

'I had to let her go.'

I thought I'd not heard properly. 'You had to – *what?*'

Right then I heard the neighing of horses and the racket of wheels.

I leapt to the window and, with both hands pressed on the glass, I saw a small carriage ride away across the snowed gardens.

32

I had not run so fast since I'd been simultaneously chased by a foul coven of witches and the Prime Minister's assassins.

I stumbled along the corridors, all the way to the long gallery where the Devil's mark had appeared painted in blood. I darted towards the back doors, opened them wide and ran into the mighty blizzard.

The wind pushed me with an incredible strength, forcing me to zigzag across the lawns.

'*Follow that carriage!*' I hollered as the snow hit me, the flakes now turned into dense clumps of ice. '*Follow that—!*'

I looked about me, squinting, but saw no one around. Not that I could trust my eyes; the blizzard blurred everything in sight. I shouted again, but I could hardly hear my own voice.

Recklessly, I followed the deep tracks the carriage had left in the snow. I thought of calling for help, but the wind would soon erase the trail.

I ran to the gardens' borders, past the back gate and into the main road. All I saw was a uniformly white blur, not even the other side of the street was visible. I ran on, my eyes straining to see the tracks on the ground. And then, when I next looked up, a grey ghost appeared before me; a blurry square, charging against me just as I became aware of the stomping of hooves.

When I made out the shapes of the horses, they were but a couple of yards away. I yelled, instinctively covered my face, and hurled myself sideways.

I felt a battering on my shoulder as I hit the ground, heard the wheels cracking and skidding on the snow, and my body rolled uncontrollably across the road.

For a moment I lay there, face down, my nose touching the disturbed ice as I panted.

Again I heard the horses neighing, and a distant voice yelped, '*Did we hit him?*'

I stumbled upwards, my shoulder terribly sore. I managed to straighten my back, my knees still on the ground, and I looked around. Through the blizzard I could just make out the curved tracks the carriage had left in the snow as it dodged me. It had missed me by inches.

I rose to my feet and limped towards the coach.

'Ye all right, sir?' the vexed driver said as he jumped from his seat. I was about to reply but then the carriage window opened.

'*Ian?*'

I nearly fell backwards from the shock.

'*Elgie!*'

It was indeed him, sticking his head and shoulders out of the window.

'What the Dickens are you doing here?' I asked him.

'You called for me, remember?'

'Is he all right?' someone else said, pushing Elgie aside, and a second face emerged.

'*Miss Ardglass?*' I cried. '*The two of you together?*'

Elgie grinned. 'Oh, it is a jolly funny story. I was just—'

'Oh, shut up!' I cried, and pulled the driver by the collar. 'Did you see a carriage just now? Riding away on this road?'

'Aye, master. It ran past us like the wind. Nearly clashed—'

'Turn around and follow it! I'll give you a full pound if we catch it.'

I have never seen a driver get to his seat quite so quickly.

I opened the door, the wind almost tearing it off its hinges, and as soon as I closed it again, the driver whipped the horses. The carriage made a sharp turn, and the three of us were thrown sideways like marbles in a sling.

As soon as I regained some control I opened the window, only to be blasted by the snow. Just as I popped my head out, the driver took another turn. The carriage nearly turned on its side, and for a chilling moment I thought my face would get crushed on the ground.

Despite the blizzard I recognised the broad Morningside Road. We were travelling north, dodging carts and horses. I tried to look ahead, but the snow got straight into my eyes.

'*Are we still after it?*' I shouted. I had to repeat myself, almost tearing my throat so the driver could hear me over the wind and the racket.

'Aye, master. Only just!'

I shielded my eyes with a hand and made an effort to look away. I saw a multitude of blurry shadows, cabs and coaches all indistinguishable from each other, and let out a curse.

How could the driver possibly tell which carriage we were chasing? Was he just lying to me to make his money?

I cursed again as I realised there was nothing I could do but deposit all our hopes on that stranger's eyes.

I shut the window and sat back, punching the pane with utmost frustration.

'What's happening?' Caroline asked me as the carriage rattled.

'Miss McGray has fled.' I said. Both Caroline and Elgie gasped. 'She attacked a doctor and now she is going God knows where. And they found your gloves and cloak.'

Even as I said it, I realised I should not have spoken so freely in front of Elgie, but there was no time to be cryptic.

Caroline was astounded, a hand on her forehead and another clutched at her chest.

'That's impossible!' she hissed, barely able to breathe. 'You must be—'

'I wish I was.'

'But you said the garments weren't there! You said you looked!'

'And I did! They were not there yesterday. Someone must have taken them back. Only... I do not think we have any means to prove it.'

'Oh, Lord...' Caroline sighed. I told her about the scalpel too, but by then she was too drained to react. 'But it – it makes no sense,' she said dejectedly. 'None of this. How would she flee? She – she cannot be driving that carriage!'

'Indeed not,' I said. 'Someone must be helping her – or fleeing with her or... I don't know.'

Elgie looked at us with his lips parted, only half understanding what was going on.

'How did you two get here together?' I asked, if only to occupy my mind while I waited.

'I had just arrived in town,' Elgie said, 'so I went to your hotel and they told me you'd probably be at the City Chambers. I took a cab and—'

'We made it there at around the same time,' Caroline said. 'I was looking for Adolphus to tell him – what I needed to tell him. The constables said you had both gone to the asylum because of some kind of emergency. I had dismissed my driver, so your brother was kind enough to offer me a ride.'

She nodded at him, but Elgie was staring at her with a quizzical brow.

'*Adolphus*, did you just call him? Are you – are you engaged to him?'

I could not suffer that conversation. I opened the window and exposed my ears to the searing cold instead.

The pristine white of the storm was suddenly darkened by columns of smoke, and the blowing of the wind became intermixed with the sound of locomotives and steam whistles. We were riding past the makeshift Caledonian Station. I had no time to have a proper look, for we moved on swiftly, darting straight into the road around Charlotte Square – the very spot where Caroline lived these days.

She noticed this too. 'Are we going to Moray Place?' I heard her cry, and she was right. We moved on north, and again I had to get back inside, for the horses galloped madly, hugging the round, leafy circus. I caught a glimpse of McGray's façade and thought we were about to halt by his front door, but then the driver whipped the horses and we moved, if possible, even faster.

We left Moray Place behind and meandered through some opulent streets of New Town, before reaching the winding Water of Leith, the canal's stream now completely frozen.

After a few turns the carriage crossed the wide bridge over the canal. I recognised the streets that led to the Botanical Gardens, as we headed towards the street where the late Mrs Brewster had lived, but then we took another unexpected turn, this time west, onto the less-trodden roads that led to the country.

Very soon we left the city behind, and all we could hear were the whistling of the blizzard and the frantic rattle of the wheels. I looked through both windows and saw nothing but flat land in all directions, the horizon hidden behind the thick storm.

'Where is he taking us?' Caroline said, looking as doubtful as me.

The road was perfectly straight now, so I took a chance and opened the window once more. My eyes teared up instantly, but I still managed to get a glimpse of the fields. There *was* a carriage ahead of us, about a hundred yards away. It was just a blurry outline though, a smidgen darker than the surrounding sky, growing fainter and fainter with each blink.

I doubted it was even the correct carriage, but then—

A gunshot tore the air, the detonation glowing in the distance. Our horses swayed, neighing manically, and for a second I thought one had been wounded.

'Am turning back, master!' the driver cried.

'*No!*' I howled. '*Follow them, dammit! They won't shoot again!*'

I was of course lying, but the man somehow believed me and steadied the horses. I could only hope I was not sending him to his death.

When I looked back at the road, the other carriage had vanished. I let out a grunt, but then I saw it reappear, along with the shadows of some long, bulky buildings – and the roar of the sea.

'They're going to Granton Harbour, master!' the driver shouted, and as soon as he said it the shapes made sense: lengthy storehouses, a clock tower and spectral masts pointing to the sky.

The carriage ahead of us shook and bounced as it took a sharp turn to the left. I saw it had reached the coastline and now rode over some railway tracks. Our carriage did the same a moment later, our heads banging against the roof.

I could only gasp when I looked out of the window again. We were at the very edge of the land, on the slim gap between the rails and a cliff that descended abruptly into the sea.

I shivered when I looked at the choppy waters, like moving hills under the hard wind. There were two long piers ahead of us, so long that they got lost in the mist, and the waves clashed against them with brutal force, rising as tall as belfries.

'They're going to kill themselves!' Elgie cried, also staring ahead. And he was right; that carriage moved more and more erratically, shaking like a matchbox under the blizzard.

I saw it reach the east pier just as a mighty wave broke against the granite wall.

For a moment all I could see was a splash of white foam, as if the ocean had swallowed the carriage. I heard the neighing of its horses, and their outlines reappeared slowly as the waters receded. The poor beasts were rearing in panic, their forelegs shaking in the air. The carriage behind them rolled backwards and forwards, its wheels getting dangerously close to the edge of the pier.

'The driver's seat is empty!' Elgie cried. I had to squint to see, but he was right. As we got closer I also saw that the door was open and flapping under the wind.

'Where did they—?'

I could not finish the sentence. I looked on and saw two figures, dwarfed by the size of the harbour, making their tortuous way along the stone pier. One was tall and broad backed; the other small and slender.

'What are they trying to do?' I cried. 'Throw themselves into the ocean?'

Our driver took us as close as he could to the abandoned carriage, just to the point where the pier touched the land.

'Cannae go any further, master,' he shouted, already dripping water sprayed by the waves. 'Nae in this weather.'

He was right. I looked through our right window, onto the railways that served the pier. Even the trains had halted, fearing the wind might derail them.

I had but an instant to make up my mind.

I opened the door and jumped out, the snow lashing my face as soon as I took my first clumsy steps. I heard Caroline yell something, and then Elgie shouting at her.

'*Don't!* You're wearing crinolines and a corset! You'll kill yourself.'

Just as he said so I saw the sharp, jagged rocks that hugged the coast on both sides of the pier, hit by wave after wave. Shrouded in fog, the pier seemed to dissolve into nothingness, as if those two figures were stepping decidedly into death itself.

I marched unsteadily, the wind constantly pushing me sideways. A mighty wave clashed to my right and I had to drop to my knees, my hands slipping on the rock. I hung on to the cracks in the granite with my very nails, fearing that the water would throw me into the sea, to be torn apart on the sharp rocks.

The water ebbed away, leaving me drenched and deathly cold. I looked up and, through the dripping hair that had stuck to my face, I saw the two figures again. The taller one carried a rifle.

I also saw something else to their left – a faint plume of dark smoke.

I scrambled upwards and moved on, stooping and keeping my hands just a few inches from the ground, in case another wave hit me.

I soldiered on, each step carefully placed, until I saw that the plume of smoke came from a very small tugboat that swayed uncontrollably next to the pier. Its chimney, painted red, seemed to be the one speck of colour left in the world.

'*Stop!*' I shouted, but the two figures were too far off to hear me.

As I ran on I saw they were heading to a very old wooden dock, precariously nailed to the pier. The entire structure seemed to bend under the blizzard, its boards mere splinters that the storm could snap like reeds. And the tugboat was hitting it time after time, the vessel nearly capsizing with each wave.

The two figures ran onto the tattered dock. A sudden gust of wind hit us all, and the slender figure dropped on her knees. I had no doubt as to who she was.

'*Stop!*' I shouted again, as loud as I could. I was some thirty yards from the dock, so I abandoned all caution and ran frantically. '*Stop!*'

The taller figure, clearly a man, heard me then. He held the rifle up with one hand, and with the other he helped Pansy get to her feet. He fired to the sky and for an instant I stopped. As soon as I resumed, the man let go of Pansy and used both hands to aim the weapon at me.

It was Tom, Clouston's most trusted orderly.

I halted just a few yards from them and raised both palms.

'I am here to help!' I shouted.

Tom kept pointing at me, offering his arm to Pansy while still gripping the rifle, and they continued to march towards the end of the dock. The tugboat hit it again and I felt the wood shake under my feet.

'You cannot sail in this weather!' I cried, following them at a distance. '*You'll kill her! You'll kill yourself!*'

'Ye want to help?' Tom shouted as he walked backwards. 'Keep away! And don't follow us!'

They took a few more steps and then reached the edge of the dock. The gunwale bounced up and down, a desperate sailor pulling the one feeble tether that kept them from drifting away.

Tom, still pointing the rifle at me, guided Pansy to the vessel, her small hands gripping the man's raised elbow.

I thought I could not feel any colder, but a renewed chill took hold of me when I saw the poor, slender girl standing precariously on a single foot, stretching the other outwards and trying to board the moving boat.

'*Stop!*' I shrieked, stepping closer. '*This is madness!*'

Pansy went still then, as if the blizzard had frozen her limbs. She put her foot down, turned slowly on her heels and pulled back the hood that until now had concealed her face.

Her bonnet blew in the air and her dark hair flapped violently in the wind. Her eyes, amidst the white blizzard, were like endless wells.

And then, as a large wave clashed behind her, she spoke.

'*Madness, Mr Frey?*' she cried.

I froze. I had never heard her speak before. Her tones were rich and deep, her voice cutting the storm like a knife.

'*Could you never guess?*' she shouted, a grin spreading across her face. '*I am not mad!*'

The blizzard roared on, as if the very elements had decided to join her cry. The waves broke around us and the clumps of snow seemed to hit us even harder.

I felt pins and needles on my hands and face, and I was unable to move.

Pansy's chest was heaving, and even though she grinned, her eyes also welled up with tears, as if she had yearned to spit out those words for years.

'I have *never* been mad!'

We stared into each other's eyes for God knows how long, her breath steaming up in the air, until she turned her back on me once more.

For an instant she did not seem to care about anything, not even her own life, for she leapt lightly off the dock, and only seemed to land on the tugboat out of sheer luck.

I wanted to run to her, but could only take a step forwards before Tom shouted.

'*Don't follow us!*' he repeated, now aiming directly at my forehead. He too jumped onto the boat and the sailor at once let go of the rope. I saw it slide around the dock's cleat and fall into the sea as they sailed away.

I was finally free to run to the edge, where I stood for a good while, battered by the storm.

The tugboat moved swiftly, growing fainter and fainter with each gust of wind, and well before it reached the end of the harbour, it vanished into nothingness.

33

Caroline wrapped me in a thick blanket while Elgie poured me a generous measure of Scotch. I was about to receive the tumbler, but my entire body shook with a thunderous sneeze. Right in front of my armchair, the innkeeper poked the logs in the roaring fireplace.

We were in the dim parlour of the harbour's inn, only the hearth and a smudged sconce lamp lighting our grim faces. The wind still blew hard outside, and the steamed windows gave us a blurred, eerie view of the tall waves.

I took the tumbler and had a good glug. The burn of the liquor, foul as it tasted, was exactly what I needed.

'It makes perfect sense!' I mumbled, pressing my lower lip against the glass. 'Perfect sense indeed... How could I have been so blind for so long?'

Caroline stared at me, standing very still by the fire. Her eyes were fearful.

'You may leave us now,' she told the innkeeper. The man bowed and walked away rather reluctantly, obviously hungry for gossip. Our driver, now getting dry in the kitchens, would surely tell him the tale in detail.

I stared at the crackling flames, my mind spinning.

'Her behaviour suggested it all along,' I mumbled on. 'One

day she was heard talking and the next she'd be as absent as ever. One day she was an empty vessel and the next she'd provide us with crucial pieces of information for our cases. It was simply too convenient...'

I recalled that the orderlies had heard her speak to Lord Joel: last year, right before the man murdered his nurse and fled the asylum. And Pansy's condition had worsened since then. Of course it had – the man had been her father! She must have known. Before escaping he must have told her everything we now knew. And more.

I looked accusingly at Caroline.

'You knew it, didn't you? You've known all along!'

'*Knew?* What are you talking about?'

'That your sister is not mad.'

Elgie gasped, his mouth wide open. Caroline, on the other hand, needed a moment to make sense of the words. She opened and closed her mouth, and yet all she could utter was a throaty, 'What?'

'She just told me,' I said. 'Right before she jumped onto that boat.'

Caroline looked from side to side, as if suddenly lost.

'But she is – she *is* mad. Of course she is mad.'

Elgie had to steer her to the armchair opposite mine and help her sit.

'You know she spoke once, do you not? To your father. *Her* father.'

'*What?*' Elgie cried, nearly dropping the bottle of ghastly Scotch. I shushed him.

'Did she never talk to you?' I asked Caroline. 'During your night visits to the asylum? Did she never tell you she is not mad?'

'She has never spoken to me! Not a word.'

I was going to shrill '*Has she not?*', but Miss Ardglass seemed about to collapse.

I gave her time. Elgie offered her a glass of Scotch but she pushed it away.

'Pansy . . .' she whispered. 'She has to be mad. *She has to!* If she wasn't – Her parents – I mean, her mother and the late Mr McGray – that would mean she *did* mean to—' Poor Caroline shook from head to toe. 'I can't even say it. It's too horrible.' She took a few troubled breaths. 'She could have been delirious just now! All mad people say they're not mad.'

Caroline went silent for just a second, and then jumped to her feet, propelled by sheer anxiety.

'She *did* say she wasn't mad! Adolphus told me. When Dr Clouston first saw her, right after she—' Again she shuddered. 'She said she wasn't mad.'

'She said it had been the Devil,' Elgie mumbled. 'Everybody's heard that story.'

Caroline rested a trembling hand on the mantelpiece. 'And now the Devil's mark appears . . .'

We remained silent for a while, hearing just the blizzard and the crackling fire.

'There was a man with her,' Elgie said. 'The one driving her carriage.'

'Tom,' I said. 'One of the asylum's orderlies. And they boarded that steam tugboat. They clearly planned this well in advance. Clouston himself told me he *had to let her go.*'

Caroline frowned. 'So he knew.'

'Of course he knew!' I said, stretching my arm so Elgie could refill my tumbler. 'How could he not? He has treated her for the past six years. And Miss Smith must know too. No wonder she has been acting so strangely.' I looked sideways. 'Though she may not have known all along.'

Caroline stared into the fire. 'Should we tell Adolphus?'

'No,' I said immediately. 'At least not yet.'

'But you said before—'

'I know what I said, but this changes everything! Think about it: the sister he has visited for years, the reason he became obsessed with the occult, the reason he became a detective inspector and championed his idiotic *odd and ghostly* subdivision... Can you imagine his devastation if he finds that the girl has been pretending all this time?'

Caroline shut her eyes. 'It would destroy him,' she mumbled, and once more we all went silent.

Elgie was the first to speak.

'She may still be mad, for all we know. That Clouston man could have had other reasons for letting her go. She is being accused of murder!'

Caroline let out a bitter sigh. 'I cannot believe I am now praying for her to be truly insane. And she could have gone anywhere!'

I swirled the tumbler and mused as I watched the liquor form gentle tears on the glass. 'Maybe not anywhere,' I mumbled. I stood up, walked slowly to the window and wiped the condensation from the glass. I took a moment to stare at the endless waves and the insistent blizzard.

'They sailed north,' I said. 'In a pathetic little tugboat. They cannot go far in this weather. Perhaps – perhaps they never intended to sail far. Perhaps they only meant to cross the Firth of Forth.'

'Have they not opened that new bridge recently?' Elgie asked. 'To connect Edinburgh with the north side of the bay?' As he said so, I pictured the map of Scotland in my head.

'Not yet,' Caroline told him. 'The papers said it will open next month, but the bridge itself is ready. They have been running trial trains across.'

'Still, not yet open for regular people,' I said. 'And if we assume they only meant to cross the bay...' I drew the path in the air with my index finger, and then turned to Caroline. 'Could she have gone to Dundee? The McGrays' hometown?'

Caroline lifted her chin as if she'd just picked up a scent. 'Yes! They could have.'

Elgie shook his head. 'She cannot be hoping to hide there forever. She'll know people will make the connection quickly, like you just did.'

'Indeed,' Caroline said, 'but she could be going there looking for something. Money or some possessions to take on.'

I stared hard into the storm, still unable to see the end of the harbour. 'Or she might be after something entirely different.' I sighed. 'Miss Ardglass, you know Scotland better than either of us. How long does it take to travel to Dundee?'

'A full day, surely.'

'And with the new bridge?'

'Oh, yes! Well... I'd say some five hours. Maybe less, if you hire a four-in-hand carriage.'

'Elgie, do you have any money on you?'

'Oh, not much at all, brother. Just pocket money, you know – about twenty-five pounds.'

I grinned and ran to hug him. '*Good Lord!* That will take us comfortably to Aber-bloody-deen and back!' I looked at Caroline. 'If I depart right now, across the bridge, I might even get there before Miss McGray does.'

Caroline shook her head. 'What if she is not heading there?'

'At least we will know for sure. And I'd be back by this time tomorrow, so it would not be an insurmountable waste of time. Not that it makes any difference – I am not even allowed to investigate anymore.'

I began pacing around the parlour, already thinking of the practicalities. 'Do you know the address?' I asked Caroline.

'Gosh, no. They locked up the property right after the –

incident. Adolphus has never been back. I believe the house has a proper name, but he hardly ever speaks of those things in detail.'

'Nor can we blame him,' I said.

'Well, it will not be difficult to find,' Elgie jumped in. 'That family is infamous. You'd need but to ask where the house of the demented McGrays is!'

'True!' I said. 'God, Elgie, I am glad you are here.'

'Why, thank—'

'Especially since I will need someone to come with me.'

'What?'

'Miss Ardglass should stay. Nine-Nails will be a loose cannon. We need someone to—' I nearly said *comfort him*, but it would have been far too vulgar. 'Someone to make sure he is all right.'

Caroline nodded. 'Yes, you're right. And I can also make up some excuse to explain your absence. If he knows where you're heading, he'll go right after you.'

'Good,' I said, gulping down the last dregs of that disgusting spirit. 'Come, Elgie. We have no time to lose.'

Sadly, I was too quick to cheer. The storm brewing in Edinburgh was far worse than that nasty blizzard.

34

On her way back to Morningside, still in the same cab that had taken her to Granton Harbour, Caroline had plenty of time to think up her story.

No one at the asylum had seen her, so there was no need to tell Adolphus she'd been with Mr Frey at all. If asked, Caroline would simply tell half the truth; that she'd looked for Adolphus at the City Chambers, and that the officers had told her where he'd gone. The hardest part would be to feign shock at the things that had happened in Morningside.

The worst of the blizzard had passed, but the snow still fell thickly when the cab halted by the front gate. The driver, warmed up with whisky and handsomely bribed to keep the frantic race secret, helped her alight.

An officer raised a palm as soon as Caroline, tightly wrapped, approached the front gate.

'No one's to get in, ma'am.'

'I'm here to see Dr Clouston.'

'Sorry, no one's to get in.'

'*Then drag me out if you dare!*' she yelled, stepping in with resolute strides.

The officer followed her, his hand raised as if to seize her by the arm, but he did not dare touch the refined young lady.

Caroline crossed the long entrance hall, took the first turn, and found what looked like the wreckage left by a tempest. Two of the long benches, where the more impoverished visitors would usually wait to see their relatives, had been thrown and smashed into splinters. A young nurse with two blond braids was sweeping the debris.

'What happened here?' Caroline asked her, the officer still behind her back, prattling on and on that she should leave.

'It was that Mr McGray, ma'am,' the young nurse said, clearly annoyed by having to clean up the mess. 'Some peelers came. They told him he couldnae touch any evidence or som'it like that. He went mad, made all this mess and then stormed away. His wee sister's gone missing, did ye know?'

Caroline did not bother to reply. She lifted her skirts and dodged the smashed wood. She hoped nobody would ask why her hem and shoes were quite so muddy.

The constable, still after her, gathered courage to brush her sleeve with his fingertips. 'Ma'am, ye cannae—!'

'*Don't touch me!*' she barked. The man tripped on a piece of wood and nearly fell backwards.

Caroline marched on through the familiar corridors, her heart pounding. She found Clouston's office soon enough, the door wide open.

'You knew!' she cried as she stormed in.

Clouston was giving instructions to a junior doctor, and both men stared at Caroline with confusion. Clouston dropped the documents he'd been holding, and the sheets fluttered onto the floor as the man lost all colour.

'*Leave us!*' Caroline snapped at the younger man. Clouston told him something in whispers and the younger man walked away.

Caroline peered out of the office to make sure no one was eavesdropping, shut the door and snapped again.

'You knew! All this time you have known that my sister's not—'

'*Be quiet!*' Clouston hissed. His smooth scalp had gone red, the veins on his temples palpitating. '*Do you want everyone in the blasted building to hear?*'

Suddenly aware of his outburst, Clouston smoothed his jacket and adjusted his tie. Caroline noticed a crumpled shirt on a nearby chair. The doctor had just changed into clean clothes.

He spoke on with forced politeness. 'Leave, Miss Ardglass. I beg you. I will not deal with this right now.'

'You will have to! I have just learned that—'

'*Get out, dammit!*'

And with that thunderous shout Clouston strode around his desk, grabbed Caroline by both arms and shoved her out. He slammed the door and Caroline could only stand there, astonished, her nose less than an inch from the polished wood, as she heard him turn the key.

She knocked, shouted and then growled out of sheer frustration. Just as she rested her forehead on the door, she heard footsteps behind her.

It was Miss Smith, bringing a bottle of brandy and a tumbler, her greying hair dishevelled. As soon as she saw Caroline, the head nurse turned pale. Both women looked into each other's eyes for just an instant, but that was all they needed to realise all that was happening.

Caroline felt her jaw drop. 'So you also know!' she cried.

Miss Smith tried to say something but no sound came out. She made to turn on her heels, but Caroline grabbed her by the wrist and Miss Smith dropped the glass, which shattered on the wooden floor.

'Since when?' Caroline pressed. '*Since when?*'

Miss Smith panted, looking from side to side. 'Not here, miss. Not here.'

Caroline was panting too. She forced a few deep breaths, and as soon as she gave a brief nod, Miss Smith pulled her down the corridor to a small broom cupboard. Miss Smith pushed Caroline in, followed her and shut the door behind them, the bottle of liquor still in her hand.

'Did you find her, Miss Ardglass?' the nurse urged in whispers.

'You'd better not know. All that matters is I've heard the truth. *How could you not tell me—?*'

'I've only known for a wee while myself!'

Caroline took a step back, feeling terribly cold.

'So ...' she whispered. 'It is true—' She gulped, and then shook her head. She did not have the strength to deal with all the implications there and then. 'Since when have you known?'

'Last summer, and only because Mr McGray gave me a wee vial. He said it contained some miraculous waters from some loch up north.'

Caroline nodded. 'Oh, yes. Loch Maree.'

'Aye, miss. Mr McGray told me it was supposed to cure all kinds of madness. That even Queen Victoria had used it. I handed the vial to Dr Clouston and then – I didn't mean to, but I saw him about to chuck it into the fire. I was so shocked that he had to tell me everything.'

Caroline covered her mouth and had to allow herself a moment to take in the news. Her mind was becoming exhausted.

'Does Pansy know – that you know?'

Miss Smith shook her head. 'We didn't have to tell her immediately. She was in the Orkneys back then.'

'True.'

'It was only when she was brought back, in January, that the doctor told her. It would have been impossible for me to keep on tending to her without – God, the poor creature!'

Caroline looked down, her stare fixed on the thin strip of

light between the door and the floor, until she felt a pain on her forehead. She'd been frowning hard all this while.

'Did she—' Caroline gulped, her chest growing cold. She did not want to ask the question, not even think about the possibility, but she must. 'Did Pansy actually murder the McGrays? I mean – we know she did, but – did she really *mean* to do it? Was she aware of what she was doing? Is she a mur—' She looked down, biting her lips.

'I don't know, miss. Dr Clouston said the less I knew the better for everyone. I still feel goosebumps when I think about all that. And after all these years working here, I am not easily shocked.'

'Is that really all you know?'

'Yes, miss.'

'Do you swear?'

'Yes, miss!'

Caroline rested the back of her head on the dusty wall. Again, she found herself wishing that Pansy were truly insane.

'I suppose the police took my garments?'

'Aye, miss. There was nothing I could do. They said it was all evidence to present at the courts. And they also found a torn dress that belonged to Miss McGray.'

'Lord!' Caroline panted. 'And – Mr McGray?'

'He went berserk, as you'll know by now, and then stormed away to keep on looking for his sister.'

'Did he talk to Dr Clouston?'

'No. The doctor—' Miss Smith could only bite her lip.

'Avoided him,' Caroline mumbled, struggling to think amidst that whirl of tension. She looked up. 'Do you think Clouston knows where Pansy went?'

'If he does, I wouldn't know.'

'*Are you lying to me again?*' Caroline yelled, shaking Miss Smith by the arms.

Her voice travelled across the corridor, and at once a young orderly opened the cupboard door. The young man cast them a puzzled look before he spoke.

'Miss – Miss Smith, they're looking for you.'

The head nurse welcomed the interruption, pulled away from Caroline and stepped out.

'For me? Who?'

'Some peelers. Well, they were looking for that Nine-Nails man, but we told them he's nae here. Then they asked for Doc Clouston or someone in charge, but we cannae—'

'Yes, yes, I'll attend them,' Miss Smith concluded, already heading to the main hall, if only to avoid Caroline asking her more questions. 'What do they want?' she asked.

The orderly seemed keen to share the information. 'They say there's been another death.'

Caroline tripped when she heard that. The orderly even had to hold her arm.

'Another death!' she cried, exhausted after the torrent of bad news. 'Where? Who?'

The young man shook his head. 'I didn't hear more, miss. Well – only one more thing...'

'What?' she urged.

'They said –' the orderly lowered his voice – 'that the Devil's mark has appeared again.'

35

The four dark horses galloped frantically across Forth Bridge, on the narrow gap between the two new railway tracks.

The mighty steel beams, sharp and unforgiving, rose to our left and right like stark embodiments of the new industry. The wind blew through them, making some disturbing screeches, as if nature itself protested against such intrusion on the landscape. And the waves roared many feet below, unable to reach us.

It had taken a few lies and some sterling to bribe the bridge engineers, but in the end they agreed to turn a blind eye to our crossing.

Elgie offered me some of the bread and cheese he'd insisted on buying before we departed, and I was only too glad he was with me; I did not have a head to think of those practicalities.

'What do you think we might find there?' he asked as we shared the improvised meal.

'I do not want to think about it just yet,' I said, though my mind would not rest.

Six years, a voice kept saying in my head. Nine-Nails had gone through six full years of sleepless nights, facing bereavement, loneliness and ridicule. Six years of his life fighting for what had now turned out to be a lie. What could that do to a man so hurt already?

And along with that voice came the eerie vision of Pansy's eyes.

Even if we found her and managed to bring her back – what would we achieve? It now seemed impossible to prove her innocence; not without tainting Caroline's name too.

And if Pansy had told the truth at the harbour and she was not insane, she would have to be tried for multiple murders. Including the McGrays'.

I stared at the bridge ahead, through the narrow front window. Beyond the driver and the horses' manes, the clouds gathered ominously above the hills, as though we were riding into a black cave.

Pansy might be better off out there, I thought. Gone forever.

'Ian...'

Elgie's voice startled me so much I nearly choked on the cheese. He did not wait for my reply.

'I think we're being followed.'

He was looking out the back window, clenching a piece of bread with apprehension. I leaned closer to the glass and, despite the condensation on our side and the drops of half-melted snow on the other, I saw them too.

A couple of faint, fuzzy lights in the distance.

They seemed to float over the railways, at times brighter, at times more diffuse, like the glow of the sun when seen from under water. They must be lanterns, held by shaking hands that struggled to keep up with us.

'Oh, for goodness' sake!' I grunted. I slid the glass of the front window, the harsh wind and snow immediately hitting me on the face. '*Can you go any faster?*' I asked the driver, having to shout over the blizzard.

'Ye sure, master? Ye don't wanna tire the beasts if ye wanna get to Dundee.'

'Do it. I think we are being followed.'

The man jerked a little, perhaps to look over his shoulder – from that angle and in the inclement weather, I could not really gauge his movements.

'Ye sure?' he asked.

'Yes, dammit!'

'Sorry, master, I see nothing.'

'What? We have just—'

I did not finish, but jumped back inside and wiped the condensation from the back window. I saw the railway tracks rolling behind us, the sharp edges of the bridge's steel beams and the dark sky above.

The lights had vanished.

36

The mark had been cut deep into the man's right cheek.

Fine, dexterous slashes that reached the muscle. And then the skin had been peeled off like that of an orange, leaving exposed flesh, sinew and some bone.

Under the ongoing blizzard, the corpse of the young man was already half buried in snow, his skin the colour of death, so the Devil's mark looked like a red beacon.

Caroline saw it even from the carriage, before the driver halted on the other side of the road. Not waiting for his help, she pushed the door open, jumped onto the snow and walked briskly towards the cluster of constables. They were surrounded by an even wider ring of reporters, and Caroline had to elbow her way through.

A dark overcoat flapped in the wind, and for a blissful instant Caroline thought it would be Adolphus. Then the man turned, and she saw waves of auburn hair.

'Ye cannae be here, ma'am!' one of the officers told her, blocking her path.

'I am looking for Inspector McGray,' Caroline replied.

'So is everyone else,' said the man with the auburn hair. Caroline knew he was the superintendent, though she did not remember his name. He came closer and nodded to the constable, who went back to the dead body. The superintendent spoke in a lower voice. 'What do you need him for?'

There was a gust of stronger wind, the snow momentarily thicker, and Caroline had to wrap her cloak about her more tightly as she gulped.

'It is – a personal matter.'

The superintendent furrowed his brow, studying Caroline's face with much more attention than she would have liked. It took him a moment to speak.

'Related to Miss McGray, perhaps?'

He kept on staring at Caroline until she had to lower her gaze. Could he have spotted her resemblance to Pansy?

'Personal, I said,' she snapped. 'Unless you want to interrogate a lady.'

The superintendent cleared his throat. 'Do excuse my manners, Miss...?'

'Ardglass,' Caroline said, but at once regretted volunteering her name. She was not thinking straight.

'Do excuse me, Miss Ardglass,' the superintendent reiterated. 'As you can see, we are under terrible pressure. In answer to your question, we have not seen Inspector McGray for a while.'

Caroline moved an inch sideways, catching another glance of the red mark, so similar to an eerie face with horns.

Just as she felt her heart skip a beat, the superintendent blocked her view.

'He was here, though,' he said, speaking slowly, as if he feared he might say too much. 'Just a few minutes ago.'

'And you had to send him away, I suppose,' Caroline added with impatience.

The superintendent tilted his head. 'How do you know that?'

'I've just been to the asylum.'

'Then you probably know that Miss McGray...' The superintendent left the rest implied.

300

'Indeed,' Caroline said, looking again into the man's eyes. She felt he could see right through her.

'Miss Ardglass, what is your connection to–? Forgive me, I don't need to know. Yes, you are right. We had to send him away. He is not to continue this investigation.'

'Where did he go?'

'He did not tell us. He stormed away. He must be looking after—'

Again, he left things implied, nervously eying the keen correspondents.

'Have you any idea where he might have gone?' Caroline asked, not caring to disguise her desperation.

The man's face went sombre. 'No. Have *you*?'

They remained in silence, the wind battering them without pause.

Caroline felt the cold seep into her chest, took in a trembling breath and then stepped back. She'd find nothing there.

'That mark is different,' she said as she turned on her heels. 'Someone else has done it!'

And as she rushed back to the carriage, she heard the superintendent raise his voice. His tone was one of resignation.

'We know, Miss Ardglass. It may not make any difference, though.'

37

Either the blizzard had abated, or we'd simply left it behind. The sky was still shrouded in dark clouds, but at least the wind did not shake the carriage anymore.

We rode due north for hours, all the way to Perth. We had to navigate through its very centre to reach the one bridge that crossed the River Tay, and then we turned east.

Night fell soon after, and without any stars above us, the only light was our driver's bull's-eye lantern. It showed us but a dozen yards ahead: a lonely, snowed road that then vanished into utter blackness.

Elgie was becoming more and more restless, peering out the window as he fidgeted with his hands.

We hardly spoke for the best part of two hours, until a faint, yellowish glow appeared on the clouds ahead of us.

'Is that Dundee?' he muttered.

'I hope so,' I said. 'I have never been to the place.'

A battered sign soon proved it so, and we rode into the McGrays' hometown without ceremony.

I could hardly tell where the town began, the houses were quite sparse. Just as we reached the first row of terraced dwellings, somewhat busy with pedestrians and other carriages, the driver turned left and took us along a parallel, less-trodden road.

I'd asked him to avoid the busier streets, well aware that a four-horse carriage is a rare sight. Luckily that road – fittingly named Blackness Avenue – had no street lamps at all.

Still, we could not avoid being seen for long. Our road soon merged with another one called Scouring Burn (Dundee truly had some grim names for her streets), where the bustle of an industrial port town began.

At least we should blend in. Despite the hour, the streets were packed with all manner of carts, coaches and cabs. I saw everything from businessmen in fur coats to pedlars carrying beer barrels on their backs. They were all accustomed to those wintry nights, impervious to the wind that, though not too strong, was icy and laden with tiny specks of snow. Even in Edinburgh most people would have sought refuge on an evening like this.

We reached the town's main church, its Gothic steeple only covered in snow on its west side – the blizzard had clearly hit this part of the country as well, quick and unforgiving, the snow sticking on everything it touched and freezing into a solid white crust.

Around the church there were many Georgian buildings, rather similar to those in Edinburgh's New Town. I shall never admit it to McGray's face, but his town's High Street was not excessively shabby.

Just a street past the church, the driver found a sheltered spot to park, in a little square flanked by shops and trade houses. He slid the front window open.

'Dundee, master. This is as far as I can go without directions.'

I looked around, the square brightly lit by gas lamps, some people already turning their heads to see our four panting horses.

'I will ask the locals,' I said, wrapping myself in my overcoat.

'*What?*' Elgie cried. 'Are you really going to venture into these savage—?'

'*Oh, shush!*' I snapped, for some people on the street had already heard his plummy English accent. 'Just wait here, and don't talk to anybody!'

He snorted. 'As if it were the most alluring experien—'

I shut the door then and heard no more.

As I strode away from the carriage I saw we'd parked just off one Crichton Street. On the left-hand side there was a bank – a thriving business, as suggested by its gilded sign and the polished brass bars on the windows. It was already closed for the day, but the tavern across the street bustled with activity.

Through its steamed windows I recognised the figures of many men in dark suits either smoking, holding glasses, cackling boisterously, or doing all the former at once. That establishment must be the bankers' den.

I took a deep breath. 'Come on, Ian. One last time...'

I pushed the door open and was instantly hit by a solid wave of heat, loaded with smoke and the stench of stale beer, sweat, naphthalene and cheap bay rum.

I had barely set one foot on the stained floorboards when all the chatter and laughter ceased.

All eyes turned to me, unblinking. The chubby man behind the bar stopped pouring Scotch, men's pints frozen halfway to their lips. For a moment the only movements were the trails of tobacco smoke ascending to the ceiling.

A very tall chap, middle-aged and rather smartly dressed, swayed in my direction.

'Ye lost, lad? Yer nae from 'round here!'

For an instant I thought it was McGray talking; the exact same tones and inflections.

'Erm – good evening—' There was an explosion of laughter, my refined accent (they called it something else) instantly noted. I cleared my throat, overtly conscious of my own voice. 'I am looking for... you might think it odd—'

'*You maaaahight think it aurrrrrdd!*' someone mocked in the distance.

I grunted, tempted to storm out, but I forced myself to finish. 'I am looking for the McGrays' house.'

There was a split second of silence, instantly followed by whispers and scornful laughter.

'Nine-Nails McGray?' the man in front of me asked. His nose was mighty red from the liquor.

'Yes,' I said. 'I believe he is – rather well-known around here?'

There was more laughter, and the man quite forwardly tapped me on the shoulder.

'Och aye, he is! Yer after Cleaver Hoose.'

'What?'

'Cleaver Hoo—' The man cleared his throat. 'The estate's called Claverhouse, but awbody calls it Cleaver Hoose.'

'Do you mean *house*?'

'Aye. I guess yer after the hoose where the wee lassie – *went dead mad; butchered and sliced her mum and dad . . .*' That last part he said in song, and some of the more intoxicated men joined in.

'Erm, yes,' I said. 'That sounds like the place.'

The man threw his head backwards and let out a cackle. 'Och, yer nae even close, lad!' He put his arm around me, and as he did so he spilled a good deal of his ale on my shoes. 'Stay for a wee drink and I'll give ye directions.'

He was already signalling the barman to pour me something.

'I do appreciate it, but I do not have time for—'

'Aaaaih doo noorrrt haaaarrrve taaaaaaime . . .'

'*I do not sound like*—!' But even as I said so, I heard what they meant.

The barman, perhaps the only sober man around, leaned over the sticky counter and spoke to me in a lower voice. I could barely hear him as the men continued their strident song.

'Ye a peeler?'

He passed me a very small measure of whisky, only to humour the drunkards. I took the greasy tumbler and nodded.

'Is it because o' tomorrow's news?' the man said.

'Tomorrow's?' I cried, and the man suddenly looked suspicious. 'Sorry,' I said. 'I have been travelling all day. I have not heard any – developments.'

'Ye ken about Auld Nick's marks, reicht?'

Thankfully, I was well-versed in their vernacular to know that he meant the Devil.

'Yes, of course I do.'

The man leaned closer to me, lowered his voice further and pointed discreetly to one of the pub's corners. 'That lad over there. See 'im?'

'Brown suit, scarlet nose, a pint glass in each hand?'

'Aye. Billy. He works at the local papers. After a few drinks he told me he'd got a wire,' the man checked the clock on the wall. 'That must've been – two, three hours ago. From Auld Reek – from Edinburgh, I mean.' He looked sideways, saw that the tall, drunken man was now distracted with a second round of the McGrays' song, and then leaned a little closer to me. 'Ye ken the McGray lass escaped, don't ye? And yer looking for her?'

I looked down and swirled the glass. Even if it had been clean, I wouldn't have been able to take a drink. My silence must have been confirmation enough.

'Did she do it, then?' the barman asked.

'Do what?'

The man smirked, mistaking my ignorance for secrecy.

'Och, ye ken what I mean! That dead body they found on the streets near the madhouse. With the same Auld Nick's mark we've seen in the papers the past few days. Ye—'

306

My jaw must have dropped abruptly, for the barman went silent and pulled away for a moment.

'Another death?' I mumbled, already sure Pansy could not have done it. I had followed her; right from the asylum to the harbour. It would be up to Nine-Nails to investigate it – that is, if he could possibly think clearly now that his sister had disappeared.

'Ye really have nae heard?' the barman asked.

'As I said – I have been travelling all day.' I took a deep breath, feeling a renewed pang in my chest. 'Do you know how to get there? That Cleaver House?' I saw the man torn between giving me the information and fishing for more gossip. 'It is *urgent*,' I said through my teeth.

'Aye. Awbody here kens the place.' He hesitated again, until I made to turn on my heels. 'Alreicht, alreicht. Go west past the kirk, all straight till ye see the signs to Dundee Poorhoose. Now, *don't* go there. Keep to yer richt on Pitkerro Rood—'

'Pit-*what*?'

'Och, I'll write it doun for ye—'

He tore a piece of brown paper from a poorly wrapped bottle and scribbled down a few lines with a blunt pencil. He folded it and slid it in my direction.

'Thank you,' I said, pushing the greasy tumbler back at him. I'd only managed a single step when the tall drunkard grabbed me by the shoulder.

'Och! Ye won't stay for another tune?' he howled while the rest of his friends screeched '*poor Adolphus howled in pain, his finger hanging by a vein...*'

I have never wished more that I carried a gun. Thankfully, the barman shouted behind our backs.

'Oi, Colin! *Here!* I'll refill yer pint!'

The drunkard forgot about me at once, and I scuttled away while the lyrics turned darker and darker.

As I walked back to the carriage I unfolded the brown paper and let out a grunt. I could hardly make sense of that horrendous spelling. I only hoped my driver knew how to read.

Even as I opened the carriage door, I could still hear the muffled voices singing:

> '...*though he'd never tell,*
> *he saw the Devil rushing back*
> *to his murky Hell*...'

38

Caroline spent the day searching everywhere, Nine-Nails always one step ahead of her.

Right after talking to the superintendent, and still shaken by the sight of the most recent victim, she looked in Morningside. Some residents told her they had seen Adolphus, looking for 'the mad lass' and aided by a couple of constables. Caroline had to desist, for people cast her suspicious stares as soon as they realised who she was looking for.

She tried New Town, in case Adolphus had gone home. George had not seen him, but he suggested Caroline tried asking at the Ensign Ewart. There, the cab driver had to make the enquiries for her, for a respectable young lady could not possibly set foot in such an ill-reputed establishment. Neither the landlady nor the regulars had seen Adolphus since the night before, however.

Caroline then went to her own apartment in Charlotte Square, in case Adolphus had been looking for her for some reason. Joan gave her a mighty scolding for leaving the place unchaperoned, and then insisted on joining the search. By that time the evening editions were already circulating, the entire city aware of the new murder and Pansy's disappearance.

To Joan's dismay, Caroline decided to enquire at the police

headquarters, and they made it there just as the clerks were leaving for the day. They told them that Adolphus *had* been there briefly, not too long ago, talking to the superintendent and demanding to be allowed to keep on investigating his sister's case. The superintendent had refused, and McGray had thrown a mighty tantrum.

At least one of the clerks had heard Nine-Nails grumble something about going home, and Caroline and Joan immediately headed back to Moray Place.

Caroline bit her lips and wrung her hands all the way there, nearly snapping her fingers.

She'd not spoken to Adolphus since convincing him they needed Mr Frey, after which she'd embarked to London. It seemed the entire world had changed since then, and Caroline dreaded what she might find now.

'You'll be fine, gal,' Joan whispered, while pulling Caroline's hands apart, fearing she might hurt herself. 'You'll be fine. You'll all be fine.'

Caroline attempted a smile. Joan's words were kindly meant, but they still sounded hollow.

The carriage turned into Moray Place, the circus now draped in fog that would only get thicker through the night. Instantly Caroline looked for McGrays' façade: only one of the windows, the one that looked into the messy library, was lit. Quite dimly too.

'Wait for you again, ma'am?' the exhausted driver asked as he helped her alight for the umpteenth time that day.

'Yes,' Caroline said, and at once lifted her hem and rushed up the front steps. Old George opened the door, holding a gas lamp, for the house seemed to be plunged in darkness. The man looked very tired, the light trembling in his hand.

Caroline placed a hand on his wrist. 'Is he here?'

'Yes, miss, in his reading room. But if I were ye—'

Caroline made her way into the dim corridor. She could already hear the racket; books being thrown and chairs being dragged.

The door to the library opened with a creak, as though pushed by a ghost, but then Adolphus's golden retriever emerged, whimpering, and trotted towards Caroline to lick her fingertips. She patted its head, standing still by the partly open door and feeling how her heartbeats quickened.

She forced a deep breath – and stepped in.

McGray, his back turned to her, had just tossed a heavy book into a carpet bag, the thud making Caroline jump.

'Dammit, *George*! *Whoever's out there, ye can tell them to go fuck—!*'

He saw her then, and looked abashed for a split second. His shoulders dropped and all the former fury turned into exhaustion. He let go of the little book of maps he'd just been holding, and sat, or rather sank, onto a nearby cabinet.

Caroline took short, ginger steps towards him, the dog whining as it clung to her skirts. She saw Nine-Nails cover his brow, as if ashamed of his temper.

Hesitantly, she reached for his hand. It took some effort to pull it away from his face, bring it down and interlace their fingers. His were deathly cold.

'I'm sorry,' she whispered. 'I'm so sorry.'

Caroline saw the remains of a torn newspaper on the floor. It had been crumpled and trampled on, but she could still make out the news it told. Base, cruel language to narrate the day's facts. It made her stomach burn with anger.

She looked at their interlaced hands instead. Hers was a tiny morsel engulfed in his.

'I'm—' She gulped and thought of Joan's words, recalling how hollow they'd sounded despite the woman's best intentions, and Caroline said no more.

Adolphus must have understood. He squeezed her hand a little more – incredible that he could curb his strength to such subtle movements – and then he lowered his head, pressing his now cleanly shaven cheek against Caroline's forehead.

They remained thus for a while, as Caroline let the warmth of her hand seep into his.

Neither was fond of long speeches about ardent love or undying devotion. They preferred a quiet, understanding silence, as they'd discovered during that first visit in the last days of December. Adolphus had called on her as soon as he heard she'd decided to live alone. It was meant to be a single, short visit, but like so many times in his life, things had not gone as planned.

'That blasted body appeared right after Pansy ran away,' he mumbled, glaring at the newspaper. 'They're already trying to pin it on her.'

Caroline kicked the scraps of newspaper under the nearby sofa. 'I saw that mark. It could not have been Pansy. I mean – it could not have been her from the very first mark. And that last one was different.'

'Nae branded but cut out.'

'Yes.'

Caroline felt Adolphus's hand squeeze hers a little tighter.

'Did ye see it when ye talked to Trevelyan?'

She started. 'Did he – did he tell you I was there? I thought he didn't know my—' She then recalled having volunteered her name, and her heart skipped a beat.

Adolphus rose to his full height, and when he pulled his face away, Caroline felt her own skin go cold.

'Were ye looking for me to tell me Pansy's gone to Dundee?' he asked, looking at her with an odd expression.

Caroline opened her eyes wide. 'What?'

Adolphus did not speak. He simply stared at her, his eyes inquisitive, and Caroline could not think what to say.

'How did you know?' she whispered, though what she really wanted to ask was how *much* he knew.

Adolphus stared at her for a moment, before letting go of her hand. He then went back to his carpet bag.

'We asked people in the neighbourhood,' he said while he continued packing. 'Right after Pansy fled. They told us they saw a carriage getting away, and then some dandy boarding another cab and chasing it. That could've only been Frey.'

Caroline looked sideways, the scene still clear in her mind.

'That wasnae a discreet chase,' Adolphus went on. 'We asked many people and followed the trail here – even George heard the racket! And all these New Town twats love their gossip. It wasnae difficult to track them all the way to Granton Harbour.'

Caroline could not contain a gasp. When she finally looked at Adolphus, his pupils, catching the light from a sconce lamp, seemed to be on fire.

'Ye were there,' he said. 'The keeper at the harbour's lum tended to ye and Frey. And some other sissy Londoner.'

Caroline took a deep breath, surprised by her own anxiety. After all, she'd come here to tell him everything.

'We saw her leave, yes,' she spluttered, and Adolphus leapt closer to her.

'Was she all right?'

Caroline shut her eyes, her heart pounding as she recalled Mr Frey's account.

'She wasn't injured. One of the orderlies—'

'Tom. Aye, he went missing too. Was he with her?'

'Yes. He threatened Mr Frey with a rifle. They jumped together into a tugboat and sailed off.'

'Fuck!' Adolphus cried, rubbing his face. After a moment's hesitation he shook his head and began throwing hunting gear into the bag.

'Are you going to follow them?' Caroline cried.

'Och nae! I'm takin' ye to Seville so ye can buy me another horse.'

Caroline's mind was so muddled it took her a second to get the sarcasm.

'Are you sure?' she said. 'Mr Frey is following her. If Pansy really went to Dundee, he will handle it.'

Nine-Nails let out a bitter chuckle. 'Somebody once told Percy he couldnae handle a teapot without a cosy.'

'That – may be right, but – Adolphus, they are *hours* away. By the time you get to Dundee, Pansy might be long gone. And we are not even sure that's where they headed in the first place.'

'Where else could she have gone?'

Caroline bit her lip. The golden retriever, still stuck to her skirts, whimpered, as if able to feel her doubt.

'I don't know,' she said, 'but Dr Clouston might.'

Adolphus nearly sprained his neck when he looked up. 'Clouston?'

'Yes. I can assure you he knows far more than we all think. He might know where Pansy went.'

Adolphus dropped the carpet bag, pondering. 'I did try to talk to him, but—'

'He avoided you?'

'Aye, but I thought he was just too damned shocked by the—' Adolphus tilted his head. 'How d'ye ken he avoided me?'

Caroline gulped, suddenly feeling cold. The golden retriever let out a last whimper, before scuttling away.

'Miss – Miss Smith told me.'

Adolphus was astounded. For a few seconds he could not even blink.

'*Miss Smith?* How d'ye even ken her name? Ye've never talked to her! Ye told me ye talked to nobody when ye sneaked in to see yer dad!'

Caroline's eyes welled up with tears. The moment she'd feared so much was finally upon her.

'I – I do know her. And I know many other things I haven't told you yet. You—'

There was a sudden racket then, coming from the streets – a carriage and the neighing of horses, soon followed by George shouting.

Adolphus went to the window and looked out. Caroline went after him.

'I do need to tell you now,' she cried. 'This cannot wait another—'

'What the *fuck*'s he doing here?' Adolphus snapped, and then turned on his heels and stormed out of the library.

Caroline was going to run after him, but before doing so, she looked through the window.

Even in the thick fog, she saw the glow from the street lights reflected on a pale, smooth scalp.

39

'This is the furthest north I have ever travelled,' Elgie said, wrapping himself in one of the dusty blankets the driver had lent us.

We'd left Dundee well behind. The town was now but a ghostly glow barely visible through the back window, the wheels rattling frantically on the frozen road.

Soon there was nothing but black night around us, only occasionally interrupted by the lonely lights of remote dwellings. Like before, the driver's lantern would only show us the most immediate surroundings, but the wind and the silence suggested we rode across flat, uninterrupted grassland, now surely covered in snow.

The monotony was interrupted by the trickle of a river, and I saw we were crossing a narrow stone bridge. The road ascended gradually from then on, taking a gentle turn west.

I leaned closer to the window and saw the faint outlines of leafless trees, and then, emerging slowly, a low stone wall covered in moss and snow.

The driver slowed down and pulled the carriage closer to it, pointing the lantern at the stones. He halted a moment later, in front of a tattered wooden gate.

I could tell it had been opened years ago, never to be shut again, for there were dark, thorny brambles tangled around and through the old planks. It was the entrance to a small side path that led into solid blackness, like the entrance to a cave. I felt a pang of anxiety when the driver said, 'This is it, master. Cleaver House, as they told you.'

'Take us in,' I told him, and so he did. The horses neighed and snorted, as if fearing to tread there.

'Are you sure this is the place?' Elgie whispered, staring at the unkempt path. 'Rather the middle of nowhere.'

'I am not sure of anything anymore,' I answered, for a moment thinking that perhaps the man at the pub had lied to me. Though I *had* travelled much further north, I too felt as though we were at the end of the world.

The wilderness gradually gave way to birches and conifers, the evergreens rustling in the wind, and the rustic stone walls that edged the path suddenly changed into smooth granite.

The track and the walls ended, after another turn, in twin pillars crowned by elegant stone globes. Beyond, slightly darker than the night itself, was the outline of a wide Jacobean-style house, with steep gables and very tall chimney stacks.

My heart skipped a beat when I saw a couple of lit windows on the upper level. I could tell it was a single long room, lit by a modest, flickering fire.

Elgie saw it too, and gasped.

'Will that be her?'

Before answering, I looked at the grounds, the snow flat and smooth around manicured evergreens. The snow, I noticed, was undisturbed.

'It could be a servant,' I said. 'I see no other tracks ... and someone has definitely looked after these gardens.'

Those were the lawns Dr Clouston had visited more than six years ago, perhaps on a similarly dark night, right after Pansy's incident. And he would have been far more frightened than we were now.

The carriage followed a curved path lined with small hedges. We halted in front of a flight of granite steps, also flanked by stone banisters and carved globes. The moment the wheels stopped, a raven cawed in the darkness, followed by the sound of flapping wings that faded in the distance.

I took a deep breath as I opened the carriage door. At last we had made it, after what had felt like years of journeying.

'Ready?' I asked Elgie, and he started.

'What do you mean *ready*?'

'I cannot go in there on my own.'

'The driver—'

'Needs to look after the horses and the bloody carriage. Unless you feel capable of defending them if Miss McGray and her brute appear.'

Elgie looked from side to side, then grunted and opened his door.

The driver was lighting a second lantern, which he handed to me. 'Want me to go in with youse, master?'

'No. Stay alert. We may need to leave in haste.'

The man nodded stoically, unlike Elgie.

'What do you mean in haste?' he whispered as we rushed up the steps. I preferred not to answer.

The steps led us to a little terraced garden that surrounded the property. I raised the lantern and we saw well-trimmed yews and rose bushes hugging the house's walls. There was also an imposing, gnarly ivy that climbed almost all the way to the intersecting gables.

'I thought they were paupers,' Elgie muttered.

'Not at all. McGray still owns a distillery not far from here.'

I looked up at the lit windows. Behind the mullions I caught a glimpse of a grimy wall and ceiling. I stared for a moment, hoping to see someone's shadow projected against the plaster, but there was only the flicker of the fire, so we walked on.

As we walked around the house, part of me felt as though we were about to enter some mythical place – like a Pharaoh's tomb, or some fortress mentioned in ancient tales. Behind those very walls Pansy had gone berserk; she'd murdered her parents and chopped off her brother's finger.

And those foreboding walls, amidst the cold and the dark, seemed to deserve their reputation in town.

Behind the next corner we found the stone porch, the year *1826* carved on the ornate gable. Below was a dark oaken door.

I thought of knocking, my hand already raised, but decided not to. Instead, I reached for the doorknob and twisted.

It was unlocked.

An icy breeze blew around us and the cold seeped through the skin on the back of my neck, all the way to my bones and marrow. I pushed the door gently, the hinges making a faint creak. I took a few careful steps in and we were met by the smell of damp, dust and old furniture.

The one trace of light came from a substantial staircase, but the rest of the dwelling was pitch-black.

I raised the lantern and we saw the floorboards, clean but ridden with woodworm; curtains neatly arranged but frayed and faded; and the plaster on the walls dotted with damp at the upper corners. The general feeling was that of a house that did her best to remain standing, but was gradually losing a long battle against decay.

I shivered, the place only a little less cold than the fields outside.

'I have this feeling –' Elgie whispered, his breath condensing before him – 'that we should not be here.'

'Don't be ridiculous,' I said, and walked on before the same fears took hold of me.

'Ian!' Elgie said then, pulling me by the elbow.

'Oh, would you please—?'

'Look!'

He pointed to our left. I saw an otherwise elegant door, long ago ripped off its hinges, taking some of the plaster with it. It had been propped back in place and boarded up with coarse wooden plinths, secured in place with bent, rusty nails.

'That must be the room,' Elgie muttered. 'Where – where it all happened.'

'Indeed,' I whispered, but then turned hastily on my heels and headed to the stairs. I did not even want to stand near that door.

The wooden steps creaked loudly under our feet, Elgie starting with each noise. We saw many frames hanging on the walls, all the paintings covered with old sheets.

My brother grabbed my arm.

'Can you hear that?' he said as softly as he could.

I halted, listened, and nearly gasped – not one, but two sounds.

One was a faint, rhythmic creak. The other, a tad clearer, was an irregular, very soft rattle.

It made me think of teeth falling into a tin bucket.

I tensed my lips and nodded at Elgie, indicating he should stay behind me. He did so and we climbed the next flight of steps.

We made it to a long landing and then, before I had gathered enough courage, there it was, right before my eyes: the door where the light came from.

It was ajar.

I felt Elgie's hand clutching my shoulder, his troubled breath on the back of my neck. The clatter sounded more clearly, and the rhythmic creak came and went along with an intermittent shadow beyond the threshold.

I took a long, deep breath, and then spoke with a firmness that surprised me.

'Hello, there?'

The noises stopped. The shadow went still.

We waited there, holding our breaths for what felt like a painfully long time, but there was no reply.

'We mean no harm,' I said, already raising my palm, as if preparing myself to appease a wild beast.

No reply. We only heard another clatter – another *tooth*.

I took a step forward. 'We would like to come in,' I said, my voice trembling at the last words. I stretched an equally trembling hand and pushed the door.

I shuddered when I saw the occupant.

A mightily old woman, seated on a rocking chair, her legs wrapped in a threadbare blanket.

She reminded me of the elder witches, her skin leathery and creased, her hair white and brittle. Even though she was sitting, her head and her shoulders were bent forwards, so I could only see her protruding cheekbones and a nose reddened by decades in the cold. Her hands, blotched and bony, were clenched on her lap. She'd been shelling pods of dry beans, tossing them into a pewter dish by her side.

I took a quick look. The room had been turned into a kitchen, bedroom and living room, with sacks of beans and oats in a corner, and a heap of firewood stacked next to the hearth.

An old servant, I gathered, and McGray must pay someone to bring her supplies.

Just as I thought of him, the woman lifted her head.

'Master?' she said with an infirm voice.

I gulped. 'I – I am afraid we are not—'

'*Told ye before!*' she snapped, making Elgie jolt behind me. 'Am nae leaving!'

I shut my eyes for a moment, trying to recollect the many times Joan had told me the McGrays' tale. She had mentioned George, and also a female servant.

'Betsy?' I asked.

She must be, for she spoke more confidently.

'I told ye, I'm nae leaving! *This is the auld master's home!*' and she clenched the arms of the rocking chair, as if that could plant her more firmly on the ground.

I felt so sorry for her. I could picture the aging woman painstakingly cleaning and maintaining that house for the past six years, all alone, perhaps in the hope that her master returned one day.

'It's all right,' I said softly as I knelt in front of her. 'We've not come to take you away.'

'I'm nae leaving!' she repeated, her lower lip pushed out.

'Of course, of course. We are just looking for the girl Amy. Pansy.'

The woman clenched the chair more tightly and bent her head further.

'She won't be here,' she said bitterly. 'They took her to the madhouse.'

'I know,' I said. 'It was all very sad.'

Betsy nodded with a grunt. I leaned forwards a little, trying to look into her eyes, but the woman recoiled.

I was afraid to ask the next question.

'So, Miss Amy...' I whispered slowly. 'Has she not been back?'

For a moment there was no reaction, and I waited with held breath.

The woman laughed then, the sound bouncing across the walls and soon turning into a reverberating cough. For a moment I thought she'd choke to death in front of us. Thankfully the cough faded and she wiped the corners of her mouth with her sleeve.

'*Back?* She'll ne'er come back! Nae after Auld Nick was in this hoose.'

The name came out as a growl, sending a shiver down my spine.

'*The Devil?*' I whispered, frowning. 'Has the Devil been here?'

Betsy chuckled. 'As if ye didnae ken. 'Course Auld Nick has been here. I saw him!'

'You *saw* the Devil?'

The woman nodded with anxiety.

'Aye, but I didnae have the courage to tell anyone.' She moved her jaw from side to side, as if deliberately trying to dislocate it, her yellowish teeth catching light from the fire. 'I thought they'd take me to the madhouse too, like they did the poor lass. She was the brave one – she 'n' her brother.'

She went silent. I was going to say something, but then Betsy let out a tearing scream.

'*But I don't care now!* Ye cannae take me to the madhouse for telling the truth! *Aye!* I saw him with my own eyes! The boy Adolphus did too.'

I took a couple of deep breaths, my heart pounding.

'Yes,' I said. 'Yes. I know he did. He – he told me himself.'

It was true. Right at the end of our first case, McGray had confessed to it, but I had always thought he'd imagined it somehow. After all, he claimed it had happened right after he found his parents dead on the floor and after Pansy had mutilated his hand.

'Where did you see him?' I asked. 'Was it – in the room where it all happened?'

The woman's chest shook. I thought it was the prelude to another fit of coughing, but it turned out to be just a throttled laughter.

'Aye. I saw him crawling away; slithering through the window like a black lizard! Youse will think I'm mad, but I saw him. *I saw his horns!*'

She looked up at Elgie when she said that, and for a moment I caught a glimpse of her eyes, veiny and ridden with cataracts. I heard Elgie jump, perhaps hitting himself against the doorframe, but I did not take my gaze from the woman.

'But I kept quiet,' she mumbled, clenching her hands. 'I kept my mouth shut 'n' it's been eating me inside e'er since!'

I nodded, my pulse finally slowing down. Everything she'd said, word for word, matched McGray's statement.

'I believe you,' I said. 'I have heard the story before. I believe you.'

It seemed to work. Betsy took in hissing breaths as she slowly bent her head down, like a turtle returning to her shell.

She was slightly unhinged, I thought. Maybe because of her solitude, or the impact of those events, or the burden of not telling a soul what she thought she'd seen. Either way, she had no reason to lie.

'Do you mind if we – have a look in that room?'

She shook her head. 'The library's been boarded up for years.'

'Yes, we saw, but we can try to—'

Betsy grunted and waved a hand, as if saying she could not care less. She then focussed on the dry pods again, patiently chucking beans into the pot.

I rose gently. 'Thank you, ma'am.'

She did not even flinch.

When I turned around, I saw that Elgie was as pale as a bleached bone. I squeezed his shoulder.

'Come on,' I said, and I had to pull him out of that eerie room.

'Miss McGray is obviously not here,' he babbled. 'Can we go now?'

'No. I want to inspect that library.'

'But it's all boarded up!'

'Then we are breaking in! The driver must keep some tools in the carriage.'

'But—'

'I *must* look. I may never again come this close to finding the truth.'

40

'*Begone, youse bastards!*' George was shouting by the door, his lamp held up high while Joan and the boy Larry brandished broomsticks as if they were truncheons.

Caroline only saw them for a second, before Adolphus planted himself on the threshold and obscured the view.

'Ye heard the lad!' he growled. '*Piss off!*'

His dogs, both the golden retriever and the far more menacing mastiff, ran out to flank their master, barking like wild beasts.

Caroline peered through the gap between Adolphus's shoulder and the wall, and saw that her carriage was now surrounded by two other cabs, from which four tall, sturdy men had emerged. Their faces were all weathered and covered in dust, as if they'd just been working at—

'The quarry,' Caroline whispered. She tilted her head sideways, the better to see, and she found the bald fiscal, dwarfed among the burly workers, standing on the house's front steps.

The man was wringing his bowler hat, his knuckles jutting through his leather gloves. No wonder she'd seen his scalp through the window – the man was dripping perspiration, and his face quivered with a disturbing blend of fear and seething rage. Caroline thought he looked like someone about to jump off a cliff, forced to do so in front of a cackling enemy.

'I am only here to convey a message,' he said, his voice a constricted grunt.

Adolphus moved forwards. 'I got one for ye: tell yer bastard prick of a son he needs to show up at the City Chambers to-morrow. Trevelyan will question him himself.'

Pratt nearly tore his hat in two. He took a deep breath.

'My message—'

'We all ken yer brat's a blithering idiot. *He led us to his stinking hovel himself!*'

Caroline saw lights appear in the neighbouring houses, people peering through their windows and some servants from their front doors.

Pratt scowled.

'*My son did nothing!*' he hissed.

'Did nothing right!' Adolphus said after a cackle. 'Just like his sad auld man. Ye must be veeery proud.'

Pratt, unexpectedly, let out a chuckle. 'Just as you are of your sister?'

There was a wave of laughter, not only from the miners, but from some of the nearby houses too.

'I know the police have evidence,' Pratt added. '*Hard* evidence found in your sister's chambers. And hearing that you shot the Lord Provost's—'

'*Och, fuck off!*' Nine-Nails butted in, and then patted Joan and George, who returned inside. 'And go *convey messages* to yer bitch of a—'

'Someone wants to see you,' Pratt had to shout, trotting path-etically up the steps.

Adolphus turned around and seized him by the neck.

'Tell them to fuck off too, or I'll—!'

'It's Lady Anne,' Pratt whispered.

Caroline felt her jaw drop slightly, unable even to let out a gasp, and in the split second it took Nine-Nails to react, she saw that the brawny miners had rushed to protect the fiscal. For some reason, that man was now glaring directly at her.

Adolphus let out a loud, '*Ha!* Ye tell that auld bitch she can—'

'*For her sake*,' Pratt howled, nodding at Caroline, and then continuing in a low voice, 'I would not ignore Lady Anne's call. And I'd go quietly.'

Caroline had to shut her eyes. How much would her grandmother know?

Everything, most likely.

When she looked again, Caroline found everyone staring at her; the miners, the drivers and the servants. And Adolphus's eyes flickered from her to Pratt.

He gripped the man's neck more tightly, pulled him to, and hissed a couple of inches from his face, 'Are ye playing games, Pratt? Remember, every time ye've tried to mess with us, ye've ended up as scorched as my grandma's festy cock.'

The man gagged a few times, barely standing on his tiptoes. And yet, he managed a triumphal smile.

'No games, Nine-Nails. Lady Anne's the only person who can help you now. All you have to do is see her. Ignore her – and all of you will be doomed. *All* of you.'

He said it softly, in a cold, matter-of-fact tone, which made it all the more disturbing.

Adolphus pondered. He looked at Caroline from the corner of his eye, and she could not conceal her angst.

'What's he talking about?' he whispered. Caroline looked around, all eyes still on her, and for an awful moment she could not bring herself to speak.

'Very well,' Adolphus whispered, pushing Pratt away. The man nearly fell on his back, but no one was looking at him.

Everyone stared at Adolphus as he strode swiftly into the house. He came back within seconds with a gun in his hand

and, making sure everyone saw it, he checked that the cylinder was fully loaded.

Caroline shuddered, but then forced herself to lift her chin.

'We'll go in my carriage,' she said, already heading there, but one of the miners blocked her way.

'He must come alone,' Pratt snarled, and then gave her a hyena's smile. 'Your grandmother's bidding, Miss Ardglass.'

A cold hand touched hers, and Caroline started. It was Adolphus.

'I'll be back soon,' he said, his tone reassuring. 'I'll just tell her to her face she can sod off.'

Caroline moved a little closer. 'You cannot go!' she whispered, her entire body shaking. 'There's – there's something I need to tell you—'

'She won't wait for long!' Pratt said loudly.

Adolphus looked deep into Caroline's eyes, his own irises flickering. She saw his confusion … and a sudden shade of mistrust. How could she blame him?

'I'll be back soon,' he repeated, then patted her on the shoulder and walked down the steps before she could say a word.

'I don't want trouble,' Caroline's driver said when he saw Adolphus opening the cab's door.

'Then drive!' he snapped, hopping in.

As soon as he had shut the small door, Caroline felt as if the street had gone a shade darker, the fog a little thicker. The other men jumped into their respective cabs, followed by Pratt, who gave her one last bow of the head.

As they set off, Caroline again felt hands gently holding her by the arm. It was Joan this time.

She said nothing, though. The woman simply stood next to her, while they saw the three carriages ride around the circus and become lost in the thick mist.

Caroline only managed to move a hand, clumsily covering her mouth as the full implications of the summons dawned on her.

She'd had so many chances to tell Adolphus the truth. So many evenings spent together; so many days…

And now it was too late. Now he'd hear it all from the twisted lips of Lady Glass.

She knew, with all certainty, she had just lost him forever.

41

The plinth cracked at the first pull, the wood dry and dusty. The driver moved it away, and then pried the next one with his crowbar.

I held the lantern next to him, Elgie coughing behind the clouds of dust.

The door nearly fell forwards as soon as the man retrieved the last board, but I held it with my free hand.

'Thank you,' I said. 'You can leave us now.'

The man arched a brow. 'Ye sure, master?'

'Yes.' I nodded at the crowbar. 'Do keep that handy.'

He weighed it, hesitant to leave, but in the end he nodded and walked away. I waited until I saw him disappear through the front door.

'Hold this,' I told Elgie then, handing him the lantern. He was fanning the dust with his handkerchief, and I wondered if I'd looked as soft as him when I first arrived in Scotland.

I propped the door against the wall and then peered into the room. It was pitch-black, the smell of damp and dust much stronger there. Elgie gave me the lantern back, and once more I led the way into the darkness.

The light cast long shadows around us, all the surfaces grey and fuzzy, for everything in that room was covered by thick layers of dust – even the cobwebs that hung from the ceiling. The layer on the carpets felt like a cushion under my feet.

'They must have boarded it up right after the incident,' I said, feeling a renewed shudder. 'Never opened again until now.' I must be treading on the very spot McGray had stood when he caught his first glimpse of that night's gore.

'I thought there had been an inquest,' Elgie said.

'Yes, but clearly they never inspected the place. They must have thought it was pointless after Miss McGray was declared insane.'

I strode carefully. The air felt a little colder there, and also *charged* with something I could not quite identify. Like some eerie presence that had lingered there, locked between those mouldy walls.

To my right there was a large sofa, with papers and books still strewn among the cushions. I could not even tell the colour of the upholstery anymore. The wall behind it was lined with crammed bookshelves, one of them collapsed in the middle. And there was also a tall cabinet, like the one my late uncle used to keep his hunting gear.

To my left there was a window, boarded up like the door had been. That would be the window through which the Devil had allegedly escaped.

I walked to it, drawn by some morbid magnetism, and then I raised my free hand and touched the boards. They were fitted quite snuggly, but I still felt an icy draught coming in. They had never replaced the glass, and the shards still lay on the sill and the carpet below.

'Would the Devil need to smash a window?' I mumbled, looking down.

Any marks of steps would be long gone, but I still looked closely, wiping the dust with my feet as I stepped back to the centre of the room.

'A nice Persian rug,' I said, revealing the green and brown pattern, until—

Elgie gasped.

I'd just disturbed the dust that covered a dark, almost black stain. I squatted down and, repressing a retch, wiped the dust ahead of me.

I uncovered the entire stain, almost three feet wide; a pool of blood that had seeped into the rug's fibres, dry and caked after six years.

As I wiped the dust, my hand touched something. I started, for a ghastly instant thinking I'd just found McGray's missing finger. I wiped more dust from what turned out to be a metallic rod.

'A fire poker—' I mumbled. I was about to lift it, but before doing so I gauged its position. It lay right next to the stain.

Elgie panted. 'Gosh! Is that what Miss McGray used to—?'

He could not finish the sentence, so I nodded.

'McGray's mother, yes. That is what the depositions from the inquiry said.'

I also remembered that McGray had sorted the burials himself, and I felt a tremble. Had he also had to remove the fire poker from his own mother's body?

'Let's go,' Elgie whispered. 'I don't want to be here.'

I leaned down, examining the wrought iron closely, though I did not dare touch it. I saw that it was an expensive, very ornate piece, but when I found the tip, I went still.

'What is it?' Elgie asked me.

I forced myself to touch the cold iron. 'This is rather blunt.'

'Yes. Most pokers are.'

'No, I mean – you'd need a lot of strength to pierce someone's body with it.'

Picturing the scene at once made me queasy. I looked up and

lifted the lantern. I saw, just some six feet away, the dark hovel of a wide fireplace. I rose and went closer.

'McGray could definitely kill a man with a fire poker,' I mumbled. '*I* would struggle...' I looked at Elgie. 'You certainly could not. Even less Miss McGray. She was fifteen back then, and presumably as dainty as she is now.'

Elgie frowned. 'She did look rather petite on the harbour. Are you saying...?'

I let out a growl. I had known that fact for more than a year. I'd heard it time and again, read it on the official documents, and yet I'd never pondered on the mechanics. I could understand McGray not wanting to analyse the nuts and bolts of his mother's slaughter, but *I* should have known better!

I shed light on the fireplace. There was an eerie collection of antlers and skulls hanging over the mantelpiece, all covered in clumps of dust, their hollow eyes seemingly staring at us, intruders.

I looked down, to the grille and the hearth.

There were several pokers there, all propped vertically on a stand, some with the sharp ends upwards. I looked at the spikes in turn and then back at the stain on the floor. The distance was about the same as a person's height.

Elgie's curiosity was stronger than his fear. He too came to the hearth and stared at the set of instruments.

I felt a discomfort growing in my chest, part dismay and part disgust.

'Oh, Lord!' I said. 'Could it all have been an accident?'

I thought my voice had echoed across the room, but it had not. It was another sound. It lingered, then faded and came back. I realised with a chill that it was a throaty laughter.

'No...'

The soft, breathy voice came in like a freezing draught.

Elgie and I turned swiftly, both nearly losing our balance, too shocked even to gasp.

There she was. Standing like a spectre under the threshold, holding a thin candle that sharply delineated her pale face. Her black dress and cloak merged into the surrounding shadows, as if her hands and slim neck where those of a floating ghost. Her eyes, also dark, were like tunnels letting through fragments of the gloom behind her.

Her pupils moved in circles, gauging the room as if she saw it for the first time. Then they fixed on me, and I felt a chill.

'There were no accidents,' she whispered, her voice dreamy. 'I really am the reason they're dead.'

And she tilted her lips slightly, halfway to a blood-curdling smile.

42

Pansy stepped in, her tread light, the candle holder firm in her hand. Once more she appeared to be floating.

Elgie finally managed to draw in a breath, his chest heaving with dread.

'Go,' I whispered into his ear, but he did not move; he simply stared at Pansy, without blinking. She was approaching slowly but steadily.

I had to push my brother to one side, and only then did he react. He took faltering steps, moving in a circle and keeping as far from Pansy as he could. He stumbled against the sofa, lifting a cloud of dust. Elgie panted and raised his palms in Pansy's direction, as if pretending to fend off a lion.

She seemed not even to notice him. Her eyes were hooked on me, as intense as they had been at the harbour, her pupils shaking. I could not possibly tell whether she was insane or not.

Elgie reached the threshold and stopped. I nodded and mouthed, 'Go.'

I regretted it the instant he disappeared, for it happened just as Pansy reached the dark stain on the carpet. She stopped and lowered her eyes.

I cannot describe her expression. Her lips were parted, her brow ever-so-slightly furrowed, and there it was again – the hint of a smile, as though she were staring at the world's greatest irony.

I realised the perfect amalgamation that her face was – Caroline's eyes, Lady Anne's poise and frame, Lord Joel's cheekbones, McGray's pointy chin... They were all in her.

Pansy bent down, startling me. She stretched her free hand and seized the fire poker.

Her hands reminded me of Lady Anne's, with sharp knuckles and long, thin fingers, the veins bulging as she easily picked up the wrought iron. She raised it slowly, the sharper end of the poker pointing upwards.

Suddenly she did not seem quite so dainty, the instrument not so blunt.

I gulped. 'Miss McGray—'

Pansy drew in a hissing breath, gazing at the fire poker as if it were the strangest object she'd ever beheld. She brought the candle closer to it and, with a shudder, I understood her fascination.

Even after six years, the tip still looked slightly darker than the rest.

'It looks the same,' she mumbled, stunned by the fact. She looked around, nearly dropping the candle, and hissed, 'Everything here looks the *same!*'

She began spinning, pointing at the objects with the poker.

'The antlers, the broken shelf, the books – even that blasted feather on the sofa.'

She signalled it and I saw an elongated shape, half buried in the dust. I guessed it was a pheasant's feather, perhaps from her father's hunting spoils. The most trivial of objects, but Pansy now glared at it, her cheeks turning from white to red. Her body began to tremble with uncontainable rage. She bared her teeth and then growled, her voice rising with each word.

'People die and get buried and rot in the ground – *yet everything here looks the same!*'

Her eyes quivered, pooling tears that she could not quite shed. As gently as I could, I raised an appeasing hand.

'Miss McGray—'

She pointed the poker at me, turning her head so fast I thought she'd snapped her neck. She held the instrument, brandishing it like a spear, and pointing it directly at my chest. At once I felt a phantom prickle, right on the spot she was about to stab, which increased with each judder of her hand.

Pansy took a tiny step forwards. She did not dare tread on her mother's blood and instead walked around it, each careful step muffled by the dust. The boards under the rug creaked then, and she halted. It was as if the sound reawakened her for a moment. She looked sideways, like a hound listening for prey. She soon looked back at me, her eerie expression back, now accompanied by troubled breaths. But she did not walk on.

She simply stretched her arm to bring the poker closer to my chest.

Even through the wrath, through her animalistic panting, and despite that rusty instrument ready to stab me in the heart – I could already tell.

'You—' I whispered, my mouth dry. 'You did *not* do it.'

Pansy went still, her tremors and her breath halting. Her rage briefly turned into shock. In the deep silence I thought I heard voices upstairs – had she heard them too? – but I'd have no chance to dwell on them, for Pansy's lips stretched in an unnerving smile.

'Oh I did. I did, all right!'

She nodded, slowly at first but then frenetically. And as she did so, the girl retreated, stepping backwards and bringing the poker closer to her eyes. The thought of her stabbing her own smiling face made me tremble far more than any threat to myself.

The candle shook in her hand until it slipped from her fingers and fell to the floor. As dust and carpet began to catch fire, Pansy raised a hand to cover her brow. She gathered air, just as she'd done at the asylum a few days ago, only this time nothing would contain her.

She let out a howling scream; the most dreadful, most anguished sound I had ever heard. It came from the depths of her stomach, shrilling and incessant, ascending to the ceiling and bouncing on the walls.

She dropped the poker, the thud barely audible under her wail.

It was the fire that made me react, spreading fast on the dust as Pansy sank to her knees. I put my lantern on the floor and rushed to stamp on the flames. As I did so, I seized Pansy by the arms and held her before she dropped to the floor. She was deathly cold.

Her shriek did not stop, and all I could think of doing was to steer her to the dusty sofa. I carefully placed her there, and just as her lungs ran out of air, I heard the thud of heavy steps behind me.

I looked over my shoulder and saw the tall, burly figure of Tom.

'*Let her go!*' he commanded, pointing his rifle at me.

'Oh, for goodness' sake!'

'*I'll shoot you!*' he shouted. I noticed he carried a heavy bag on his shoulder, perhaps with Pansy's money and possessions.

I let her go, took a deep breath and moved away with my palms raised. By then her howl had faded and the poor girl coiled up on herself, rubbing her chest as if desperate to warm up her insides.

'We came to help you,' I said, looking alternatively at them, and then nodded at the bag. 'I see you came here for provisions, but where will you go now?'

'That's none o' your business,' Tom interrupted, the rifle firm in his hands.

'This cannot end well. For either of you. Tom – how could you agree to this? The police will go after you. Did Clouston not tell you?'

Pansy drew in a hissing breath. With my nerves shattered, that was enough to silence me.

'Go,' she mumbled. I thought she meant me and I was about to retort, but then she spoke again. 'Go, Tom. Please. For a moment.'

He snorted. 'I'm not leaving you with—'

'*Go!*' she shouted, with a shrill that again made me doubt her self-proclaimed sanity.

Tom took a deep breath and, most grudgingly, lowered the rifle.

'I'll be guarding the door,' he said, glaring at me even as he propped it back into place.

The man gone, the only sound we could hear was the barely audible hiss of a draught; the icy air coming through the boarded window.

That was the sound I'd heard before while standing next to her: that gentle, never-ending murmur, like that from a seashell.

The superstitious would tell me I'd always known of this moment; that I had always been destined to stand here and now.

I stepped away from Pansy, pretending to reach for the lamp. In truth, I did not want to stand so close to her, especially since she began so stir on the sofa, again rubbing her chest, looking very much like the mad girl everyone believed her to be.

'I'll tell you,' she said between choked breaths. 'I'll tell you everything, Mr Frey. All that happened here.'

43

The carriages rode briefly north and then turned east, very soon leaving behind the lights of Edinburgh.

McGray kept hold of his gun, a finger on the trigger at all times, thinking the miners might simply be driving him away to murder him in quiet.

No, too many witnesses, he thought. Everyone at Moray Place had seen them fetch him and all the snooty neighbours had heard it was Lady Glass who'd summoned him. If the old crone wanted him dead, she would have been far more discreet.

Unexpectedly, the dark countryside did not sound quiet. McGray heard the echoes of steam engines and machinery, and as the carriages reached the summit of a small hill, he saw what appeared to be the crater to an ancient volcano.

It was Craigleith Quarry, lit from below by the countless men who worked there well into the night. McGray saw the chimneys spewing smoke, the spiky hoists retrieving stone from the depths of the earth and, as the carriages approached the edge of the chasm, he also saw the workshops and houses built at the base of the pit. They seemed like matchboxes with mere specks of light for windows, and the men who walked down there, carrying lanterns, made him think of meandering glow-worms.

The carriages rode towards the main workshops. They were a

hive of activity, the conveyors and silos lit by countless gaslights, where the workers crushed, cut and cleaned the sandstone. McGray winced at the crates of explosives piled so close to steam engines and naked flames, their sulphurous pong floating in the air.

They took a turn to a yard where half a dozen carts were being loaded with flagstones, brick and rubble. The measly horses, their eyes covered so the incessant activity did not frighten them, seemed inured to the noise.

The carriages continued on to an adjacent yard, much closer to the edge of the quarry. There were enormous blocks of sandstone there, already cut into perfect prisms and arranged in neat stacks, thrice the height of the men who ran around them.

There was Lady Anne.

McGray saw her seated among the angular boulders and surrounded by her tallest workers, like an ancient druidess about to perform some sort of sacrifice within a stone circle.

Her men had installed a little table next to her cushioned chair, everything covered with clean blankets, so her ladyship's dress and plumed hairpiece did not get blemished with the fine dust. There was something on the table, the size of a small crate, also covered in sheets, but McGray did not have time to ponder on it, for someone else caught his eye.

Another man was standing there, shorter and much thinner than the miners and foremen. His black suit, like Lady Anne's mourning attire, stood out amidst the dust.

Dr Clouston.

McGray felt a pang in his chest when he recognised him. The doctor glanced at the carriages but then lowered his head, his eyes fixed on his shoes. His expression was that of a man standing by the gallows.

The carriages halted, forming a semicircle around Lady Anne's table, and McGray hopped off at once.

'*Doctor?*' he cried, and Clouston let out a burst of steaming breath.

'I'm so sorry, Adolphus,' he muttered, unable to look him in the eye. 'I'm sorry for every—'

'*Shut it!*' one of the miners snarled at him.

McGray turned to Lady Glass and found her wrapped in black bear furs. Her butler stood next to her, holding a silver tray with a cut-glass decanter. As McGray approached, he poured more claret into the lady's glass.

'Saved yer best claret for this?' McGray barked, making sure she could see his gun.

Lady Anne pulled a little smirk, but did not reply. Instead, she made a slight nod to a muscly man who stood nearby, clearly her foreman. He shouted some command, repeated by others in the distance, and within seconds the entire quarry came to a halt. The natural silence of the countryside took over, and Lady Anne smiled with satisfaction, able to silence the world with the smallest movement of her chin.

'Good evening, Adolphus,' she said, before taking a leisurely sip.

'Speak quickly,' McGray snapped, 'so I don't have to look at yer shrivelled hide for too long.'

Lady Anne grinned in earnest, as if to show off her creases.

'Before I speak, I shall show you something.'

She nodded again, and the foreman rushed to lift the cloth and reveal what sat on the table.

In the dim light, it took McGray a moment to make out what the object was. When he did, he gasped.

A gleaming typewriter, its brass keys and levers catching the glow from the nearby lamps.

'What?' McGray mumbled, as all the facts took shape in his mind. The swirl of thoughts even made him sway.

He took a step forwards, but right then a dozen guns were pointed at him.

Lady Anne made another gesture. Her foreman picked up the typewriter, heavy even for him, and before McGray could even utter a syllable, the man strode to the edge of the cliff and threw the artefact into the abyss.

'*Wait!*' McGray yelped as he darted forwards, for an instant not even thinking of the guns aimed at him, and two men had to run and restrain him.

Amidst his grunts, they heard the rattle of the typewriter, ever dimmer, as it rolled down the cliff.

'You'd better not do that again,' Pratt told Nine-Nails from a prudent distance.

The men let go of McGray then, and for a moment he simply stood there, surrounded by those hostile characters and the remorseful Clouston.

McGray took a few troubled breaths, forcing himself to calm down; to think. He let out one last sigh as he covered his brow.

'Of course,' he whispered. 'Of course it was ye! Ye sent all those notes to the newspapers! This weasel Pratt told ye everything – his bastard brat told him what he'd been up to – and then ye prattled away like a sodding parrot!' He snorted. 'Just like Percy said – there had to be a scheming, methodical fucking viper behind it all!'

He turned to face Pratt, the man cowering behind a particularly rough-looking miner.

'How did yer wee rat do it? How did he brand the bodies?'

Pratt chuckled. 'It was the Devil, was it not? I thought that would be your preferred theory: the lurking *demon* that—'

'Oh, shut up, Mr Pratt!' Lady Anne interjected. 'You do live up to your name sometimes.'

Her men, even her butler, let out barefaced giggles, but they all went quiet when Lady Anne spoke again.

'I did not bring you here to tell you who did what and when and why, so that you could then run and chase certain idiots.' She glanced at Pratt when she said this, then took a long swig of claret and looked back at McGray. She smacked her lips in a repulsive manner.

'If I've owned to typing those letters, it is only to prove that all I am about to say is true. Starting with the fact that you have no evidence to absolve your snotty mad sister.

'That typewriter would have been your only link. It's a *shame* you won't be able to take it to a specialist in London to pair it with the letters. Not that you were even thinking of searching my residence, were you? You probably thought it was some stupid lunatics' doctor who'd typed them.'

McGray felt his insides set on fire. His gun still lowered, he squeezed his finger on the trigger. How tempting it was to shoot the damn woman there and then, even if her men shot him straight away. A swift end. Tempting indeed.

'Did ye type the damn things yerself?' he hissed.

'Oh, I did. I find those new contraptions truly amusing.'

'And ye didnae snap yer fucking mummy fingers?'

Lady Glass sneered. 'Mock my age, Adolphus, but that is my greatest strength. I've seen it all. I can tell the trivial from the transcendental. The fool from the wise.'

She took another drink, and savoured it in her mouth as she looked him up and down. The tendons on her neck contracted repulsively as she swallowed.

'You, Adolphus, are a fool. A scared child; too scared to confront what's been staring him in the face for years. Idolising your father, ignoring how he treated your slag of a mother—'

McGray raised his gun at once, pointing directly at Lady Anne's left eye.

'*Insult them one more time,*' he hissed, just as all the other guns

344

were raised too, '*and I swear I'll blow yer damn brains out! Seeing them one second before I die will be well worth it!*'

Lady Anne lifted her chin as if to offer him a better shot. Her eyes glimmered with pleasure and contempt.

'A fool, gentlemen,' she said, pointing at him with her glass. 'Did I not just say it?' She took another sip while her men laughed. 'Your father was a fool too. A despicable fool. You remind me so much of him. He pulled the same idiotic face of yours the last time I talked to him. Coincidentally, that was also the day he died.'

The words lingered in the icy air, McGray's own fingers going numb with pins and needles.

Without noticing, he lowered his gun a little. 'Ye *what*?'

He barely managed to say the words, his eyes flickering from Lady Anne to Pratt and then to the butler. They were all astonished too.

The only person who did not seem shocked was Dr Clouston. McGray was going to ask him why, but he could not put the sentence together; not while Lady Glass grinned at him, her eyes bulging and her teeth bared. She looked like a snake that had just administered her venom.

'Yes, Adolphus,' she whispered, leaning slightly forwards. 'I was there.'

44

'I think of that day all the time,' Pansy murmured. 'Every morning when I wake up and every night when I go to sleep... I so dread going to sleep—

'My poor father – Mr McGray, I mean. Even after all these years, I still call him my father. He'd been edgy for days and days. I could tell something was wrong. He was always short tempered, especially to my mother, but not like this.

'I needed to talk to him. He trusted me more than he did anyone else; told me things he never told anyone else. He told me of my poor mum's miscarriage, soon after my brother Adolphus was born. He also told me they never laid together after that. Well – except for that *one* time, when I was – well, when he *thought* I was...

'One day he sent all the servants away. He always gave them some free time whenever we came to this house, whether it was for the summer or for a hunt, or just to get away from the nasty snobs in Edinburgh, always calling us "rustic upstarts" behind our backs.

'He sent them away to the public house, so I knew it was the perfect time to speak to him in private. I asked Adolphus to go out riding with me, but only to get him out of the house. We rode to the lake. God, how I remember that!

'It was warm and the sunset was beautiful, just a few clouds in the sky. That was the last sunset I saw from here. And the last time I ever spoke to him. I only – I only wish I'd kissed him goodbye...

'But I couldn't. I pretended to be tired and came back. The house was deserted. There was only Betsy in the kitchens, having a nap. No sign of my mother. I came here...

'God, I came here. I'll never forget those instants before I knocked on the door. I heard thuds – one after the other, like a drum. And then I heard a whimper and wood shattering and books tumbling about.

'I opened the door and – my mother was right there. Right there! With her back against the bookshelves. And my father had grabbed her by the neck. He...

'God!

'He was punching her in the stomach. He...

'I shrieked!

'I ran to him and begged him to stop. I even tried to pull him away, but he pushed me so hard I fell backwards and rolled on this sofa.' Pansy picked up the feather, studying it as she wiped the dust off. It really was a pheasant's, only dyed black.

'Strange,' she whispered, 'the things one remembers. I remember stumbling upon this even while he was hitting her, and I remember the sound – the *sound*! I still hear it in my head. I covered my ears and pulled my hair and screamed! No wonder they all thought I was mad.

'I ran to the kitchen, grabbed the biggest cleaver and came back. I heard Betsy run after me so I locked the door. It was so foolish of me but – I wasn't thinking. Somehow I just didn't want anyone to see. I just ran to Father and begged him to stop. I don't even know if I was making any sense, and Father was so incensed he did not hear me. He kept hitting my mum and I had to – I had to cut him in the arm! *I had to!*

'God... I cut through cloth and skin and he only let go of my mother then. The poor thing. I remember her limping to the fireplace, gagging and choking.

'Father growled. He was clenching his arm; dripping blood all over the carpet. The *hate* in his eyes. No one's ever looked at me like that.

'I stepped back. I saw his blood had spilt on my dress and I shrieked. He came closer to me. He didn't look himself. He looked like a monster. And I remember his words – the words of a monster too.'

45

'Your fool of a father was my business associate for a number of years,' Lady Anne said, raising her glass to have it refilled. 'He did – let's call them *under-the-table* deals for me.'

'Och, ye fucking liar! My father was a—'

'Self-made man?' Lady Anne jumped in. 'Risen to wealth astonishingly fast? Bought his own distilleries and farmland – even a townhouse – all within just a few years? Did that never strike you as questionable? Too good to be true?'

McGray lowered the gun a little further, feeling a nasty chill take hold of him.

Indeed, he had never doubted his father's success. Why would he? He'd been a child back then.

'He was very efficient,' Lady Anne said, 'but I knew he couldn't be honourable. Men like him never are, so I dealt with him carefully and kept him happy.' She stared at nothing for a moment, a growing bitterness burning in her eyes as she swirled the glass. 'And yet, he betrayed me.'

'Ye must have deserved it,' McGray blurted out, already fearing he'd be wrong.

Lady Anne picked up on his doubt, and smiled. 'You've been to Cobden Hall, have you not? That's in *Lancashire*?'

She made the annotation with sarcasm: McGray would never

forget that ruined property at the foot of Pendle Hill, where a band of witches had nearly taken his life. Lord Joel had been killed there, on that same night.

'My family's ancestral home,' Lady Anne said, 'which I only managed to get back centuries after it was stolen from us, and I only did so to take revenge on those witches.

'I knew that those crones still used the manor for their rituals, so I acted through intermediaries and lesser-known conveyancers so the damned coven didn't know who was taking the property from them. I also needed agents to bribe the crooked judges in Lancaster. One of those agents was your late father.'

Her smile widened. McGray, though riled, could not speak.

'You see where I'm going, don't you?' Lady Anne said and then took another leisurely sip of claret. The corners of her mouth were becoming stained with it, as if she were feeding on blood.

'Part of your father's payment,' she went on, 'was a loan and a substantial discount to buy one of my best properties in New Town. *Your* current house.'

McGray drew in a deep breath. He did remember being stunned by his father buying such a sumptuous house. He'd been in his early twenties by then, yet still, the idea of his adored father being unscrupulous had never even crossed his mind.

Lady Anne chuckled. 'But that was not enough for him, and that was how he chose to betray me.' She leaned forwards. 'Do you remember the visit I paid you right after your father died? To claim back my property? *He* was there!' She nodded at Dr Clouston, whose eyes were still fixed on the ground. 'And he had the gall to threaten me! *Me!* Even though I could destroy his career and reputation at the snap of a finger. You, doctor, must have known the old McGray had swindled me to get hold of a property like that!'

Clouston clenched his fists as he hissed, 'I did not. But even if I had, I would have still—'

'Oh, do shut up,' Lady Anne snapped, before turning back to Nine-Nails. 'It was your father who told the so-called witches I had taken Cobden Hall from them,' she said, 'after I refused to give him more money and sign the Moray Place property off to him, even though he still owed me more than half its value.'

'*My father had no contact with witches!*' McGray cried. 'I would have heard, after all these years investigating witchcraft and buying auld books on the black market!'

'He may not have contacted the witches directly, but he mentioned my name at the right times and places. It reached the witches' ears and they turned against me. Or, rather – they turned against my son.' She gripped her glass tightly, as if deliberately trying to crush it. 'It may have been the witches who turned him insane with their charms and their poisons, but your father was the one I'll always blame. He was the one who led them to him! He was the one who destroyed his life! And my Caroline's.'

The name echoed in between the sandstone blocks, along with Lady Anne's noisy slurps. She had abandoned all manners and now drank long and deep.

McGray felt dizzy, struggling to take in all those facts. Caroline must not know that the old Mr McGray had caused her father's demise. If she found out, would her rage extend to him? Would the son have to pay for the sins of the father?

'It was much later that I found out what your father had done,' Lady Anne resumed, while her butler poured her more claret. 'Five or six months after my Joel had to be locked up; the same summer your sister –' the woman sneered – '*lost* her mind.'

Clouston leapt forwards, but the two miners who flanked him rushed to seize him. One gave him a not-so-soft blow to the kidneys, well calculated just so that the doctor could not speak on.

Lady Anne smirked with pleasure. 'I, of course, had to confront your father,' she resumed, 'so I went all the way to his farm near Dundee, where you all were at the time. But I needed to meet him alone.

'I'd done my homework and knew that your father let his servants get drunk there from time to time. I found the tavern they frequented and I asked the landlord to tell me when they arrived. Once they were there, I set off. I didn't want anyone to see me, so I went there in my smallest carriage – a two-wheel cabriolet, freshly oiled so it hardly made a noise. And I did find your father on his own. Even you and your sister were out. Do you remember?'

McGray raised a brow. Of course he remembered that late evening; that last ride with Pansy in the rolling countryside, before their entire world shattered. 'Even if all that shite yer telling me is true,' he said, 'and ye were there, what does that have to do with Pansy?'

Lady Anne laughed, softly at first, but it soon turned into a frank cackle. She even spilt some of the claret as her echoes travelled across the quarry.

'Plenty, you poor fool! I've not even begun to tell you about your mother!'

46

'Amina Duncan was a social climber and a slag.'

McGray immediately thrust himself forwards, charging like a locomotive. The men must have expected it, for they seized him before he could even raise his gun. Two miners had to pull at each arm, while McGray grunted and writhed with fury.

Pratt took a few small steps into the shadows, subtly getting closer to his carriage.

Lady Anne waited patiently, savouring short sips of claret until McGray's growls subsided a little.

'During my son's initial fits of madness,' she said, for the first time looking slightly saddened, 'my poor Joel ... he babbled. He told me things. So many things—' The woman drew in a breath. 'I knew your mother's family, the Duncans. Like your father they were all social climbers, but *she* – oh, the presumption of aspiring to marry my son! They met at a town assembly where your late grandfather was a steward. *A steward!* And yet your mother approached my son and tried to ensnare him with her arts and her allurements. What a viper she was!

'At first I thought Joel would simply have his way with her, like young men do, and then forget about her. But he didn't. I had her followed and it soon transpired how serious the situation was becoming. I could tell she'd soon force him to propose.

Luckily, I intervened just in time. I managed to send my Joel to the continent to visit that sickly Lady Beatrice, whom I had eyed for him a few years earlier.

'In the meantime, it was *I* who introduced your father to the Duncans. Mind, this was before he betrayed me. In fact, back then the timing seemed simply ideal, with the old McGray on the rise – in part, thanks to his dealings with me. I still remember old Duncan's face, your grandfather's, when I told him about James McGray's businesses and how keen he was to marry soon. He started courting your mother at once, and very publicly. I had but to write a letter to my son telling him those two were already engaged. He didn't believe me, but a few other acquaintances in town confirmed it for me.

'And then I needed but to forge a couple of letters from France, where Lady Beatrice lived with her aging mother, to make people believe she and my Joel were soon to be married. I sent them to a few key gossip-mongers in town, and very soon everyone treated it as fact.

'I adore rumours and gossip; you plant the seed and it takes hold like darnel.

'Once Joel and your mother thought the other was engaged to someone else, everything fell into place. Old Duncan was keen to marry his little vixen into money, so he rushed the union between her and your father. By the time my son came back from Europe, those two were already married.' Lady Anne lowered her gaze, a shade of guilt finally appearing on her face. 'The news hit him hard. Much harder than I expected. He even took rat poison the very day he heard *you* had been born.' And then the guilt vanished, replaced by derision. 'As much as I loved him – he too was a fool. It took me nearly three years to get him to marry Lady Beatrice, but marry he did. I only wish that little cow had been a little less sickly so she could have given him a male heir. I tried to find him another wife but he refused. He'd finally grown some gumption – too much for his own sake. He took Caroline away and they spent the next ten years trotting about in Europe.

'Your mother, I heard, had a miscarriage not long after she had you, and then there were no more children. I thought *good, no more spawn of James McGray in this world* and then, ten years later, that Amy brat was born.'

McGray stopped struggling then, every muscle in his body suddenly going limp.

Lady Anne's grin stretched to an eerie breadth, her teeth looking like sharp fangs. 'How suspicious,' she whispered, 'that Amina McGray gave birth to a child after ten barren years, and –' she laughed – 'nine months after my Joel paid a brief visit to Edinburgh.'

Pansy brought a hand to her chest as her eyes shed a torrent of tears. 'He – he said he was not my father! He said that my mother was a whore and I was the spawn of an adder! I didn't understand at first. He had to say it twice, all the while dripping blood from the cut I'd given him. I don't remember if I said something, or if I whimpered or cried, I only remember I dropped the cleaver.

'I must have mumbled something about it being impossible, or not believing it, because he turned to my mother and shouted that *she* would tell me the truth. Only she couldn't speak. But the way she looked at me – so loving and so ashamed and so sorry… it was true. She didn't need to say it. She did try to speak, but Father went to her again and I went after him. He saw me and he slapped me! Stabbed arm and all.

'I don't even remember the pain. I just remember that I fell on my back, and then I saw him coming at me. He picked me up and was going to hit me, just like he'd done Mum. My mum… she cried like an eagle and lunged at him. He dropped me back to the floor and I heard them scuffle. He pushed her to the fireplace, and it was then that—'

Poor Pansy stared at the fireplace. I don't know for how long, but she did not blink or breathe throughout, so still that she looked like a pale block of marble. Then she took in a troubled breath, her body stirring as if stricken by the coldest draught.

'She only let out this – wee whimper. Like a puppy that's got strangled. I didn't understand at first. She was just there – suspended in mid-air, just over the stand with the fire pokers, flailing her arms. Father stepped back. He was still clenching his fists but – not so tightly now. He... he probably didn't believe what he'd just done.

'My poor mother jerked. *God* she looked like a pierced fish! She gagged and I saw blood come out of her mouth. And still she managed to stand up. The – the poker was stuck through her back. That's how deep it went... *My poor mother!* She tried to walk to me. She said – "*Sorry*".

'And then she dropped to the floor. Face down. Right there. And no one's ever even bothered to clean up her blood.'

47

Pansy gulped, her lip trembling. 'Father and I just stared at her. I... I will never forget that silence; how the poker swayed like a pendulum for a wee while – and then it stopped. And I noticed I couldn't breathe, and when I managed, it was just so I could scream.

'And Father – I don't know why I still call him that! He looked at me in that silly way – *like a child!* Like a stupid child that's just shattered some vase! I felt this fire – my entrails burning. I picked up the cleaver and jumped up. And everything is a blur after that.

'I think... I think I *did* lose my mind. For a wee while. I remember brawling with Adolphus – I didn't even notice what I did!'

Pansy sprang to her feet, the memory shaking her to the bone, and I could not contain a gasp. I wanted to approach her, perhaps pat her on the shoulder or say something comforting, but the way she fidgeted, pacing frantically in circles and rubbing her chest as if trying to shed some nasty mange, made me take a step back. How could I possibly help? How could anyone soothe the guilt of having maimed her own brother?

*

'*Fuck off!*' McGray barked. He felt a rush of blood to his head, his heartbeats pounding in his ears. It all had to be lies. Well crafted, of course, but lies nonetheless.

'As I said, my Joel told me this as he began to lose his mind. He knew Amy was his. He knew she was his bastard. And that your mother was a loose—'

'*Shut up!*' McGray hollered, his voice darting like a gunshot as he thrashed in the miners' grip.

Lady Anne smiled. 'What an irony it was – that your *half*-sister should end up locked in the same madhouse as him!'

'Yer lying. Yer just a two-faced auld bitch!'

Lady Anne, however, could not have been more pleased by the cursing.

'Do you want to hear the rest? How your sister never really lost her mind? How she killed your parents after she found out about her origins?'

McGray shouted a torrent of abuse, his voice travelling all across the quarry, until Lady Anne's foreman approached and hit him in the stomach with the butt of a rifle.

'You will hear it, whether you like it or not,' Lady Anne said with a side smile, while McGray bent down, precariously held by the workers, and groaned in pain.

'And as I said,' Lady Anne resumed, 'I went to your sorry farm, told my driver to park in a nook of the garden, where nobody would spot him, and I went in. I told your father everything before he could throw me out.

'Just like you, he didn't believe a word I said. I told him to call his trollop of a wife and – oh, stop writhing like that! Get used to it. Everyone will call her that from now on. Your father brought your mother into the library. He even made me hide in this dreadful cabinet where he kept his barrages. In the haste I lost a plume from my hat.

'And from there I heard it all. How that vixen admitted to

her filthy frolics. She said she never loved him. Never liked him. Never even cared for him! She said he revolted her and she only married him because she was forced to!' Lady Anne lounged back, for an instant her hatred turned into pity. 'That was the one time I felt some sympathy for her. I lived through the same thing when I was young. I understood her perfectly.' She stared into the night, perhaps summoning bitter memories, but her smirk reappeared when she looked back at McGray. 'And he beat her,' she said with scorn. 'Not once or twice – many times. He was beating her to a pulp when your bastard sister came in and they all skirmished like the wild animals they were.

'I don't know who killed who. I just stayed in the cabinet until you arrived and she did – *that* to your hand. I only opened the door slightly when I heard her run out and you drop to the floor. I scrambled out, entirely numb after all that time hidden there, and I had to break a window to get out. Fortunately, my cabriolet was close enough, and all your servants were inside chasing your mad sister, so nobody saw us leave.'

McGray looked up, so dumbfounded he could not blink or breathe. He could only look at Lady Anne as her smile widened.

'But *you* saw me,' she whispered, in a manner that made everyone around shudder. 'I know you did.'

The scene flashed before his eyes: the dark silhouette, blurred against the twilight sky beyond the shattered window. The spasmodic, animalistic movements. The …

'You thought I was the Devil. And that the plumes on my headpiece were the Devil's horns. You said as much right before you passed out. Do you remember?'

The silence was utter and deep, and Lady Anne savoured each moment of it. She must have spent years hoping she could one day tell him all this to his face. And she'd saved it for the most convenient moment.

'Of course you don't remember!' she sneered. 'You were already broken. But I had to be sure, so I made a few secret enquiries on the following days. I even talked to one of your gardeners. He didn't mention my name at all, which was a relief; I knew you would have made a mighty scandal if you'd recognised me. And it was then that I realised your bastard half-sister must have seen me too, for she told everyone she'd been possessed! Common, stupid folk, just like you. She too thought I was some demon!' She brought the glass close to her lips, for a moment musing over the bouquet. 'Who would have said it back then?' she whispered with pleasure. 'Perhaps I really *am* the Devil.'

48

'What happened then?' I murmured. 'What is the next thing you remember?'

Thankfully, the question brought Pansy back to focus. She halted and looked at the door.

'I ran through there. I saw people in the house ... I – I even think I saw a shadow, someone who looked like the devil ...' She shook her head. 'And then all I remember is being curled up in my bed, and that I still had the blade in my hand. I sat up and stayed there for God knows how long. I felt thirsty at some point, but there was no water in my ewer. That was all. That was all my mind could think of: the thirst – until I heard a key turn in the door. I hadn't even noticed that they'd locked me in.

'It was Dr Clouston ... I knew him, of course. He was a very good friend of the family. So I also knew what he did for a living. I knew he treated the insane.' Pansy gasped then, as if touched by icy water. *'Just realising he'd been called!* That they had sent for him to take me to the madhouse! He said he was here to help me, but I sensed his tone. He was treating me as if I were a mad beast. I felt enraged. And ashamed. I – I nearly killed him too.'

Pansy went silent, finally wiping her tears with her sleeve. I realised I didn't have a handkerchief to offer.

'But you did not,' I said soothingly, and she shook her head.

'Only because I was too weak by then. I don't know for how long I'd been locked in my room; no food or water. I simply collapsed, and Dr Clouston must have given me laudanum or something to keep me docile. The next thing I remember is waking up at home, back in Edinburgh, and going back to sleep almost at once. I woke up again, God knows after how long, in some strange room at the asylum. And until last spring, I never left the place.' She bent her head exhausted after the tale she'd told me. And yet – it was as if the beast had gone, the burdens somewhat lifted just by telling them out loud.

I moved slowly, not to startle her, and sat by her side. 'Did you tell Dr Clouston what had happened?' I asked. 'You must have.'

'It was days before I could make any sense. But yes, I did.'

'And then you two decided to keep it all a secret?'

'No, not us both. I had the idea. *I* begged him. He'd already been at the Sheriff's Court. He told me they wanted to try me for murder.'

'So you decided to pretend?'

'*How could I not?*' she barked, though instantly recoiling. It was as if she could not measure her tones and gestures anymore, unused to holding long conversations with strangers. She took a few deep breaths, and as she spoke she shed renewed tears. 'I had mutilated my brother. I had killed my so-called father – *he* had killed my mother. She had lain with another man and I was a bastard ... If people knew ... To the world we'd be an entire family of disgraced harlots and murderers.' She shook her head. 'I'd rather let people think I was insane. That I was the only one to blame. The one bad apple.'

Though it all made sense, I was still open-mouthed. 'But – at what cost?' I whispered. 'To spend the rest of your life locked in an institution? Staring out the same window year after year?'

Pansy shrugged, pulling a side smile. 'It did not matter

anymore, did it? I had lost everything already. There could be no happy ending for me; not after all that had happened. Just like there can be no happy ending for me now. I don't know how many times I've wished I had the courage to – just end it all. A swift, neat ending.'

The yearning with which she said that made me shiver.

'Everyone's lives would have been easier. Dr Clouston's, for instance. He's kept my secret, even if it has caused him all manner of trouble. Miss Smith, lately... you yourself have had to go through so many trials because of me!' She turned her head away, unable to meet my gaze out of sheer guilt. 'And my brother –' she wept – 'my poor brother... he is the one I've dishonoured the most. All these years he's visited me; brought me flowers, presents, my favourite sweets, talked to me as if I were – *normal*.' She cried in silence for a moment, which was more heart-breaking than frantic sobs.

'I cannot argue your brother's devotion,' I said. 'All he has done he has done for you, ever since—'

'*But why!*' Pansy shouted, again making me jump. '*I thought he would hate me!* How could he not? Anyone else would have despised me! I maimed him and killed his parents and brought shame to us all!' Pansy covered her face. 'If he finds it's all been a lie... *God*, if he finds I've been pretending all these years, and that I'm not even his full sister!' Her chest began to heave. 'That is why Dr Clouston helped me flee. That is why he asked Tom to bring me here, so I could gather my mother's jewellery and savings.

'Now I'll just set off; disappear somewhere far away. I might bring Betsy with me. And Tom and Clouston can make up some story – tell everyone I turned violent and forced Tom to bring me here.' Finally she looked at me, her eyes flickering with desperation. 'You can help them! Adolphus will believe them if you vouch for their story. My brother trusts you.'

My frown could not have been deeper. 'I – I do not know what I could possibly tell him. He *will* try to find you, no matter what we say.'

'*I don't know!*' she cried, jumping to her feet and walking in circles like a caged creature. Sane she might be, but six years locked in a mental institution had definitely left their mark on her. 'Tell him – tell him that I died! Yes. Tell him I died!'

I shook my head, not knowing what to answer, and the poor girl flung herself to her knees right in front of me.

'*Please!* What else am I to do? Even if I go back and they don't hang me for all these murders – I'd still have to explain him all I've just told you.' She trembled from head to toe. 'And I don't want him to know. I'd kill myself if he finds out. I don't want him ever to know!'

49

'I knew she wasn't mad,' Lady Anne said, enunciating each word with delight. 'Shocked and upset beyond belief, yes. But not mad.' She snorted, her eyes sombre. 'And I had seen plenty of madness by then.' She eyed Clouston. 'The good doctor here – he knew as well. And he must have known from very early on. Did you not?' But she did not give him a chance to reply. 'When I heard the brat had been declared insane and would not be tried, I knew Clouston here had lied and forged documents again. Did you learn the trick from the favours you did for me and my son?'

McGray stared at the doctor, desperate to hear what he might have to say, but Clouston remained silent, not meeting his eyes. He simply stared at Lady Glass with a wrath he could barely contain.

'Of course you did,' she mocked. 'I was tempted to expose you both, and I didn't, simply because of my own son's involvement. I don't need the world to know that the Ardglass and the filthy McGrays have common offspring. So I simply sat back and watched you.' She looked at McGray. 'I even felt sorry for you. Lied to and manipulated by your only *friend* in town and by your one living relative.

'Not only did they deceive you, but they also let you carry on with your idiotic investigations on demons and ghosts and ghouls. They let you become an oddity; shunned and laughed at by the entire country.' Lady Anne's voice became a screech. 'And every time you visited that horrible little bitch, she was pretending! He too! Even writing false medical reports to uphold the charade!'

McGray was breathing like a locomotive, his exhalations like bursts of steam. His brain was jumbled, drained of all energy. He'd never felt this way before – utterly paralysed by confusion and hatred and disbelief; unable even to thread a few thoughts together.

It was simply too much to deal with, and yet Lady Anne kept probing with her devilish tongue.

'Can you forgive them?' she was saying. 'Can you forgive *her* after all her deceit?' she let out a short, piercing cackle. 'What am I saying? Of course you will! She's still your half-sister. And even if she wasn't... You're a fool. And that's how I have you in my hands now.'

The words lingered in the air, muddled with the rest of that foul speech. It took McGray a moment to take in that last sentence.

'*In yer hands?*' he repeated and, as if saying the words out loud had untangled his thoughts, the entire situation made sense. 'Och, ye fuckin' conniving bitch! What d'ye want from me?'

Lady Anne grinned, her lips and teeth now stained with the dark red of the claret. 'Leave my granddaughter alone.'

McGray took a step back. '*What?*'

'Go and marry what you deserve – some debauched trollop like your dead mother.'

'How d'ye...?' And again the men had to restrain him.

Lady Anne simply tapped on her glass to have it refilled, seemingly bored of McGray's outbursts.

'I've had Caroline followed all this time,' she said as soon as he calmed enough to listen. 'Since you both came back from – was it the Isle of Wight? And I bribed her silly scullery maid too. I know exactly how many times you've visited her and what you've talked about. I know you gave her a pauper's ring. I know everything!'

McGray could not conceal his surprise. He remembered the dull, almost stupid-looking scullery maid, but only because Joan always complained about her.

'You look astounded to learn all this about your depraved relatives,' Lady Anne said while Nine-Nails reflected. 'Well – I was ten times more stunned when I learned the sort of rascal Caroline had chosen. She might have done so only to spite me, mind!'

McGray scoffed. 'Like father like daughter, I'd say! Am sure ye too liked a wee bit o' muck back when yer inexpressibles were still—'

'*Oh shut up!*' Lady Anne snarled, turning her face to one side. 'As sickening and prosaic as you father!'

'Which only confirms what I was just sayin' about yer inex—'

'*Listen!* Before I ask my men to throw you down this cliff!' The old woman leaned forwards. 'I have the power to clear your sister's name. Point the fingers in the right direction. We have the evidence and the right witnesses for that. But they will only speak if I tell them to.' She took a leisurely sip, pleased and yet exhausted. 'And if you don't oblige,' she went on, 'I will let the world know everything I've just told you. About your mother's infidelity and that your sister was never insane to begin with. And then she'll be tried for *all* these deaths—'

'Including the poor dead bastard ye planted near the asylum this morning?' McGray barked. 'He got killed here, right?'

Lady Anne was too clever to admit it out loud. But she did pull a blatant smirk.

'Och, let go!' McGray roared, and with one final pull he finally managed to set himself free. The workers rushed to seize him again, but Lady Anne raised a hand.

McGray snorted and smoothed his coat. He took a step closer to the old woman, his chest swollen with pride.

'I'll never be bossed around by an auld dried crow like yerself. Ye can do whatever the fuck ye want. Pansy's run away. As long as she's gone and safe I don't give a shite what people think.'

Lady Anne laughed in earnest. 'Do you honestly believe I did not think of that? We've dispatched people to bring her back. They should be in town by tomorrow morning!'

'D'ye think I'm an eejit? Yer bluffing!'

The woman arched an eyebrow. '*Am I?* You were not the only one who saw her flee. We know Mr Frey is following her. The little monster went back to Dundee, did she not?'

McGray could not answer. He had reached the same conclusion himself.

'Yes,' Lady Anne reiterated. 'My men might be there even as we speak, and I doubt that the swashbuckling Mr Frey will be able to fend them off by shaking his hanky.'

McGray covered his brow, the miners around him now mocking with scorn.

Lady Anne raised her voice, like a judge pronouncing sentence. 'Leave my granddaughter alone or see your bastard sister hanged. It is as simple as that.' She indulged in a long drink and then smacked her lips. 'You don't have to answer now. I know your "wee" brains will need time. You have until the morning to decide, before they arrive in Leith Harbour. If I haven't heard from you by then, we shall hand Amy to the police expediently, along with all the evidence Mr Pratt sees as convenient. She *will* be tried for multiple murders.

'And even if you refuse, like the stubborn scoundrel you are, I will still get some satisfaction. It would be a tragedy to see my

Caroline married to a pig like you, but at least I'd get the joy of seeing your bastard sister hang.'

She waved a hand, signalling the men to take McGray away. To their surprise, Nine-Nails did not resist. He simply looked back at Lady Anne while the miners led him back to the carriage.

'I've never, ever said this to anyone, *ma'am*...' he said in a dark, guttural snarl, 'but ye *really* are one diabolical cunt.'

50

We all needed some time to recollect our thoughts.

Tom and Elgie rejoined us and we all gathered in the shady dining room, lit by a single oil lamp. The old table had been recently polished, and there were twelve services carefully laid out, ready for a banquet that would never come.

Tom passed around a little flask. The liquor, though rather coarse, was just what I needed. I passed it to Elgie, who gave it a sniff and then pushed it away.

'Oh, don't be a goose!' I said. 'I am sure Oscar Wilde drinks worse.'

He still refused, unable to take his eyes from Pansy, who'd installed herself at the head of the table.

'I suppose...' I said, turning to Pansy, 'you already know that you and Miss Ardglass—'

'Are half-sisters? Yes. And that my father was Lord Joel.'

'Did he tell you?'

'Yes. The night he escaped. When he–' she sighed – 'when he killed that woman.'

She trembled, so I offered her the flask, but she too refused it.

'He had always known,' she said, looking at my extended hand. 'That ring you wear—'

'It was his. I know.'

'You can imagine how I felt when I saw you had it. My mother gave it to Lord Joel after I was born. I suppose Caroline gave it to you?'

'Yes, but I doubt she knows the significance.'

'She couldn't have. Only my mother and Lord Joel knew, and it was he who told me. He took it off before he fled. Dr Clouston must have handed it to Lady Anne –' Pansy sneered – 'my grandmother.'

How difficult it was for her to say that.

'How come he only told you after years in the asylum?' I asked her.

'Well, he *was* insane for most of the time. It was painful to see, even back then, when I thought he was just a stranger. He had this constant frown, like he was always aching. I can't remember the first time I saw him. It must have been months after I arrived. And he had been locked up a while before that.

'I remember he liked his books and the nurses made him read aloud in the function room. He had a wonderful voice; really deep and calming, and he enunciated beautifully. I really enjoyed his readings. At some point he heard my name and made the connection. I remember he was particularly kind to me. And the stories he read were my only escape; his books were my last window to all the things in the world I'd never see for myself. My favourite was Wilkie Collins.

'The nurses noticed and began asking him to read just for me from time to time. Sometimes in the dining room; sometimes in the gardens. Those were the only happy times I had in there. I liked being visited by my brother, but as you can imagine, those occasions always came with dreadful memories.

'And Lord Joel was pleased too. He told me so. He'd lost his mind, but at least that gave him the chance to spend his last years reading for his second daughter. I hope that was at least a small consolation. The poor man had such a sad life. I know it doesn't justify his crimes, but – I understand where all his hatred came from.'

My memory travelled back to the very instant of Joel's death. With his last breath he'd told us Pansy's words.

'You asked him not to do any of that,' I whispered. 'You asked him to stay, did you not?'

'Yes, but he said it was too late for him; that his life was already ruined. I knew exactly how he felt.'

I nodded. 'Did Dr Clouston know Lord Joel was your father?'

'Only after I told him. I couldn't have lived with yet another secret, especially after learning that Lord Joel, had just died. It was then that I really felt I'd go insane. Years of incarceration and then learning those facts ... Even Adolphus's visits became an agony. That was why Dr Clouston had to send me to the Orkneys.' She showed the slightest hint of a smile.

'I hate to admit it, but it did me good. I'll never forget the first time I saw the sea – another horizon – after years locked in the same rooms, only able to walk in circles; the same corridors and the same gardens ... I remember I cried. I almost felt free.'

She must have, I thought, and then a great deal of memories came to mind. All the times she'd acted in unfathomable ways in front of me – they all flashed through my head.

'I suppose I should thank you,' I said. 'For all the clues you gave us.'

Pansy let out a shy chuckle, her face unexpectedly illuminated. 'I hope my messages weren't too cryptic.'

I laughed. 'Sometimes they were!'

The gloom seemed to lift for a second, but then all the immediate pressures rushed back into my head. The Devil's mark, the gloves, the cloak, Caroline's visits ...

'Speaking of riddles,' I said, 'all those pieces of evidence we found in your room – I knew they were not under your bed. I searched for them myself! You were there.'

'Yes, I could tell that was what you were doing.'

'What happened?' I soon regretted those words, for Pansy's chest began heaving.

'Dr Harland came in yesterday morning. He doesn't treat me, so it surprised me, but there was nothing I could do. I just sat by the window, pretending like I always do. Trying not to stare at him, until—' Pansy clenched her fists on the table, some of the madness I'd seen before again taking hold of her. It was so sad to see how the confinement had affected her behaviour. 'I heard him hammering the floors and I couldn't sit still anymore. I turned and saw him kneeling by my bed. He had a cloth bag with him. I saw my sister's cloak sticking out. I recognised it immediately!' She took hissing breaths, again on the verge of insanity. Elgie had to cover his mouth not to whimper. 'I stood up and saw what he was doing – ripping up the boards and hiding all those things under my bed! That damned weasel! *There was a scalpel too!*'

This last she uttered in a deafening shriek. I had to stand up and place a hand on her shoulder.

'Here,' I said softly, offering her Tom's flask. 'Have a drink. Please.'

She did so, wrinkling her face at the burn of the spirit. Locked in the asylum since she was sixteen, it might well have been the first time she tried the stuff neat. I waited for a moment before speaking.

'So you confronted him?' I asked, and she nodded.

'I told him to get out. He was shocked I'd spoken – but then he pushed me! I fell backwards and saw him pouncing on me. I had to grab the scalpel and—'

I squeezed her shoulder a little, and whispered. 'It is fine, you do not need to tell me more.' I made her take another sip, as if feeding medicine to a young girl. At last she calmed down.

373

'So it was *Harland* who murdered the inmates!' Elgie said, despite his tension.

'I don't know,' Pansy mumbled. 'He must have. Tom?'

The tall man shook his head, looking at me. 'Everything I told you before is true, sir. I think he must have, but I couldnae be sure. And those marks – we have no idea how they could appear. I saw Mrs Brewster before they took her to the kirk. I helped put her in the coffin. She'd nae been touched.'

I pondered for a second. 'We thought that someone within the asylum might have branded the bodies as a means to bring attention to the body snatchers,' I said. 'Link them to the smear of blood on the walls.' I turned to Pansy. 'Was it not you, Miss McGray?'

She gulped. 'No, I swear. As you can imagine, there was very little I could do while keeping up my act. And like everyone else in the city, I have no idea how those marks could have appeared.'

I perked up, recalling what I'd told Dr Reed at the City Chambers, right before all the mayhem began.

'I think I do.'

All heads turned to me. Elgie and Tom looked baffled, but Pansy was astounded beyond explanation.

'You do?' she whispered.

'Yes. Or at least – I think I have a promising lead. Yesterday, just before going to the asylum, I asked our forensic man to carry out a few experiments. If the results are what I expect... Miss McGray, we can still prove your innocence!'

Pansy gathered her breath, her eyes glimmering. I could tell she wanted to believe, but at the same time did not want to raise her hopes too high.

'She should still hide,' Tom said, also incredulous. 'At least while she gets cleared.'

'Indeed,' I said, looking at Pansy. 'We can hide you and send for you as soon as it is safe. Do you agree?'

Pansy frowned, clearly unused to hearing good news. She then gave the slightest of nods, and immediately I jumped to my feet.

'Good! I need to go back to Edinburgh and tell your brother. He will never find this evidence I told you unless I guide him to it. If you tell me where you are planning to hide, we can—'

I did not get to say the rest. We heard the neighing of horses and the rattle of wheels. We all turned our heads to the window, and then heard gunshots.

51

Pansy and Elgie gasped, I jolted and Tom raised the rifle.

'*Who's there?*' old Betsy shrieked from upstairs.

I reached for my breast pocket, instinctively looking for a weapon, but of course I had none. Even my little notebook was not there.

There was more racket in the gardens. I heard men laughing and then the sound of cracking wood coming from the entrance hall – the main door being crushed to splinters. And then we heard stamping boots breaking into the house.

Tom stepped forwards, pointing the rifle at the dining-room door. We heard the footsteps approach, and Elgie and Pansy clustered on each side of me, both grasping my arms.

I saw a flicker of light appear on the floorboards, coming in through the gap under the door. It had the golden hue of fire, and it came and went erratically, perhaps blocked by many moving feet.

We all breathed in frantic pants, staring at the door without blinking.

The rough voices murmured and giggled, like nasty children getting ready for the worst misdemeanour, and I felt pins and needles in my fingers.

There was a mighty thud then, the very ceiling joists shook, and the door slammed open.

A dozen men stormed in, all holding guns and torches. Pansy and Elgie shrieked and I pulled them closer to me, my heart throbbing.

'*Stop right there!*' Tom hollered, but the men only cackled as they spread out, forming a tight circle around us. I saw their begrimed faces and their nasty smiles.

Tom swung the rifle from left to right.

'Don't get any closer!' he cried, but the men continued to spread, their body odours filling the room. They left the door clear and three more chaps came in, they were pale, thinner and wrapped in expensive overcoats. One of them wore a hat that covered most of his face, and when he removed it I recognised young Martin Pratt. With the one flourish of blond hair left on his forehead, he looked like one of the apostles at Pentecost.

He recognised me at once. 'Inspector Frey!' he said with the slurred, slightly nasal voice of the upper-class. 'Will you care to move? We just want the mad girl.'

'*You won't take her!*' I barked, but I knew how pathetic I must sound. The begrimed men, clearly miners, cackled again, just as we heard irregular footsteps through the ceiling.

Martin's lips twisted in the most arrogant of smiles. 'I'm afraid we're your only way out,' he said with a scathing smile. 'Your driver took off. Scared and bribed. Good combination. Now, if you tell this brute to stop pointing his—'

'*Back off!*' Tom snarled the instant Martin took a step forward. The young man chuckled. 'You can only shoot one of us.'

'Then make sure it's *him*,' I said.

There was a flash of fear in Martin's eyes, but he gulped and pulled another mocking smile. 'Oh, be reasonable, Mr Frey. We'll do nothing ominous. We'll just surrender this girl to the police. You know – follow the proper procedures.'

'*Get away!*' Tom insisted, his finger already on the trigger.

The other two upper-class men looked at each other, apparently not knowing what to do. They must not have expected one of us to be armed.

Martin sighed. 'Oh, don't make this drag on. You know you won't get—'

'*Not drag it on?*' Tom shouted. 'Very well. Get out on the count o' three!'

Tom pushed the rifle a mere inch in his direction and Pratt Junior jumped backwards.

'Aye, all the way out!' Tom cried. '*I'll count to three!*'

Martin and his colleagues might have looked tense, but the miners did not. A couple of them even seemed keen to see which rich student we might shoot first.

'*One!*'

We all jumped at Tom's growl, and the flames of the miners' torches shook as if agitated by a sudden gust of wind.

Martin opened his mouth, but Tom shouted again.

'*Two!*' He aimed directly at Pratt's forehead.

There was absolute silence for a seemingly endless time. I heard my own bated breath, I felt the pulses of Pansy and Elgie as they squeezed my arms, and then a drop of cold sweat rolling slowly down my back.

I saw Tom's finger twitch on the trigger; saw the tendons on his neck tense up, and then his entire torso swelled as he gathered breath to deliver his last—

'*Damn youse all!*' Betsy cried like a banshee from the darkened hall, Tom started and at once three miners pounced on him. One pulled the rifle upwards, the rest hurled themselves upon us, and the entire world became a blur of hands, torches, foul breaths and screams.

'*This is the master's home!*' old Betsy howled amidst the mayhem. I shrieked and felt the grip of many hands on my arms and legs, pulling me up as I saw a miner seize Pansy by the waist and lift her from the ground. The girl writhed and yelled, and I heard Elgie shout something but I could not see him. Tom shot the rifle and I felt plaster from the ceiling rain on us.

'*Bastards!*' Betsy roared. '*Bas—!*'

The woman went silent just as I realised that my feet were not touching the floor. The miners were carrying me away! I twisted and thrashed in the air, and caught a glimpse of a torch on the floor, the carpet and chairs catching fire.

I saw three men holding Tom and giving him a mighty beating with the butt of his own rifle, and beyond, just for a fraction of a second before they dragged me out of the room, I saw Elgie's blond hair, the rest of him obscured behind many shoulders covered in soot, the men shaking like vultures fighting over carrion.

'*My brother!*' I howled. '*Don't touch my brother!*'

I could not see or hear his voice anymore, the men around me cackling and chanting as they carried me through the entrance hall.

'*Is she dead?*' I heard Pansy scream then. '*Did you just kill her?*'

I could not see what she meant, for the men pulled me out of the house and flung me onto the snow. They did the same with Pansy, the girl landing next to me. I reached for her and surrounded her with both arms. The poor thing was deathly cold.

Amidst the light of the torches, I saw Martin's shadow approach.

'*My, my!*' he cried in mawkish tones. 'I thought you didn't speak? Did you all hear that? *The "mute" mad girl speaks!*'

He bent down to say something else, but Pansy gargled and spat right into his eye.

Martin jumped backwards, for a moment whimpering as if stricken by acid. The miners and even his classmates instantly burst into laughter, and the young man snarled as he wiped his face with his sleeve.

'*You'll regret that, you little bitch!*' he hissed, darting towards her, but I stretched an arm and pushed him away.

'*It won't be wise to touch her!*' I shouted. 'Not if you really *are* taking her to the police.'

Martin straightened his back, frowning as if I'd asked him to do the most complex mathematics. He really was not very bright.

'I hope that woman is fine,' I added, nodding at the house. '*And if you dared touch my brother I swear I will—!*'

'Och, shut it!' one of the miners snapped. He pushed Martin aside, let out the loudest whistle and began shouting orders to the other men.

A moment later I saw three carriages come from behind the house.

The miner who had taken over – someone called him Angus – pulled me upwards, and I helped Pansy stand.

'Just enjoy the ride, boss!' the man Angus told us, opening the door of the first carriage with a mocking flourish. 'Neither o' youse might be alive by this time tomorrow.'

52

Caroline felt her chin drop.

That woke her up, but she was rather glad. She'd been having an awful nightmare, all about fire.

She sat up, her neck sore after hours on that frayed chaise longue, and looked at the dim room. It was the little parlour Joan had once adapted for visitors – not that Adolphus received many – with low tables, ornaments and cushioned seats. Now the vases only contained dead blooms and the main sofa was taken by crates of whisky bottles. Without Joan around, the house was slowly reverting to its old masculine disarray.

Caroline heard quick footsteps and realised the door to the corridor was ajar. It opened slowly and she saw Larry, the young servant boy, peeping in. He smiled bashfully and then shouted over his shoulder.

'The lady's awake!'

'Don't bother her!' Joan shouted back from the corridor. 'Go fetch that coal!'

Larry jumped and dashed away, carrying a pewter bucket that rattled as he ran to the back door.

Joan came in then, bringing a breakfast tray bursting with freshly baked treats. Caroline glanced at the clock on the wall. It was just past five o'clock.

'Didn't you sleep at all?' she asked.

'How could I,' Joan grumbled as she displayed the tea set, 'with the master out there meeting that old hag?'

'Has he not been back yet?'

'No, miss. I think he—'

Someone knocked on the front door then; frantic, insistent blows.

Joan and Caroline looked at each other for an instant, and then they both sprang up and ran to the entrance hall.

'Could that be him?' Caroline said.

'Don't be daft, miss. Why would he knock on his own door?'

Old George was already at the door. He opened it, letting in fluttering snowflakes and the cold air of the early morning. The skies were still pitch-black, but the street lamps outlined clearly the frame of Dr Clouston.

'Doctor!' George cried. 'Come in.'

'Thanks, George,' Clouston said, handing him his hat as soon as the man shut the door. He looked deathly pale, rims so dark around his eyes they almost looked like bruises. And his gesture worsened when he saw Caroline and Joan, their faces expectant. 'Adolphus never came back?' he asked.

Caroline frowned. 'Did you know he was away?'

Clouston nodded nervously, his hands shaking.

'Your grandmother summoned me as well. I was there.'

Caroline brought a hand to her chest, open-mouthed.

'Come, doctor,' Joan said. 'You look like you need a cup o' tea.'

She had to steer him to the parlour, Clouston moving dreamily, as if only just aware of his surroundings. He stumbled against the low table as he sat down, nearly knocking the tea service.

Caroline sat next to him. 'What happened?' she urged.

Clouston went a shade paler. 'Your grandmother –' he gulped, staring at Joan's hands as she prepared his tea – 'she told him everything.'

Caroline gasped. '*Everything*, you say?' she muttered, a sudden nausea taking hold of her. 'Everything about Pansy and me and … *her* not being—?'

She wanted to say *not being mad*, and *not being Adolphus's full sister*, but the words choked in her mouth.

'Yes,' Clouston said, and then he eyed the engagement ring on Caroline's hand. 'That too.'

Her first impulse was to cover it, but she realised it was pointless. She toyed with the jewel for a moment, wincing as she pictured the scene in her head: all the things she had concealed for months, all the things she'd feared so much even to whisper, suddenly being shouted out with spite. She pictured the rage burning on Adolphus's face, his clenched fists, the awful things that must have gone through his mind … what he must now be thinking of her … She shuddered. 'How could she know of *this*?' was the only sentence she could articulate, and only because she was staring at the ring. She briefly recalled Adolphus kneeling on the snow-covered Calton Hill when he presented it, and the memory made her chest ache.

'Lady Anne said she had you followed,' Clouston replied as he pushed the teacup away, he too looking queasy. 'And that she bribed your scullery maid.'

'That bloody Tilly!' Joan cried at once. 'I knew it! I didn't want to tell you, miss, but that lil' wench always seemed to be snooping.'

Caroline only dwelled on that for a second, her head whirling with questions. 'Why did my grandmother do this? Why *now*?'

Clouston took a deep breath. 'Your grandmother claimed she has evidence to exonerate Amy. She wants to trade it.'

'*Trade it?*'

'Yes. The condition is that you break your engagement.'

'*The auld bitch!*' George snapped unapologetically.

383

Caroline pulled back a little, as if Clouston's words had been embers.

'I see,' she whispered, looking down and feeling her cheeks heat up. 'That's why we wanted to keep it a secret; at least until we'd married. We knew she would oppose.' When she looked back at Clouston, the man had turned green. 'Is there something else?'

Clouston gulped, sweat rolling down his temples.

'Oh, have a drink!' Joan said, forcing the teacup to his lips. 'Like you're the patient and I'm the nurse ...'

Clouston managed a few sips, before pushing the cup away.

'Lady Anne had her men follow Mr Frey,' he said. 'She claimed they'd find your sister and bring her to – *justice*.'

'And she will make us keep our word,' Caroline whispered, having trouble breathing. 'She will find ways to make us—'

There was a racket then, the main door being slammed open, and unmistakable footsteps stamping across the hall.

Caroline's heart skipped a beat, an icy sensation spreading in her chest. Everyone had gone still, their mouths open and their eyes pointed at the library, already hearing the sound of books and boxes being thrown. And they all winced at every thud.

How strange, Caroline thought: they all cared for Adolphus, and yet they were all so scared of him.

Scared of what? a little voice said in her head, and she recalled the time he'd showed up at her apartment, cleanly shaven for the first time, looking a little bashful.

With tears welling up, she sprang to her feet and strode briskly to the library.

Joan ran after her, Clouston's teacup still in her hands, and the doctor followed, though he was so shaken old George had to offer him an arm.

Caroline saw the dogs run out of the library, the retriever

whimpering. Not a good sign, but still she pushed the door open and stormed in.

She felt another pang in her chest when she first saw Adolphus. His skin, already with a shade of stubble, looked ashen, his hair was dishevelled and his coat dotted with snow.

He had just pulled open a drawer and was rummaging violently through its contents. When he looked up, his blue irises were framed by veins.

Dr Clouston came in then, and Adolphus looked alternatively at him and Caroline.

It was the most agonising moment; Adolphus staring at them with all those emotions boiling in his eyes, yet saying nothing. In the deep silence, Caroline thought she could even hear her own heartbeats.

At last he spoke. 'Henry Irving might want youse in his damned theatre.'

His voice was soft, his tone sombre and deeply hurt. Caroline had never seen him like this: clearly burning on the inside, and yet despondent and drained of life. She would have preferred a roaring outburst.

'I was going to tell you,' she whispered. 'I really was! But it wasn't just something I—'

'I'll deal with youse later,' Adolphus interrupted, his voice inexpressive. He straightened his back, and Caroline saw he'd just retrieved a second gun and two small pouches full of ammunition.

'I had no other choice, Adolphus,' Clouston said, mopping sweat from his temple. 'You must understand! If I hadn't kept your sister's secret—'

Adolphus walked closer to him. It was not a sudden or threatening movement, but the doctor still went silent.

'I said – *later*.'

As he spoke, Adolphus filled the gun's cylinder, pressing each bullet in with a force that might have crushed bones.

'What are you going to do?' Caroline asked, and he gave a bitter smile that made her shiver.

'Investigate.'

'What?' she cried. 'But the superintendent said you were not to—'

'I ken what he said.'

Adolphus took a step forward and everyone moved aside. He walked back to the entrance hall and Clouston rushed after him.

'Lady Anne said they'd bring Amy back today. *Today!* What are you planning? They might surrender her to the police before—'

'*I'll beat them!*' Adolphus roared, bursting at last. He waved the gun and, for a horrid second, Caroline thought he was about to use it to beat Dr Clouston to a pulp. 'If they don't want me to investigate, they can fuck themselves. If they don't let me see the evidence, I'll bloody steal it. If they bring Pansy and put her in a damned cell, I'll find a way to get her out!'

He paused, took a deep breath and put the gun in his breast pocket as he opened the door. He glanced at Caroline from the corner of his eye.

'I'll get her out... *Even* if she lied to me too.'

He turned away and rushed to the back stables, where he readied Onyx, his black horse, at staggering speed.

As she saw him mount, Caroline repeated his last words in her head. *Even if she lied to me too...*

Was that his way of telling her he'd eventually forgive?

She wanted to look into his eyes. One look might be enough to tell. But Adolphus spurred the horse, never looking back, and galloped away, his dark outline quickly swallowed by the thick fog.

They all remained at the back gate for a moment, snow

fluttering around them, until they heard a raucous voice coming from across the circus.

It was the boy Larry, running manically back to the house, not a single lump of coal in his bucket.

'*Mrs Joan!*' he cried, '*Mrs Joan!*'

She sprinted forwards to receive the boy. She still had the teacup in her hands but she dropped it to hold him by the shoulders.

'What is it, lad? You're as white as a ghost!'

Caroline stepped forwards too, the cold seeping into her chest.

'Everyone's carrying firewood to Salisbury Crags!' Larry cried, struggling to catch his breath. 'They say they'll burn the witch and the Englishman. Someone told them they'll be arriving in Leith any time now!'

53

McGray banged the door of the Reed household, so hard that some of the windows of the neighbouring houses began to light up. Young Dr Reed lived conveniently close to the City Chambers, on a narrow close that intersected the Royal Mile.

To McGray's surprise, it was a sour-looking woman who opened the door, face puffy and eyes bleary. She'd wrapped tightly in a frayed shawl, in a pathetic attempt at covering her night shimmy. The woman gave into a wide yawn, rubbing her eyes. She half opened one, her knuckles still on her other socket. McGray was about to say something, but the woman growled over her shoulder.

'*Wesley! It's that Nine-Nails man!*'

And saying no more she turned on her heels and went back in, leaving the door ajar.

McGray stepped into a dim corridor with a narrow staircase. Reed appeared seconds later, also in his nightclothes, and rubbing his eyes as if consciously imitating the mannerisms of his mother.

'Inspector, sir! Are you here for the results? Don't worry, the experiments will be ready by now. Just give me a minute to put on a—'

'Experiments?' McGray echoed. 'Results?'

'Yes. The experiments Mr Frey asked me to – did he not tell you?'

McGray frowned. 'We've nae spoken since yesterday morning.'

That got rid of any grogginess on Reed's face.

'Have you not? Oh, God! You will *really* want to see this, sir! It is exactly what Mr Frey and I suspected.'

McGray only gave Reed enough time to put on his shoes and a coat, and they both galloped on Onyx's back towards the police headquarters. It was so early the front courtyard was desolate, its corners dotted with clumps of snow. The only person around was Constable McNair, zealously guarding the gate. His freckles turned bright red as soon as he saw them.

'Sir! Yer nae supposed to be here!'

McGray snorted. 'Och, I ken. I erm... *forgot* something yesterday.'

McNair swallowed, clearly torn. He was one of McGray's most devoted colleagues, but...

'They gave us direct orders, sir. I'll be in deep shite if I—'

McGray held the young man by the shoulders. 'All right, laddie. I really like ye, so here's what we're going to do. If the super asks, I'll tell him ye tried to stop me and I kicked ye in the baws and then sprained yer arm. Whether it'll be the truth or a lie, that's entirely up to ye.'

McNair pondered for a moment, while McGray slowly tightened the grip around his clavicle.

'Go on,' he muttered, and McGray and Reed rushed inside.

They made their way across the desolate hall and down to the morgue, where Reed lit his small desk lamp. McGray saw the cavernous room, all the dissecting tables cleared.

'Where are the bodies?'

'They were decomposing badly,' Reed said as he brought a

covered tray from a nearby cupboard, 'so I had to release them yesterday; back to Greyfriars Kirk. Mr Frey said it was—'

'Fine, fine. Tell me what ye have there.'

Reed placed the tray on a worktop and removed the cloth on top.

McGray could not repress a gasp, for it contained uniformly sized pieces of rotten meat, all arranged in a neat line.

'Och, that looks like the ingredients for the Sunday stew at Calton's Jail!'

'I don't think they get meat this nice, sir. It is fine pork belly. A real waste, but all I could find in such haste.'

'That looks really fresh,' McGray said, looking at the chunk on the furthest left. 'But that nasty one in the middle...'

He had to bend down, look closer and blink a couple of times to believe it.

'*Fuck!* That's the exact same colour as the marks on the bodies!'

Reed grabbed a pair of tweezers, picked the most stained piece and brought it closer to the light. Half the meat was pink and plump, but the other half looked grey and stiff.

'And the same clean edges too,' Reed said, pointing at the border of the stain with his little finger. The narrow outline of the stain, as in the marks on the corpses, also looked milky white.

McGray stared at it for a while, not even breathing, before he managed a whisper.

'How did ye do it?'

Reed went to one of his shelves and came back holding an amber jar with a red label.

'*Caustic ash!*' McGray exclaimed. 'Like the stuff they use to make soap?'

'Indeed.'

'Ye must be joking!'

'No, sir. Incredibly simple. Incredibly available. And it was extremely easy to create the effect.'

'*Easy?* To make that soddin' mark appear like magic?'

'Indeed.'

'*How?*'

Reed looked rather smug. 'I made a sort of paste with the stuff; added only enough water so I could apply it with a brush.' He reached for a pestle and mortar and showed it to McGray. There was a small brush in it, its horse-hair bristles corroded away.

'But people *touched* those bodies,' McGray said.

'I know. I only applied it for a matter of minutes and then wiped it off. In fact, the stain appears more clearly when the paste is only left on briefly. The one I just showed you is the best, and I only left the smear for five minutes. That sample on the right I left for an hour and you can barely see a shade of it.'

'Why is that? Makes nae sense.'

'It is odd indeed, but logical – left for longer, the flesh absorbs the chemical and the burn is spread across the skin layers.'

McGray arched an eyebrow, still sceptical. 'And these didnae appear instantly?' he asked.

'No. Caustic acts very slowly; that's why it's so dangerous. I had a couple of minor burns myself, back in my student days. My skin didn't show marks until after a few hours.'

McGray snorted. 'I bet yer fingers didnae look grey like this!'

'No, and that's why I didn't make the connection before. Living skin turns red. Dead skin doesn't react. It simply gets – sort of *cooked*. Similar to the way the acids in the stomach digest food. That is why those sections of the skin seemed to corrupt more quickly.'

McGray covered his mouth. He *wanted* to believe Reed. It all sounded terribly sensible, and yet... it was such a simple answer. Too good to be true.

'Ye sketched the marks, right?'

'Yes, sir. I'll get them.'

Reed pulled the file from his cabinets and spread the sketches on another table.

'They're a true rendition,' he said with a clear hint of pride. 'I traced them directly from the bodies.'

'Exact same size and shape, are nae they?' McGray asked, reading the margin notes.

'Yes. Identical to one thirty-second of an inch.'

McGray bent down, staring at the detailed sketches. More than ever, the little cloven hooves looked like squinting demons laughing at him.

'To be identical like these,' he said, 'they must've been *stamped* with something.'

'Yes, I thought so too.'

McGray rose up, looking alternatively at the samples of pork, the jar of caustic and the sketches.

'Ye can only do this if ye ken very well what this stuff does to a dead body.'

'Indeed,' Reed prompted, 'and very few people would. There are many books that describe caustic burns on the living, but I can't think of a single one that deals with what the substance does to a corpse.'

McGray instantly recalled Frey vomiting at Surgeons' College.

'They use caustic to clean skeletons!' he mumbled. 'For exhibits and such.'

'Oh, yes. I still remember the reek, from back in my student days.'

McGray stroked his chin. 'Now ... auld Pratt was with that bitch Lady Glass last night—'

Reed frowned. 'E-excuse me?'

'And they said they had the right evidence and witnesses. So it cannae be Pratt Junior they were intending to frame.'

McGray snapped his fingers. Even though he'd suspected it all along, he felt a twinge of excitement at seeing it confirmed. 'So it *was* Harland,' he said.

'*Dr Harland?*' Reed asked, but McGray was not listening.

'Things must've gone sour between him and the body snatchers! So he branded the bodies to frame them! Just like Frey said – it was meant to catch the attention of the police.'

'I know Dr Harland studied at Surgeons' College,' Reed said. 'If he ever worked preparing specimens, he must have seen how caustic worked on dead bodies. Many times, perhaps.'

'Indeed,' McGray whispered, for the first time in days feeling a glimmer of hope.

But still, he needed *evidence*.

'The stamp,' he mumbled, then pointed at the sketches. 'Laddie, what can ye think would have that shape? Something that could've been used as a seal.'

Reed blew inside his cheeks. 'God, many things! A real goat's hoof? Perhaps a deer's, from some hunting trophy? I've also seen walking canes with ferrules shaped as cloven hooves.'

'Aye, and for the marks to be identical, Harland must have used the same thing both times. Perhaps he hid it somewhere – kept it for future jobs – or Pratt Junior took it and that's the evidence Lady Glass mentioned. In which case – *shite*, I'll never get hold of it if they have it!'

'Or he may have destroyed it,' Reed added.

McGray pulled at his hair, his hope swiftly turning into despair.

There were a thousand routes and possibilities, only a single true one. And right then Pansy must be approaching Edinburgh. She might have docked already for all he knew.

McGray paced frantically. He felt the burden on his shoulders, and yet he had no time, no grit left... and maybe not enough brains to solve this. If only he could have one more day; one more *hour*.

'Think,' he mumbled, standing still and shutting his eyes. 'Harland… marking the bodies with something… If he hid it, which is the best I can hope for, it could be any-fuckin'-where! The asylum, his house – other places!' He growled, picturing a steamer about to dock at Leith Harbour.

Immediately he opened his eyes. '*Damn!* Nae time to search. I'll have to beat the truth out o' the bastard!'

He took a deep breath, and then stormed out of the chamber and into the morgue's ante-room, ready to gallop to Morningside.

'*Sir, wait!*' Reed yelped just before McGray reached the stairs. 'I think Mr Frey did a good job at recording Dr Harland's activities. That might help you.'

'What?' McGray asked, while Reed frantically searched through his desk's drawers.

'Yesterday, when he asked me to do these experiments – he wrote down what he wanted me to do in this wee notebook of his…'

'Did he?'

'Yes. He was going to tear the sheet out, but he left in such haste he forgot it and left it here.'

Reed produced the notebook and McGray received it as if it were made of gold.

'Och, laddie, I could kiss ye! Percy writes *everything* down!' He shoved the notebook into his breast pocket and rushed to the stairs, but then turned around one more time. 'Reed, make sure ye document all yer experiments in detail. At least it will prove Pansy couldnae have marked the bodies.' He climbed one step and then turned again. '*And tell no one!* Nae even Trevelyan. I don't want Harland or Pratt planting caustic ash in my sister's bedroom!'

'Yes, sir. I'll—'

But McGray heard no more. He climbed the stairs two at a time and then darted out of the building. Constable McNair shouted something but McGray did not hear him. He simply jumped onto Onyx's back and spurred him along the Royal Mile, dodging the sleepy pedestrians that began to fill the street.

Along with the stomping hooves and the wind whistling past him, Nine-Nails thought he heard some child shout in the distance—

'Come come! We're goin' to burn the witch!'

54

Even along the sumptuous Queen Street, at the heart of New Town, Caroline saw a couple of carts crammed with people chanting a strident rendition of the 'Lament for the McGray Clan'. She felt a shiver when she saw a boy, not eight years old, carrying firewood and being egged on by his father to chant the dire verses.

Fortunately the cab turned then, halting by the front door of the Ardglass mansion.

Caroline jumped off, climbed the steps and knocked hard at the door. As she waited, she regretted not having taken a set of keys before moving out.

The door opened just an inch and she saw the snooty face of Halston, the stiff butler.

'Do you have an appoint—?'

'*Step away!*' she screeched, kicking the door so hard she nearly ripped the little chain off its hinges.

Halston only moved a little faster, and as soon as Caroline heard him pull the chain and locks, she flung the door aside, the edge hitting the man on the head.

'Haughty, useless idiot,' she grumbled as she rushed past him. 'When the old hag dies you'll be the first dusty knick-knack to go!'

Caroline remembered the old house being cold, but not quite as icy as it was that morning. She rushed to the wide staircase, to her grandmother's bedroom, but as she crossed the landing she saw light already coming from the old lady's study. She rushed there and pushed the door open.

'*Why are you doing this?*' she barked.

Lady Anne, behind her desk, was living up to her reputation – a large glass of claret in one hand, while with the other jotting numbers in a long ledger.

She looked up, ready to scold the intruder, but when she recognised her granddaughter, the woman smiled.

'Why are you doing this?' Caroline insisted after a deep breath.

Lady Anne put down the dripping pen. 'Why do you want to marry sludge? Our ancestry dates back to the War of the Roses, and yet you—'

'You will fix this.'

Lady Anne grinned, lounging back in her seat. 'I *am* fixing it.'

Caroline snorted. 'Don't play games with me, you old cow!'

'Why, you already have his charm!'

'You're only doing this—'

'*I'm only doing all of this for you!*' Lady Anne howled, jumping to her feet and spilling red claret all over her papers. 'So that you and your children can have a future! All the trouble, all the tribulations, all the *expense* I went through to keep your father's insanity a secret! All that was for you! So you could marry well. Nobody wants an infected vessel for their children.

'And for what? So that you'd throw yourself at *him* at the first chance! Of all the manky rascals in the world, you had to choose *him*!'

'Forget about me!' Caroline snapped. 'Pansy is your grand-daughter too. My father's—'

'*She is your father's bastard!* And raised by the filthy McGrays.' Lady Anne reached for the decanter, her hand trembling with wrath as she refilled her glass. 'I tried to let it go. God knows I tried. All men have their dirty offspring; it would have been foolish to expect my Joel to be different. But I couldn't. And I couldn't because of *you*. Every time I saw you I saw *her*. It was as if they slapped me in the face every day! The rascal that condemned my Joel to insanity and the trollop that ensnared my son...' Lady Anne had to take deep breaths, a hand clutched at her chest, as if she was about to have a heart attack. 'They say you can't choose your parents, but you can't choose your children either –' she glanced at Caroline – 'or your grandchildren.'

She bared her teeth, and then stared into nothing as she took another sip. After smacking her lips she looked back at Caroline. 'Why do you even care about her?'

Caroline closed her eyes for a moment, clenching her fists.

'I don't have time to explain basic humanity to you. You *will* fix this. You'll go to the harbour and tell your men to take Pansy away.'

Her grandmother let out a piercing laugh. 'Why would I do such a thing?'

Caroline lifted her chin and squared her shoulders. She was not quite as tall as her grandmother, but close enough.

'Because if you don't...' she said, 'I will take her place.'

Lady Anne opened her mouth, showing her stained teeth, ready to burst into laughter. But before she uttered any sound, she realised Caroline was serious. The grin twisted into a growl.

'*Don't be stupid!* How could you possibly?'

Caroline walked around the desk, feeling taller with each step.

'I'll tell everyone the truth. I'll tell them that Amy McGray is my half-sister and that I have been visiting her in secret. Just like I used to visit –' she imitated her grandmother's grin – '*your mad son.*'

Lady Anne opened her mouth ever so slightly, drawing in a throttled breath.

'And then,' Caroline added, 'I'll tell everyone I killed that poor man, and the worker you dropped near the asylum.'

Her grandmother cackled at once. 'Oh, you stupid, stupid imp! No one will swallow that!'

'They will when I tell them that the gloves and cloak they found in Pansy's room are mine. The gloves' lining is embroidered with my initials. They will even think I took after my insane father!'

She took a little step forward, for the first time in her life forcing her grandmother to back off.

'Your son's insanity revealed,' she whispered, 'and your granddaughter tried for murder. How would you like that to end the Ardglass line?'

Lady Anne, for once, was rendered speechless. For a moment she simply looked at her granddaughter, her upper lip raised as if she were smelling something foul.

'You wouldn't dare!' she hissed. 'You're just a silly brat with a big mouth.'

Caroline simply stared on, not even blinking.

'*You'd hang!*' Lady Anne screeched. 'Or spend the rest of your days in a filthy cell.'

Caroline smiled. 'Yes. And the McGrays would be free forevermore. Think of that.'

Lady Anne pretended to laugh. 'You wouldn't—'

Caroline took another step, startling the old woman. 'A risky gamble, is it not?'

They stared at each other for a while, in a silent duel of wills, until Caroline snatched the glass from Lady Anne's hand, had a long drink and wiped her lips with her sleeve.

'I'll be waiting at Leith Harbour,' she said. 'If I don't see you there giving the order to your men ...' There was no need to say more.

Caroline put the glass down with a bang, turned on her heels and walked out of her grandmother's study – for the last time in her life.

55

McGray had never galloped quite so fast to Morningside.

Onyx managed to cover the three miles in about twenty minutes, and even as McGray jumped off its back, the horse seemed only slightly out of breath.

'I envy ye,' McGray said as he tethered it, and then ran to the main entrance. As he climbed the steps, he saw the clouds above the asylum, so thick and dark it could have been midnight.

An orderly attempted to cut his path. 'Sir, we were told we shouldnae—'

'*Back off!*' McGray barked, drawing a hand to his breast pocket and showing just a third of his gun.

The orderly immediately froze, as did the few nurses and patients that stood around.

McGray cast them a cautionary glare before rushing upstairs. He went straight to Harland's office and slammed the door open.

The man was not there, his desk crammed, as ever, with paperwork.

McGray did not repress a frustrated growl, keen to throw the first punch at the blasted doctor's face. He turned around, ready to search for Harland in every corner of the building, but then halted.

'Good chance to sneak,' he mumbled, and then shut the door, making sure he put the latch on.

McGray went to the desk – the one he himself had kicked – and spotted the hastily fixed legs. He pulled all the drawers and rummaged through the contents. Only paperwork. There could be something there but he had no time to go through each sheet of paper.

'Should've done this from the very fucking start!' he mumbled as he went through the cabinets. He was hoping to find a jar of caustic, or perhaps a receipt for the stuff, or whichever trinket Harland might have used as a stamp. He found nothing of the sort.

Of course. Harland would not be so stupid as to leave such crucial evidence lying in his office, surely not even in his home.

McGray let out a furious growl, let himself drop into Harland's chair and rubbed his face in desperation.

Someone knocked at the door then.

'*Sod off!*'

'It's me, sir. Miss Smith.'

McGray laughed bitterly. 'Did ye hear me, or should I repeat myself?'

The head nurse began pleading for him to let her in, but McGray purposely did not hear. He bent forwards, resting his elbows on his knees and covering his brow, making his best effort to think. The noise from the corridor, where people were beginning to cluster, made it all the more difficult.

'Percy's notes!' he whispered, and immediately pulled the little notebook from his breast pocket and looked for notes about Harland.

It might have been because the woman kept shouting behind the door, but the first name McGray found was Miss Smith, scribbled many times all across a lengthy account of her conversation with Frey.

Miss Smith had been the one who'd prepared Mrs Brewster's body. She had dressed the old lady and done her hair. She had been present when Dr Clouston put a sprig of laurel and yew on the lady's hand. And then they had—'

McGray jumped up and opened the door, so swiftly that Miss Smith had no time to pull back her fist and he had to seize her by the wrist.

'I need ye,' he spluttered, pulling her in, and as he shut the door he saw Clouston appear behind her.

'Adolphus! I need to tell you—'

'Shut up!' McGray snarled as he locked the door again. He turned to face Miss Smith and showed her Frey's notebook. 'Says here ye dressed Mrs Brewster.'

Miss Smith's chest swelled. 'I – oh, sir, I am so sorry for all the—!'

'Och, forget about that! I need ye to tell me—'

'*Adolphus!*' Clouston shouted at the top of his lungs, knocking desperately. 'People all over town are saying Amy will arrive in Leith Harbour. That they want to intercept her to lynch her! And that—'

'*Fucking shut up!*' McGray hollered, silencing everyone in the corridor. He turned to Miss Smith, pointing at the door with his thumb. 'That true?'

Miss Smith bit her lip. 'Yes, sir. I think so. That's what I wanted to tell you. People are—'

McGray raised a hand. He felt his heart thumping as a myriad of thoughts and complications spun in his head, an imaginary clock ticking in the background. He felt he could not quite breathe, and had to shake his head and force himself to focus.

He was so close. He could feel it. Then again, he could not ignore those warnings. If he did not find anything of consequence within minutes, he'd dash to the harbour and help Pansy.

'Miss Smith, tell me, and quickly – ye prepared the lady's corpse, right?'

'Yes.'

'And then ...' McGray pointed at the exact line in Frey's notes. 'Says here ye and Clouston left the body unattended. Out o' respect?'

'Yes.'

'For how long? It doesnae say here.'

Miss Smith again bit her lip. 'I don't know – it couldn't have been long.'

'An hour?'

'Oh God, no! Much less. Twenty minutes at most.'

'Good. Did ye see Dr Harland in that time? Perhaps sneaking into Mrs Brewster's room?'

'N-no. If I had I would have told Mr Frey.'

'D'ye ken where Harland was? What he was doing?'

Miss Smith looked from side to side, frowning and then closed her eyes tightly.

'I – I'm so sorry, sir. I don't know. I was so busy I just—' She looked up. 'We could check his shifts or—' She opened her eyes wide. 'Mr Frey! He questioned Dr Harland right before talking to me!' And she pointed at the notebook just as Clouston began banging on the door again.

'Adolphus! Should I tell that man Trevelyan—?'

'*Give me a fucking minute!*'

McGray passed the pages so quickly he tore a few. He found the name soon enough, followed by upsetting notes about Harland's threats against Pansy.

McGray closed his eyes for a moment. Even amidst the tension, he felt a renewed fire in his stomach when he realised Frey had known everything – Pansy's origins and Caroline's visits – for quite a while. No wonder he'd forced him to leave Harland alone.

'Adolphus!' Clouston shouted, and McGray opened his eyes again. He went on reading, turning pages and fishing for facts. Frey's records spoke in length of Harland's impoverished circumstances, but said absolutely nothing about his movements before Mrs Brewster's funeral.

'Useless soddin' notes!' he growled. 'Typical Frey – "*Uuh! Even Dr Harland's desk is a dilapidated antique in the awful Queen Anne*—"' He looked up, nearly spraining his neck.

'Are you all right, sir?' Miss Smith asked while Clouston repeated his pleas, but McGray did not listen to either of them.

'Queen Anne-style furnishings ...' he whispered, staring at the old desk. He felt a rush of blood in his head. 'They had spindly legs – carved as talons and paws and—'

McGray looked at the chunky blocks of wood nailed to the desk. He then pushed it against the wall and flung himself to his knees, bending so low his nose nearly touched the dusty floorboards.

There it was: the Devil's cloven hoof!

Not one, but four of them, the furniture's legs clearly dented on the floor. That desk must have stood there for years. He remembered Reed talking about walking canes with ferrules carved as hooves.

McGray sized the nearest mark with his hand, his chest tingling with excitement. Those were the shapes he'd seen on the bodies; there was no doubt. And Reed's sketches, traced from the bodies, would prove to be perfect matches.

'So Harland cut the legs off,' McGray mumbled, slowly rising his head, 'then dabbed them in caustic and used them as seals, as if to brand cattle.' He looked at the desk and its new makeshift legs. 'He probably used only two; one for Mrs Brewster and one for MacDonnell, and then decided to get rid o' them all.'

When McGray looked up, he found Miss Smith clutching a hand at her chest.

'Dr Harland repaired that himself,' she said. 'I saw him bring the blocks. He moaned about everything here being eaten by woodworm.'

McGray shoved the notebook back into his pocket. 'We have to keep those boards safe. It must be the police who take them away, ye understand?'

He opened the door then, to tell the same words to Dr Clouston, but he had no chance. Harland was elbowing his way through the nurses. The gash on his cheekbone, crossed with five stitches and caked with blood clots, looked like a bulging caterpillar, the skin around it all the shades of red and purple.

'*Are you retarded?*' he barked. 'The police said you have no right to—!'

He went silent then, looking over McGray's shoulder. His eyes went straight to the floorboards.

Harland turned so pale the stitches and bruises seemed black in comparison. He opened and closed his mouth, unable to speak, and McGray had no trouble pushing him outside.

'*You have no right to search!*' he finally shouted. 'You—!'

'*Shut it!*' McGray yelped, raising a hand as if to smack him. Harland crouched, guarding his face with a forearm, but the fire in his eyes did not diminish. He tried to push past McGray when he saw him close the door.

'That's my property there! You have no right to—!'

'*Everyone heard that?*' McGray shouted over Harland. 'All the shite in there is his!' He then grabbed him by the collar and lifted him to his toes. 'I really didnae think ye'd be stupid enough to admit to that!'

Harland twisted and jerked until McGray let go of him.

'Get some keys,' he told Miss Smith, who at once nodded and dashed away. McGray turned to Clouston. 'Nobody gets in there until the police come. Ye hear me? If ye still have any thread of decency!'

Clouston raised his chin, like a soldier called for duty. His pupils flickered and he tensed his lips, as if he wanted to say a thousand things but had to force himself into silence.

'I'll guard it myself,' he said at last. 'Like I have guarded—'

McGray raised a hand and Clouston started, thinking he'd punch him, but Nine-Nails only rested it on his shoulder.

'I ken ye have,' he said swiftly, not meeting the doctor's gaze.

'*You have nothing on me!*' Harland interrupted, his voice a guttural growl. Again he tried to get to the door but McGray pushed him away. 'Anything in there could have been tampered with! Or planted, or – *broken* by the inmates!'

McGray frowned slightly, unable to hide a sudden doubt. He'd thought that was all the proof he needed, but...

'*That's right!*' Harland cried, each word raising the temperature in McGray's blood. 'Anyone could have sneaked into my office! *Anyone!* I seldom lock it. Whatever you claim you found there will only explain how your sister did what she—'

McGray burst in a roar and charged against Harland, pinning him against the hall's opposite wall. Everyone around gasped or yelped, and a couple of orderlies rushed to try to pull him away.

Harland, at the core of the skirmish, was laughing.

'I'm right,' he said, savouring each word. 'You know I'm right.'

McGray grunted and stepped back, far angrier at his own shattered hopes than at Harland. He covered his brow and took a deep, hissing breath, everyone around him scared and silent.

'Is this – a bad time?' someone interrupted behind their backs.

McGray looked up slightly, still trying to calm down, and saw the plump figure of Reverend Hunter, from Greyfriars Kirk. The man's shoulders were peppered with snow, matching his neat crown of white locks, but his cheeks and round nose were bright red.

'It is a terrible time, reverend,' Clouston replied. 'If you'd please come back—'

'I am so sorry, doctor, but I must talk to you right away. I need money for a coffin.'

McGray winced. 'Wha— *Fuck off!*'

Reverend Hunter wrung his leather gloves.

'Sorry, inspector, but I must insist. Your colleague Mr Frey said I was not to use Mrs Brewster's original coffin. The poor soul needed burial and I don't have ready cash. I had to beg the undertaker to lend us—'

McGray snorted, strode briskly towards the chubby man and grabbed him by the arm, ready to send him away. But just as the minister began to protest, Nine-Nails went perfectly still.

'D'ye still have the auld coffin?' he mumbled.

'Yes, inspector. You saw it yourself. It's still sitting in my sacristy. And I cannot—'

'*Shush!*'

McGray let go of him and quickly produced Frey's notebook. As he looked for the pages, Miss Smith came back with the set of keys.

'Ye prepared the lady's body,' he told her. 'And Clouston came in to put some sprigs in her hand. Says here—'

'Laurel and yew,' Clouston said. 'I remember it vividly. I took them from the gardens. I had no shears with me so I had to tear them from the trees.'

Harland perked up then. The way he moved closer to McGray, slowly and utterly silent, made McGray think of a slithering snake.

'Youse left Mrs Brewster alone, then?' McGray went on, though looking at Harland from the corner of his eye. 'She was left alone until the coffin arrived?'

'Yes, sir,' Miss Smith said.

'The one time her body was unattended,' McGray said, pointing at Frey's same observation. 'So she must've been branded right then!'

He exhaled, staring at the ceiling. Once again he was tantalisingly close to the truth, but still nowhere near finding absolute, irrefutable proof. That entire trip to the asylum would be a dreadful waste of time, when he ought to be heading to Leith Harbour to help Pansy and—

Something shifted in his mind. McGray pinched the bridge of his nose, trying to remember.

'Laurel and yew...' he mumbled, recalling a little vial Frey had left on his mantelpiece. 'but we only found the yew...'

Then the idea took full shape. It was a feeble, dangerous plan, but he'd have to take the risk.

He moved closer to Miss Smith, consciously turning his back to Harland.

'Miss Smith, ye saw this lanky sod lurking around Mrs Brewster's room, right?'

The head nurse stared at him in confusion, and McGray pressed a finger on a random page.

'*Says here,*' he grunted, and he lowered his head to make a discreet wink. 'Ye told Frey. *Right?*'

It took Miss Smith a second to understand that McGray wanted her to lie, and even then she was only able to mumble a befuddled *aye*.

McGray turned back to Harland, who suddenly appeared standing a little closer, as if he'd moved by magic.

'What a sad attempt of an inspector you are,' the young doctor said. 'Even if this bloody wench is telling the truth, there is no way you can prove the mark was made there and then.' He bared his teeth. 'Is there?'

McGray was finally able to smile. 'That's where yer wrong, laddie.' He turned the page. 'Miss Smith, ye told Frey ye saw the laurel still in the lady's hand when she was at the kirk.'

This time Miss Smith answered with full confidence. 'I did, sir. Right before she was buried.'

'We found a few wee spots on Mrs Brewster's hands, between her fingers. The same colour as the mark on her face. That means ye spilt some o' the *stuff* – ye ken what stuff I'm talking about – on Mrs Brewster's hands!'

Harland's jaw dropped, the man staggered beyond words.

'Of course ye didnae see it then,' McGray said. 'The marks only appear much later, and ye must have been in a hurry.' He looked at Frey's notes. 'If she was buried with that wee sprig, it must've fallen off her hands when the snatchers moved her.'

He looked at Harland, the doctor just a few inches from him now, craning his neck to look into the notebook.

McGray pulled it away. 'If ye spilt on the lady's hands with – ye ken *what*, ye may well have spilt on that leaf too.'

'You're making all of this up!' Harland hissed.

McGray's smile widened. 'Och, I'm nae. And if ye spilt on that laurel leaf, it must have stained! Luckily those leaves last for weeks; hence their meaning "eternal life". It will still show that stain. And if it's still inside that coffin, perhaps caught in the lining—'

Harland shuddered, his face going from pale to a sickly shade of green. Clouston moved closer to him, ready to catch him if he fainted, but then Harland twisted his torso, reaching for one of his lab coat pockets, and McGray caught the briefest glance of a shining scalpel.

Harland hurled himself against Nine-Nails, and with a swift movement plunged the thin blade between McGray's ribs.

56

McGray sank to his knees as everyone around him gasped and screamed.

His eyes teared from the pain, and he caught a blurry glimpse of Harland running like the wind along the corridor. *'Catch him!'* he screeched. Clouston and Miss Smith knelt by his side. He saw a couple of orderlies go after Harland, but not nearly as fast as he himself would have run.

'Don't move,' Miss Smith urged, and only then did McGray realise that the scalpel was still plunged into his torso, his coat, waistcoat and shirt pierced cleanly by the blade. 'I will pull it out. I need you to—'

'Wait!' McGray snapped, feeling stabs of pain with every twitch of his body. He looked for Reverend Hunter's face. 'Go to yer kirk. He'll try to destroy the evidence!'

The priest seemed about to vomit. 'What? If you're expecting me to guard a blasted leaf from a lunatic doctor that throws stabs left, right and cen—'

'Fuck, go!' McGray roared, but instantly coiled up and pressed a hand against his ribs.

When he looked up the minister had vanished, and Nine-Nails could only hope the man had listened to him.

'Bring that, quick!' Clouston said, and McGray saw that a

young nurse had already fetched bandages. He grabbed a folded one and gave it to McGray. 'Bite this.'

No more explanation was needed. McGray did so and, before he could even blink, Miss Smith pulled the scalpel out in one rapid movement.

McGray's growl echoed throughout the corridor, his entire body shuddering from the pain. Miss Smith then began dousing alcohol on a handful of cotton wool.

'Nae time for that,' McGray snapped, trying to stand, but Clouston pushed him down.

'At least let us dress it. What use will you be, bleeding yourself to death across Edinburgh?'

McGray felt the impatience clutch at his chest like yet another physical pain but, much to his dismay, he had to nod. He pulled his tartan waistcoat and shirt open himself, ripping out buttons and tearing fabric.

Miss Smith worked quickly, cleaning the wound, pressing a cloth on the gash, and then Clouston helped her roll the bandages hastily all around McGray's ribs. They did it in such a rush half of his shirt ended up clumped under the strappings.

McGray clambered up as soon as Miss Smith tied the last knot, immediately feeling a searing pain. He pressed on none-theless, limping stubbornly towards the stairs.

'What about Amy?' Clouston asked, striding next to him. 'And this mob that claims they'll—'

McGray winced as he took the first step down. He had to accept Clouston's arm to support himself.

'Send someone to the City Chambers. Ask them to tell Trevelyan that I implore him to send men to the harbour. Also send him Harland's address. Someone should guard the place in case he goes there.'

'Of course. Will you go to Greyfriars?'

McGray sighed, picturing Pansy being surrounded by police

officers and angry pedlars. He was well aware that he might be making the worst possible decision.

'Aye. I need that evidence safe. That's the only way to save her from a trial.'

Once on the ground floor, McGray moved more quickly, limping his way out. When he walked out of the building two orderlies came to him, panting.

'He took a horse from the stables,' one spluttered. 'We saw him gallop to town.'

'Course he did,' McGray muttered. 'Help me.'

The orderlies and Clouston had to push him up onto the saddle, and McGray screeched, feeling as if his entire torso tore with each movement.

He patted Onyx's neck and whispered into its ear. 'Be gentle with me, laddie.'

He spurred the horse on and, despite the pain, made it gallop at full speed.

57

Lady Anne poured the last drops of claret left in the decanter and then banged it on her desk three times, to signal she needed more.

'She wouldn't dare,' she grunted, picking up her glass and pacing towards the window. 'She wouldn't.'

The street lights were still on, shedding their pathetic amber light on the snowed street, the thick clouds swirling as if about to deliver a thunderstorm. She'd heard a few people cry 'burn the witch', and she would have smiled, had Caroline not stormed in with her threats.

Lady Anne gripped the glass more tightly. She relished in the irony of the old McGray's bastard being burned as a witch, but what use would it be, if her own granddaughter got herself tried for the murders of two nobodies? Locked up for life. Childless. Her ancestry disgraced.

'She wouldn't—'

But this time Lady Anne could not complete the phrase. She had a sip of claret instead, thinking of Caroline's jaunts across Europe, and then Windsor. And before that, her infamous trip to the Lancashire wilderness, right into the den of the very women who'd turned Joel insane.

That girl was a reckless, headstrong, stubborn creature.

Very much like her father.

Very much like Lady Anne herself.

Even that little bastard Amy, feigning madness for years and years, lying even to her brother, had shown much of the Ardglass character.

'*May she join her mother in hell!*' Lady Anne hissed, downing the rest of the claret in one gulp.

Her butler stepped in, already bringing more wine.

'I want a carriage ready,' Lady Anne barked even before the man had swapped the decanters. 'Now! One of the small ones. I don't want to draw too much attention.'

The butler frowned. 'It will take a while to fetch the driver. He is not yet—'

'*Now!*' she yelped.

The man bowed. 'If it helps you, ma'am, there is a small coach at the back door. One of your contractors from the quarries. The pedlar is demanding payment, else he won't deliver. His coach is full of crates, and the smell of—'

'Good!' Lady Anne interrupted. 'For once they're timely.'

And she left the study with brisk steps, letting out irate snorts as she realised she was about to thwart one of her own most clever schemes.

She'd have to err on the side of caution, but just this once. Just to protect her kin, even if that meant having to intercede for a damned McGray.

'That is,' she mumbled, 'if those indigents don't burn her first.'

58

Leith Harbour's lighthouse appeared on the horizon. A fuzzy, milky spark amidst the darkness.

I saw it from the rusty steamer, as the miners shoved Pansy and me up the stairs to the deck. At least they'd given her a blanket, but after hours and hours crouched in a dingy, claustrophobic compartment, unable to sleep, we were both numb and bleary-eyed.

'Quick!' barked the burly miner called Angus. He pushed Pansy forwards and she tripped on the last step. I only just managed to catch her as she fell.

'*Don't touch her!*' I shouted, but the men around us simply cackled.

It was no time for decorum: I put an arm around Pansy's shoulders and pulled her closer to me.

'I will not leave you on your own,' I whispered.

I heard the clinking of pewter, and saw Martin Pratt and the other medical students clustered at the prow. They were all wrapped in excessively thick bear-fur coats and drinking from steaming mugs.

'Nearly there!' Martin said, raising his mug and spilling hot brandy. The others joined him in a puerile chorus.

Pansy turned her face away, trembling with anger. All I could do was squeeze her shoulder a little more tightly.

She placed her hand on mine. Just for an instant. And then she hid it again under the blanket.

The steamer reached the long piers then, the waves clashing against the high stone walls, the lighthouse right over our heads, and Pansy stared at them with awe. Even then, despite all our fears, she could not contain her wonder at such a vast view.

I did not share the emotion, for I noticed something eerie in the air. I could not tell what it was, but it was akin to that oppressive sensation one feels right before a mighty storm.

I also heard the murmur of a crowd coming from the docks. Something was wrong.

The voices were agitated, but also excited, in a manner that chilled my blood.

It was too foggy to make out any shapes. All I could see were many lights ahead of us, perhaps torches, teeming like a swarm of fireflies.

'*Burn the witch!*' the children cried, and Caroline started on the carriage seat.

They were not far from the harbour now. She could already see the lighthouse in the distance, beyond the snow-covered roofs, and hear the roar of the waves and the steamers.

And the agitation increased as they got closer. More men chanting horrid songs about the corrupt police, more children and women cackling and shouting the name McGray. Caroline saw a few people jerking the newspapers, the sign of the Devil printed all across the pages.

She could feel their rage. Something debased, inhuman and cowardly, that only surfaced in the crowds but never in the individual: a latent monster, ever looking for a chance to emerge.

The carriage reached the end of Bernard Street, took a turn, and then Caroline had a first proper view of the harbour. She could not contain a gasp. The docks were lined with torches, hundreds of them, all gathered at the very edge of the waterfront. To her left was the long channel, bordered by the tall breakwaters that led to the lighthouse and the open sea; to her right, she saw the straight lines of Albert Dock. Both sides were alight with twinkling specks of fire, the hubbub of the crowd rising each time they saw a vessel appear.

Caroline felt a cold fear in her chest, just as a group of young men ran past her cab, punching it as they rushed towards the waterfront, cheering and bringing more torches.

'A public execution,' she whispered.

There were even carriages of the gentry, parked haphazardly on the yards surrounding Albert Dock, their well-to-do occupants ready to witness the spectacle.

Caroline opened the front window. 'Park over there,' she told the driver, and her own cab joined the lines of morbid gawkers.

She already knew there was nothing she could do.

59

Each stride felt like a new stab into McGray's ribs, Onyx galloping at breakneck speed along the north side of the Meadows. And with the pain, McGray felt an unbearable pang of anxiety: Harland had but to crush a little laurel leaf to clear his name, and then Pansy would be damned forever.

McGray turned left then, following the hedged Meadow Walk, and as he dashed north, towards Greyfriars Kirk, he spotted another horse, more than a hundred yards ahead, dodging carriages and pedestrians in a manic race.

The rider wore a white lab coat, almost glowing under the street lights.

'*Harland!*' McGray roared. His voice resounded over the racket of the street, and the man looked back briefly. McGray could not quite make out his face, but he did not need to.

'*I see ye!*' he shouted.

Harland spurred his horse with all his might, the agonised neighing piercing the air.

McGray charged on, moving swiftly and yet gaining ground at a frustratingly slow pace. He unsheathed his gun, ready to test his aim, but just then Harland entered the busy esplanade where the road joined George IV Bridge.

Harland nearly clashed against a hefty landau carriage. His

horse reared, almost sending him to the ground, and when it landed back on its front legs, its chest hit the side of the carriage so forcefully McGray heard the wood crack.

Harland's horse sprinted madly, moving in erratic circles in the middle of the bustling road. People, carts and other riders tried to move aside, crashing against each other, the entire street now in chaos.

McGray aimed his gun, but people constantly got in the way. All he could do was spur Onyx.

Harland then let out a rasping, desperate howl, let go of the reins and clumsily jumped off the horse's back.

He fell on his knees, rolled on the mud and dragged himself away from the stomping hooves.

'*Stop!*' McGray cried, raising his gun, if only for show.

Harland saw it, still on all fours, and then sprang to his feet and ran towards Greyfriars gate, while everyone around him let out frantic cries.

McGray made it to the esplanade but had to slow down, his path cut by horses and clumsy passers-by. He dismounted, his eyes fixed on Harland as the man recklessly crossed the road. He hid momentarily behind the statue of Greyfriars Bobby, before darting forwards.

A tall stagecoach approached at speed, just a few yards away, but Harland ran right in front of it. The driver had to pull the reins so hard that his gloved hands must have bruised, and the horses only just managed to stop, their muzzles hitting Harland on the shoulder.

He halted for an instant, stunned, as if he could not believe his luck, and then looked back. His eyes met McGray's, and Nine-Nails ran to him at full speed, but still at a considerable distance. Harland allowed himself a smirk and then staggered forwards.

He was struck that very instant.

A cart, concealed by the stagecoach, rammed him from the side. Harland fell sideways and his body momentarily disappeared under the wheels and trampling hooves.

It took the entire street, even the cart driver, a few seconds to realise what had happened.

McGray went still, paralysed by the sight. The cart slowed down several yards away, and McGray saw a muddy lump move sluggishly on the ground.

He ran closer, just as a woman standing nearby let out a piercing scream. Many voices followed. McGray, forgetting his own pain, knelt down next to Harland, and what he saw made him shudder.

Harland lay on his back, all his limbs bent at odd angles. McGray could not tell where his left hand ended and the mud began, and the only colour amidst the murky brown was the crimson spurt of blood that the man spat out.

He looked at McGray and immediately began coughing. He tried to move, but all he managed were pitiful shudders.

A cab halted behind McGray, but he did not notice it. A man jumped off and placed a hand on his shoulder.

'Take him to the yard,' he said softly. It was Reverend Hunter.

Only then did McGray see the crowd that was gathering around them.

'Come on,' the reverend insisted, and McGray nodded.

He pocketed his gun and then slid his hands under Harland's torso, moving as gently as he could, but the poor man still cried in agony. McGray lifted him slowly, his own ribs searing with pain. He noticed every crushed bone, every trampled bit of flesh. Harland's arms dropped limply and his torso trembled, oozing blood from somewhere underneath his clothes.

'*I didnae see him!*' the cart's driver cried, rushing to help McGray. '*That other damned carriage!*'

'We ken,' McGray muttered, while Reverend Hunter told

people to move aside. He closed the wrought-iron gate as soon as they entered the lawns.

'This way,' he said, pointing to the temple. The old sexton was at the entrance, and he too rushed to help.

They went into the nave and the minister ran to the sacristy. He soon came back with several old blankets, perhaps from the donations for the poor. He spread them on the floor, making a bundle for a pillow, and McGray, aided by the driver and the sexton, gently laid down what was left of Dr Harland.

The man spat out another gush of blood just as they helped him rest his head on the blanket. He coughed and choked, until Reverend Hunter lifted his head and supported it under his own knee. The minister whispered something into the sexton's ear, and he rushed away, and then Hunter began murmuring prayers.

McGray simply knelt to one side, dumbfounded, and the cart driver sat on the floor and buried his face in his hands, sobbing in misery.

Harland coughed and grunted, staring at the vaulted ceiling.

'Where did it all – go wrong?' he said, tears rolling down his face. 'I – I could have had it all – I—' and then he began weeping like a young boy. McGray, despite everything, felt terribly sorry for him: still a young man, educated at one of the most respected universities in Europe, surrounded by colleagues who'd gone off to treat wealthy patients and lead distinguished careers. How soul destroying it must have been to hear their news while he was working at the lunatics' asylum, dealing with the worst cases of insanity in the country, forever waiting for a promotion or a breakthrough that would never come.

Harland looked at McGray, fear and regret and anger stirring in his eyes.

'I – tipped off the medical students – once,' he grunted. 'After an inmate had died. Easy money, just for whispering secrets in a tavern. Harmless. And the more I did it, the easier it got. Even the professors respected me again. But—' A drop of blood spilled from the corner of his mouth and Reverend Hunter cleaned it with his handkerchief. 'There were never enough bodies, no matter how many I told them about. So – I rushed things.'

He shed copious tears, eyeing the altar. The sexton returned, bringing a small decanter, and something else McGray did not quite see. The minister took the bottle, opened it and dabbed Harland's lips with tawny port.

'MacDonnell – I – I taunted the man. I knew his ailment; how to – wield him. I left him messages on rags, telling him to do my chores. I used rags from the laundries – and bandages—' Harland looked at McGray and gulped. 'I took one of your sister's dresses for that too. I – always had her in mind in case I needed a scapegoat. I knew you wouldn't let her be prosecuted. I didn't even need to convince you she'd done it. But I had to play that card much sooner than I thought...

'Martin told me that the police – you – were on our tracks. I shouldn't have sent them to this graveyard so many times... I knew it would be very easy to incriminate me. You and your colleague suspected me from the very start! I told Martin so, but he didn't care. Neither he, nor the damned professors. They just wanted more bodies!

'At first I refused, but they threatened to tip you off. All they'd need was to send you an unsigned message and you'd be after me. And even if I told on them, and by a miracle managed to convince the courts they were guilty as well –' Harland gulped, making a revolting noise as the fluids accumulated in his lungs – 'I was the one who'd rushed those inmates' deaths! I'd be tried for murders! Martin and Grimshaw might lose their licences; maybe spend a few years in jail, but I would more than likely hang!

'They knew it, so they forced me to deliver another body. Mrs Brewster's. Even if they thought you'd almost certainly track her corpse. I had no other choice but to incriminate your sister, so I marked Mrs Brewster in a way that made you all suspect her. In a way that seemed – unnatural.'

He coughed again, and again Reverend Hunter wiped a trickle of blood from the corner of his mouth.

'And then MacDonnell began blabbing! On the same night I knew they'd be disinterring the old woman! And I panicked. I panicked!'

His chest heaved, each breath a true effort.

'I left a rag in MacDonnell's room, telling him – die. I even soaked it in laudanum to lull him. As always he stuffed his own mouth with it and then he couldn't even scream when I stabbed him!

'And I let him bleed – like I'm bleeding now. And I used his blood to draw the same mark on the wall. Almost a full hour passed before that silly girl found him!'

He shed a renewed burst of tears. Reverend Hunter had to wipe them with the back of his hand, for his hanky was now soaked in blood.

'I marked him while his body was in the storeroom. I wanted you to be certain it was the Devil's mark – only then Martin stole the corpse. I'd met Martin the evening before and I was stupid enough to mention where the body was being kept. It never even crossed my mind that he'd dare break in and take it, but you were right – Mrs Brewster's body was in your custody, so they needed a replacement. He must've taken MacDonnell right after I branded him – before the mark appeared. Martin could only have seen it when the corpse was already at the college. He—'

Harland wrinkled his face, stricken by a stab of pain. And while he caught breath, McGray pondered.

Professor Grimshaw must have seen the mark and thought it was the perfect chance to incriminate Harland: they could not accuse him openly, given their own involvement, so they'd simply sent the piece of skin to the papers, along with an anonymous note that mimicked Harland's hand.

Frey had been right McGray thought, *the skin and the typed documents had come from two different sources, each working to their own agenda.*

The clever bastards.

'Martin told me they'd pinned the guilt on me,' Harland went on, his voice a rasping whisper by now. 'That they'd lead you straight to me.

'It was then I decided I'd not take risks. I gathered my evidence – not the wooden hooves; those I'd burnt already – and I took them to your sister's—' Harland began vomiting blood. Not a spurt like before, but a slow, continuous ebb. He shut his eyes while the minister placed a gentle hand on his forehead.

Behind him, the sexton revealed the other item he'd fetched.

McGray gasped.

It was a single laurel leaf, still crisp and green even after five days, but blackened at the centre.

The stain, following the natural veins of the leaf, looked as sharp, dark and symmetrical as an inkblot.

Solemnly, as if it were some sacred relic, the sexton handed it to McGray, who produced Frey's notebook and inserted it in between the pages.

Feeling slightly guilty, McGray approached the minister and whispered.

'Can ye repeat all this in court, rev'rend?'

The man nodded, though never taking his eyes from Harland.

McGray was too tired to smile. All he managed was a sigh of relief. The statement of a minister would never be put to question.

Harland shook then, gagging on his own blood.

The end would not be peaceful.

60

I heard the shouting even before we entered the harbour, growing louder and louder as we approached the waterfront.

'*What the hell is that?*' one of the college students hissed, pointing at the swarm of lights.

Martin could not answer. He was open-mouthed, his mug tilted until he spilt all his brandy on the deck.

When we passed the lighthouse the torches began to stir, following us as we sailed on between the long piers. The fog cleared slightly and we caught the first glimpse of people running along the wharfs, pointing excitedly at our steamer. We heard not only their shouts, but also the dull noises of a crowd beyond.

'Why are all those people here?' Pansy whispered, her breath coming out in short puffs of condensation.

'I have no idea,' I said, though I had a disturbing inkling.

'*What the hell's all this?*' the miner Angus yelled behind our backs. He marched towards Martin and slapped him on the back of his head. 'Ye never said all o' bloody Edinburgh would come to greet the damned witch!'

'I don't know!' Martin whimpered. 'Someone must have prattled!'

'*What a fuckin' genius!*' the man barked, smacking him not once but twice. He turned to the weather-beaten captain. 'Move faster and make it look like we're heading to the west docks, so that those bastards gather over there. We'll turn to the Albert Dock as late as we can. That should give us some advantage.'

'Cannae do that, lad. This vessel's too wee to take a sharp turn,' the captain said. 'We might cap—'

'*Just do it!*' Angus howled. 'Lady Glass promised us a hundred pounds if we delivered the madwag to the peelers.'

'But—'

'*I said do it!*' and Angus pushed the captain in the direction of the helm. 'I'll shout ye when it's time.' He then strode to the prow, casting Pansy and me a mocking look. 'Youse better hold on to something.' He sneered at Pansy. 'Especially *you.*'

Terrified as she looked, she bared her teeth at him. 'I could jump overboard just so you can't get your damned reward!'

I looked around, feeling the ship already speeding up, and all I could do was rush to the nearest gunwale and cling to it, locking Pansy in my arms. The poor creature was panting in a disturbing blend of anger and fear.

'It will all be all right,' I said, feeling her tremble against my arms. 'Just stay with me.'

'*They're coming!*'

'*That one there!*'

Caroline's heart froze at the screams, while the crowd around her burst in blood-curdling cheers. As soon as her carriage halted, at a vantage point in front of the Albert Dock, she opened the carriage door and peered out, hardly aware of the icy wind and the fluttering snow. She raised a hand above her eyes and saw two steamers on the canal, both heavily lit and moving swiftly on the choppy waters.

'Which one is it?' she asked out loud, her voice quivering.

Right next to her was a middle-aged gentleman, wrapped in an expensive coat, also perched by his carriage door.

'That one, miss. To our left. Care to borrow these?'

He offered her a pair of opera glasses. Caroline snatched them and looked towards the canal.

She saw it was an old, rusty steamer, rather small, and that there were many figures on the deck, but it was too far to make out any faces.

'Bad luck, miss,' the gentleman said, twirling his perfectly manicured moustache. 'Looks like they'll take them to the west docks.'

'The west docks?'

'Yes. Look at them. They are already steering there, to the Victoria Dock. We won't get much of a view from—'

Caroline jumped from the carriage, nearly tripping on her skirts, and sprinted forward without thinking.

'*Miss Ardglass!*' the driver shouted. 'What are you doing? *They'll crush ye!*'

'*Miss Ardglass?*' she heard the gentleman cry, but she had not time to look back. She simply lifted her hem and ran on, diving into the maddened crowd.

'Steady!' Angus shouted from the prow as we sailed at speed.

I looked over my shoulder, for Pansy and I were on the gunwale opposite to the shore, and my heart skipped a beat.

We were so close to the pier I could make out people's faces and, despite the roar of the steamer, I could hear the dreadful things they shouted at us. Martin and his chaps were on that side, holding on for dear life, the young Pratt about to burst into panicked tears.

I looked back to my side, but the prospect was not any better. The entire harbour opened up over there, ablaze with moving torches, their reflections dancing on the choppy waters. I recognised the outlines of Albert Dock, lined with countless specks of light.

'Steady!' Angus repeated.

My heart pounded, only then realising how sharp a turn that would be. My hands were cold and numb, piteously gripping the wet, slippery gunwale.

Pansy looked left and right, her entire body shaking and the blanket about to slip down her shoulders.

I saw the entry to the west docks then, dozens of steamers ahead of us. But Angus remained at the prow, holding a reckless stance.

I waited, not blinking, clenching my hands and holding my breath, until the prow reached the entry to the harbours.

Why did he not give the order?

I felt Pansy's blanket fall off her shoulder. I moved a hand to retrieve it and—

'Turn!'

The shout drilled my ear, and immediately I felt our side of the boat rise up, the motion throwing me away in a circle as Pansy too was flung sideways.

I fell to my knees, hanging by the gunwale with a single hand. I heard Martin's whimpers behind me, along with the splash of the waters and the roar of the steam engine as it propelled us in that manic veering.

My fingers began sliding off the wet surface, the momentum still throwing me sideways. I grunted and clutched my other hand on the deck boards, clinging to the cracks in the wood with my very nails.

Caroline ran on, breathing heavy and elbowing her way through the crowd. Somebody pulled the opera glasses from her hand, but she did not even stop to see who'd done it.

She headed to the bridges that connected the two sides of the harbour, but even from a distance she could tell she'd never be able to cross them. They were both brimming with people.

Caroline stopped, feeling she could cry with despair, people pushing her constantly as they all rushed to the bridges too. And from the street came more carts and carriages to join the mayhem.

What a horrendous display of madness.

She forced a deep breath, wringing her hands as she looked around and gauged her options.

As she turned she saw a small group of officers clustered at a nearby corner, and though they stayed clear of the turmoil, even more frightened than she was, Caroline could only think of appealing to them.

She dashed in their direction, but she'd hardly run a few yards when a shout came from the nearest bridge.

'They're turning!'

Caroline halted and turned around, but she was now surrounded by so many people she could not even see the canal.

'They're turning!' someone else echoed, and the words spread all across the crowd in an instant.

Caroline had to balance on her tiptoes. The wind brought the sound of splashing water and the roar of engines, but all she could see was a vague shining: perhaps the lights of the turning steamer.

She turned again, set on talking to the police, but the crowd was now moving like a solid wall, people pushing her backwards. They almost lifted her into the air, carrying her towards Albert Dock.

'Officers!' she cried, waving a hand. *'Officers!'*

If they heard her they preferred to do nothing. They could not have reached her even if they had wanted to.

And now Caroline found herself trapped in that sea of people, forced to follow them and unable to get away. Like a blade of grass tossed around by a mighty torrent.

*

I felt a hand pulling me by the lapel. It was Pansy's, and she caught me just as my fingers slipped off the gunwale.

'Hold on!' she cried.

We had taken a ninety-degree turn and were now sailing swiftly eastwards. The boat fell back to position, the momentum throwing me back towards the gunwale. Martin and his colleagues fell too, rolling to our side.

I clambered up clumsily, my hands sore, but I still locked them on the gunwale, on either side of Pansy.

'Look,' she said, pointing to the shore.

The ruse had worked: people had clustered on the bridges, but they were now running back to Albert Dock, from this distance looking like a thick liquid slowly moving in a tilted jar.

The boat sped up, and though I nearly fell sideways, I welcomed the hurry. We'd have but seconds to moor, disembark and flee from that hellish port.

'Is it possible for the police to catch us first?' Pansy asked.

'I hope so,' I muttered, not believing my words.

We entered the dock then, and I saw many lines of carriages dotted all along the waterside.

'The gentry also want to see the fray,' I mumbled.

Ours was the only ship entering the wharf at the time, so all eyes were on us. I heard the roar of the crowd, and saw the first torches already reaching the dock. Very soon the place would be bursting with people.

And we'd not even found a spot to dock.

Lady Anne's carriage broke its way onto the harbour-side just as the people gushed off of the bridges and towards Albert Dock. From her raised seat, and despite the stinking crates cluttered to her side, she saw the rusty funnel of the incoming ship.

'There!' she told the driver through the front window, and the man whipped the horses. 'Five peelers to contain this horde,' she said bitterly as they rode past the scared officers. The driver meandered through the crowd, finding the last pockets of space and halting behind the lines of carriages. As soon as he stopped, Lady Anne opened her window and leaned her head and shoulders out, the carriages in front of her blocking most of the view.

'Lady Anne!' someone cried from afar. 'Is that you?'

She saw an older gentleman approach, and she recognised his twirled moustache: one of her wealthier tenants, though she did not recall his name. She gave him an impatient nod, not bothering to talk, and then looked nervously at the dock.

The man cleared his throat. 'Ma'am, I just saw your granddaughter!'

'*What!*'

The man stepped back at her yelp. 'She was here,' he said, peering curiously into the carriage, his eyes drawn to the piled crates.

Lady Anne grunted. 'Are you sure?'

'Absolutely. I just talked to her. I even lent her my opera glasses, but she—'

'*The stupid fool!*' Lady Anne hissed. 'Where is she?'

'I – I'm afraid I don't know, ma'am. I saw her run into the crowd and I lost her.'

Lady Anne opened her mouth to screech, but right then the crowd screamed in anticipation. She looked back at the dock and saw the ship's rusty funnel. It was slowing down.

'*There!*' Lady Anne cried, and the driver moved on.

The boat took another sharp turn and then moved astern briskly between two large paddle steamers. We crashed against the dock, and Pansy let out a yelp as our bodies shook with the impact.

At once the miners and two sailors ran desperately to the gunwale, bringing ropes to secure the boat. Martin Pratt and his colleagues, though visibly shaken, surrounded Pansy and me, all three pointing guns at us. I could only laugh at them, the young men struggling to keep their balance as the captain steered the boat sideways, the hull repeatedly hitting the dockside.

I heard shouting, so close it could have been right next to my ear, and when I turned I saw the miners already throwing punches at people trying to climb onto the boat.

'*God,*' Pansy whispered, and I tightened my grip around her.

The brawny Angus lifted a hefty boarding plank and, aided by the captain, they fanned it left and right to oust the mob. A couple of people threw their torches at us and Martin let out a high-pitched cry, staring at the fire dying on the drenched deck.

I took a step backwards, pulling Pansy with me. I even considered jumping overboard. How cold could the waters—?

There was a gunshot then, and the crowd screamed.

I heard the neighing of horses and the piercing notes of police whistles.

'There!' Pansy said, pointing to our right, and amidst the rows of carriages I recognised a moving shape, darker, taller and wider than the rest.

'A prison van!' I cried with inexplicable relief, seeing it barge through the crowd.

'*Here!*' the captain roared, still wielding the plank, and the van steered in our direction to halt abruptly right before our boat, its wheels cracking loudly. The barred windows seemed a heavenly gift, and I saw a familiar face in the driver's seat.

'McNair!' I cried. '*Here!* It's me!' and people at once began mocking my accent and shouting that I was the man who'd performed dark magic at Calton Hill Jail.

Caroline immediately recognised Mr Frey's voice. It had come from the steamer, where the prisoner's van had just halted. Amidst the crowd she could only see the coach's dark top, but she still caught a glimpse of a lanky ginger policeman climbing

433

down. As he did so, the man raised his arm and shot to the sky. The crowd let out a synchronised screech, stopping still for a moment.

It was then that Caroline recognised the only moving carriage. Her grandmother's.

She saw Lady Glass sticking her head out of the window, pointing at the van and shouting orders to her driver.

Caroline somehow found the strength to elbow her way through the crowd, shouting and squeezing through any gap she could find.

'Hop in, sir!' McNair told me as soon as he jumped off the driver's seat. He opened the back door of the van, and another two officers came out.

The captain threw down the gangplank then, but people instantly jumped onto it, and the constables had to thrust themselves forward to fight the crowd. Within a blink there was a mighty skirmish before us, the plank shaking and cracking as people and officers threw punches at each other.

I led Pansy to the ramp, and just as I attempted to set foot on it, a man leapt forwards, trying to grip my arm, but amidst the fight he lost his balance and plummeted into the water.

McNair shot into the air a second time. The crowd hesitated for a moment and I seized that instant to dart forward, holding Pansy firmly by the waist.

We ran down the gangplank, stepping on the very edge to dodge two young men fighting the police.

One of them pushed Pansy, who, in turn, pushed me, and I grunted and waved my arms frantically, feeling the vertigo as my entire body leaned into the void.

And then a small hand grabbed me by the collar and pulled me back.

'Caroline—' Pansy muttered even before I'd taken in her

sister's face. Caroline's hair was dishevelled, her dress torn in places, as she helped me take the last few steps to the ground.

Someone pushed her sideways and Caroline fell to her knees. The officers ran to help us, the crowd pouncing on us, and Caroline disappeared under feet and torches.

The moment I lost sight of her, Pansy screeched like an eagle, her voice cutting the air like a knife.

'*Caroline!*'

And, for an instant, it was as if time stood still.

Lady Anne heard the name and nearly sprained her neck when she turned in the direction of the cry. The word echoed across the dock, each syllable loud and clear, and the crowd went briefly silent.

I was the first one to move, pushing Pansy onto the van.

'*Where is she?*' Pansy screeched, trying to run back out, but I had to get hold of her, my mind already reeling with what the crowd might do if they caught us out there. I pushed Pansy into the van and reached for one of the doors.

I only just managed to shut it, but the other door got pulled away by the crowd. McNair had to plant himself by the door, his arms spread to keep the people at bay. I could only guess what had happened to his missing gun.

'*Where is she?*' Pansy screamed again, just as people began to shake the van from side to side.

I rushed to the open door and tried to grab it, but hands seized my arm and tried to pull me out of the van.

I roared, stretching my hand, the edge of the door just a few inches from my fingertips. It moved then, coming closer to me, and I gripped it immediately and pulled it shut.

It was then that I saw a small, gloved hand reaching between the window bars, and Pansy and I caught a glimpse of Caroline's pale face.

'*Go!*' she commanded breathlessly, before the crowd again pushed her aside, and then I heard thuds and bumps, as if people were crawling on top of the coach.

From her vantage point, Lady Anne saw Caroline run to the back of the van, just an instant before the doors shut.

'Stop!' she commanded, and the driver did so, right behind the prisoners' van. 'Where's my granddaughter?' she asked, and the driver shouted something she could not quite catch.

Caroline had vanished. Lady Anne strained her eyes, but could not tell whether the girl had jumped into the van or the crowd had trampled on her. All she could see was a mass of thugs surrounding the carriage and shaking it as if trying to tear it apart.

Lady Anne nearly opened her door, but then she saw a couple of intoxicated men climbing on top of the police carriage, and one of them, torch in hand, made his way to the driver's seat.

The man felt for the reins, and when he found them he lifted them in the air, as though they were a trophy, and the crowd burst in deafening cheers.

'*Off to the Crags!*' he howled in a slurred voice, and then he whipped the two horses, and the beasts moved in a wide circle.

'*Burn the witch!*' the crowd hollered once and then again, and Lady Anne saw the tall carriage dart away from the harbour.

61

McGray rushed into the City Chambers, gripping the minister's signed statement and a little pouch containing the stained leaf.

But the place was deserted.

McGray limped about, pressing his free hand to his ribs, and looked left and right. There were papers and litter scattered on the floors, as if the entire police force had fled mere minutes ago.

He heard approaching footsteps, and saw Dr Reed emerge from the door to the stairs. The young man rushed to him.

'Goodness! What happened to you, sir?'

McGray looked down. His bandages had loosened, his blood now mixed with that of Harland, and also the mud from the road.

'Never mind,' he exhaled. 'Where's everyone?'

'Off to Leith Harbour,' another voice said, coming from the end of the hall. McGray saw Dr Clouston, coming towards him with the most tired steps. He was panting and mopping sweat from his temples. 'I just told Superintendent Trevelyan. Not that I had to. The entire town knows what is happening.'

McGray felt a prickle of fear. 'Is she here?' he whispered. It was difficult to breathe, the anxiety building up in his throat. 'Is she in Edinburgh?'

'I think so,' Clouston said.

'I saw Trevelyan leave,' Reed added. 'And before that I heard him sending people to Salisbury Crags. People from the area came to tell us there was a mob gathering there. All bringing firewood.'

McGray took a hissing inhalation. 'And I've been –' he looked at the statement and the pouch – 'I've been wasting time on *this*!' He dropped them in Reed's hands. 'Keep this shite safe.'

'What is this?' Reed asked.

'The evidence we needed. Getting it might've cost Pansy's life!' And McGray turned around and stumbled away.

'*Wait!*' Clouston shouted, trotting behind him. 'You can't ride like that! You'll bleed yourself to death!'

But McGray did not listen. He simply ran out, crossed the courtyard in a few painful strides, and mounted Onyx, feeling the bandages loosening.

Caroline found herself on her knees, not daring to rest her hands on the ground lest people crushed her fingers. She saw many legs, all rushing away, following the stolen van.

Someone grabbed her by the arm and Caroline squealed with fear.

'Ye all right, miss?'

It was the tall, ginger constable.

'Yes,' Caroline said, a hand on her chest trying to catch her breath. She looked up and saw her grandmother's carriage as it turned away, moving slowly amidst the crowd. And at once she thought of something.

'Can you do me a favour?' she asked the officer.

'Yes, miss. Though we have to help—'

'Tell my grandmother *I* was in that van.'

'Excuse me?'

'*Please!* She knows Miss McGray is innocent. If she thinks

438

I'm in danger she might talk to your superintendent. He might do something to stop this!'

The constable's eyes glowed with understanding.

'She's over there!' Caroline cried as she pointed. 'That's her carriage.'

'Right away, miss. Ye wait over there.'

The constable nodded at a small cluster of carriages, where a few gentlemen were toasting on the spectacle. Caroline went towards them, careful to hide behind their coaches.

A man with a mighty torch came dangerously close to Lady Anne's carriage, and the driver desperately kicked him way.

They were moving at a sluggish pace, everyone rushing after the police carriage.

'Lady Anne! Lady Anne!' someone cried in the distance.

She looked out of her shut window. It was a young driver she'd never seen before, so she simply tapped the front window.

'Go away!' Lady Anne's driver shouted back, but the man trotted on.

'I lost the wee Miss Ardglass, ma'am!' he cried. 'Your grand-daughter!'

'*Stop!*' Lady Anne barked at once and then opened her window. 'My Caroline? You brought her here?'

'Yes, ma'am. But she went into the crowd and I lost her. I tried to look for her but – I only found these...'

The man handed her a pair of trampled opera glasses. They were bent, covered in mud, and one of the lenses had cracked.

Lady Anne took them, open-mouthed, as she recalled the words from the older gentleman.

'*Ma'am!*' another man shouted then. A lanky constable, running frantically towards her. 'Yer granddaughter – she hopped into the prisoners' van!'

Lady Anne felt her jaw drop as he took in a throttled breath.

'Oh, that's where she went!' the unknown driver cried. 'I was looking for her on the other side of the—'

'*Shut up!*' Lady Anne snapped, her hands now trembling, and she turned to the officer. 'You! Are you sure? She's in *there*? *I'll flog you to a pulp if you're lying!*'

The constable took a deep breath. 'I was right in front of the van's doors,' he said firmly. 'I saw exactly what happened.'

Lady Anne lost all colour. Her lips, stained with claret, looked almost black. She peered into the distance, but she could no longer see the stolen coach. As she grunted she reached for her hip flask, but she could not find it amidst the cluttered crates.

'Here comes the superintendent, ma'am!' the constable cried then. 'He might help you.'

Lady Anne looked at where the ginger man was pointing, and saw several policemen on horseback, as well as a cart full of officers. Among them was the superintendent, the only one wrapped in a black overcoat. Lady Anne had seen him before, and recognised his auburn hair.

'Go to him! *Now!*' she cried, banging the front window, and the carriage moved forwards.

She did not even look back to thank the constable and the young driver; she simply fixed her eyes on the superintendent, fearing she might lose him.

They reached him soon though, and Lady Anne saw the man staring around, regarding the incensed crowd with sheer disgust.

'*Superintendent!*' she shouted, waving her hand and sticking her head out of the window. '*Here!*'

Trevelyan saw her and steered his horse in her direction. 'Are you all right, madam?' he asked, his voice tired.

'*My granddaughter is in that carriage!*' Her desperate screech travelled across the street and people turned their heads to her. '*Those damned thugs took her!*'

Trevelyan looked all around. There was an unnerving hope-lessness in his eyes.

'I know,' he muttered.

'You *know*? Do something!'

Trevelyan fanned his hand towards the dispersing crowd. 'Do you want me to hang all these people, madam? Or merely incarcerate them?'

There were some brazen laughs and calls for 'Lady Glass!'. She let out a roar. '*Don't you dare give me wit, you little—!*'

Trevelyan made a little bow and moved his horse away.

'*Is it money you want?*' Lady Anne hollered. '*A house?*'

Trevelyan pulled the reins and remained still for a moment. Lady Anne began to grin, but then the man turned his head back, his look so sombre even Lady Anne shivered.

'*Money?*' he repeated. 'Do you think money will solve this? *This is out of control!* My men are outnumbered!'

'*You must do something!*' she shouted, punching the windowsill like a wilful child.

Trevelyan chuckled, all bitterness. 'We'll go to the Crags, but there is very little we can do now.'

'Nonsense! This is your job!'

'Indeed. A job we cannot do. Thanks to *you*, madam.'

Lady Anne bared her teeth. '*Me!*'

'*Yes!* We know it was your miners who spread the news. They've been rousing people all over town since last night.' He looked around again, nauseated. 'This is all your doing, madam. Enjoy your harvest.'

And the superintendent turned around, moving away for good.

Lady Anne felt a hollow in her chest; a desolation she'd never experienced before, expanding swiftly until it swallowed her whole.

62

'Arrest those men!' Caroline heard the superintendent shout. From the corner of her eye she saw three young men, all wearing fine clothes, jumping off the now-abandoned steamer.

Half a dozen constables ran in pursuit, and very soon seized the terrified chaps.

'We didn't do anything!' one of them whimpered, withering as the officers dragged him closer to the superintendent. He saw the men with repulsion from the height of his mount.

'You "escorted" Miss McGray here, did you not?' he asked, but the balding chap only whined. 'I see. We'll let the courts decide whether it was right or wrong – and I guarantee that your father will *not* preside over that inquest. Take them away!'

The superintendent then steered his horse in Caroline's direction, and she immediately hid behind the nearby carriages, fearing Trevelyan might tell her grandmother he'd seen her.

The ginger constable came over to her. 'Did you hear that, miss? The super says there's nothing we can do.'

'I did…' she mumbled. 'They'll take her to the Crags – and Mr Frey too – and they'll…'

Caroline had to cover her mouth, already picturing a hellish bonfire.

Her driver came over. 'Miss Ardglass! There you are! I've been looking for you everywhere!'

'Will ye be all right if I leave ye now, miss?' the constable asked. 'The super will need me.'

Caroline nodded and saw the man go away.

The driver sighed in relief. 'So glad to see you, Miss Ardglass! I'll go tell your gran—'

'*No, don't!*' she cried at once, and again her mind went still.

What could she do? The police themselves could do nothing! She covered her face, shuddering with anger and impotence. How useless, how dwarfed she felt.

And yet, she could not simply stand there while her sister and Mr Frey were burnt on a pyre.

'Take me to Salisbury Crags,' she spluttered.

'E-excuse me?' the driver stammered. 'That's where all that mob is going!'

'You heard me!'

McGray galloped along Canongate, the road eerily quiet.

He saw stars in the corners of his eyes, and bursts of sparks with each stride of the horse. He did not look down at his wound, but he knew he must be bleeding profusely, finding it ever harder to grip the reins.

Onyx was knackered too, snorting and panting after all the mad races of the day. His strides grew slower and slower as they dashed eastwards, the poor beast finally pushed to its limits.

McGray saw the gloomy spires of Holyrood Palace, right at the end of the road, and swiftly turned right.

As he did so, the buildings gave way to the ominous outline of Salisbury Crags and Arthur's Seat, right ahead of him. In the dim morning the jagged, dark boulders looked like dormant creatures.

McGray spurred the horse, for a moment thinking he was

seeing more stars. His heart skipped a beat when he realised they were torches. Hundreds of them, lining the edge of the Salisbury cliffs.

'*Damn!*' he cried. He should have gone there first. He should have tried to disperse that mob; think of the legal case later.

He cursed his own stupidity as he galloped on, without a plan or an inkling as to what he might do.

I was only glad the drunken 'driver' steered the van so fast and madly, for at least the mob could not keep up with us. Else they'd be battering the wooden walls to splinters.

Pansy and I had crouched at the centre of the coach, for people kept throwing ghastly things at the barred windows, shouting 'burn the witch' on and on. There was stuff dripping down the sill, and I tried not to think what that might be. I only dared look out for a moment, when I felt we were riding up a slope. I saw no buildings, only the dark, thunderous clouds.

I surrounded Pansy with an arm, and the girl reached for my signet ring.

'I'm so sorry,' she whispered, looking at the emerald with teary eyes. 'It's my fault you're trapped here.'

I tried to breathe, just as frightened as she was.

'It is not your fault people behave like this,' I whispered. 'You are not responsible for the worst of humanity.'

And as I said so, a chilling thought finally sank into my head.

We *were* about to die.

The police could not contain that mob. McGray could do nothing. Even proving that Pansy was innocent would make no difference now.

My body trembled, shaken by an icy sensation I had not quite felt before.

I took Pansy's hand and wrapped it in mine, trying to keep it warm.

A little kindness for our last moments.

'I lost them, ma'am!' Lady Anne's driver shouted.

The woman bounced on her seat, gripping the opera glasses so tightly she felt prickles in her joints.

'Just go to the Crags!' she snapped back, wishing she could have a drink.

She stared at the crates piled next to her, and grinned. She had all she needed. Those thugs would not win.

63

The slope grew steeper, the van bouncing more and more as we moved off the road.

I rose then, to take a look through the bars. I could see the lights of the city, hundreds of yards below us, and realised we were riding at the very edge of the Crags.

The glow of torches came in through the windows, and we heard blows land against the van's walls, people beginning to gather around us as the coach slowed down.

Pansy reached for my hand, and I took it again, the frightful chanting enveloping us, ever louder.

The wheels stopped then, and we heard strident cheers.

Just as he felt like fainting, McGray reached the foot of the Crags.

He saw the outline of the van even from the distance. It had halted right at the edge of the cliffs, before a dark mound that was bounded by quivering torches. The lights clustered around the coach, and McGray retched in sheer fear.

He spurred on Onyx and the exhausted horse took its first strides up the tortuous slope. McGray then heard a racket around him. Carts, full of people and pulled by rested horses, began to overtake him.

The van shook, people punching it and pulling it around, and I saw many hands trying to get us through the bars.

A beast of a thousand fingers, eager to crush us just for the pleasure of it.

I saw the pyre then, behind the bars and all those ghastly faces. It was a makeshift mound of logs and chip wood and old furniture, sections of it already ablaze.

They were pushing us towards it.

McGray at last saw the pyre, or rather guessed that was what that blur was, already catching fire to one side.

'Nine-Nails McGray!' someone shouted then.

'*Get him!* He wants to save the witch!'

The voices sounded muffled, everyone moving around him like a dizzying twirl. They all looked blurred. They all spun before his eyes, stretching their hands towards Onyx and trying to pull the exhausted horse back.

A carriage overtook him then, lustrous black amidst the dull greys.

McGray thought he caught a glimpse of a plumed hat.

Like horns.

The things they could do to us if we ended up in their midst, I thought, the most disturbing images rushing to my head.

The world around me was not any better. Someone was banging the back doors with a crowbar, and many hands pulled the bars of all the windows, trying to rip the van apart.

Pansy clung to me, shedding panicked tears as we heard the old wood crack.

I tried to take a deep breath through my mouth, but the air choked in my throat.

I realised, all my joints numb, that there was only one thing left to do.

'Run to the pyre,' I whispered. 'As soon as I open the doors.'

Pansy looked at me in horror, her lips trembling. I swear I felt her body go cold. But then she looked at the shaking doors.

'We'll be safer there—' she whispered. She frowned and then looked back at me, shedding renewed tears.

I attempted a smile. 'I'll stay with you,' I said, my voice quavering. And I hugged her a little more tightly.

Caroline popped her head out of the carriage window and her heart skipped a beat.

She was still hundreds of yards away, and yet she could see the convicts' van being jerked from side to side.

And she also recognised the jet-black outline of a familiar horse.

I took a deep breath, squeezed Pansy's hand and took a ginger step closer to the doors.

'Are – are you ready?' I whispered amidst panting breaths.

Pansy gulped, gave a quick nod...

And I lifted the latch.

McGray hit the edge of the crowd, and people instantly began shouting his name. They pulled at his legs and his saddle and his reins.

He grunted, feeling ever weaker, and when he looked up he saw the police van, tantalisingly close, but surrounded by a solid mass of thugs.

The doors flung open, people pulling them outwards, and I gripped Pansy as we leapt towards the pyre.

I threw her upwards, the girl shrieking and clambering onto the mountain of scrap wood.

As soon as I let go of her I felt many hands on my arms and legs, but instead of seizing me they pushed me upwards, to the summit of the pyre.

I met Pansy there, the poor girl shielding her face.

And people began throwing torches at us.

'Like I told you!' Lady Anne commanded as her carriage cut through the crowd. 'Get as close as you can, leave the carriage and then get out. These bloody fools will take care of the rest.'

'Aye, ma'am. But you should get off now!'

'*Not yet!*'

The heat was searing.

A torch landed by my feet, the wood around it at once catching fire. I grabbed the log and threw it back at the crowd. Pansy desperately tried to smother the flames with the hem of her dress.

More torches flew in my direction and I let out a desperate sigh.

We would not last long.

Lady Anne was just some fifty yards from the pyre. She could even see that there were people on top. Mr Frey, clearly, and a silvery shape next to him. Her heart pounded when she realised it was a white dress flapping in the wind.

She still gripped the opera glasses, so she rushed to open the front window and peered through them.

The cracked lens was useless, but through the other she managed to see that slender figure, kneeling on top of the firewood and stamping flames with her skirts.

Lady Anne's chest ached with despair, but then the figure turned and she had a good view of that pale face.

'That's not Caroline,' she mouthed, trying desperately to gather some air.

'That's not Caroline!' she uttered, but barely making any sound. She had to stick her arm out of the window and poke the driver's leg.

'Turn around!' she managed to shout. '*Turn around!* That's not my granddaughter!'

'Ye sure? That really looks like—'

'*Yes, I'm sure!* Turn around! That bastard can burn to cinders for all I care!'

She shut the window just as the driver turned the carriage around. For a moment she had a privileged view of the pyre from her side window, the flames growing taller and brighter, girl and man crouching on top.

Lady Anne had just begun to smile, but then her driver hollered.

An old cart, loaded with roaring men, clashed against her carriage, lifting it on three wheels and ramming underneath. The crates plummeted onto her and flooded the air with the sulphurous stench of their contents.

'*Pansy!*' McGray howled. He could see her on top of the pyre, her dress glowing above the approaching flames.

He tried to spur on his horse, but a sea of thugs had surrounded him, pulling Onyx in all directions. The horse shook, letting out piercing whines. McGray felt the blood from his torso drip down his own legs, and a sudden nausea took hold of him.

He realised he was about to faint, and he'd fall into that frenzied swarm of people.

Someone gripped him by the torso, and McGray howled in pain.

*

Lady Anne tried to push the crates, the unbearable weight crushing her ribs.

'*More firewood!*' someone shouted, and people at once began tearing apart the cart that had just crashed. Another cluster of people rushed towards her carriage – yet more wood for them.

'*More firewood!*' Caroline heard, her carriage still hundreds of yards from the burning pyre, and she hollered in despair.

Pansy's skirts caught fire and she shrieked.

I tried to smother the flames with my bare hands, but more and more torches rained on us. I felt my feet and my elbows on fire, and all I could do was crouch around the poor girl, trying to shield her with my body.

My face seared in the heat. My eyes stung—

Lady Anne tried to reach for the front window, but she could no longer see her driver. All she saw were incensed faces battering the glass, and many hands trying to rip off her carriage doors. The hinges were already giving way.

The thugs shattered the glass, shards flying onto Lady Anne's face. And just as quickly, the first sparks from their torches made their way through the gaps, landed on the crates, and the sulphurous powder came to life.

64

The explosion resounded throughout the mounds, the fire billowing and spreading in a majestic ball of blinding light.

Caroline's carriage halted, the horses rearing and neighing, the driver unable to control them.

McGray's Onyx was thrown sideways by the expansive wave, throwing him to the snow as people shrieked and ran for dear life.

The air filled with tearing screams and darting debris – burning plinths and wheels flying across the sky, as the fire swelled and consumed the people around it; charring carts, wood, flesh and bone.

An invisible hand pushed me and threw me in the air, the roar of the explosion drilling my ears as I rolled down the pyre, my body plummeting through the very flames.

My cheekbone hit the ground, damp and yet hot from the blast, and for an instant I could hear nothing but a constant, high-pitched buzz.

People lurched away, many of them turned into living torches, screeching in agony and jerking their burning limbs.

I too was on fire. I squealed and crawled away from the flames, and then rolled madly on the slush.

Some saw me and followed my example, but many simply ran on, their bodies engulfed in flames. I could see their mouths opened wide, but I could not hear their screams. My very mind was numb, unable to thread thoughts together, until I saw a piece of white cloth, its edges aglow, flutter in front of me.

'Pansy!' I shouted, even if I could not hear my own voice. I looked around, still on all fours, as the dark morning turned into a glowing furnace.

The mob at once forgot their resolve, and as they ran for shelter, Caroline's carriage could finally make its way through.

She heard police whistles coming from behind, but did not turn to see. She kept her gaze ahead, staring at the pyre. It now looked dwarfed by the second tower of fire next to it, so bright Caroline could not even see a hint of what might be left of Lady Anne's carriage. All she could see of it were the burning splinters that still rained all around.

'There!' she cried at the driver, though there was no need; the man was already driving there, the air growing hotter as they moved forwards.

Caroline felt the heat on her face, as if she were about to plunge her head into an open kiln.

'Pansy!' I roared, and despite the scorching heat I felt a crippling shiver all across my body.

I desperately looked around, but there was only fire and smoke and despair. I tried to jump to my feet, but I collapsed after a single stride, my limbs shaken and my skin seared.

The shouting began to trickle into my ears, intermingled with the roar of the fire and the continuous buzz, and all I could do was try to crawl away from the still-billowing fire.

I looked back as I did so, and saw the half-stricken pyre,

pathetic in front of the main explosion, now completely engulfed in flames.

A dull sound made it to my ears, coming and going, until I felt something cool touch my hand. I heard the sound again, low-pitched, and it suddenly turned into—

'Mr Frey!'

I looked up, only just able to make out the words. Right there, inches from my eyes, were Pansy's.

She was trying to pull me away, her face and hands covered in soot, her dress scorched and muddy.

I only had time for one relieved exhalation, before she pulled me again. I could not stand, so I dragged myself miserably across the ground, Pansy towing me by the arm.

I heard hooves and wheels, and then another cry in the distance. Those words I could not catch, but I saw Pansy rise up and wave frantically, jumping on her tiptoes.

Someone ran past us then, pushing me aside, and it was as if the blow finally unblocked my ears.

I wish it hadn't, for the roar of the flames and the tearing screams of the people struck me like a physical punch. I heard the whistles of police officers, their shouting and their galloping horses.

The sound of wheels stopped. I turned around and saw a small carriage just a few feet away. The door opened and Caroline jumped out.

She ran towards Pansy and the two sisters clashed in a tight hug. I saw Caroline clench her teeth as she shed a gush of tears, her dark eyes still staring at the column of fire. They were finally together – though not for long.

Pansy pulled away and stuttered. 'He's hurt!'

Caroline nodded and they came to me, each pulling one of my arms, and together they helped me to my feet and into the carriage. They had to prop me on the seat, for my legs felt like they were made of rags.

'Where is Adolphus?' Caroline asked as she shut the carriage door.

Pansy and I exchanged muddled looks.

'*Adolphus?*' Pansy echoed.

'Was he here?' I asked too loudly, for I still could not hear properly, and I saw Caroline turn pale.

'Yes!' Caroline cried. 'I saw him near the pyre. Just before the explosion.'

There was nothing Pansy or I could say.

The carriage was already moving, so Caroline stuck her head out of the window.

'*Go back!*' she shouted. 'We need to find Adolphus!'

McGray lay on the ground, face up, looking at the stormy clouds and the glowing cinders that fluttered all around him.

He felt his own heartbeats, both in his chest and on his open wound. Each one ached like a stab, but fortunately they were slowing down.

People ran past him and puffs of black smoke rolled above his head, but everything appeared to move gently and slowly. There was almost an elegance to it.

He saw some shadows gather around him, but he could not make out any faces. They must have lifted him in the air, for the sky began to shift. He could no longer feel his body. What a bliss that was – all the pain ebbing away.

For the briefest of moments he recognised two pairs of eyes, wide and dark, and so similar they could have belonged to the same person.

So they were both well.

Adolphus smiled, or at least thought he did. He let out a long breath, and then the world turned peaceful and silent.

455

Epilogue

The snow had finally stopped, the rolling Gloucestershire land-scape now as smooth as white velvet. Even the clouds had begun to retreat, patches of blue sky visible on the horizon.

I looked at the gentle slope ahead of me, dotted with leafless oaks and ascending gently to my small dowager's house. Its pale granite was framed by the dark woods beyond, thin trails of smoke coming from the two chimneys.

Despite the idyllic views, the morning was bitterly cold, so I wrapped myself more tightly in my fur-trimmed coat and walked on. My wrist ached terribly as I plunged my cane on the thick snow, my knee still sore from the fall. I only wished it had been the other leg, so I did not have to use my bad hand to support myself.

Mad barking came from behind my back, and two furry fig-ures darted past me, their paws disturbing the otherwise pristine snow.

'*Slow down, you brutes!*' I shouted.

Tucker, the golden retriever, halted and looked back at me like a guilty child feigning innocence. Mackenzie, the drooling mastiff, simply ignored me and ran on.

'Just like his old master,' I said with a sigh.

I caught up with Tucker and patted him on the head. At least the beasts were grateful. I might even get used to looking after them.

'Go on,' I said, and the golden retriever resumed his race. '*Slow dow*—*!* Oh, never mind.'

The dogs reached the house well before me and settled themselves on the wide portico, their tongues hanging out and their breath steaming in the air.

I made no haste, though. I enjoyed those morning strolls, and finally I understood why my awful brother Laurence liked his walking canes so much. I might keep using mine – ebony with a silver collar – even after my knee healed. If a distinguished landowner cannot indulge in an expensive cane, who can?

Foolishly I climbed the first front step with my lame leg, a stab of pain instantly taking hold of my knee, and I let out a loud growl.

The door opened.

'Mr Frey!' cried Caroline, rushing to help me. 'We saw you were coming.'

She nodded at the parlour window, which had a direct view to the estate's main house, half a mile away.

'Since I set off?' I asked.

'Almost. We knew it would take you a while. It gave us time to prepare the tea. Do come in, it is jolly cold out here!'

We stepped in, the dogs again rushing past me, and—

'*Your master is here!*' Caroline barked. 'How long will it take you to take his coat?'

The young maid, whom I'd hired expressly to look after the dowager's house, ran to receive me.

'And bring the tea service to the parlour,' Caroline commanded. 'None of those soggy scones.'

The girl curtsied and left as quickly as she could, while I gave Caroline a bemused look.

She'd taken to bossing around all my help as if she were the lady of the estate; even my staff at the main house. I must admit I rather liked it – she pointed out errors, got things done faster, and the servants grew bitter against her rather than me.

'Oh, sorry,' she said then, steering me to the parlour as one does an invalid. 'Presumptuous of me. Would you like tea or something stronger?'

'Tea will be fine,' I said. 'It is hard enough to walk already.'

She helped me sit down on one of the green velvet sofas just as the maid came in with the tea service.

'This was my late grandmother's favourite room,' I said, nodding at her portrait on the wall.

'I can see why,' Caroline said as she prepared my tea. I could not help noticing her engagement ring when she poured the milk. She must have lost some weight, for the diamond now drooped to one side.

She passed me the cup and saucer. Milk, no sugar. So she remembered.

The dogs came in, with the confidence of the estate's masters, and lay down by my feet.

Caroline threw them some pieces of scone, and we sipped our teas in silence for a moment. I was conscious of the warmth of the room, the lovely snow-covered views and the delicious scent of the brew. A far cry from the hell we'd been though in the past days.

I indulged in that calm bliss for a moment, before I put the cup down and asked the impending question.

'How is he?'

Caroline also put her cup down, folded her hands on her lap and let out a relieved sigh.

'He's only just come around.'

I gasped. '*Has he?*'

'Yes. Pansy is with him now.'

I made to stand up, looking at the ceiling as if thinking I

458

could see through it, but I felt another stab of pain in my knee and I had to lounge back. Still, I let out a long, relieved breath.

'Finally,' I whispered. 'Have you spoken to him?'

'No, not yet,' she said. 'Poor Pansy was so eager to talk to him I – I just left them alone.'

'Of course,' I said, and a very awkward silence followed.

I noticed Caroline was wearing a bottle-green velvet dress, as if to match the sofas.

So she was not even mourning her grandmother.

I nearly commented on the fact, but preferred not to. I imagined Caroline would resent Lady Anne for the rest of her life – acrimony intermingled with guilt, as her eyes suggested.

'You may stay here for as long as you need,' I said, keeping to a safe topic. 'So can McGray and Pansy.'

Caroline smiled, though with a hint of bitterness on her face. 'Thank you, Mr Frey. But I will have to go back to Scotland soon. Arrange the finances and so on.'

I only nodded. Lady Anne's death had been in all the papers from London to Inverness, given the extraordinary circumstances in which it had happened, and every single article speculated as to the extent of her wealth. It even piqued *my* curiosity, to be frank. Especially since Caroline was now her sole heiress, and soon to wed Nine-Nails McGray. I might get him drunk one day and ask him.

Just as I thought of that we heard hasty footsteps from the stairs.

I was expecting to see another servant, but it was Pansy who stepped into the parlour. I stood up carefully, bowed, and only then did I take a proper look at her.

The girl wore a dark burgundy dress, clearly influenced by her sister. The material was sombre and much more elegant than the pinks and pastels she used to wear at the asylum, and it highlighted her pale skin, as well as her dark hair and eyes. I noticed how reddened they were; poor Pansy must have cried her eyes out, her cheeks rosy and her lips dry.

She curtsied, but could not bring herself to meet my gaze.

'Mr Frey,' she mumbled, still clenching a hankie. 'My brother wishes to speak with you.'

Her stark formality was like an invisible hand pushing me backwards. I looked cautiously at Caroline, who simply gave me a quick nod.

I bowed again and walked up the stairs, wincing at each step. Soon I'd be reminded that I had been the luckier one.

As soon as I reached the first floor I heard an unmistakable growl, coming from one of the guest rooms. I went there and found McGray in the four-poster bed, squinting as the man-servant attempted to reposition the pillows under his back.

'What the *fuck* are ye doing? A blootered camel would be a better nurse than –' he saw me then, his eyes also reddened, though not quite as much as Pansy's. 'Piss off,' he told the young servant.

'But sir, your back needs—'

'*Piss off, I said!*'

The young man jumped at that and rushed to the door.

Before he went out I whispered into his ear, 'I shall pay you extra for these days.'

His eyes conveyed that all the money in the world was not worth this, but he had the composure to bow before he shut the door.

I let out a sigh and stepped closer to the bed. McGray's torso was still heavily bandaged, his arms and face dotted with multicoloured bruises.

We exchanged looks for a moment, but neither of us said a word.

I was torn between being earnest or making a silly joke

– something about it being time *he* got injured instead of me. McGray must have been going through a similar conflict.

After a while he offered a hand to shake. His four-fingered one. I took it and he squeezed mine with affection. My wrist was sore but I put on a brave face.

'I thought that was the end, Percy!' he exhaled.

I smiled, turned to pull over a nearby chair – which also gave me a chance to wince at leisure without him noticing – and sat next to him. There was a bright stream of light coming through the window, the glow from the white fields reflected into the room.

'It very nearly was,' I said. 'You lost so much blood we had to inject you with some fluid. I really thought we'd lost you. Caroline and your sister did too.'

Our swift escape from Salisbury Crags, while the fire still roared, flashed in the back of my head. I knew I would dream of angry mobs, bonfires and torches for the rest of my life. I could only hope that the nightmares abated as the years passed.

'Was I really out three days?' Nine-Nails asked.

'Indeed. I am only glad I did not have to look after you throughout.'

'I'd be dead if ye had. Even with yer two bloody weeks o' study at Oxford!'

He made to chuckle, and by some divine justice that caused him a mighty spasm. He winced and pressed a hand on his still-sore rib.

'Let me arrange that,' I said and, taking advantage of him being crippled by pain, I managed to adjust the pillows to support him better.

Rather grudgingly, he let out a sigh of relief.

'I need to ken something,' he said, keeping his eyes shut. 'The evidence. Did ye—'

'Why, yes! That was some quick thinking, McGray. I thought

you'd never string all the facts together.' I allowed myself a smirk. 'How fortunate that you had my notes!'

McGray just pulled a face. 'What happens next?' he asked, never keen to delve into the brilliance of my deductions.

'The inquiry will be ...' I counted with my fingers – 'either tomorrow or the day after.'

'*What!* And ye won't be there? What the—'

He tried to sit up, but again the pain was too much for him.

'You do need to learn to calm down!' I said. 'And yes, I am making the most of the fact that you cannot move.' I pushed him back onto the pillows and for once he did not put up a fight. 'The inquiry will be a mere formality. Everyone knows already that this will not go to the courts. Reverend Hunter's statement will suffice. It was lucky that Harland—'

I did not finish the sentence. I had read the minister's account, and could only imagine the agony that Dr Harland had gone through.

I shook my head. 'The Sheriff's Court will never put to question the statement of a man of the cloth. And even if they did, the physical evidence ties up all the loose ends: Reed's experiments, the marks on the bodies... the laurel leaf... the marks on the floor in Harland's office...'

'So they'll jail that wee Pratt bastard?'

I had to take a very deep breath to deliver my next sentence. 'It – it is not that simple.'

McGray frowned. 'What ye talking about?'

'The Lord Provost, I hear, is doing his best to keep the situation very hush hush. The fact that you shot his nephew—'

'*The damn weasel asked for it!*'

I sighed again. 'You know how the world spins. The Lord Provost offered to forgo your – misdemeanour, but only if we do not press on the body snatching matter. Martin and his friends will go free with a slap on the wrist, and all the deaths and crimes will be pinned on Harland.'

McGray snorted. 'How convenient for them that the poor sod died!'

'Even if he had not,' I said, 'I think he would still have become their scapegoat. It would only have taken a few well-coordinated lies, and men like that blasted Professor Grimshaw have years of experience teaming up against anyone who defies them. Like that poor Eustace Murray. He will have to go and study elsewhere, for his own sake.' I shifted in my seat. 'That reminds me – I need to write some letters to my professors in Oxford. I am hoping they will take him on. I still think he'd be a fair anatomy illustrator.'

McGray shifted a little on the bed, unable to find a comfortable position.

'Speaking o' useless pretty boys,' he said, 'what happened to yer brother? Pansy told me a wee bit about yer trip, but nae all.'

I shuddered at the mere memory of that dreadful night: poor Elgie surrounded by a band of thugs, all craning over him and jerking like hungry raptors.

I sat back and sighed. 'He is fine. I was convinced that those miners were beating him to death; it turns out they were fighting over his jacket and his shoes. They took his cufflinks, his pocket watch, his money… he had to wait at your parents' farmhouse while Tom walked all the way to Dundee to get some help.'

'Lucky laddie.'

'Lucky? To him it was a tragedy! He won't stop moaning that Sir Arthur Sullivan gave him the cuffs he lost.'

'And Tom… I guess he was well enough to walk those miles.'

'He has a broken rib, but he managed. He is quite resilient.' I half smiled. 'Just as much as your housekeeper Betsy.'

'Och, aye! Pansy said—'

'She is fine. Elgie took care of her before help arrived. The thugs gave her a good smack and she had a fall, but she was much better the day after. Clouston, you must know, thinks she cannot continue to live there alone. He suggested you send her to his clinic in the Orkneys.'

McGray sighed. 'That'll take some convincing. But aye, we should get rid o' that house too. There's only bleak memories there...'

His eyes drifted towards the window and for a moment he watched the sparse snowflakes flutter in the air. His pupils flickered, perhaps following his darkest recollections.

He began pooling tears, but he swiftly blinked them away.

'It wasnae the Devil,' he whispered, and then had to clear his throat. 'That thing I saw... all those years ago... nae Devil...'

I kept silent, for I knew just how difficult it was for him to say those words.

'All these years,' he went on, 'pondering, wondering – having nightmares about that damned shadow – reading every book on the occult – and it was nothing but that auld bitch Lady Glass and one o' her sodding plumed hats. All those wasted years...'

A bittersweet realisation indeed. Pansy was well, but she and he had spent six years separated, tortured and vilified – all for nothing. Now she'd come back to him, but at the cost of finding out that his father had never been the hero he'd built up in his memory; that his mother had never wanted that marriage; that she'd been miserable since before McGray had even been born.

The silence that followed was charged with tension, but there was something I'd been yearning to say all these days.

'McGray... do not be harsh on your sister. She—'

'*Harsh?*' he snapped. 'Why would I be harsh on her?'

'Well—'

''Cause she let everyone blame her for our parents' deaths? Cause she locked herself in an asylum for years to protect me from a pathetic truth? *She* was the braver one, keeping it all to herself! If she'd told me, *I* would've taken the blame! I would've told everyone I'd done it all.'

I made a small nod. 'Perhaps she knew that.'

McGray chuckled bitterly. 'Aye. She kens how fucking stubborn I can be.' He let out the longest, most guilty exhalation. 'She's the one who should be harsh on me.'

Unprecedentedly, and despite all my very English awkwardness, I knew precisely what to say.

'Time to look ahead, is it not? To stop dwelling on the past and wondering what happened that night – or what could have happened had things been different. You are free now.'

Nine-Nails had to look away, frowning deeply and once more pooling tears. I pretended I did not notice.

'Pansy is already doing very well,' I said.

McGray cleared his throat and rubbed his eyes with one swift move of the arm.

'Is she?'

'Oh, yes. She is quite shy in front of me, but with Caroline – she talks. *A lot.* I have heard them: it is as if she is trying to make up for all the wasted time. They are already planning a trip to Seville to get her a Carthusian horse like yours.'

McGray smiled. 'Aye, that'd be nice.' He nodded at the window. 'She must love it here, after all that time locked up.'

'She does,' I said, remembering Pansy's first day on the estate, running on the snow with her arms wide open. Even her brother's dogs could not keep up with her.

Nine-Nails was about to say something, but then his face went sombre.

'Wait – I *heard* her.'

'Excuse me?'

'Pansy. I heard her scream at the Crags. People heard her! If people ken she's nae insane – will she be tried for—?'

465

'No, no,' I said, raising a palm. 'Who could blame someone about to be burned alive for screaming?'

'But now that she's out o' the asylum—'

I shrugged. 'I would not worry about that. We might tell people that the trauma of the bonfire and the explosion brought her back to sanity.'

'*What?* Ye joking? Who the fuck's going to swallow that idiots' tale?'

I laughed. '*You*, of all people, asking that question?'

'I'm serious!'

I nodded. 'I know, I know. But again, I would not worry too much about it. I doubt that the cowardly thugs at the harbour and the Crags would be the sort of people to solicit a trial reopening in court. There might be some trouble from Lady Anne's workers, though. Clouston told me they heard everything the old crow told you.'

McGray clenched his teeth. That must be a night he was desperate to forget.

'Caroline told me she will bribe all those men,' I said. 'Clouston will point them out. That is one of the many financial matters she needs to resolve in Edinburgh.'

McGray leaned forwards a little. 'Then she must go there soon!'

'Yes, she will. And I am sure she can afford to bribe them quite handsomely. Lady Anne left her cartfuls of sterling.'

Nine-Nails smiled bitterly. 'At least that bitch's hoarding will be put to good use.'

I gave a cheeky smile. 'I am glad you are not too scrupulous about spending her wealth. After all, she nearly *was* your grandmother-in-law!'

'Fuck off!'

'And thanks to her, if you have any sons, they shall be little barons!'

McGray, too drained to bounce back, just let out an angry
'*pff!*'

Sadly I could not torture him any longer, for then we heard
a rapping on the door. I turned and it opened before I could
say anything.

It was Caroline, closely followed by the young maid. The
girl brought a tray with a steaming broth, and Caroline wore a
mighty frown.

'Excuse me, Mr Frey, may I *please* see my future husband
now?'

The clear hint of jealousy nearly made me chuckle, but I had
to contain myself.

'Of course, Miss Ardglass,' I said, jumping to my feet. I eyed
the maid. 'I trust you will be properly chaperoned.'

Before I could step away McGray stretched his arm again,
and we had a final handshake.

'Thanks again,' he muttered.

I only nodded, no further words needed, and as I went to the
door I said, 'Like I already told Miss Ardglass, you may stay here
for as long as you need to recover.'

McGray frowned. 'Really?'

'Yes. The advantages of owning a large estate – you can linger
for weeks on end and I will not even have to deal with you.'
I reached for the doorknob, shutting the door as I delivered
my last sentence. 'And if you do become bored, we can always
discuss how to dispose of all your ghastly witchcraft tatters.'

Nine-Nails simply shrugged. 'Nae. Auld habits die hard.'

I limped down the stairs, still laughing at my own jokes. To my
surprise, I found the manservant standing by the parlour door.
He looked on edge.

'What is it?' I asked, and the young man eyed the room.
Pansy was there, sipping her tea and staring at the window, a

melancholic look on her face. McGray's dogs lay around her, sleepy as ever.

'What is it?' I repeated.

'Is she not mad?' he mouthed.

I chuckled. 'No more than I am!'

And, despite my pained knee, I went straight in to prove my point.

'Miss McGray!' I said, as jovial as I could. She looked up, managed a coy smile, and then focussed on her cup.

It reminded me of that very first day I'd seen her. Our eyes had also met for a mere instant, before she looked away and a mighty row ensued.

'Are you well?' I asked, making my way to a nearby sofa. She only nodded, and then my mind went completely blank. We simply sat there in awkward silence. I thought of pouring myself some tea, but somehow could not come to it.

How ironic. Pansy and I had clambered onto a blazing pyre, faced hundreds of frenzied people who wanted our blood, and yet a small parlour and a tea set proved more intimidating foes.

Then I remembered—

'I have something that belongs to you,' I said rather triumphantly as I reached for my breast pocket. 'Here.'

Pansy gave me a puzzled look, and then saw the little signet ring I was offering. She recognised it at once, but did not seem to react; she simply stared at the polished emerald. The young woman was just about to turn twenty-two, but her eyes already held a depth well beyond her years. I realised that, no matter how long I got to know her, I might never be able to guess what went through her mind.

She stretched out a hesitant hand and I passed her the jewel. My fingertips touched her palm for an instant, and I must admit I twitched.

Her expression shifted too. She kept on staring at the gem, a slight tremble in her hand. Her lips parted, and for a dreadful second I thought she was about to have another fit.

'How could I ever thank you?' she whispered, her eyes glinting with tears. 'All the things you went through because of me. All the times you risked your life ... your wrist and your knee ... and I – what can I ever do to repay you?'

She clenched the ring and brought it close to her chest.

Astonishingly, again I knew precisely what to say.

'Live your life. That will make all the trials worth it – your brother's, yours and mine. Like him, you are free now. Go live your life.'

Pansy could not answer. She frowned and looked sideways, tears rolling down her cheeks. I offered her a handkerchief and she wiped them hurriedly, rather embarrassed by my presence.

'I shall leave you now,' I said. 'I—'

And just as swiftly my mind went blank, so I simply stood up and made my painful way to the door, but Pansy spoke then.

'Mr Frey—'

I turned around. 'Yes?'

She gulped and wiped her last few tears, all the while staring at the ring. 'This is a man's ring,' and she slightly opened her hand as she said so.

'I – yes, I know.'

Pansy raised her hand. 'You should keep it.'

Unconsciously I took a step back, recalling all the history that the little gem stored.

'Oh, no! That – it is a family heirloom. I could not—'

'*Please*,' she insisted, lifting her hand a little further. 'My sister gave it to you – and I want you to keep it too.'

I made to lift my hand, but then hesitated.

'You don't have to wear it,' Pansy insisted. 'Just keep it – to remember I will always be in your debt.'

I saw her lips trembling and I could not refuse. I approached again, received the ring and hastily shoved it back into my pocket. I could not even utter a thank-you.

'Good day, Miss McGray,' was all I could think of saying, and I made my way to the door.

'Mr Frey—' she said a second time. When I turned, I saw her wringing my hanky in her hands, her cheeks ever-so-slightly blushed.

'Yes?'

She gathered air. 'Will you – will you join us for dinner?'

Her dark irises flickered for a moment, until she managed to lift her chin and look into my eyes.

And she smiled.

Author's Note

The Devil's Mark was inspired by a personal injury.

Early on in my PhD, I spilled my fingertips with a concentrated sodium hydroxide solution. There was no pain or discomfort – my fingertips just felt soapy – so I didn't wash properly until a few minutes later. By the evening, I had a very nasty rash, and in the following days my skin turned slightly grey, as if dipped in ashes, and then began to peel off. Eventually, I realised that the soapy feeling had in fact been the outer layers of my skin getting dissolved. Yikes!

Unlike acids, caustic corrodes slowly, and while there are countless studies dealing with chemical burns on living tissue, I had the same problem as Frey – I found no papers on the effect of sodium hydroxide on corpses.

In the end I had to perform the same experiments as Dr Reed, also using a small piece of pork skin – I am sorry to say this book is not 100 per cent vegan. Reed's observations and methodology are entirely based on my own. I also tested caustic soda on a laurel leaf for the final description. Laurel and yew do symbolise eternal life, and I can attest that after weeks of the experiment, my leaf still looked green and crisp, with a lovely, well-defined stain that was almost pure black.

Most of this book was written during lockdown, so I had to

rely on digital maps, memory, previous notes and old photos for most of the geography of Edinburgh. For the interiors of Surgeons' Hall, in particular, I had to resort to the imagination, since the place has undergone dramatic changes across the decades.

The final scene atop Salisbury Crags was partly inspired by the tragic events in Tlahuelilpan, Mexico, in early 2019, and also the mild ochlophobia I have developed in recent years, exacerbated by the global pandemic. Penning that sequence really was a sort of therapy.

Indeed, working on this last Frey and McGray case kept me sane and focussed in the thick of the crisis, and I cannot thank you enough for all the time and emotion you have invested in my books. It is an indescribable sense of achievement to wrap up this mammoth piece of work, especially knowing that for more than twelve years I remained true to the original story arc. I planned the big denouement well before I even began working seriously on *The Strings of Murder*, and I have dropped clues here and there throughout the series. I challenge you to spot them!

And though I do not want to stop, my word count reminds me to conclude. I really hope to see youse soon, my dear lassies/laddies/ladsies, either in new pages or in these ones again, if you ever wish to revisit Ian, Nine-Nails and the whole gang. They will always be happy to see you back.